I0633722

BEAR TRAP

A JON SMITH NOVEL

BOB ASHER

BOB ASHER

Printed in the United States of America
First Printing 2022
Second Edition 2024

ISBN-13: 978-1-958115-03-9
ISBN: 978-1-958115-00-8 (Paperback)
10 9 8 7 6 5 4 3 2 1

NGA OCC - Approved for public release, 21-024
Why is that statement here and what does it mean? You can find the answer at the end of the book, but be warned, if you look now, you may see some spoilers.

This is a book of fiction. Really, I had to promise the US Government that it was. The names, characters, organizations, places, events, and incidents are either products of my imagination or are used fictitiously.

Book cover design by semnitz (semnitz@gmail.com)

Interior Formatting by 100Covers.

To: Sierra Kilo, thank you for your patience and unwavering support while I locked myself up in my office at night to write this story.

CHAPTER 1

0200Z (0500HR AST)
OUTSKIRTS OF MOSUL, IRAQ

Jon was the fourth man in a tight stack of seven standing in the dark along a pockmarked, cinder block wall outside the back door of a battle-damaged two-story house. Tonight, he and his teammates were wearing black Iraqi Army Special Forces uniforms. He yawned quietly as his stomach growled. He had been awake and on the move for over thirty-six hours. The only thing he had eaten was an unheated MRE spaghetti entrée ten hours earlier. All he could think about was food and sleep. Despite the early hour, the temperature hovered just over 100°F. Sweat flowed steadily from under his helmet and into his eyes before dripping off his nose into his beard. Under his body armor, his pale pink skin was steaming. He grabbed his plate carrier below his neck and pulled it out and back like a bellows several times to force some fresh air under it for a little temporary relief. He was standing nut to butt behind his swim buddy, Clint.

He and his team were hunting Quds Force terrorists sent from Iran to plant improvised explosive devices, or IEDs, on the area roadways. These explosively formed penetrator-type IEDs were effective against mine-resistant vehicles and tanks. Their bombs resulted in the maiming and deaths of over 150 civilians and soldiers in the preceding month.

Jon wiped the sweat from his eyes with his Nomex gloved hand and sucked a mouthful of warm water from the drinking tube attached to his CamelBak hydration pack. He reflexively re-coiled and closed his eyes as a powerful stench assaulted his senses. He had been subjected to another one of Clint's silent but deadly gastronomic attacks. In response, Jon pulled his collapsible baton from his plate carrier and slid it up between Clint's inner thighs and pressed it against his perineum. Through his night vision goggles, Jon saw Clint spring to his tippy toes and clench his cheeks.

Clint swatted the baton away and quietly said, "Asshole!"

Jon chuckled under his breath. The team leader began counting down from five seconds with his left hand. When he got to zero, they would breach the door and kill or capture the tangos —more likely kill, but a couple of prisoners for the interrogators would be preferable.

As the leader signaled three, the eight-inch-thick wall in front of Jon exploded, sending concrete shrapnel and an explosively formed penetrator flying from a fifteen-inch-diameter hole. Clint's head vaporized, spraying Jon's face and night vision goggles with hot blood, tissue, and bone. Some went in his mouth, causing him to gag. He froze for what seemed like an eternity. His mind screamed at his body to move, but nothing happened.

The operator behind Jon yanked him back out of the way and yelled, "Frag out!" as he threw two grenades into the hole. They exploded and the breacher blew the door.

The stack flooded through the smoky opening. Jon spit the coppery-tasting lump of brain matter onto the sand and wiped his face. His goggles were covered with the goo, and he flipped them up out of the way. He stepped over Clint and followed the team inside. They quickly swept the house, killing tangos. Tonight, there would be no prisoners. As the Team searched the house and gathered intel, Jon ran back outside to check on Clint. Maybe he hadn't seen what he thought he had. Jon pointed his flashlight at his friend then immediately turned away, retching uncontrollably until nothing remained.

CHAPTER 2

1950Z (0750HR PETT)
PETROPAVLOVSK-KAMCHATSKY, RUSSIA

The helicopter pilot, struggling to see through a blurry green tube, flew west over a dark, foreboding world. Light green specks in the center of the tube grew larger and brighter every second. Soon, the dark green curtain passed behind him, and the specks surrounded him from the front and below. They were now so bright they overpowered his night vision goggles, and he raised them out of the way. Lieutenant Maks Yakov asked his copilot, Lieutenant Yaroslav Saveli, for the landing checklist as he lowered the collective with his left hand and pulled back on the cyclic with his right to slow his helicopter and transition to a landing profile. He scanned the snow-covered landscape as he began his landing approach to an empty parking lot next to a small cinder block warehouse on the Kamchatka Rybachiy Nuclear Submarine Base in eastern Russia. A low overcast sky obscured the glow of the sun as it slowly approached from below the horizon. The lot's lights were still on. A half-meter of snow blanketed the ground and buildings, but the temporary landing zone in the middle of the lot had been plowed clear. As soon as Yakov landed, he saw nine soldiers push open the heavy old doors to the warehouse. Then they double-timed it toward his decrepit gray and white Ka-27PS Helix-D SAR helicopter.

The Helix featured a coaxial rotor system with two counter-rotating three-bladed main rotors mounted to a single mast. The system eliminated the need for a tail rotor to provide antitorque. It was considered innovative when it first flew in 1973. The aging Helix was a workhorse that had room for up to sixteen soldiers in its cabin, but it looked odd compared to the world's other helicopters with tail rotors. Actually, it was the most butt-ugly helicopter ever produced, appearing as if it was about to fly apart.

***

Inside the warehouse, the driver of a green Ural-4320 general-purpose off-road 6×6 cargo truck watched as the soldiers leaned their shoulders into the rusty doors. He screwed the top back on his thermos and dropped it on the seat next to him. As the large diesel rumbled to life with plumes of black exhaust, he put his truck in gear and followed closely behind the soldiers as they hurried to the helicopter. He made a quick 180 and backed up to about ten meters from the spinning rotor blades and stopped. He hopped down out of the cab, ran to the rear, and jumped into the canvas-covered truck bed. He slid the soldiers' heavy packs and equipment cases across the slick bare metal truck bed to the soldiers. They slowly carried them under the rotor arc to the helicopter's cabin. Only one large green canvas equipment bag remained in the truck. Before the soldiers could return, the driver dropped the bag inside a stack of truck tires in the front of the bed. When the soldiers came back from the Helix, they saw the truck was empty except for the stack of tires.

The driver jumped down from the bed and yelled, "That's everything!" over the roar of the helicopter as he closed the tailgate. He climbed back into the cab and drove away, smiling to himself. The soldiers would be hundreds of kilometers away before they realized anything was missing. The tire stack trick had made him a tidy sum over the years. He didn't know what was in the bag yet, but it had to be worth something. Whatever it was, he would sell it in town or possibly, if it was field gear, sell it to other soldiers. They were always losing personal gear like gas masks, helmets, or canteens when they went out on field exercises. His prices were cheaper than what the Army would charge them to replace their lost equipment.

***

As the pilots, Yakov and Saveli, waited for the soldiers to load their equipment into the cabin, Saveli looked out his right door's window and propped his right boot up against the cockpit window frame above the pedals. He exhaled heavily on the freezing cold window to fog it over and drew a frowning face in the frost with his gloved finger. He peered over the face at the gray sky and said over the intercom system, "Maks, this is the stupidest fucking thing I've ever heard of. They can't seriously expect us to do it. It's crazy."

Yakov had his head turned around to the left and was watching the soldiers carry their gear from the truck to the cabin of his helicopter. He was trying to estimate the weight of their gear to determine how it would affect his weight and balance and fuel calculations. If it was too heavy and loaded too far forward or aft, it might affect his ability to control the helicopter. Plus, too much weight would burn more fuel, and he might run out before arriving at the destination. He knew his crew chief would make sure the gear was loaded safely, but he still kept an eye on everything. He was ultimately responsible. He also wondered what the soldiers' mission was, but he knew not to ask. Whatever it was, he thought it must be extraordinary. He swung his head back to the right to look at his buddy, Yaroslav, and saw the frowny face on the window.

Yakov chuckled. "Well, obviously they do because here we are. I'm not happy about it either, but we have our orders."

Saveli turned to look at Yakov. "I only have three months to go, and I already have a job lined up. You know I'm getting married in a couple of months. Everything is planned and paid for. Polina will kill me if something goes wrong."

"By the way, I still haven't received an invitation." Yakov feigned disappointment.

"Polina hasn't mailed them yet, but you know you're invited. I told you months ago." Saveli swiveled his head back to the right to look at the darkening sky again. "I think the weather is getting worse. We should hurry."

Yakov nodded his agreement. He didn't say so, but he knew Yaroslav would never leave the Navy. It was the Saveli family business. His father, uncles, and both grandfathers had all been career Navy officers. He had ancestors who had served in the Czar's Navy. They would disown him if he got out. No, his buddy, Yaroslav, was a lifer just like him.

The soldiers had efficiently transferred their weapons and equipment from the truck into the helicopter's cabin and then climbed aboard. The helicopter's crew chief climbed in behind them and slid the door closed, blocking the cold wind. He threw a heavy-duty nylon cargo net over the pile of equipment in the center of the floor and duckwalked around the cabin securing it to the cargo tie-downs recessed into the floor. The net would keep the cargo from shifting while they were maneuvering in the air.

Yakov watched the crew chief perform his duties and was satisfied the cargo and soldiers were properly loaded. After he verified the truck had driven clear, he took off, heading back to the east away from the base and out over the gray ocean toward his ship. As they went feet wet, Yakov passed the controls to Saveli. He thought if Saveli was busy flying, he might stop whining. They took turns on the controls over the next several hours flying over the water. The low overcast sky combined with the gray ocean made it difficult for them to see the horizon. They flew along at 150 meters above the water using their flight instruments to avoid getting vertigo.

In the cabin, the soldiers sat stoically. They were used to dealing with the boredom of waiting for hours on end. Hurry up and wait was a practice exercised by all military organizations around the world. They weren't cold, wet, or hungry, and no one was shooting at them, so they were content. When they grew tired of being bored, they took advantage of the time and went to sleep. Professional soldiers could sleep anywhere: lying on a concrete floor or sitting in a muddy fighting hole. It didn't matter. Some could sleep while standing in formation.

***

Yakov and Saveli continued to fly their Helix out into the foreboding Bering Sea. With every passing kilometer, Saveli was pulled closer to his personal mental abyss. After 800 kilometers, he reached his limit. "We are fucked, Maks! We are going to die out here on this stupid fucking mission, and no one will ever find us!" Saveli yelled as he pounded his fist against his door. They had passed the point of no return over two hours ago.

"Calm down, dammit! You are a naval officer, not a little girl hiding from Baba Yaga!" Yakov chided his copilot without taking his eyes away from his instruments and the ocean in front of him. He regained his composure and said, "Stop whimpering and help me find the ship."

"Maks, please, let me call the ship and ask them for a vector," Saveli begged softly as he reached for the radio switch.

Yakov swatted his hand away. "No! We have our orders! Keep looking!" Finally, with twenty minutes of fuel remaining, Yakov spotted the frothy wake of their ship churning away from them to the east. It was right where it was supposed to be. He called for the landing checklist. Saveli read it off and signaled it was complete.

Yakov circled the Udaloy-class guided missile destroyer, Admiral Vinogradov, and landed on the fantail.

Even though the temperature was below zero, the soldiers hopped out of the helicopter and stretched their legs while it was being refueled. Some of them did calisthenics to get their blood flowing again, and because time was an issue, they asked for and received permission to urinate off the fantail of the ship instead of going inside to use the head.

The ship's mess men brought out hot food for them to eat on the next leg of their trip. It was a special treat—beef and potatoes from the captain's mess. Yakov had never seen this done before. With refueling complete and the soldiers back aboard, he prepared to take off. A deck crewman approached his door and handed him a note. It was from the captain of the Vinogradov, and it asked him to orbit the ship once before he departed. Yakov wondered why. He took off, and as the helicopter approached the bow, he saw the captain and thirty of his sailors manning the rail in their navy blue dress uniforms. They were all standing at attention, saluting in the freezing weather. The hair on the back of Yakov's neck stood up and goose bumps covered his body. A great honor had been bestowed upon him and his crew. Yakov pulled the helicopter into a hover fifty meters off the starboard side of the ship parallel to the formation and pedal-turned the helicopter to the left to face the formation. He pushed the cyclic forward with his right hand to dip the nose down to return the salute. Next, he pedal-turned back to the right, and they proceeded on their mission.

"So, I guess we're really doing this," Saveli said glumly as he watched his home away from home slide away from view as the Helix accelerated.

Yakov smiled as he punched his friend on his left arm. "This is a great honor, Yari. Aren't you filled with pride?"

"Maks, the Captain honored us because he thinks he'll never see us again," Saveli replied.

They continued on their mission for four more hours and another 800 kilometers heading east across the Bering Sea without seeing another aircraft, ship, or living being. Flying over the sea for eight hours with no visible horizon was physically and mentally taxing, and the longer they flew, the more anxious they became. They were bone tired. When they were first assigned to fly the mission, Yakov had been excited to be selected, but now he silently wondered if Saveli might be right. They were down to thirty minutes of fuel remaining before they would be forced to ditch into the ice-cold water, which would mean certain death. They arrived at the planned rendezvous point, but there was nowhere to land. They saw gray sky and gray waves in every direction.

Yakov squirmed nervously in his seat. He was growing more concerned by the minute as he watched the needle on the fuel gauge slowly sweep toward empty. Back in the cabin, the soldiers sat peacefully. Some were reading paperbacks, some were sleeping. Ignorance was bliss. Yakov slowed to ninety knots to conserve fuel and entered a wide right-hand orbit over the rendezvous point.

"Where is it? They're supposed to be here already!" Saveli yelled. His head swiveled back and forth as he frantically scanned the sea. They were on their fourth orbit and down to fifteen minutes of fuel remaining when Saveli pointed and shouted, "There! At one o'clock and 500 meters, it's a periscope!"

Yakov slowed down and adjusted his orbit over the periscope. The submarine's hull slowly broke the surface as it continued churning ahead at a leisurely five knots. Two officers and a sailor wearing dark wool overcoats appeared in the bridge atop the sail. The sailor attached the blue and white Russian Navy ensign to the halyard and hoisted it aloft. One of the officers shined a steady green light at the helicopter to signal it was cleared to land. Yakov called for the landing checklist, confirmed the parking brake was set, and began his approach to the exposed black hull between the rudder and the sail. The BS-64 Podmoskovye's beam was just under twelve meters, which gave Yakov little margin for error. The submarine wasn't designed to have helicopters landing on it, but this was an unusual mission. Yakov made a slow approach to the deck and landed the helicopter gently behind the sail.

"Yari, go with the soldiers. I'll stay at the controls until you are inside," said Yakov. There was no reason to risk both of their lives shutting down the helicopter.

Saveli looked wide-eyed at his friend Maks for a second, realizing he might never see him again. Then his instinct for self-preservation propelled him out of the helicopter.

Yakov kept the rotor head spinning at 100% RPM to maintain control of his helicopter until the soldiers and his crew had unloaded their equipment and disappeared inside the hatch near the sail. As Yakov reached to shut down the engines, the #2 engine flamed out on its own from fuel starvation. He released his seat harness and pulled both engines' levers to the shutoff position before jumping from the helicopter and running for his life toward the open hatch. As soon as he dropped down inside the hull, a young sailor dogged the hatch and slid down the ladder behind him. The sailor on the bridge pulled down the ensign and dropped through the hatch, followed by a baby-faced lieutenant who secured it.

***

The submarine immediately began submerging, and within seconds, it vanished beneath the waves, leaving the helicopter bobbing up and down momentarily in the swells. The captain watched through his periscope. He wanted to be certain the helicopter sank without damaging his boat.

Like most helicopters, the Helix was top heavy and soon rolled upside down with its wheels pointed skyward like a dead cockroach floating in a bathtub. It quickly filled with water and, within another minute, succumbed to the sea.

CHAPTER 3

Two snowmobiles slowly emerged from the trees on the south side of frozen Eek Lake. The embroidered patches and badges on their dark blue parkas clearly identified the drivers as Alaska State Troopers. They followed the cones of light produced by their headlights as they traveled cautiously across the frozen surface. Cautiously, but also with a sense of urgency and purpose. They had been dispatched on this mission by their president on a matter concerning the nation's security. They felt proud and honored to be tasked with the mission. They rode directly across the four-mile-wide lake toward a cabin on the north shore.

***

Inside the cabin, Mark Lange woke from a deep sleep as he lay in an old recliner. The dry brown leather was cracked along the seams and groaned as he shifted. He rubbed the sleep out of his eyes and scratched his two-week-old beard. He scanned the dimly lit, wood-beamed ceiling as an orange glow flickered around the room from the fire burning in the massive stone fireplace. The logs were nearly reduced to ash. Soon, he would have to put more logs on and stoke the fire. It was a nice old cabin, but it didn't hold heat very well.

Mark really didn't want to get up. He was fully clothed except for his boots, and he was toasty warm under his covers. The weather outside reminded him of his infantry days in the Army when he was stationed in Germany. He spent many cold nights in a two-man pup tent snoring the night away. It would be brutally cold with two feet of snow outside, but inside the tent, zipped up in his fart sack, he would sleep like a baby. Germany had some harsh winters, but it was worth it. He had a lot of fun in Europe. He and his girlfriend, Micha, explored Europe from the D-Day beaches on the Normandy Coast to the southernmost tip of Italy. At the end of his three-year assignment, he married her and brought her home to the States. Now they had been together for over twenty years and had a boy and girl in college.

Mark tried, but he couldn't go back to sleep. Something was wrong. He wasn't sure what, but after twenty-one years in the Marshals Service, he had learned to trust his gut. As he sat there with his eyes closed, his thoughts drifted to another night seven years earlier when trusting his gut had saved his life. He had led a multijurisdictional fugitive task force. The team had lawmen from federal, state, and local law enforcement agencies deputized by the Marshals Service.

That night, he and his team were hunting members of the Gangster Disciples street gang on the South Side of Chicago. He chased the gang's leader, a hardened criminal called T-Dawg, into a condemned house. It was an abandoned 150-year-old three-story brick house built at the beginning of the population explosion after the Civil War.

He had his Glock 23 pistol and Maglite out aiming to his front as he made his way through the dilapidated house. His arms moved in unison with his eyes as he scanned the hallway. He was about to go through a doorway on the third floor to what had originally been the master bedroom when the hair on the back of his neck stood up. He slowly retraced his steps. He had backed down the hallway about ten feet when the floorboard beneath his boot creaked softly. Instantly, the wall three feet in front of him exploded from the blast of both barrels of a sawed-off 12-gauge shotgun. He thrust his Glock through the giant hole and shot the fugitive five times before he fell to the floor. Mark rushed down the hall and through the door. He pointed his pistol and light at T-Dawg just in case he needed to take follow-up shots. He saw the man lying dead on his back. The fugitive's left hand was in the pocket of his ragged blue jeans where he had the extra buckshot shells. His tattooed right hand still held the grip of the open shotgun. T-Dawg was the fourth fugitive Mark had killed during his career. Now, he tried to push this memory out of his thoughts.

He listened to the fire as the recliner cradled his body. He was a big man, and his feet hung out beyond the end of the footrest. He was covered by a green wool army blanket and his Woobie. The Woobie was an old woodland-camouflaged insulated poncho liner from his Army days. He thought it was one of the best pieces of gear the Army ever issued. At least as important as the M1 Garand rifle or the Abrams tank. Mark was drifting off to sleep when he heard the far-off sound of a snowmobile, faint but getting louder. His eyes popped open.

"Wake up, we've got company!" he yelled to the others in the cabin as he sat up and slid his feet into his boots. He sprang out of the recliner and hurried to the window next to the front door. He pulled the curtain back and saw two sets of headlights slowly approaching the cabin from across the frozen, snow-covered lake. He hiked his left foot up on the edge of the end table next to the window and tied his boot. Then he tied the other. He subconsciously felt for the Glock on his right hip and pulled on the end of the magazine to make sure it was properly seated. This situation didn't feel right. It was odd to get visitors at the cabin, especially in the middle of the night. They hadn't seen anyone around the cabin in the week and a half they had been there.

Moments later, the other two half-dressed deputy U.S. Marshals came out of the bedroom they were sharing. Next, their protectee came out of the larger bedroom.

As he pulled on his flannel robe, he squinted through his glasses and asked in his thick Russian accent, "What is happening, Mark?"

As Mark kept watch at the window, he briefed them. "I see two snowmobiles approaching us from across the lake. It looks like they're taking their time. You guys gear up. When they get here, I'll go out and talk to them. Doc, please, wait in your room until I give the all clear."

Two minutes later, the snowmobiles stopped about 100 feet from the cabin and shut off their engines and headlights. Mark continued to watch them from the dark window.

As the men climbed off their machines, one called out, "Hello, in the cabin. I'm Alaska State Trooper Darrin Logan. We have a message for Deputy Marshal Lange."

Mark cracked open the door and yelled, "I'm Lange! I'll be out in a minute!" He closed the door and turned to his partners, Kevin Bass and Ronnie Dillon. "You guys stay in here with the doctor. I'll see what they want."

They both nodded, and Kevin responded, "Roger that, Boss," as he pulled back the charging handle on his M4 and let it slam forward, chambering a round. The M4 was a magazine-fed select fire rifle commonly carried by the military and law enforcement capable of firing semiautomatic or a three-round burst. It had a 14.5-inch barrel, a thirty-round magazine, and a collapsible stock.

Mark looked back and smiled at Kevin. "If you shoot me in the back, I'm gonna beat your ass."

Kevin returned the smile. They had been working together for five years and coming up to this cabin every winter for the last three years with the doctor. Up until now, it had always been without incident.

Ronnie said, "I'll keep the doctor company. Come on, Doc." He led him to the bedroom door.

Mark grabbed his parka off the coat rack next to the door and zipped it up. Then he pulled his black leather shooting gloves out of the front pockets and put them on. The gloves had a Kevlar lining to help resist cuts and were made to fit tight.

Mark opened the heavy wooden door and stepped out onto the covered porch that ran the length of the cabin. He took two steps down into the deep packed snow. He turned on his big Maglite and pointed it toward the snow-covered ground in front of him as he walked out to greet the troopers. The flashlight reflected enough light that he could see the embroidered patches and badges on the troopers' blue parkas. He relaxed a bit.

Mark stopped about ten feet from them. "I'm Mark Lange. What brings you guys out here so late?"

The one on the right said, "I'm Darrin Logan, and he's Howard Johnson," as he motioned to the other trooper.

"No shit." Mark smiled at the trooper standing ten feet to the left of Logan as the old motel chain came to mind.

Johnson nodded. "Howdy."

Logan reached into his parka pocket and pulled out an envelope. He offered it to Mark. "We were told it was very important that you get this message tonight."

Mark looked down to take the envelope. He never saw Johnson raise his pistol.

***

"Kevin, what's happening out there?" Ronnie asked from the doctor's bedroom doorway.

"Mark's talking to them. Fuck, it's freezing," Kevin said as he spoke through the six-inch opening in the doorway. He grabbed his jacket off the hook and quickly put it and his gloves on. He peeked out through the crack, making sure to keep his rifle out of sight. He saw one trooper offer Mark something, and then as Mark reached for it, the other trooper inexplicably shot Mark in the head. He saw Mark's limp body collapse to the snow. Kevin gasped for air, and his eyes bugged wide. The sudden violence shocked and momentarily confused him, but his training and combat experience in the Marine Corps threw him into action. It was as though a switch had been flipped on in his head.

Ronnie heard the shot and shouted, "Kevin, what happened?"

Kevin didn't hear him because his heart rate immediately spiked, and he experienced auditory exclusion, his mind filtering out Ronnie's voice because the threat was in front of him on the snow, not behind him in the cabin. He braced his rifle against the doorframe and squeezed off well-aimed three-round bursts at the troopers who were already diving for cover behind their snowmobiles. He concentrated most of his rounds on the trooper who shot Mark. The old feelings from Afghanistan came rushing back—fear mixed with exhilaration and an overwhelming urge to attack. As he fired, he formulated a plan to wipe out the troopers, but of course, he knew they weren't really troopers. They were out in the open except for the snowmobiles, and they only had pistols. Plus, Mark's flashlight had landed on an area of hard crusty snow facing the troopers. It lit them up for Kevin and blinded them. He would keep shooting until he killed them. He wanted to punish them for Mark. Kevin lowered his rifle slightly to load a fresh magazine before the first ran dry. As he inserted the new magazine, something massive hit him in the face with the force of a sledgehammer, and he crumpled to the floor.

***

A white-clad sniper lay prone on the frozen lake less than 100 yards away to the right of the cabin. He rose to his feet and dusted the snow off the front of his smock and trousers. He began slowly slogging through the knee-high snow toward the cabin. Even though the target's head was small, he had no trouble hitting it. The .308-caliber bullet put a small hole below the target's right cheek then ripped the left side of his jaw away from his face as it exited below his left ear. His weapon wasn't a military sniper rifle. It was a Remington 700 with a Leupold scope, like the ones thousands of American outdoorsmen owned.

***

Ronnie was standing in the doorway to the doctor's bedroom when he heard the sickening crack of the bullet that hit Kevin's face. Kevin's head slammed into the doorjamb before his limp body fell back into the cabin. Ronnie screamed involuntarily at the sight. He'd been hired right out of college and had only been a deputy marshal for two years. He had never been involved in a shootout, much less seen anyone murdered. Now, he was scared out of his mind. He locked himself in the bedroom with the doctor and drew his Glock. He thought of calling for help on the satellite phone, but remembered it was out there with Kevin. He knew if he tried to get it, he'd be cut down too. Besides, help wouldn't come in time anyway. It would take hours. His mind raced as he tried to think of an option where he and the old man could survive. He considered jumping out of the window and running for his life, but he couldn't leave the doctor behind. He would rather die than do that. "Doc, get behind me!" Ronnie yelled as he walked backward to the other side of the bed and tried to cover the door and window with his pistol. He knew he had at least two adversaries to deal with.

***

Outside, Logan carefully advanced on the cabin. He stepped onto the porch and leaned against the doorjamb.

Standing over Kevin's gurgling body in the doorway, Logan glanced at the bloody mess of a face and shot him in the chest to finish him. He called out, "Dr. Karpinsky, are you alright?" There was no response. He called out again, "Doctor, are you alright?"

A shot rang out from the bedroom, and Logan flinched as he jumped back out of the doorway onto the porch.

CHAPTER 4

0630Z (2130HR AKST)
BEAVER CREEK LODGE,
HOMER, ALASKA

"Good evening. I'm Jon Smith. I have a reservation for one of your three-bedroom lodges," he said to the clerk behind the highly varnished pine wood counter.

"Yes, Mr. Smith, we've been expecting you. I'm the night clerk. My name is Billy. I just need your credit card and your signature, and you'll be all set."

Jon handed him his plastic. Billy stuck the credit card into the chip reader and then handed it back to Jon. Jon grabbed the stylus off the counter with his quivering right hand and hastily scribbled his name on the digital registration pad.

"Can I show you to your lodge?" Billy asked as he held out the key to Jon's lodge.

"No thanks. I have a car. I'm sure I can find it." He didn't want Billy to see all the gear he would be unloading into the lodge, especially the black Pelican rifle cases. He walked outside and hopped into his rented black Ford Explorer and drove off, following the signs leading to the lodges. As he turned off the tree-lined trail, his headlights fell on the large three-bedroom log cabin. It had all the amenities and a west-facing deck on the beach.

Jon parked next to the freshly shoveled porch steps and made several trips back and forth to get all his bags and cases inside. He planned on being in Alaska for a month, so he had packed heavy. He had looked forward to this vacation for months while he was in the Sandbox. The deployment had been rough, and he hoped to never see Syria or Iraq again, but that was unlikely given his occupation. His mind lingered on the night two weeks earlier when Clint had been killed. The memory of his teammates carefully placing Clint inside the black vinyl body bag was burned into his brain. He could still taste the bitter copper. He had lost friends and teammates over the years, but this one hit him harder than the others. The tremors started the next day. Clint was a devout Catholic. He left a wife and seven kids behind. The Agency made sure the Team came home in time to attend the ceremony unveiling Clint's star on the Memorial Wall.

The wintry weather in Alaska was a welcome change, plus no one would be trying to kill him. Jon had the lodge to himself for the first week. That would give him some time to decompress and, if he was lucky, maybe even be bored for a day or two. Hopefully, the intermittent tremors in his right hand would go away before the others showed up. He didn't want to answer any uncomfortable questions. Oddly, the shakes only occurred while he was out of harm's way. When he was operating, he was rock solid. The following week, his buds from the Teams and the Agency would start arriving, and then the fun would really kick off. Since he had gotten there first, he claimed the master bedroom. Rustic oversized wood furniture sat on the oak plank floor. A floor-to-ceiling window faced the beach next to a stone fireplace. It was much nicer than he was accustomed to. He threw his jacket across the overstuffed red-and-black plaid chair next to the king-sized bed and unpacked his gear. Two of his buddies would get the smaller bedrooms. The others would share the other two lodges they had reserved.

Ten minutes later, he was done unpacking and walked into the fully stocked kitchen. He opened a door with a frosted glass pane that had the word "Grub" etched on it and flipped the light on. He knew what he wanted as he scanned the shelves. He found a can of deluxe mixed nuts and a big bag of pretzels. He backed out of the pantry. Next, he went to the refrigerator and opened the door. He smiled as he pulled out a Blue Moon Pale Ale and twisted the cap off. He didn't see a trash can and was too tired to look for it, so he left the cap on the granite countertop. He walked into the living room and placed his snacks on the massive pinewood coffee table in front of the sofa.

Jon pulled his holster off his waist and placed it next to the pretzels. The holster held his .45 ACP caliber Glock 30 SF. The pistol had become a part of him over the years, and he felt naked without a weapon within arm's reach. He didn't have PTSD, no matter what the doctors said. He slept fine. He wasn't afraid or paranoid. He was pragmatic and liked being prepared. For him, it was like wearing a seatbelt when he was in a car. He didn't think he'd be in an accident, but if he was, he'd be ready. It was always better to have a gun and not need it than to need it and not have it.

He sat down on the overstuffed sofa and kicked off his Merrell's. He grabbed his snacks and put his feet up on the table. He leaned back with the TV remote and started flipping through the channels on the eighty-inch flat screen attached to the wall. He settled on a rerun of Hawaii Five-O. The fingers on his right hand started to tingle like they were about to go numb. He rubbed his hands together and made a fist a few times until his hand felt normal again. Then he noticed his hand didn't shake while it held a beer. Maybe it was a sign.

When the commercial ended, the leader of the Five-O Task Force, Lieutenant Commander Steve McGarrett, appeared on the screen. Jon smirked at TV's idea of a Navy SEAL. Somehow McGarrett had left active duty in the Teams and was immediately hired to lead an elite police unit without ever having been trained at a police academy or having any law enforcement experience. Then the governor of Hawaii gave his unit the authority to violate all of their suspects' civil rights. Somehow, McGarrett never had to write a police report or testify in court and explain his actions. Jon wondered if the show even had a technical advisor.

McGarrett had just jumped off of a twenty-foot-tall building without breaking any bones, and Jon had downed about half of his beer when his head slid back against the sofa cushion and his eyes closed. Fifteen minutes later, he was sound asleep when the sonar ringtone on his cell phone jerked him awake. He groaned as he pulled the phone from his shirt pocket and checked the caller ID. His Aunt Faye was calling.

"Son of a bitch," he cursed and declined the call.

He turned off the phone and dropped it on the sofa next to the pretzels. He was almost back to sleep when it magically came back to life and started ringing again. This time before he could silence it, he heard a helicopter outside approaching the beach, and then the windows on the back of the cabin began to shake.

Resigned to his fate, he answered the phone. "I guess the helo's for me." Helo was Navy speak for a helicopter.

"Sorry to interrupt, Jon, but you'll have to postpone your leave for a couple of days. Duty calls. Just leave your gear there. Everything you need will be provided," the gravelly voice said before hanging up.

Sometimes he felt like one of Charlie's Angels, always getting called and assigned to missions without any advanced notice. He wondered if Mister Gravel Voice ever went on missions himself or if he just sat on his ass in Virginia and sent others.

Jon put his boots back on and stood up. He stretched his tall, well-muscled frame and scratched his gray-haired head with both hands. He turned off the TV and retrieved his pistol. He took a step then reached back to grab his beer before walking to the bedroom to get his parka. He walked through the kitchen and out of the lodge through the sliding glass door onto the cedar deck facing the beach. He could barely see the white and orange helicopter sitting on the beach behind the lodge in the dim light provided by the porch light. The rotor wash peppered his face and the back of the lodge with sand and an occasional pebble. He squinted, chugged the rest of his beer, and left the empty bottle on the deck railing before he headed across the patchy snow-covered beach.

The Coast Guard Jayhawk helicopter's crew chief was waiting at the edge of the rotor arc and ushered him aboard. As soon as they were inside, the cabin door slid closed. Three crewmen were in the cabin area with Jon. Besides the crew chief, there was another crewman and a rescue swimmer. The swimmer handed him a Toughbook secure laptop. Instructions on how to log in were taped to the top. The helicopter sprang from the beach and nosed over to accelerate over the water. The takeoff seemed unnatural to Jon, and he thought they were dipping way too close to the water. He was about to say something to the crew chief when he saw the lights from the lodges falling away from the window in the cabin door.

Jon wondered if they had a new copilot they were trying to get trained up. Usually, these Coasties were shit hot. He had flown a lot with military helo guys, and it always amazed him how they could operate these complicated beasts at night while wearing night vision goggles. From his experience using NVGs, depth perception was tough while looking through the goggles. The field of view was only about 40°, and the best vision you could get from them was about 20/40. Everything had a green fuzzy, out-of-focus look to it. If a pilot's unaided vision was tested at 20/40, the flight surgeon would make him wear glasses while flying, but at night on NVGs, the pilots were flying all night long with 20/40 vision. The pilots had to scan outside of the cockpit through the NVGs and then quickly look under the goggles at the instrument panel. Their heads were on a swivel, constantly sweeping back and forth to the side and out front and to the instruments as they tried to cover 180° with the 40° FOV goggles. It's a wonder they didn't have constant neck problems and headaches.

Jon fumbled around under his seat in the dimly lit cabin until he felt the seatbelt and secured it around his waist. He tugged on the rescue swimmer's sleeve and gestured for a cranial and inflatable life vest. The cranial was a flight deck helmet the boatswain's mates and other deck crewmen wore on the flight deck to protect them from head injuries and hearing loss. It was a tan canvas and foam rubber-padded helmet with hard plastic shells over the forehead and back of the head separated by sound-suppressing cups over each ear. The boatswain's mates usually had goggles attached to theirs to protect their eyes from debris flying around on the flight deck.

The swimmer gave Jon a look that he translated to, I think you're a pussy, and then reached into an olive drab, or OD, green parachute bag and fished out a cranial and vest for him. Jon hesitated for a second, trying to decide which to put on first, and then decided any action was better than inaction. He put the cranial on his head and secured the Velcro chin strap. Then he tried to put the vest on and figured out it wouldn't fit over the cranial, so he had to take it back off. He hoped the pilots would do him the courtesy of waiting until he was ready before they decided to crash into the water. Eventually, he got the vest and cranial on. He leaned back in his seat and tried to relax. He'd made it through a twenty-year career in the Teams and never went down in a helicopter. He sure didn't want to do it tonight in ice-cold water miles from land.

CHAPTER 5

0630Z (2130HR AKST)
HOMER, ALASKA

Alaska State Trooper Eric Fuller was only three and a half hours into his shift. He was patrolling north of the city of Homer in a worn-out white Ford Crown Victoria. He was driving back and forth down Sterling Highway bored out of his mind. The nights went by slowly when he wasn't busy stopping cars and answering calls for service. It had been slow the last few nights because of the shitty weather, but the snow had stopped falling, and the weather was improving. He thought people might start coming back out on the streets again. The only vehicle on the road with him tonight was a state-owned snowplow that passed him going in the opposite direction.

Eric's cell phone rang. He put the free hot cocoa he had just picked up at the Stop and Rob in his cruiser's cupholder and answered, "Hello."

It was one of the dispatchers, Jenny. "Eric, you need to come back to the station. Rick needs to talk to you." Rick was Sergeant Richard Baderman, the watch commander.

"What for?" Eric couldn't remember doing anything bad enough that it would warrant the watch commander pulling him off the street, but it must be bad news if he wanted to talk to him immediately. You never got called in during the middle of your shift and told you were doing a great job. It just didn't happen.

"I don't know, but it seems important. Could you go by Mike's house and ask him to come in too? He's not answering his phone. Also, stay off the radio. If you need me, call back on your cell phone."

Mike worked with Eric and was his best friend. "OK, I'll swing by his place then come in." He hung up and made an illegal U-turn across the snow-filled median. Snow was thrown out onto the freshly plowed pavement as his car's back end spun around too far to the right. He overcorrected a couple of times before he straightened out and accelerated down the empty highway. Eric picked up his cocoa and sipped it. He thought it was good Baderman wanted Mike too. If there was any trouble, he was great for taking the heat off of everyone else. His friend, Mike, was a shit magnet. If you were ever in trouble, all you had to do was go stand next to him, and the trouble would leap off of you onto him. Mike sucked in trouble like a black hole sucks in, well, everything.

CHAPTER 6

"Do you want some ice cream?" Jocelyn Gillis asked her fiancée, Liam. She was standing in front of the refrigerator with the freezer door open in their one-bedroom apartment. It was kind of late for her to be eating, but she had gotten home from work an hour earlier, and she needed to unwind for a while before going to bed. She had the weekend off, so she could sleep late in the morning. She tended to be cold all the time, so she was wearing gray sweatpants and a black wool sweater to go with her puffy orange Garfield slippers. She was also the proud owner of two Sphynx cats. Known for their lack of hair, they also tended to be cold. To compensate, she kept the thermostat set at a balmy 75°.

Liam wasn't cold. He was wearing a threadbare gray Rams T-shirt and blue gym shorts. He was sprawled out on the sofa in his bare feet about ten feet from the kitchen table watching his hometown team, the Anaheim Ducks, getting their asses beat by the St. Louis Blues.

He replied, "Chocolate, please," right before the doorbell rang. Without turning his head away from the TV, he said, "Somebody's at the door."

Jocelyn walked by the sofa and flicked the back of his head with her middle finger and said, "What? Are your legs broke?"

"You were already up," he replied.

"If you weren't so beautiful, I'd throw your ass out," she said jokingly.

Liam looked like a modern version of Thor from Norse mythology, minus the beard. With his looks, he could have starred in the next Point Break movie.

Jocelyn grabbed her Glock 23 pistol from its holster on the catchall table next to the door and raised the small piece of black construction paper she had taped to the door to cover the peephole. She kept the peephole covered to prevent someone from using a reverse peephole viewer to see into her small apartment's living room. She had one of her own she used at work. She peered through the peephole and smiled. She unlocked the two deadbolts and opened the door. "Come on in, Jerry. You're just in time for ice cream," she said.

Jerry was Special Agent Woodrow T. Jerome and Jocelyn's partner in the Counterespionage Section of the FBI's Counterintelligence Division. He was still wearing the dark gray suit he had worn to the office that morning. Over the suit, he wore his black London Fog trench coat. It was his unofficial FBI uniform. Jerry was a tall, fit thirty-five-year-old black man. With his wire-framed glasses and conservative haircut, he looked more like an accountant or lawyer than a spy hunter.

Jocelyn and he had been teamed up as partners for almost three years and worked well together. They weren't like the FBI agents on TV that were constantly bucking the system on the verge of being fired by the Office of Professional Responsibility. They were GS-13 journeyman agents, which meant they were highly trained and competent law enforcement professionals. They were also the working class of the FBI that actually went into the field and did the dirty work.

"I'm sorry, Jocelyn, but we have to go back to work," he replied. They had both put in a twelve-hour day before she left for home. He stayed after because it was his turn to do the paperwork.

"What's going on?" she asked.

Jerry looked past her at Liam. "I really can't talk about it here. It's classified. I can say I was still at the office when I received a call from the Director's office and was told to go over to the White House and see the Director. When I got to the gate, the Secret Service waved me right in and directed me to park in front of the side entrance. They escorted me to the Situation Room in the basement. The Director was sitting in there with the President, the National Security Advisor, the White House chief of staff, and the chief justice of the Supreme Court. The Director handed me a handwritten search warrant signed by Chief Justice Robertson. We have to execute the warrant ASAP. Get dressed, and I'll brief you in the car."

"OK, give me five minutes." She headed for the bedroom. She had never been to the White House and was excited to be involved in something so high-vis. She scrambled around her bedroom getting ready. Normally, she was more organized, but she hadn't expected to go back to work until Monday morning. Fifteen minutes later, Special Agent Gillis came out of the bedroom in her unofficial FBI uniform: a navy blue pantsuit and sensible shoes. She wanted to look good in case they were called back to the White House after executing the warrant. She found Jerry and Liam sitting on the couch eating chocolate ice cream and watching the hockey game. Jerry was rooting for the Blues.

Liam took his wallet off of the coffee table and said, "Here you go," as he handed Jerry twenty bucks.

Jerry put his bowl down on the coffee table and stood up. "It's a pleasure doing business with you. Thanks for the ice cream."

"No sweat, Jerry. Have my girl back before curfew."

Jocelyn bent over, kissed Liam goodbye, and told him not to wait up for her, not that she thought he would. She put her holstered Glock on her right hip and grabbed her black London Fog trench coat and purse before they headed out the door. As she and Jerry walked down the drab hallway on the fifth floor of her outdated but reasonably priced apartment building, she pulled her poufy black wool cap and leather gloves from her coat pockets and put them on.

"What was the money for? Were you betting on the game?" she asked.

Jerry smiled. "No, we bet on how long it would take you to get dressed. I knew you would get dressed up for the White House." Then he asked, "How long has the elevator been broken?"

"What do you mean?" Jocelyn gave him a confused look.

"The kid in the lobby said the elevator was broken."

Now Jocelyn smiled as she stopped in front of the elevator door and pressed the down button. "Was he about sixteen years old and wearing a red Nats baseball cap?"

Jerry eyed her suspiciously and nodded his head.

"That's Edwin. He lives in the building. He's mildly autistic and he thinks he's funny, but hey, at least you got your cardio in for the day. So, what are we doing tonight?" she said as they stepped into the elevator.

They were alone so Jerry started explaining, "The CIA has a scientist on vacation in Alaska named Karpinsky. Every year he goes up there for three or four weeks. He's a Soviet-era defector, and they think the Russians are going to try to snatch him because the NSA intercepted a message to one of their submarines in the Bering Sea mentioning his name. He has a three-man security detail of deputy marshals protecting him. He lives alone in a house in McLean. We're going to search his house to see if we can determine if he is really a potential victim or possibly a double agent. We have to do it tonight while his neighbors are asleep so they don't see us there."

"So, this is a black bag job," Jocelyn guessed.

"Yes, except this one's legal," Jerry replied as he held up the warrant.

Black bag jobs were covert operations where agents would sneak into vehicles, homes, and offices without their owner's knowledge or permission to gather intelligence or evidence. Back in Hoover's day, black bag jobs were commonplace and accomplished without a warrant. Evidence collected without a warrant couldn't be used in court, but it could still be valuable for counter-intelligence purposes, and Hoover wasn't above using the information for political blackmail. These operations still occurred, but the Bureau had become much more circumspect.

After the elevator door opened onto the first floor, they walked briskly across the lobby and out onto the sidewalk. Jerry's car was parked a half block down the street. They braced against the chill and hurried to the car. Jocelyn had to jog to keep up with Jerry's long stride. Even though it was freezing cold, Jerry took off his trench coat and threw it onto the back seat. Then he and Jocelyn got in Jerry's Bureau car, which in this case was a dark gray Chevy Impala. Jocelyn kept her jacket and hat on and immediately turned the heat up to the maximum setting.

It took twenty-three minutes to travel the eleven miles to Dr. Oleg Karpinsky's home at 6721 Pine Creek Court in McLean, Virginia. Just before Jerry turned onto Pine Creek Court, he turned off his headlights and relied on the parking lights to navigate the rest of the way. The house was a two-story with light gray siding and four bedrooms that sat on a cul-de-sac with three similar homes. It was built in the 1930s on a half-acre lot that backed up to Kirby Park. The streetlight in the circle was on, but shadows from several large red cedar trees covered the driveway in front of the garage door. The two-car garage was in the left half of the basement, and stone stairs on the right side of the driveway led up to the first-floor main entrance.

Jerry pulled the Impala into the driveway as close to the garage door as he could to take advantage of the shadows. He reached into the back seat to grab his coat. After they climbed out of the Impala, they both put on a pair of disposable black nitrile gloves.

While they climbed the steps to the front door, Jocelyn said softly, "I wonder how this guy can afford a million-dollar home while working for the CIA."

"He's also a practicing psychiatrist, and he wrote a couple of books on something called remote viewing. They're used as textbooks by some major universities," Jerry replied.

The house was dark, and they looked through the windows on the front porch. Jocelyn didn't see any movement, so she rang the doorbell. The last thing she wanted was to break into the wrong house and get shot by a scared homeowner. No one answered. Jerry glanced back at the other houses to see if they had drawn any attention, but the neighborhood remained quiet.

"Do you know if he has an alarm?" Jocelyn asked.

"I don't know for sure, but I don't see a sign in the yard or any decals on the windows," Jerry replied.

Jocelyn pulled a black neoprene mouse pad from her coat pocket and dropped it on the porch. She lowered her left knee onto the pad, clenched a small plastic penlight between her lips, and went to work on the deadbolt with her lock-picking kit. The Bureau had trained her to pick a lock within a minute or two. Jerry turned his back to her and attempted to block anyone from seeing her activities. Even though they had a warrant, they didn't want anyone to know they had entered the house. If Karpinsky was innocent, it would cause him unnecessary embarrassment with his neighbors, and if he was guilty, it might tip off the Russians that the Feds were on to him. In less than a minute, she pushed the door open and they stepped inside.

"Not bad," Jerry said as he locked the door behind them. He shined his small flashlight along the doorjamb and then to the corners of the entryway. "I don't see any alarm sensors on the jamb or motion sensors in the corners. I think we're good."

They purposely left the house lights off and relied on their flashlights to clear the house. After they were satisfied that they were alone, they began their search.

Jocelyn stopped in the first-floor hallway and asked, "Are you cold?"

"No, why?"

Jocelyn walked over to the thermostat on the wall. She shined her light on it. "The thermostat is set at 72°. If you were going out of town for a month in the middle of the winter, wouldn't you lower the thermostat down to 55° or so to save money on your heating bill?"

Jerry shrugged. "Maybe he just forgot."

"My dad always says, 'In police work, we call that a clue.'" Jocelyn's father had been a police officer for the last thirty-five years. When she told him she wanted to be a cop, he advised her to go federal. He told her the pay and benefits were the best anywhere, and she would deal with a better class of criminal. Plus, she was too smart to spend her first five years on the job in uniform patrolling a beat. She would have been bored to death writing speeding tickets and barking dog summonses. She followed his advice and never regretted it.

Next, Jocelyn walked over to the home office. Karpinsky didn't have a separate medical office out in town. He saw his patients in this room. She stopped at the double pocket-door entrance and shined her light around the room. It was a large room decorated with an abundance of expensive wood trim. A large Persian rug covered the polished oak plank floor. The wall to her right was covered completely by a built-in mahogany bookcase overflowing with books. Next, she examined the wall to her left. It was Karpinsky's "love-me" wall. It was covered with certificates, diplomas, awards, and photos of him with important people from the academic and intelligence communities. He wasn't a covert CIA employee. He used his status as a Russian defector and CIA scientist to help sell his books and grow his list of patients. A large antique desk and plush brown leather swivel chair faced the doorway from the far wall. Two brown leather chairs sat in front of the desk, and a matching couch sat to the right. Everything in the room was a testament to Karpinsky's gravitas.

Jocelyn sat down behind the desk and began going through the drawers. She pulled a black-and-white speckled school composition book from the center drawer. Karpinsky used this one to keep track of his household bills. Each page accounted for a month's expenses. She flipped to the last page of entries in the ledger and discovered the expenses for the month of February had not been paid. He had stopped a week before he left on vacation. That meant he had some bills that would be more than a month overdue when he returned home from Alaska.

She called out to her partner, "Hey, Jerry, come here."

He came downstairs from the master bedroom. "What's up?" he wondered as he entered the room.

"Clue number two." She showed him the ledger and explained what she found.

"It sounds like he doesn't plan to come back. I didn't see anything unusual upstairs. I'll check out the bookcase," Jerry said. He walked over to the wall and pulled a book down from the top left corner of the bookcase. He thumbed through it to see if anything would reveal itself.

Jocelyn pulled on the bottom drawer on the right side of the desk, but it was locked. She checked the other drawers for the key but came up empty. She pulled out her lock-picking set and in a few seconds had the drawer open. It was full of green hanging file folders. She grabbed a random folder from the drawer and opened it up on top of Karpinsky's closed laptop. She gasped out loud at what she saw and covered her mouth with her hands.

Jerry turned to check on her. "Are you alright?"

Jocelyn nodded without lifting her eyes from the folder. It contained a stack of very graphic police evidence photos and news articles about a young woman named Kimberly Jansen from Annandale, Virginia, who had been brutally raped multiple times and later committed suicide. The first photo she saw on the stack was of the naked victim lying on her bed with her head hanging over the edge. Her dead eyes were staring at the camera. The folder also contained her profiles from Facebook and several other social media platforms.

Jocelyn pulled another file from the drawer. It contained similar photographs and news clips about another woman who had been sexually assaulted. She pulled the remaining files out of the drawer one at a time; eventually, all of them were stacked up on the desk. There had to be over a hundred files, and all contained pictures and news articles about women around the world who had been raped and abused. Some of the news articles were from obscure newspapers and in languages she had never heard of. Then she noticed a row of small stars drawn below the women's names on the file folders. Some rated four or five stars. Others only rated one or two. Jocelyn thought the folders didn't look like academic research; they seemed like the trophies of a sexual predator. She struggled to remain professional, but the files pissed her off.

"Jerry, this whole drawer is full of photos, reports, and news clippings of rape and sexual assault victims. That's strike three," Jocelyn said angrily.

She opened the seventeen-inch MacBook that rested in the center of the desk and pressed the power button. After a minute, the logon screen appeared and asked for a password. She thought about typing in "Pervert" or "TheRapist" but resisted. She didn't see anything written on top of the desk that was obviously the password. She peeked under the desk blotter the laptop was on but didn't find anything underneath it. She opened the top drawers on either side of her but didn't see anything taped to the sides of the drawers or underneath them. Finally, she pulled out her cell phone and called the Cyber-Intelligence Team of the FBI's Cyber Division. They operated twenty-four hours a day, seven days a week, mostly to support investigations from FISA warrants. FISA stood for the Foreign Intelligence Surveillance Act.

A technician answered the phone. "CIT, may I help you?"

"This is Special Agent Jocelyn Gillis, 32574. I'm executing a search warrant at 6721 Pine Creek Court in McLean, Virginia. I need help accessing a MacBook laptop."

"Hi, Jocelyn, it's Cathy. Is it connected to the internet?"

Jocelyn knew Cathy because they were both members of one of the FBI's numerous Special Emphasis Programs. They belonged to the Federal Women's Program.

Jocelyn saw an Ethernet cable plugged into the side of the laptop. "Hi, Cathy. Yes, it appears so."

"OK, standby." Within a minute, the desktop appeared and began loading. "Do you want help with something specific, or should I take everything?"

"Go ahead and take it all. The owner is a defector from the former Soviet Union and, apparently, a sexual predator. Let me know if you find anything encrypted and, if so, what it says."

"Sure thing. Hey, did you do something new with your hair?"

Jocelyn was watching the cursor dart around the screen as Cathy remotely accessed Karpinsky's files. She looked up at the top of the screen and realized Cathy was watching her through the laptop's webcam.

Jocelyn smiled. "Yes. I had it styled and highlighted a couple of days ago."

"It suits you."

Jocelyn made a mental note to herself to put a piece of tape over the webcam on her laptop when she got home.

Jerry was still pulling books from the bookcase and thumbing through them looking for hidden clues. There had to be over five hundred books in Karpinsky's collection. "This is frustrating. Next time, I get the desk." His cell phone buzzed. He pulled it from his pocket and read the message. "The Agency is sending one of their security teams to take possession of any Agency property or classified material we might come across."

Jocelyn was surprised. "If we find classified material, we need to seize it as evidence so we can prosecute Karpinsky."

Jerry wiggled his phone back and forth. "The Director says to hand it over."

Five minutes later, there was a knock at the back door. Jerry and Jocelyn pulled their Glocks and went to the kitchen.

"I'll cover you from the hallway," Jocelyn said.

Jerry walked to the kitchen door, pulled back the curtain, and looked through the glass. He could make out two men in the dark. They weren't wearing suits. They were dressed like they were ready to get dirty if need be. One of them wore a black backpack. Jerry thought it looked like the bug-out bag he had in the Corps. He didn't know it, but they had parked on the other side of Kirby Park in the driveway of one of the many CIA employees who lived in the area. They walked across the park and climbed over Karpinsky's eight-foot-tall wooden privacy fence.

"Show me your creds," Jerry said through the glass. Creds meant credentials, which to the FBI meant badges and identification cards. Both men opened their wallets and held their CIA identification cards up against the window. Jerry held up his cell phone, and the flash went off as he snapped a photo of the creds and the men. The names on the creds were probably fake, but he had to try. He opened the door and stood aside to allow the two men inside.

"What the fuck!" the first man said.

Both of them were rubbing their eyes. Jerry couldn't tell if they were more perturbed by the flash or the fact that Jerry had a photo of them and their ID.

"I'm Jerry Jerome, and my partner is Jocelyn Gillis."

The first CIA officer was still seeing stars when he said, "I'm Bob Smith, and he's Bill Jones."

Jocelyn and Jerry exchanged sarcastic grins as she said, "Smith and Jones, sure, OK."

"We've been ordered to inventory anything you intend to take from the premises and if it is of interest to the CIA to seize it," Bob said.

Jocelyn led them into the office and pointed at the tall stack of green file folders on the desk next to the laptop. "Your boy is one sick puppy. He has a huge collection of photos and news clippings of sexual assault and rape victims. I know he's a psychiatrist, but his field of research is not sexual deviance. His expertise is in ESP and remote viewing." ESP stood for extrasensory perception and, like remote viewing, was considered a pseudoscience by most serious scientists and medical professionals, but the CIA had been funding Karpinsky's research for over twenty-five years. They took it seriously, and with Karpinsky's help, they had been able to glean a great deal of valuable intelligence from the United States' adversaries and allies.

Jocelyn walked around the desk and, as she sat down, saw that the laptop screen was blank, making it look like the computer was powered down. "Do you guys have the password for his laptop?"

Cathy had heard the conversation with Bob and Bill and turned the screen off. The laptop still had power, and she was recording everything that was said and whatever the webcam could see.

"No, but we'll take it back to Langley and the techs will search it," Bob answered.

"Can we have a copy of what you find? This guy may be a sexual predator," Jerry asked.

"Sure, no problem," Bob replied.

Jocelyn didn't believe for a second they would get any information from the CIA. Twenty years after the Twin Towers had come down on 9/11, there was still little trust or cooperation between the CIA and FBI. Despite the recent political scandals, the Bureau was still the nation's premier law enforcement agency, and they had to protect the Republic from the CIA's anything-goes cowboy attitude. The FBI followed the rule of law, with a few well-publicized exceptions.

The Agency traced its roots back to the Office of Strategic Services, or OSS, in World War II. They conducted espionage, subversion, and sabotage behind enemy lines. The CIA viewed the FBI's white-collar, goody-two-shoes way of operating as naive and dangerous. The Agency believed that if you weren't cheating, you weren't trying. The only thing that mattered was winning. The CIA was the worldly big brother that had to protect the family from the actions of the gullible little brother. Threats weren't to be prosecuted and imprisoned, they were to be interrogated for everything they knew and then eliminated or, if absolutely necessary, traded to get back one of their own assets. The FBI served in the light and carried badges. The Agency served in the shadows, and badges? They didn't need no stinking badges.

Jocelyn stood up and offered Bob the chair. He sat down and began thumbing through the green folders. Bill joined him next to the desk and grabbed a folder.

Moments later, Bill exclaimed, "Jesus Christ! This shit is disgusting!"

After five minutes and four victims, Bob dropped the folder he was looking at on top of the desk and tried to wipe his gloved palms clean on the front of his jacket. He looked up at Agent Gillis. "I can't believe how twisted this asshole is. If it was up to me, you guys could bury him under the Hoover Building."

Jerry asked, "Does anybody want a bottle of water? I saw some in the refrigerator." No one wanted water, so he headed for the kitchen. As he walked down the hall, he heard a metallic scraping sound coming from the other side of the kitchen. He recognized the sound immediately. Someone was trying to pick the lock on the back door. He retreated down the hall as quietly and quickly as he could and stuck his head into the office. "Someone is picking the back door," he whispered.

The others immediately turned off their flashlights and pulled their pistols. Jocelyn took charge. "Bob and Bill, go cover the kitchen from the dining room. We'll take the hallway."

The CIA men complied with her instructions. They took their positions and waited, weapons in hand, for over two minutes, which seemed more like two hours, but the lock picker was still working the lock. Finally, someone whispered something in Russian that probably meant, 'Get out of the way, idiot. I'll do it.' A minute and a half later, the door began to open slowly. Two men cautiously stepped into the dark kitchen, and the second man closed the door behind them.

Jocelyn and Jerry lit them up with their flashlights and both yelled, "FBI! Put your hands up!"

Instead of complying, both men went for their weapons, which were concealed under their coats, putting them at a distinct disadvantage. Jocelyn and Jerry were about to pull their triggers when the kitchen lit up from multiple gunshots coming from their right, fired by Bob and Bill. It was like a strobe light flickering in a nightclub. Jerry and Jocelyn fired their own volley. The one-sided gunfight lasted less than three seconds. The Russians collapsed to the floor and died immediately. Remarkably, all the rounds fired hit their marks and stayed inside the bodies. If anyone had been in the backyard looking at the kitchen windows, it would have looked and sounded like a short, muffled, but very violent, lightning storm had occurred in the kitchen. Jerry stepped forward and kicked the pistols away from the bodies with his foot. The bad guys had Glocks too. It seemed Glocks were ubiquitous in the world of law enforcement and espionage. The only real disagreement was what caliber of Glock to use: 9mm, .40 S&W, or .45 ACP.

Bob pulled two black modular integrated communications helmets, or MICH, with dual-tubed night vision goggles attached from Bill's backpack. "We'll go outside and have a look around."

"Make sure you announce yourselves when you come back," Jerry said.

Bob and Bill put their helmets on and flipped on their NVGs. "Wilco," Bob replied.

Jerry noticed Bob and Bill had suppressors on their pistols as they went out the back door.

"Give me your cuffs," Jerry said.

Jocelyn handed them over with her left hand while she pointed her Glock at the closest body with her right. Jerry stepped around the bodies, being careful not to step in the blood, and locked the back door behind them. Jocelyn continued to cover the bodies with her pistol while Jerry handcuffed them.

Jocelyn realized her hands were shaking, her ears were ringing, and her heart was pounding out of control. She tried to summon some saliva to her dry mouth, but her tongue stuck to her teeth. She concentrated on slowing her breathing. She had never shot anyone before, and she dearly hoped these were actually bad men who needed killing. She asked, "Have you ever had to kill anyone before?"

Jerry used his left forefinger to push his glasses back against the bridge of his nose. "Not since Afghanistan."

Jocelyn knew Jerry had been a captain in the Marine Corps. He had commanded a combat engineer company. He and his Marines spent a lot of time repairing roads and clearing improvised explosive devices. When they weren't occupied by engineer duties, they served as infantry.

Now that the bodies were handcuffed, Jerry checked to see if they were actually dead. He held the fingers of his nitrile gloved left hand to the carotid artery of each man to check for a pulse. As Jocelyn's father would say, both men were DRT, or dead right there.

"I can't stop shaking," Jocelyn said.

Jerry bent over to go through their pockets. "That's normal. It's the adrenaline. You'll calm down in a little while." A minute later, he said, "Their pockets are empty. No wallets or cell phones, nothing. Not even rings or neck chains. Either someone drove them here or they hid their car's key fob outside somewhere."

"It's too bad we had to shoot them. I would've liked to get some information from them," Jocelyn said.

"They wouldn't have talked to us anyway. They would have just waited for the Russians to make a deal for them," Jerry replied.

"I wasn't going to talk to them. I was going to sit in the corner and listen while Bob and Bill talked to them. And if they got rough, I was going to whisper to them to stop while I wrote down everything the Russians said." Jocelyn pulled out her phone. "I'll see if CIT can ID them."

She snapped photos of both of their faces with her cell phone and called CIT. "This is Special Agent Jocelyn Gillis, 32574. Let me speak to Cathy."

Cathy came on the line and said excitedly, "Are you OK? I heard gunshots!"

Jocelyn realized Cathy was still listening to them through the laptop. "Yes, we're fine. We just killed two guys that broke into the house through the back door. They don't have ID. I'm sending you their photos. Let me know who they are."

Two minutes later, Cathy called back, "They're both Russians assigned to their embassy. They have diplomatic passports, but they don't have diplomatic immunity. The gray-haired guy is Yura Boleslav. He's a cultural attaché. The other guy is Yegor Georgy. He's an economic analyst. We have small files on both of them. They've been here for about a year but hadn't done anything interesting until tonight."

"Thank you, Cathy. I'll talk to you later," Jocelyn said before she hung up.

"Why would the Russians want to break into Karpinsky's house?" Jerry wondered out loud.

"For the same reasons we did. They want to know whose side he's really on. They want to know if they can trust him or not," Jocelyn replied.

Bob and Bill knocked on the back door and announced themselves. Jerry let them in and told them the two dead guys were low-level Russian diplomats.

Bob rotated his NVGs up out of the way. "Which means SVR."

Bill also raised his goggles and nodded in agreement. SVR— or more specifically, the SVR RF—was the Foreign Intelligence Service of the Russian Federation tasked with external intelligence gathering and espionage activities. It worked in coordination with the military intelligence service, the Main Intelligence Directorate, or GRU, in contrast to the more well-known FSB, which worked within Russia and was responsible for counterintelligence, internal security, border security, counterterrorism, and surveillance.

Bob said, "We had a look around. I don't think anybody heard the shooting. Control advised that no one has called the police yet. For the time being, we know something the Russians don't. These guys are probably supposed to check in in a couple of hours—four at the most. If they don't, the Russians will know we're on to them."

Jocelyn noticed Bob and Bill weren't the slightest bit flustered after killing the Russians. It was like another day at the office for them. "Let's give the local police credit for stopping a burglary and killing the burglars. We can put out that the dead suspects are unidentified. That should give us some time."

Jerry pulled out his cell phone. "I'll call the Director and tell him what happened. Hopefully, he'll go along with your idea." He made the call and explained what had transpired, including the fact that the CIA officers had also participated in the shoot-out. The Director agreed with their course of action. The Director then called the chief of the Fairfax County Police Department, Ed Russell, and put the plan into motion.

"Jerry, you should move the car out of the driveway before they get here," Jocelyn said.

He nodded and headed for the door.

"What pistols and ammo are you guys carrying?" Jocelyn asked Bob and Bill.

"Glock model 23 with 180 grain Federal Hydra-Shok," Bob replied.

It was the same as she was carrying. That would make things a little simpler. All of the rounds in the bodies would be the same make and caliber.

"Good, that's what we carry," Jocelyn said.

Bob looked at Bill, shared a smile with him, and said, "Yeah, we know."

"I won't ask if your fingerprints are on the brass," Jocelyn said.

The brass was actually nickel-coated brass casings expelled from the pistols as the bullets were fired. Bob and Bill smiled again. They had worn gloves while loading their magazines so they wouldn't leave any prints behind. Their Glocks were clean, meaning they weren't registered and couldn't be tracked back to them or the Agency.

"Are you guys going to take off before the police arrive?" Jocelyn asked.

"Yeah, we'll take the laptop and go. Your techs should have had enough time to copy everything off of it by now anyway." Bob smiled.

It appeared these CIA guys were sharper than she thought.

"What about the folders?" she asked.

"I didn't see anything classified in them, so help yourself." Bob grabbed the laptop and charger and stuffed them in the backpack on Bill's back. They lowered their NVGs and walked out the back door. They quietly crossed the yard and effortlessly scaled the privacy fence.

CHAPTER 7

0635Z (2135HR AKST)
EEK LAKE, ALASKA

"Report, James," Trooper Logan, who was also the Spetsnaz commander, ordered in English. Calling him and his men Spetsnaz was technically correct but wasn't very descriptive. The term Spetsnaz just meant "Special Purpose Forces." Russia had many different types of Spetsnaz units for different missions. He and his men were members of a covert unit from the Ministry of Defense's Special Operations Forces. The unit's mere existence was highly classified. They reported directly to the Office of the Chief of the General Staff. They were trained to operate in America as Americans. None of them would speak Russian until they went back to the submarine.

Logan stood over the dead marshal named Lange and stared down at his bloody head. The left eye bugged out grotesquely. Logan thought it was a pity this man had to die. There was no animus as far as he was concerned. He had orders, and he carried them out. No more, no less. Under other circumstances, he would have happily sat in Hooter's and drank a couple or maybe eight beers with Lange while they argued about which city had the best baseball team. He liked Americans and envied their attitude of invincibility. They believed America was the strongest, freest country in the world and always would be.

He had spent a lot of time in America. His parents were diplomats serving in the Russian Embassy in DC, and he had lived in America from the time he was twelve years old until he finished college. He attended the prestigious Gonzaga College High School, where following his father's advice, he was a varsity athlete for the Eagles playing football, baseball, and hockey. One of his most prized possessions was his purple and white Gonzaga Eagles' varsity letterman jacket. After high school, he attended Ohio State University, where he graduated with a Bachelor of Arts degree in American History. Go Buckeyes!

"The marshal hit Howard twice with his M4. One round took a chunk out of his left earlobe, and the other went through his left thigh. He'll recover, but right now, he can't walk on the leg. The marshal also disabled both snowmobiles. Eldon said he can take parts from one to fix the other, but he can't fix both. It will take at least 30 minutes," the sergeant, James, replied. He was the white-clad sniper who had shot Kevin in the face.

Logan and his men had started the mission with five shiny new snowmobiles. Three for Logan and his team and two for the support team. Now his team would be down to two. This wasn't good, but they were trained to adapt. "Very well," Logan said. "Help Willie bury the bodies in the snow behind the cabin and clean up the blood, if possible. We don't want to alert anyone that we were here. Where's the doctor?"

James motioned toward the cabin. "He's inside bandaging Howard's wounds."

Logan, now with his AR-15 slung across his chest, climbed the steps to the porch, stepped over the dead marshal in the doorway, and walked into the cabin. He stood over Howard as he lay on the couch.

Smiling, Logan said, "You're slowing down, Hojo. You let the American cowboy shoot you. How do you feel?"

Howard glanced up from the sofa. "My ear stings some, but my leg is killing me. I think the bullet nicked the bone as it went through. Darrin, I apologize for screwing up the plan. I can't believe how fast the marshal returned fire," Howard replied remorsefully. He was a lieutenant and Logan's second in command.

Logan nodded. "I'd bet he was former military with combat experience. America has been at war for so long, many of their policemen have served in Iraq and Afghanistan. It's a good thing we planned for contingencies. We are down to two functioning snowmobiles, so you and the doctor will ride in the sleds. We'll leave as soon as Eldon says he's ready." Logan turned to the doctor and said, "Colonel, as you can see, we received your message. I hope this mission is worth the cost."

"I appreciate the risks you have taken to come for me, but I am certain the president will want to hear my report. I have learned a great deal during my stay in America. My research has uncovered a powerful new weapon we may use to return our country to its rightful place as a world-dominate superpower. It's been a long time since I have seen the president. I haven't talked to him since he worked for me in Dresden.

I used to send Major Pichugin to the bakery to pick up my favorite pastry," Karpinsky replied with a smile.

Logan and Hojo exchanged surprised looks.

CHAPTER 8

Lieutenant Colonel Ike Dragon was alone on a Friday night. He had the weekend off and was indulging himself. Earlier he had gorged himself on a large thin-crust sausage and pepperoni pizza, and now he was following it up with a big bowl of chocolate ice cream. He was relaxing in his recliner in his three-bedroom house on Pendleton Avenue reading a George Washington biography while Band of Brothers played in the background on the big-screen TV. He was wearing his black Army PT shorts and his favorite gray Texas Rangers T-shirt. He was actually a Cardinals fan, but he liked the shirt because it said Rangers across the chest.

His wife was visiting their daughter in Charlotte. She had given birth to their first grandchild, a little boy named Nathan.

His son, Eddy, was in his second year at the Naval Academy in Annapolis. Eddy liked to tease his old man by saying he was going to be a SEAL, but he knew better. The kid had wanted to be a fighter pilot ever since he saw Top Gun on TV when he was little.

Dragon had been in command of the 2nd Battalion, 75th Ranger Regiment for two and a half years. He had been in the Army for over 25 years, and he knew he would never be a general, so he didn't bother worrying about it. His next assignment would be as an ROTC professor of military science at the University of Missouri in Columbia. While there, he would work on his doctorate in history. Plus, the St. Louis Cardinals would be playing only two hours away east on I-70. After he retired, he planned to write books and teach, maybe even be one of those paid contributors on cable news. Life was good.

General Washington's second in command, Major General Benjamin Lincoln, was about to accept the British surrender at Yorktown and Captain Sobel was threatening to court martial Lieutenant Winters when Dragon's cell phone rang. His ringtone was from the opening of Wagner's "Ride of the Valkyries." He had liked it since he heard it in the movie Apocalypse Now.

He answered the phone, "Dragon."

"Sir, this is Lieutenant Stanley. The battalion has been activated for an immediate mission. We need to be ready for wheels up in six hours." Stanley was the battalion's duty officer tonight.

Dragon sat up in his recliner. "Have you initiated the recall roster, Tim?"

"No, sir. I called you first. I will go through the binder as soon as we're done," Stanley replied. He had a three-ring binder on the duty desk with the recall procedure printed out in a checklist. As he made notifications, he would check them off and write down the time.

"Very well. I'm inbound." He hung up and sprinted up the stairs to the bedroom. He quickly dressed in the operational camouflage pattern, or OCP, uniform he had staged on his valet chair. He threw on his fleece jacket, grabbed his bug-out bag, and was out the door in less than five minutes.

CHAPTER 9

Sergeant First Class Jim Strasburg of Company A, 3rd Battalion, 297th Infantry Regiment was having a bad day that had started almost fifteen hours earlier at 0700. Upon arriving at the armory, his battalion commander advised him the unit's weapons vault would be inspected tomorrow morning at the beginning of the unit's drill weekend. He, Staff Sergeant Nate Pope, and Corporal Allen Davis were active-duty guardsmen assigned to provide full-time support for the traditional one-weekend-a-month soldiers.

They had been at the armory all day preparing for the inspection. They were alone in the armory now. Everyone else had gone home by 1800. The weapons were easily accounted for, but over 10,000 rounds of the small arms ammunition, 9mm and 5.56 NATO, were missing. It could have been shot up during the battalion's last trip to the range, but there was no documentation. Most likely, though, was the possibility that one or more of the senior battalion officers or NCOs had taken the ammo for some unofficial firearms training. Strasburg was personally accountable for the ammo, and if he couldn't balance the books, he could kiss any chance of ever being promoted again goodbye.

"Screw it, I didn't want to be a first sergeant anyway," he mumbled. "OK, we're done. Are you guys going to sleep in the armory tonight or go home?"

"I'm staying," Pope replied.

"Me too," Davis said.

Strasburg pulled two twenties out of his wallet, offered them to Davis, and said, "Here, Allen, go to the office and order a couple of pizzas for us before they stop delivering. And, hey, no anchovies this time! Nate and I'll finish locking everything up."

Davis was sitting on a stack of wooden ammo crates with his feet dangling above the floor. He launched himself off his perch and grabbed the money.

"Thanks, Sergeant!" He bolted down the hall.

They were all hungry because they hadn't stopped to eat dinner. Strasburg thought the least he could do was buy Nate and Allen something to eat. They had worked all day without the hint of complaint. They were both fine young soldiers. In the morning, he would make certain none of the blame for the missing ammo fell on those two.

After Davis was out of hearing range, Pope said, "Jim, just say the word and I'll generate the necessary paperwork and be your witness that we expended it all at the range."

Jim looked up at the black mountain of a man. "Thanks, Nate, but I don't want you to sacrifice your integrity for me. I'm a big boy. I can take the heat."

Nate had been with the 82nd Airborne Division and served as a drill sergeant when he was in the regular Army. He had seen good soldiers scapegoated before and didn't think Strasburg should bear the blame. Although Jim had signed for the ammo, several officers and sergeants had access to the weapons vault. There was no telling when the ammo walked away.

Two minutes later, Allen yelled down the hall, "Sergeant Strasburg, there's a call for you in the office. It sounds important."

They had already finished securing the weapons vault and were walking back.

Strasburg entered the office, leaned over the desk, and took the phone from Davis. "Sergeant First Class Strasburg. May I help you, sir?"

"Sergeant Strasburg, do you recognize my voice?"

"Yes, sir, General. What can I do for you?" Strasburg had immediately recognized he was talking to the Alaska adjutant general, Major General Rodney Post, but he still spun the phone around and looked down at the caller ID.

"Sergeant, in approximately twenty minutes, a Coast Guard helicopter will land at the armory. You, Pope, and Davis are to report to Lieutenant Commander Smith for temporary duty with him that could involve combat. Outfit your men for that possibility. I know this is a shock, but this matter is classified, so I can't give you any details over this telephone. I will say that I envy you, Sergeant. I wish I was going with you. Also, give the Commander access to your weapon's vault and allow him to requisition anything he wants. This has already been approved at the highest level. Your orders and details of your mission will be available when you get to the Coast Guard Cutter Haley."

"Understood, sir, but how did you know we were here at the armory?" Strasburg asked.

"We can talk about that when you get back. Hooah, and God bless you and your men." The truth was, Post didn't know until General Harden at NORTHCOM told him so. They must have some tracking capability that Post had never been briefed on.

"Hooah!" Strasburg hung up and looked back and forth at Pope and Davis. He said with a nervous smile, "I've got some good news and some bad news. The inspection is canceled, and we are ordered to go on a classified combat mission with the Coast Guard. I'll let you decide which is which. Go get your gear out of your lockers and pack for a three-day combat mission in the field. We have about twenty minutes before they land their chopper here."

CHAPTER 10

0650Z (2150HR AKST)
HOMER, ALASKA

Eric Fuller was five miles north of Homer when he pulled off Sterling Highway. He drove down the tree-lined, snow-covered gravel driveway for about 600 feet before it curved to the left and ended at Mike Harmon's homestead. He could tell Mike had been out earlier on his tractor clearing the snow because it was only a couple of inches thick. Mike owned a twenty-acre plot. It was good, mostly flat land, and all but two acres were wooded. It even had a spring and creek running through it. Eric hit the cruiser's air horn twice to alert Mike to his presence then stepped out of the cruiser and walked over to the front door. If he surprised Mike this time of night, he might get shot.

Eric pounded on the door and yelled in his most authoritative voice, "Police, open the door!"

Seconds later, the curtain on the window next to the door fluttered slightly and Mike responded, "Fuck you, Pig!"

Eric laughed as Mike opened the door. He continued to laugh when he saw Mike standing before him wearing a yellow Speedo, green flip-flops, and a smile. Mike was covered in sweat.

"Well shit, Mike, don't get all dressed up on my account," Eric said.

Mike walked back into his living room to his weight bench to resume his workout. "You're checking out my ass, aren't you?" Mike asked.

"Yeah, it looks just like Serena Williams's. Come on. You don't have time to work out. Baderbully sent me over here to pick you up. He wants both of us in the station ASAP, and it's a big fucking secret, so don't ask me why. Get dressed and—" He paused, sniffing the air with a disgusted scowl on his face. He yelled, "Why does this house smell like ass? I'll wait for you in the car!"

The house really didn't smell bad. It was just that Mike was so easy to mess with. Eric knew that when Mike got back home, he would search the house top to bottom trying to find where the smell was coming from, and when he didn't find anything, he would clean the whole house.

Five minutes later, Mike came hustling out the door in his trooper uniform. He locked up and ran to the car. As Mike reached for the door handle, Eric lurched forward about a foot. Mike laughed and reached for the handle again, and the car lurched forward again. Mike laughed and yelled, "You are such a child!" The third time, he was able to climb in.

"Are you still wearing the Speedo?"

Mike raised an eyebrow at Eric with a goofy smile. Eric shook his head as he drove back down the driveway as fast as was prudent and then flipped on his emergency light bar as he accelerated onto the empty highway. He was a young cop doing what young cops do—violating the speed limit.

"I just started my days off. What am I being brought in for? I haven't done anything wrong," Mike asked his best friend and squad mate as they sped along in Eric's cruiser.

Eric and Mike had a lot in common. They were combat veterans. They loved hunting, hiking, and the outdoors in general. They grew up in Alaska. Both were competitive about everything, but physically, they were at opposite ends of the spectrum. Eric was white, 6'3", blond, blue-eyed, and slender. He had a triathlete's body. Mike was black, 5'9", and muscular, like an NFL fullback.

Eric swung his head to the right and replied with a smile, "I don't know. Maybe the Captain heard about your 'Guess who, motherfucker!' comment," and then turned his head back to the road.

Mike looked at him wide-eyed, and then a mischievous grin appeared on his face.

"I couldn't help it. That asshole came running around the corner of the Stop and Rob and thought he was home free until he saw my Glock pointed at his face." Mike laughed out loud. "I thought he was gonna shit himself." Stop and Rob was police code for a twenty-four-hour gas station.

"Well, whatever it is, remember the Bart Simpson defense," Eric said.

"What's that?" Mike asked.

"I didn't do it, nobody saw me do it, you can't prove anything. Besides, don't sweat it. I'll be right behind you all the way." Eric grinned.

"Yeah, I can feel you already, Dickhead."

"Hey, Mike, tell me a story."

"Fuck you!"

"Ooh, that's my favorite!" Eric said as they both laughed. For some reason, that lame joke never got old. Mike turned on the radio and tuned it away from Eric's country music station to some hip-hop crap. Eric knew Mike didn't even like hip-hop.

Eric yelled, "You did not touch my radio! Don't you know better than to mess with a white man's radio?"

Mike laughed at the reference to the Jackie Chan Rush Hour movies.

Minutes later, Eric whipped into the parking lot behind the station and slid to a stop in the captain's parking spot next to the back door. A minute later, the dynamic duo sat in the watch commander's office in front of his desk. Sergeant Rick Baderman sat with his hands folded on his desk. He reached for his white ceramic coffee mug with his name and sergeant's badge painted on it, took a sip, and got right to the point.

"I just got off the phone with the governor." He turned and pulled some paperwork off of his printer.

Mike immediately went into the spiel. "I didn't do it, nobody saw me do it, you can't prove anything."

Eric slid down in his chair with his chin resting on his hand. He turned his head to look out the window as he tried unsuccessfully to stifle his laughter.

The fat old sergeant shouted, "Shut up, smart-asses, and listen! Eric, I have orders here placing you on active duty with the Air Force."

He passed the paper to Eric.

Eric stopped laughing and sat up. He grabbed the paper. "What the hell is this?" He was in the Alaska Air National Guard, but he wasn't due to deploy again for at least another year.

Now Mike was the one laughing as he leaned over to peek at Eric's orders. Mike slapped him on the back. "Hey, man, thanks for your service."

"And Mike, here are your orders recalling you to active duty in the Marines," Baderman said with a smile as he passed the papers to him.

"Oh, hell no! No fucking way! This has got to be a mistake! I got out of the Corps over a year and a half ago! Besides, I can't leave now. I've got a lot going on with SERT! I'm leaving behind some big shoes to fill!" Mike complained as he read the order.

Eric agreed, "Yeah, you are. They're giant floppy clown shoes."

Baderman continued, "Shut up, dammit. You can both take it up with your new C.O. He's picking you up in a Coast Guard chopper at the airport shortly. Get your asses over there ASAP and standby until he arrives. And listen up.

The governor told me if you don't comply with these orders, I'm to take your badges, IDs, and weapons and wish you well in your future endeavors, whatever they may be. I did hear Walmart needs people to assemble bicycles. Apparently, this is a big deal, so don't fuck it up. And stop parking in the Captain's spot!"

CHAPTER 11

07102 (2310HR PST)
2ND BATTALION, 75TH RANGER REGIMENT
TACTICAL OPERATIONS CENTER

Lieutenant Colonel Dragon parked his black 2018 Ram 4x4 truck in his reserved parking space in front of the main entrance to his battalion headquarters and rushed into his Tactical Operations Center. He walked in front of the huge flat-screen monitor on the wall and was immediately confronted with the image of the commanding general of the U.S. Northern Command, General Pete Harden, USAF, via secure video teleconference, or VTC. Harden was at his USNORTHCOM Headquarters on Peterson AFB, Colorado.

"Good evening, Ike," Harden said in a friendly tone, though they had never met. He was an old fighter pilot and was wearing his green flight suit. He had actually been out flying an F-15E Strike Eagle earlier in the day. It was good to be king.

"Good evening, General," Dragon replied.

"We've got a hell of a job for you and your boys tonight. Major Hopkins will brief you."

A young blond-haired, blue-eyed female Air Force major wearing the OCP uniform began briefing Dragon. "Good evening, Colonel Dragon. This briefing is classified Secret. You are tasked with Operation Bear Trap. It is the consensus of the intelligence community that a Russian Navy special mission submarine identified as the BS-64 Podmoskovye intends to or has already inserted a unit of approximately ten to fifteen Russian special operations soldiers in the vicinity of Eek Lake, Alaska. We believe their mission is to abduct a Soviet-era defector, Dr. Oleg Karpinsky. Dr. Karpinsky is a scientist who conducts very sensitive research for the CIA. He is currently on vacation at a cabin at Eek Lake. He has a protection detail of three deputy United States Marshals.

"Currently, Alaska is experiencing freezing rain and heavy snow throughout the state except for the area between Homer and Bethel. Eek Lake is about thirty miles south of Bethel. We have a squad-sized force within range of Eek Lake that will be inserted by a Coast Guard Jayhawk helicopter to evacuate the doctor and his security detail, assuming the Russians don't get there first. We have attempted to contact the marshals via their satellite telephone, but it is out of service. We also have a Global Hawk en route to the cabin.

"Your mission is to assist the Coast Guard with evacuating or rescuing the doctor and his marshals. If the doctor is evacuated before you arrive, you may be retasked to capture the submarine Podmoskovye and its crew. Three C-17s are being prepared for you. They can each carry 102 of your Rangers. You will be parachuting into the Alaskan wilderness, possibly at night and into combat."

As the major was talking, Dragon's officers and senior sergeants were slowly filtering one or two at a time into the room and quietly taking seats next to and behind him.

General Harden said, "Thank you, Jen. Ike, I know we're a little short on information right now, but time is critical. I need you to get 300 of your Rangers out to the airfield ASAP, outfitted for combat and ready to jump into a fight in Alaska. We'll have plenty of time to talk about the details while you're flying to the drop zone. Of course, the plan will probably change five times before you get there. We'll be bringing in more assets right behind you as the weather improves. At 450 knots, the C-17s will get you there in three and a half to four hours depending on the winds aloft. Do you have any questions for me at this point?"

"No, sir. We'll gear up and get out to the airfield ASAP."

"OK, I'll get out of your way," General Harden replied, and the VTC ended.

Dragon stood up and turned around. He scanned the room and smiled. His executive officer, company commanders, and most of their senior NCOs were already present. Most of them were in civilian clothes. It was Friday night, and they had been in restaurants, bars, and movie theaters in and around Tacoma when their phones started lighting up.

Dragon said, "Gentlemen, you are a fine-looking group of warriors. Thank you for reporting so quickly. We don't have time to repeat the briefing right now. The short version is the Russians are operating in Alaska, and we're going to go kick their asses, rescue a CIA scientist and three marshals, and steal a Russian submarine. Unfortunately, we can't take the whole battalion, so the first two companies ready to load will go. We can take up to 306 Rangers. Sasquatch, we've rehearsed this event ten times in the last two and a half years. Tonight, we need to break our record. I want to be loaded in the aircraft in ninety minutes."

Sasquatch was Dragon's executive officer, Major Henry Henderson. He stood 6'8" and got stuck with his nickname while playing high school basketball. Even back then, he had thick dark facial hair and bushy dark eyebrows. After shaving in the morning, he still looked like he needed a shave. If he had been short, his nickname would have been Teen Wolf. Of course, every other soldier in the battalion knew better than to call the XO Sasquatch. Besides having the power to make their lives miserable, he was big enough to pound them into dust.

Major Henderson turned to the company commanders and staff NCOs and said, "Get a good head count and start drawing your weapons, ammo, and parachutes."

Every soldier in the battalion kept his gear stowed in his pack, ready to deploy at a moment's notice.

CHAPTER 12

Darrin, the snowmobile is repaired, but it may not have enough gas to get us back. James and Willie are checking around the cabin for more gas," Eldon reported to his commander.

Darrin replied, "If the twins don't find any gas in the next five minutes, round them up and we'll head back. We can stop at the unoccupied cabins along the way and check for gas, but for now, we need to put some distance between us and the cabin. It's a good thing we brought the sleds for any casualties. We will double up again with the twins, and the doctor and Hojo can ride in the sleds." James and Willie shared the same last name. They weren't related, but they were referred to as "the twins" anyway. "You'll take point with James. I'll take Willie. Also have them tow the disabled snowmobile behind the cabin and cover it with snow," Darrin continued.

***

Karpinsky walked out of the cabin and down the steps with his sleeping bag under his arm and a small black three-day pack on his back. He put the pack in the front of the sled so he could use it for a back rest and then opened up his sleeping bag. He sat down in the sled and zipped up his bag around himself. Only his hooded head and face were exposed outside the bag. His thick gray beard kept his face warm. He had considered bringing out the cushions from the leather couch to pad the sled, but he didn't want the tough Spetsnaz soldiers to think he was a wuss.

A couple of minutes later, he watched as Eldon and Darrin helped Hojo out of the cabin to his sled. Hojo had his arms over their shoulders for support. He held a couch cushion in each of his gloved hands. Hojo dropped the cushions into his sled to make a mattress and stood there on his good leg as Darrin and Eldon opened his sleeping bag for him. They lowered him into his bag like they were parents putting their child to bed. Darrin zipped the bag up snugly around his head. Being tough, experienced soldiers, they were used to dealing with miserable conditions. In fact, they were so experienced that they didn't need any more experience being miserable. So, they made themselves as comfortable as possible as often as possible.

CHAPTER 13

The MH-60T Jayhawk helicopter began its landing approach to the empty asphalt parking lot in front of the National Guard Armory. The roar of the engines was deafening, and the downwash from the rotor system threw everything not nailed down out of the way. The parking lot lights were on, and the Jayhawk's blindingly bright landing light further illuminated the area for 200 feet around the helicopter as it descended rapidly toward the neatly snowplowed asphalt.

The helicopter aircraft commander, Lieutenant Commander Harry Hand, callsign Houdini, was sitting in the right seat. He swallowed constantly because his mouth watered uncontrollably. He had a pounding headache, felt nauseous, and was afraid he might shit himself. He would have let his copilot, Lieutenant Steve

"Lizard" Dumas, handle the landing, but Lizard was even sicker than he was. If this mission wasn't so damned important, he would park the Jayhawk right here and stumble into the armory to find a nice clean toilet to sleep next to. Actually, he didn't care if the toilet was clean or not. He hoped the doc could give him something to ease the symptoms when they got to the Haley.

Earlier in the day, he and his crew had launched out of Coast Guard Air Station Kodiak into the Cook Inlet to rescue five commercial fishermen from their sinking rust bucket of a fishing trawler. They arrived on scene in time to bring three of them up with the rescue hoist before the trawler sank beneath the choppy waves. The captain and first mate had jumped over the side in their orange cold-water immersion suits and backstroked clear of the boat seconds before it sank. They looked like a couple of orange Gumbys floating on top of the water. The rescue swimmer, Petty Officer First Class Chris Savage, jumped into the ice-cold waves to save them.

After they dropped the fishermen off at South Peninsula Hospital in Homer, the weather turned real shitty, real fast, and they couldn't get back to Kodiak. They wound up stuck at the airport in Homer at the fixed base operator, or FBO. The FBO was the aviation version of a gas station and repair shop. Houdini decided to treat his crew to a late lunch in town. They all piled into the FBO's courtesy car, which happened to be a beat-up fifteen-year-old part gray, part rust Dodge Caravan, and headed to a new Mongolian barbecue place called Khan's Kitchen. Lizard swore by the place.

Since Houdini was paying, everyone went for the most expensive item on the menu—the all-you-can-eat bowl for $14.95. The crewmen stuck to the beef, pork, and chicken bowl. Lizard and Houdini were feeling adventurous, so they added seafood to their bowls for an extra $2.00 each. It tasted great, and since it was all you could eat, everyone had seconds. Some had thirds. There must have been something off about the seafood because by the time they picked up the SEAL, Houdini and Lizard were passing gas and belching continuously. Now Houdini was afraid he might soil himself or hurl all over the instrument panel, or both.

He rotated his NVGs up out of the way, wiped the sweat from his forehead with his Nomex gloved hand, and prepared to land. He brought the helo to a wobbly hover about ten feet above the ground and then bottomed the collective. The helicopter made jarring contact with the pavement. Houdini and Lizard began shutting down the helicopter immediately. They were concerned that fuel might be critical on the way back, and they didn't want to waste it waiting on the ground.

***

Smith jumped out of the helicopter as the rotors spun down and ran toward the front entrance to the armory. Strasburg was waiting there and opened the door as Smith approached. Smith hurried inside and closed the door. They shook hands and introduced themselves.

"Commander, I've been ordered to go with you and give you everything you need, but first, can I see your identification?" Sergeant Strasburg asked.

"Sure, here you go, Sergeant," Smith said as he pulled his Navy Retired ID card from his wallet. He had a whole wallet full of ID and credit cards that had the name "Jon Smith" on them. For a while, he used the name "Justin Kaice," but it caused too many questions.

Strasburg glanced at the card and handed it back to Smith. "Sir, this says you're retired."

Smith replied, "I was until tonight. I've been recalled."

Strasburg nodded and smiled. "I've already told my men to gear up for a three-day combat mission in the Alaskan bush. What are your orders?"

"We need to equip a twelve-man squad with everything they need for combat. Figure three four-man fire teams. I wrote up a list of what I think we need." He handed the list to Strasburg. "If you think anything is missing, add it to the list. We need to load the helo ASAP and get out to the cutter. Time is critical."

"Sir, what's all this about? We weren't told anything."

"I'm sorry, Sergeant, but the operation's classified. I can't tell you anything until we get out to the cutter."

"Roger that, sir. We'll load the gear on a truck at the loading dock out back. Then we'll drive it around to the chopper ASAP."

"Great. I'll go tell the crew you're coming. They might need to move some things around in the cabin." Smith headed back outside. As he walked across the parking lot toward the helicopter, he could see one of the Coasties on one knee over by the eight-foot-high chain-link security fence. He was throwing up uncontrollably. Smith stopped next to the crew chief, Chief Petty Officer Ernesto "Taco" Ortega, and pointed his thumb at the wretched soul. "Is he a new crewman, not used to night flying?"

Ortega, looking worried, shook his head. "No, sir, he's the aircraft commander, Commander Hand."

Hand walked past them on his way back to the helicopter and slowly climbed into the right pilot's seat.

Smith walked over to the open door and looked up at Hand. "Hey, man, are you OK to fly?"

The pilot was gargling spring water from a bottle. He nodded, gave Smith a thumbs-up, and motioned for him to step out of the way right before he spit the water out on the cold pavement. It froze instantly. Then he pulled the door closed without a word.

Smith walked away shaking his head. "Great! This mission keeps getting better and better!"

Twenty minutes later, an ancient green-and-black cam-ouf-lage-painted M35A3 truck, also known as a "Deuce and a Half," rumbled around the corner of the armory with its OD green canvas cover flapping in the wind and pulled up parallel to the right side of the Jayhawk. Corporal Davis hopped down from the driver's seat and hustled to the rear to drop the tailgate for Strasburg and Pope. Smith and the three air crewmen joined them, and they all quickly loaded the gear into the cabin and everyone boarded the helo.

The pilots conducted an abbreviated start checklist, also known as a shotgun start, and ran the rotor blades up to 100% RPM. They had completed the takeoff checklist and the helo was getting light on the wheels when Davis saw headlights at the entrance to the parking lot.

He gave the hold signal with his arms and yelled, "Abort!" to the crew chief.

Ortega passed the abort to the pilots.

Houdini lowered the collective and asked, "What's the problem?"

"One of the soldiers forgot something and went back to get it," Ortega replied.

Less than a minute later, Davis was climbing back into the helo with two extra-large pizzas. Strasburg and Pope both gave him a thumbs-up and pats on the back. Smith and the air crewmen looked a little pissed until they were passed a slice of pie.

They were in the air immediately heading back to Homer for one more pickup. Ortega passed a slice of pizza up to the copilot, Lizard. He waved it off and hurled into an airsickness bag. The copilot caught all of it, but Smith could smell it from his seat. Puking in a helo could be contagious. Smith had been in a Navy MH-53 minesweeper helicopter once with twenty sailors when one of them threw up. It caused a chain reaction as people started hurling all down the line to the ramp. He looked around the cabin hoping no one else would spew, but thankfully everyone was happily eating pizza.

CHAPTER 14

Patrolman Caleb Beck was a field training officer with the Fairfax County Police Department. He worked out of the McLean District, and tonight he was patrolling Sector 320, so his car or unit was called 320. A month ago, he was assigned to train Probationary Patrolman Danny Nelson. Nelson was a twenty-two-year-old kid straight out of college and the police academy. Beck had been a cop for twelve years and enjoyed training probies. He figured the more cops he trained, the better the police department would become.

Beck and Nelson came on duty at 2130 hours to be briefed with their squad at shift change and hit the street at 2200 hours. Beck was driving slowly through another subdivision with the headlights off. This was the fourth subdivision they had checked in the last two hours. He was hoping to roll up on a group of car clouters who had been hitting the area for the last few weeks. So far, no one had come close to catching them.

"Caleb, when are you going to let me drive?" Danny complained.

Beck smiled. "As soon as you learn the streets. What street are we on?"

Nelson looked around for a street sign and realized he was lost.

Beck said, "That's what I thought. What would you do if somebody shot me right now? You wouldn't know where to send the cavalry. Besides, I'm doing you a favor. If you wreck a cruiser while you're still in training, the department can fire you on the spot." Beck changed the subject. "How many tickets do you have tonight?"

"Five tickets and three warnings," Nelson replied.

Beck learned early on that Nelson liked making traffic stops. That was nothing new. All probies liked traffic because it was easy. It was low-hanging fruit. Most veteran cops like Beck felt like tax collectors when they wrote tickets. Working people couldn't afford to pay a $150 speeding ticket. He'd much rather spend his time arresting real offenders than writing tickets.

Beck could tell Nelson was bored. He became a cop to drive fast, shoot guns, and catch bad guys, not creep through neighborhoods all night looking for car clouters. Car cloutings were thefts from vehicles usually accomplished by breaking a window or opening an unlocked door. The latter tended to really piss cops off. They hated writing reports on stolen property when the owners didn't care enough to keep their stuff locked up.

"Did you hear about the four Metro cops that got arrested for robbing drug dealers?" Nelson asked. He was referring to Washington, DC, police officers.

Beck was watching for movement on the left side of the street and replied without looking at Nelson, "Yeah, I heard about it, but they're not cops anymore; they're criminals."

"Do you think they'll go to prison?" Nelson asked.

"Three of them will."

"Why only three?"

"Because the first one to make a deal will get off without jail time."

Nelson was surprised. "You think one of them will turn on the others?"

Beck laughed and stopped the car. He was incredulous at Danny's naivete. He turned to him. "Hell, yes! Cops are the easiest to flip because we have the most to lose. We're all scared shitless of going to prison. Cops get fucked and killed in prison. Most of us would eat our guns first. If you catch four cops conspiring to commit a crime, all you have to do is put them in separate interview rooms and tell them that the first guy to talk will get probation and the other three will go to prison. All four of them will talk.

"Think about it. Would you lie for me and go to prison for me? Of course not. I wouldn't do it for you either. That blue fraternity stuff is mostly bullshit. Sure, if you call out "officer down," we'll come in all guns blazing to help you, even risk our lives for you, but no one will lie for you, lose their job for you, or go to jail for you. If anyone ever asks you to lie for them, they're not your friend. You need to run from them as fast as you can. Look, Danny, you're young and dumb, but you're still a cop. If you fuck up, I'll do everything I can to help you, but I won't do anything unethical, immoral, or illegal." Beck pointed his head forward and resumed creeping the cruiser down the street. "Will they turn on each other? Ha! That's funny."

***

As the night shift watch commander, Sergeant Joe Venable, drove west on Kirby Road, he pulled his radio's microphone from unit 300's radio stack and transmitted, "320 go to channel four for 300." Channel one was reserved for dispatching officers to calls for service. Channel four was an administrative channel for the police officers to talk back and forth to each other.

"Go ahead for 320," Beck responded.

"Caleb, meet me at Longfellow," Venable replied.

Beck responded, "10-4," which meant he would comply with the instruction.

Longfellow was Longfellow Middle School on Westmoreland Street.

Three minutes later, Beck pulled up car to car with Venable on the dark parking lot in front of the school and turned off his headlights. Beck was still driving, and his trainee, Danny Nelson, sat in the passenger seat. Venable knew Nelson was getting tired of being a passenger all the time, but he wasn't about to interfere with Beck's training decisions. That didn't mean he couldn't tweak him a little bit. He smiled and said, "How come the kid's not driving?"

Beck rolled his eyes. "Please, don't get him started. What's up, Sarge?"

"Turn off all of your radios," Venable said.

Beck and Nelson turned off the car radio and their walkies.

Venable began explaining, "Three blocks from here at 6721 Pine Creek Court, an hour or so ago, the FBI shot and killed a couple of Russian spooks that broke into a house while the agents were there covertly executing a search warrant. It's very important the FBI keep their involvement secret for a day or two. They don't want the Russians to know the FBI has identified the burglars as Russian.

"We're going to respond to a fake burglary-in-progress call there, and you guys are going to pretend you shot the spies. We're going to make a big show of it. We'll call in the Air Unit and the paramedics. Then the shooting team will come in to interview you. The FBI agents will be outside the house watching any people that gather in hopes of spotting more Russian operatives. The good news is you guys will get three days off for being in an officer-involved shooting. If anybody asks you about the shooting, tell them you can't talk about it because it's still under investigation. Any questions?"

Beck addressed Nelson, "OK, forget all that stuff I said earlier about lying for anyone. This is different. It's not actually lying. This is kind of like going undercover." Then Beck looked back to Venable. "Sarge, this sounds like bullshit. Are you sure the FBI's not trying to jam us up?"

Venable shook his head. "The Chief said the Director of the FBI called him personally and asked for our help to provide cover for their operation. I'll back you up on the call. When we get there, we'll contact two FBI agents named Gillis and Jerome. Turn your radios back on and wait for the call." Venable switched his radio back on and then called dispatch on his cell phone. When the dispatcher answered the phone, he said, "Peggy, this is Joe. Put the call out."

Seconds later, the radio came alive: "320, burglary in progress."

"Go for 320," Beck responded.

The dispatcher continued, "320, burglary in progress at 6721 Pine Creek Court. A neighbor advises the homeowner is out of town on vacation, and he sees flashlights moving around inside the house."

Beck transmitted, "320, 10-76," which was the police ten code for en route.

Venable transmitted, "300, en route to assist."

Dispatch acknowledged them, "320 and 300, 10-76."

Both vehicles exceeded the speed limit on the way to the house, but they didn't use their lights or sirens. They proceeded as if they were trying to sneak up on the burglars. A minute later, Beck turned off his headlights on Poole Lane about a block from the intersection with Pine Creek Court like he would have on a real call.

The rookie Nelson transmitted, "320, 10-23." 10-23 was the police ten code that meant they had arrived.

Venable rolled up right after them and transmitted, "300, 10-23."

They stopped short of the address and approached on foot across the dead grass and between the trees. Agent Gillis was waiting for them inside the front door. She opened it as they stepped up on the porch. She invited them inside. They exchanged introductions, and Jocelyn said, "My partner, Special Agent Jerome, is in the kitchen with the bodies."

The police officers followed her into the kitchen, and she introduced them to Jerry. They all stood there too long shining their flashlights on the motionless bodies on the floor between the door and breakfast counter. The smell of blood and gun smoke still hung in the air.

Venable finally spoke first, "So, you've already identified these guys as Russian spies?"

Jocelyn replied, "Yes. This is part of a much bigger operation. We need your help to buy us some time. If the Russians find out the FBI killed their people, they'll know we're onto them and possibly change their plans. If they think you killed them while responding to a burglary call, they might not change anything, and we may be able to catch a few more of them. We need your help for a day or so."

"OK. Are you leaving or staying?" Venable asked.

Jerry replied, "We've already packed up and removed the evidence we gathered. We'll be watching from a distance to see who comes to see the commotion. Oh, do you mind giving us your handcuffs? Ours are on the bodies. Do you guys use Smith & Wesson or Peerless?"

Beck said, "Smith & Wesson," as he and Nelson handed over their cuffs.

Jerry responded, "Good, so do we. Sergeant, here, this is my card in case you need to contact us. We'll find somewhere in the area to watch from." Jocelyn and Jerry walked out the front door and disappeared into the darkness.

Venable sat down at the kitchen table. "OK, you guys glove up. I'll make the calls."

Beck and Nelson put their black leather search gloves on and sat down at the table.

Venable calmly keyed his walkie. "Radio, this is 300."

Dispatched responded, "Go ahead, 300."

Venable transmitted, "We have shots fired by police. Two suspects are down. Roll paramedics, two additional units, get the Airship up, and notify the Captain."

Beck stretched his feet out in front of himself and leaned back on the rear legs of his chair. He stuck his thumbs in his belt like a cowboy. "Well, Danny, what are you going to do with your three days off?"

CHAPTER 15

0825Z (2325HR AKST)
HOMER, ALASKA

Eric and Mike sat in Eric's cruiser behind the small terminal building at the Homer Airport. Eric had backed into the parking spot so they could see any airplanes landing on the runway. They had committed one minor act of disobedience after leaving the police barracks. Taco Bell was still open and offered free food to police officers, so they rolled through the drive-thru and loaded up on tacos, burritos, and frozen Baja Blasts instead of driving directly to the airport as ordered. They wolfed down their food because they didn't know how soon the helicopter would arrive. There was no control tower at the small airport, and they hadn't seen anything flying since they got there. It was eerily quiet, except for the cruiser's idling engine.

"I wonder what's going on," Eric said as he leaned over the steering wheel and strained to see into the darkness.

"I don't know. This is some weird shit," Mike replied as he finished his last grilled stuffed chicken burrito. He took a long draw on his drink and then yelled, "Aw, fuck, that hurts!"

Eric turned to him, confused, and asked, "What hurts?"

"Brain freeze!" Mike had his mouth open and started panting. He stuck his tongue out hoping his mouth would warm up faster.

"You're not supposed to chug frozen drinks, dumbass." Like any good friend, Eric laughed at his pain.

A few minutes later, Mike regained his composure. They sat there quietly and awaited their fate. The mood became somber. They were both a little nervous. There was no more grab ass. A few more minutes passed in silence, and then Mike farted...and the spell was broken.

Eric punched him in the arm. "That's fucking nasty. Did you just shit yourself? Oh, God! Now I can taste it! Get out of the fucking car!" He pushed Mike up against the passenger side door but couldn't get the door open. Mike laughed uncontrollably and then farted loudly again. Eric bailed out of the nice warm, putrid vehicle. He bent over with his hands on his knees and tried to summon up enough saliva to spit the nastiness out of his mouth.

Mike said, "Uh-oh! That felt kind of wet!"

Eric straightened up and laughed. "Now your yellow Speedo has a brown racing stripe." He took a deep breath, leaned into the car, and quickly pulled the key out of the ignition. "If I can't be warm, neither can you, Shit Stain!"

Mike laughed. "OK, I'm done. You can get back in," and then he farted again. "Oh, I'm sorry about that. That really was the"—Fart!—"last one."

Eric walked to the front of the car to get out of the kill zone. Moments later, Eric canted his head to try to hear better. "Do you hear it? That has to be the Jayhawk." He could hear the far-off rumble of an approaching helicopter but still couldn't see it. To him, it sounded like the HH-60G Pave Hawk helicopters his guard unit flew. He had logged a lot of time flying around in them in Alaska and Afghanistan. The roar became louder and louder. He could feel the hair on the back of his neck stand up.

Mike joined him at the front of the cruiser. He tried to pull the seat of his pants out of his crack without Eric seeing him. Seconds later, they saw a black silhouette approaching the asphalt ramp in front of them about fifty feet above the ground. The roar from the engines was incredible. They could feel it in their chests. It made a rolling landing, taxied up to within 100 feet of the car, and then the tail spun around 90° to the right so the cabin door was facing them.

They both put in earplugs and squinted to protect their eyes from the rotor wash as they walked toward the chopper. A young soldier with a couple of pizza boxes in his hands hopped out of the helo and ran past them to the tall narrow trash can outside the door to the terminal building. He folded them in half, crammed them into the can, and ran back to the helo. The crew chief came out to meet them and ushered them inside the crowded helo.

***

As the crew chief, Taco, gathered up his long cord into a coil, the left cockpit door opened and the copilot, Lizard, got out and walked hunched over toward the small strip of snow-covered grass in front of the terminal. Smith was working on his laptop and looked up just in time to see a Coastie through the open cabin door go down to his knees. He removed his helmet and heaved over and over again. After nothing remained in his stomach, he staggered to his feet and threw his helmet back on as he walked slowly back to the helo.

Smith yelled in the crew chief's ear, "Chief, is Commander Hand sick again?"

Ortega shook his head and yelled back to him over the roaring engines, "No, sir. That's the copilot."

Smith leaned back in his seat and pulled his seat belt a little tighter. He returned to the secure laptop and typed out a message alerting NORTHCOM they had a mission-critical problem with the pilots. He explained in detail what he had observed. They acknowledged his message. He hoped that meant they would resolve the problem.

Ten minutes later, Houdini located the Coast Guard Cutter Haley twenty miles off the coast in Cook Inlet. He flew the Jayhawk across the bow at 500 feet above the water and made a decelerating left turn to fly down the port side of the ship. He continued decelerating, and as he passed abeam of the fantail, he continued his turn and began his approach to land on the helo deck behind the retractable hangar. Since Hand was flying the helo, he approached from the left rear of the ship because he could see more of the deck from that side.

Smith closed the laptop and stowed it under his seat. He knew from his past experience that the helo would fly up to the rear of the deck at a 45° angle and come to a ten-foot hover over the deck. Then Houdini would drop the collective to plant the helo firmly on the deck with the brakes already set. Next, the ship's deck crew would run out and chock the tires and chain the helo to the deck.

As the helo approached the deck, it seemed too low and too fast to Smith. This was confirmed when Chief Ortega yelled at Houdini to wave off. At the last second, the pilot yanked the collective up and banked sharply to the right. They missed hitting the top right corner of the hangar with the rotor blades by about ten feet. Smith was more scared now than he had been in Fallujah getting shot at. His seat cushion was sucked up so tight between his cheeks he'd be able to use it as a flotation device. He looked up front and saw Lizard's helmet flopping back and forth as Houdini maneuvered the helo for another attempt. Lizard was clearly unconscious. Smith pulled his seatbelt even tighter and checked around the cabin for exits and handholds just in case they went in the water. He tried to take solace in the fact they were so close to the cutter. If he could get out of the sinking helo, the cutter crew might pluck him out of the water before he drowned or froze to death.

He subconsciously ranked the others according to their hypothetical ability to get out of the helo alive. The Coasties were excellently trained and equipped. Except for the sick pilots, they would get out without any trouble and could probably help the others. The two state troopers would be alright. One was a Marine, and the other was an Air Force Pararescueman, but the soldiers might be screwed. They had most likely never been through the Dunker or any advanced water survival training.

The Dunker was a helicopter simulator that sat above a training pool. It was a big metal drum. It had room inside for ten trainees strapped to their seats wearing helmets, flight suits, and boots. The Dunker would be lowered into the water, rolled upside down, and then sunk. After all motion stopped and the trainees counted off ten seconds, they would release their seat belts and swim for the nearest exit. If they got it wrong, the instructors would make them do it again. If they did it right, they would still do it again, but this time, they would all go out the same exit. If they did it right the second time, they would do it yet again, except this time they would wear blacked-out goggles so they couldn't see anything.

So, if you were a good swimmer and didn't panic, you went down three times and you were done. If you weren't a good swimmer or were prone to panic, you could be there all day being dunked repeatedly by the instructors. And, of course, the instructors would tell everyone not to kick with their boots or they might kick the guy behind him in the face, but some trainee would always panic and give someone a bloody nose. The training was a giant pain in the ass to go through, but it definitely saved lives. Thankfully, it was only required once every three years.

On the second landing attempt, Houdini overcompensated and came in extremely slow and high. He came to a twenty-five-foot hover over the deck and lowered the collective enough to start a slow descent. The tail drifted left and right until the tail wheel finally contacted the deck and Houdini dumped the collective. The Jayhawk's main landing gear slammed into the deck. The landing signal officer immediately drew the blue NVG filtered wand across his throat as a signal to cut the engines.

***

Houdini's stomach was churning. He threw his door open and leaned his head out of the cockpit to throw up on the deck, but a boatswain's mate was already in the way chaining down the helo. As a last resort, he grabbed his empty helmet bag and spewed into it. With his last ounce of strength, he zipped it up and then his helmet slumped against the doorframe. Ortega reached between the unconscious pilots and pulled back both engine power control levels and the engine fuel system selectors to the off position to conduct emergency engine shutdowns. Next, he engaged the rotor brake as the deck crew lashed down the helo.

***

Smith hopped out of the cabin into the frigid arctic wind and wiped the sweat from his forehead. He turned to look at the three soldiers climbing out of the cabin. They were oblivious. They didn't have a clue that they had almost died. Nine Coasties rushed past him to the cockpit with two stretchers and removed the pilots. They were both unconscious. One of the nine was the captain of the ship, Commander Daniel Waddle. He escorted Smith inside as the mission's weapons and gear were quickly off-loaded and moved into the hangar.

CHAPTER 16

Colonel Alfred Babcook entered the Tank and handed a document to the Chairman of the Joint Chiefs of Staff, Marine General Lee Boden. The Tank was the JCS conference room in the Pentagon where America's top military officers gathered on nights like this to discuss the nation's defense and make recommendations to the Secretary of Defense and President.

Boden sat in the center of the huge mahogany table surrounded on both sides by the other service chiefs and their top aides. The only service leader missing was the U.S. Space Force's Chief of Space Operations. He was at his HQ on Peterson AFB. Tonight, the Commandant of the Coast Guard, Admiral Kurt Schultz, was their guest. Since the Coast Guard was in the Department of Homeland Security, Schultz's office was in the Douglas A.

Munro USCG Headquarters Building in the District of Columbia and not across the Potomac River in the Pentagon with the other armed forces.

Boden said, "Thanks, Al," and read the note. He frowned and laid it on the table. He looked around the room. "We have a big problem, boys. Commander Smith reports both Coast Guard Jayhawk pilots are sick with stomach flu or food poisoning or some damn thing. They almost crashed the Jayhawk into the Haley. Now they are both unconscious. The Haley's corpsman says they won't be able to fly for at least three or four days. We have to find more pilots in the area around Homer, ASAP." General Boden turned to the Coast Guard Commandant and said, "Kurt, do you have any other pilots in the area available to fly the mission?"

Admiral Schultz shook his head. "No, we don't, Lee. The only reason the Jayhawk was in Homer was because they conducted a rescue earlier in the day and flew the injured fishermen to the hospital in Homer. The bad weather closed in on them before they could fly back to Kodiak. Now Kodiak is socked in with freezing rain."

The Vice Chairman, Admiral Shane Zeller, USN, turned to Colonel Babcook and said, "Al, get with personnel and search the database for any military helicopter pilots within fifty miles of Homer."

Babcook spun and left the room.

Boden addressed everyone around the table, "Does anybody have any ideas? How can we get our people to Eek Lake before the Russians?"

The Chief of the National Guard Bureau, General Joe Lengle, spoke, "Lee, I've got a flight of three HH-60G Pave Hawk helicopters from the 210th Rescue Squadron with 24 PJs sitting in a hangar at Elmendorf preflighted and ready to go as soon as the weather lifts. Right now, they're being hit with ice and freezing rain."

PJs were pararescuemen. They were the Air Force's famed special operators tasked with rescues on land and sea.

Army Chief of Staff General Gilberto Morales said, "I have two companies from the 2nd Ranger Battalion standing by ready to launch at Lewis-McChord, but they're being held for weather in Alaska."

Chief of Naval Operations Admiral James Richards said, "I have two fast attack boats, the Columbia and Jefferson City, en route, but neither one will arrive until after the sun comes up out there. If the Podmoskovye is there, our subs will put her on the bottom before she can escape." Richards changed the subject. "What about local law enforcement? Can they go out and retrieve Karpinsky and his marshals?"

The Chairman shook his head. "The Bethel Police Department has fifteen officers and only five are on duty, but if we asked them to help out and the Russians got there first, we'd be sending them into a meat grinder. They could run up against ten to fifteen Spetsnaz operators. Police officers are trained to limit their use of force. They aren't trained or equipped to fight highly skilled soldiers. Besides, what would we tell them? Everything's classified."

Colonel Babcook came back into the room with a manila file folder.

He showed it to General Boden. "Sir, we only came up with one possible pilot. He's a retired Army Reserve Blackhawk pilot on a cruise ship near Homer. He's fifty-five, did a couple of combat deployments to Iraq, and flew over 1,000 combat hours. He also works for NGA, so he has a Top Secret/SCI clearance."

Boden asked, "How the fuck did you find him on a cruise ship?"

Babcook smiled. "We came up empty the first time around, so we asked our friends at No Such Agency for some assistance. They found Major Thomas Adams, Army Reserve Retired. They also found an Airborne Ranger and an Air Force Security Forces sniper for the mission." No Such Agency was actually the National Security Agency, or NSA.

The Marine Corps Commandant, General Bryan McKinley, looked at Babcook. "Al, did you say Tom Adams?"

"Yes, sir."

McKinley smiled. "I know him. He taught me to fly Shitters when we were with the Flying Tigers. He was an aircraft commander and instructor when I was a new copilot." Shitters were CH-53 Sea Stallion heavy-lift helicopters, and the Flying Tigers was Marine Heavy Lift Helicopter Squadron 361. He continued, "If anybody can fly this mission single pilot, Tom can."

Boden turned to Babcook. "Go back to the NSA and get everything you can on Major Adams."

***

Air Force Chief of Staff General Dave Feingold had been sitting quietly listening to the discussion. Other than his C-17s that would fly the Rangers to Alaska, he didn't have much to offer, other than AGM-158B JASSM-ER air-launched cruise missiles. These stealthy missiles could fly over 575 miles and carried a 1,000-pound armor-piercing warhead. They were a last resort if the Russian submarine was located inside U.S. waters. Nobody wanted to blow up a nuclear submarine and cause an environmental catastrophe. General Feingold was an F-22 fighter pilot. He tended to lean forward and be aggressive, but in this case, he did the math and concluded that it was better to risk losing three marshals and a Russian defector than over 300 Rangers and Airmen in three C-17s.

He was also an ambitious man, and the only professional goal he hadn't attained was to be the Chairman of the Joint Chiefs of Staff. General Boden would be retiring in less than a year, but General Morales and Admiral Richards were favored to replace him. If he opposed the plan to use Adams to fly the mission and things went bad, he might be the only man on the JCS left standing. He made his decision and spoke up, "Gentlemen, I think we should consider other options. It's reckless to risk the lives of a dozen of our people by putting them in a Jayhawk at night with one pilot instead of two—not to mention a retired pilot who isn't checked out or current in the Jayhawk."

General McKinley replied immediately, "Dave, I'm telling you, Tom is rock solid. I'd have no problem getting in the back of a Jayhawk with him flying it tonight." He picked up the folder with Adam's military records in it. "Here's his flight history. Two yearlong deployments to Iraq as a platoon leader and company commander. He flew over a thousand combat hours during 250 missions. Three hundred of those hours were at night on NVGs. He flew everything from VIP flights to night air assaults to capture high-value targets. He has over a thousand hours from his time in the Corps flying CH-53s and over 2,000 hours flying UH-60 Black Hawks in the Army Guard. After he retired, he continued flying UH-1H Hueys for the Army Aviation Flying Museum, just for fun.

"So, he's a reserve pilot with over 3,500 flight hours. Most active-duty pilots don't get that much experience in a twenty-year career. He has a current FAA Class II Medical Certificate, and our friends at the NSA say he has flown seventy-eight hours in the Huey in the last six months."

The other chiefs sat silently and listened.

McKinley looked around the table like a lawyer making his closing argument to a jury. "Look, the marshals aren't answering their sat phone. That phone has worked every day for the last ten days they have been at the cabin, and now all of the sudden, it's not working, so chances are, we're too late and the Russians have already been there. Chances are they killed the marshals and took Karpinsky. Russian soldiers are operating on our soil and killing American citizens, and we are sitting here with our thumbs up our asses. I guarantee you, if I walked out in the hall right now and asked for volunteers to go to Alaska on a possible suicide mission to fight Russian invaders, everyone I talked to would climb over each other for the chance to go, and I'd be one of them. Besides, we don't leave anyone behind."

Feingold had no response. He'd been kneecapped by the Marine. He admitted to himself he would also volunteer to go if it were possible. He kept his mouth shut and accepted the fact that he had lost this round. He didn't want the operation to fail, but he was politically savvy enough to realize he might profit personally if it did.

CHAPTER 17

Four massive gray C-17 Globemaster III cargo planes from the 4th Airlift Squadron sat wingtip to wingtip on the brightly lit ramp of McChord Airfield. The squadron was known as the Fighting Fourth. Having been activated in 1935, it was the oldest active airlift squadron in the Air Force. Tonight, they were claiming another first. They were flying the first combat airlift mission to Alaska to deliver soldiers to oppose a foreign military force since the Japanese invaded the Aleutian Islands in WWII.

Their radio callsigns were Husky 12, 13, and 14. The cargo ramps under their tails were down, and the interiors of their cargo bays were illuminated by electrical power from four pieces of support equipment called ground power units. They produced direct current and provided electricity to the aircraft while the engines were not running. This saved fuel and wear and tear on the engines.

Three Globemasters were required to carry the 300 Rangers to the drop zone. The fourth jet was a spare standing by ready to fly if one of the other three jets developed a mechanical problem serious enough to ground it. If one of the jets broke down on startup, the Rangers would waddle out of their jet and head to the spare.

So far, Lieutenant Colonel Dragon was pleased. Normally, the three Ranger Battalions of the 75th Ranger Regiment were expected to be airborne within eighteen hours of being alerted. He had been able to recall enough of his battalion to fill the three jets to their capacity of 102 Airborne Rangers each, and they did it within his goal of 90 minutes. The Rangers stood in two columns of fifty-one behind the first three jets waiting for the signal to load up from the Air Force loadmasters. Dragon commanded the Rangers, but the enlisted loadmasters were in charge of everything that happened in the cargo bays of their jets.

The Rangers were dressed in white camouflage over their extreme cold-weather gear, body armor, and white extreme cold-weather boots. The soldiers called them Mickey Mouse boots because of their over-sized appearance. They also wore their helmets, goggles, main parachutes, patrol packs attached below their reserve chutes, and their weapon bags attached to their left sides. They had snowshoes strapped to their packs. Being stationed in Washington state, they were accustomed to operating in snow.

The Rangers were carrying a heavy burden, over 130 pounds, but no one complained. They were excited at the prospect of making a combat jump into Alaska to engage Russian Spetsnaz and capture a submarine. This was a once-in-a-lifetime opportunity, and they were eager to get in the air. At this point, their greatest fear was that the mission might be canceled before they could get in the action.

Dragon and his men had been standing in line behind the jets for about forty-five minutes in the sub-20°F weather when the air mission commander took pity on them and ordered the loadmasters to bring them inside. Dragon's knees were starting to hurt, but he was too proud to let any of the young Rangers see him show any weakness. So, he sucked it up. Finally, the loadmaster in front of Dragon walked down to the bottom of the ramp and signaled him forward. Dragon began waddling toward the ramp like a penguin with his column following close behind. The leaders of the other five columns did the same. Five minutes later, the Rangers were sitting along the walls and up the center of the cargo bay in the fold-down troop seats. The loadmasters closed the ramps. The Rangers tried to make themselves comfortable. It would be at least a three-and-a-half-hour trip once they got in the air.

Dragon saw a pilot descend the stairs from the cockpit and walk over to the senior loadmaster. The pilot said something to him, and the loadmaster pointed to Dragon.

The pilot walked over to Dragon, holding out his hand to shake. "Hello, Colonel, I'm Charlie Bright. I'm the AMC." AMC meant air mission commander. He was in charge of the three jets and all the Rangers while they were in his jets. He was also the squadron commander. Dragon could see from the blue-and-white embroidered nametag on his green Nomex flight suit that he was a lieutenant colonel and his personal callsign was Notso.

Dragon shook his hand. "Good to meet you, Charlie. I'm Ike Dragon."

"The weather's still a mess over Alaska. We're going to be waiting at least a couple of hours before we can take off. I'm going to order some bag nasties from the in-flight kitchen for my crews. Do you want me to get some for your boys too?" Bag nasties were box lunches. Normally, you would have to order 24 hours in advance for 30 or more meals, but General Harden had arranged for chow halls around the base to stop what they were doing and make box lunches. The Air Force in general had a reputation for making really good box lunches. They usually contained a big sandwich or two, an apple or orange, maybe a hard-boiled egg, a bag of potato chips, a candy bar, and a soda or squeeze box of bug juice. The bug juice was usually fruit punch.

"Yeah, that would be great if you can swing it. Thanks, Charlie."

"No problem, Ike. Feel free to let your Rangers drop their gear and get comfortable. Like I said, we're going to be waiting a while. You can come up to the cockpit and listen in on the radio traffic if you like."

Dragon turned to Major Henderson. "Pass the word for the boys to ground their gear and try to relax. The Air Force is arranging chow." Dragon shed his gear except for his rifle and pistol and made his way to the cockpit. The restless Rangers were eating their meals in less than an hour.

CHAPTER 18

Jon Smith followed Commander Daniel Waddle down the brightly lit passageway as Coast Guardsmen stepped aside to make way for their captain. The passageway was unusually crowded for this time of night. Everyone was curious about what was happening. So far, it was a big mystery. The captain had ordered internet access shutdown and instructed the crew to turn off their cell phones under penalty of UCMJ prosecution. Waddle opened a hatch, which was really only a wooden door, and stepped into the wardroom followed by Smith.

"An hour and a half ago, I was sitting in my lodge drinking a beer," Smith jokingly complained.

Waddle smiled over his shoulder. "Well, at least you had a beer. We're going to set your team up here in the wardroom." The wardroom, or commissioned officer's mess, was a room about twenty-five by twenty feet with imitation wood-paneled walls. A table long enough to seat fourteen people dominated the room. The Haley only had ten officers, so there was room for a few guests at the table. Besides eating their meals there, the room served as a recreation room where the officers could gather during their off-duty time. "I'll post a guard at the door to keep my crew out." He motioned toward the large table. Two young women were seated at the table behind their laptop computers. He made the introductions. "Lieutenant Commander Jon Smith, this is my Intelligence Team, Lieutenant Junior Grade Sarah Tuttle and Petty Officer Second Class Cindy McLemore. They are who you have been texting back and forth with from the Jayhawk. They will brief you on the details of what's going on tonight and help you get everything you need."

Like the rest of the Haley's crew, they were wearing the Coast Guard's blue operational dress uniform. They both stood to greet Smith.

Tuttle smiled and held out her right hand. "Pleased to meet you, sir."

Smith took her hand and shook it. Next, McLemore smiled and shook his hand. "I'm pleased to meet you, ladies," Smith said with a smile. He was particularly interested in Ms. Tuttle. Her long brunette hair was gathered in a tight bun behind her head. She had big blue expressive eyes. Smith guessed she was about 5'9" and 140 pounds. She was shapely but also athletic. He pulled up a chair next to the ladies. "OK, give me everything you know about what's going on out there at Eek Lake." Tuttle turned her laptop so Jon could see it better and began giving him a thorough brief. He could see she didn't wear a wedding ring.

Lieutenant Commander Aaron Finch opened the wardroom door and led Sergeant First Class Strasburg, Staff Sergeant Pope, Corporal Davis, Staff Sergeant Fuller, and Sergeant Harmon into the room. They were carrying large OD green parachute bags slung over their backs. Finch motioned toward the far end of the table. "You can unload the bags over there." As instructed, they placed the bags on the table and began emptying them. They were full of Army OCP uniforms, extreme cold-weather parkas and trousers, gloves, balaclavas, and white extreme cold-weather boots.

Strasburg asked Smith, "Sir, do you want the field gear and weapons in here, or should we leave them in the hangar bay?"

"Leave it all in the hangar bay. We'll do our precombat checks out there, and if the Captain clears it, we'll test-fire our weapons from the fantail."

Strasburg turned to the two troopers. "We packed more than we would need in numerous sizes, so grab a uniform and mouse boots in your size and go to the latrine—excuse me, go to the head—and get dressed. When you're done, report back here."

***

Eric and Mike grabbed uniforms and boots and left the wardroom. They walked down the passageway and asked one of the Coasties where the head was. He pointed out the locker room to them and continued down the passageway. They sat down on benches in front of the lockers and started changing. Mike untied his boots and kicked them off. He stood up and removed his blue uniform trousers. He bent over to pull up his socks as a Coastie came into the room to get a towel from his locker.

The Coastie stopped in front of his locker, noticed Mike's ass in the yellow Speedo, and asked, "Do you play tennis?"

Mike stood up and faced him. "No, why?"

The Coastie shook his head. "No reason," he said then turned quickly and left the room.

Eric laughed.

Mike looked at him questioningly. "What?"

Eric replied, "Nothing." He changed the subject. "Hey, why do you think we're here? What's this all about?"

Mike pulled his stiff new OCP trousers on and buttoned them up as he thought for a moment. "Well, I doubt the radical Muslim fundamentalist jihadists or the Mexican drug cartels have gotten this far north yet, and the North Koreans would starve to death before they got here, so my money is on the Russians, Chinese, or Romulans."

Eric nodded his head like he was indulging an imbecile. "OK, why the Romulans?"

Mike smiled and explained, "Captain Kirk's a Canadian, and the Romulans don't want to drop in right on top of him and give up the element of surprise, so they came next door to Alaska."

Eric was tying his mouse boots and responded, "Wrong. William Shatner's a Canadian. Captain Kirk was born in Iowa, but even if you were right, why wouldn't they just blow him and Canada up from outer space with their plasma torpedoes?"

Mike said, "I guess you're right. It must be the Russians or Chinese."

Eric laughed. "C'mon on, Serena, let's get back to the wardroom."

CHAPTER 19

It was a hot moonless night. First Lieutenant Tom Adams was flying in a formation of three Black Hawk helicopters operating with NVGs. He and his friend, Captain Terry Bergman, piloted the lead helicopter. They were flying south from Balad Air Base 300 feet above the ground at 140 knots. The cockpit doors were removed, and the cabin's doors locked back in the open position to keep their passengers from overheating. With the doors closed, it could get to over 120°F in the cabin even at night. The chalk two helicopter was flying about 300 feet off to the right side of the lead helicopter at the four o'clock position. The chalk three helicopter was flying about 300 feet off to the left side of the lead helicopter at the eight o'clock position.

Their mission was to insert a platoon of infantry on a farmhouse outside of Baqubah, Iraq, to capture a high-value target, or HVT. The HVT was a bomb maker responsible for the wounding and deaths of over fifty soldiers. He had been burying his improvised explosive devices, or IEDs, on the roads and highways surrounding Baghdad. His weapon of choice was old 105mm artillery shells left over from the Iran-Iraq War. So far, the mission was going well, and Bergman was pleased with the performance of his aircrews. Bergman was a member of U.S. Army royalty. His father was also an Army aviator and a lieutenant general. He was the superintendent at West Point.

The helicopters were blacked out except for their infrared slime lights. These lights showed up bright green to the pilots wearing their NVGs but were invisible to people on the ground. They had a heads-up display, or HUD, monocle attached to one tube of their NVGs. The HUD allowed the pilots to monitor their instruments without looking under the tubes at the instrument panel. Two kilometers from the landing zone, the chalk two and chalk three helicopters moved into trail formation behind the lead helicopter, chalk one.

Terry Bergman read out the landing checklist from memory over the intercom system, or ICS. "Tail wheel switch locked, parking brake off, crew, passengers, and mission equipment check."

One kilometer from the landing zone, Tom Adams lowered the collective and pulled back on the cyclic to begin his air assault landing. Chalks two and three tucked in close behind him. The helicopters intentionally landed hard and fast in a tight triangle formation about 100 feet from the farmhouse. Immediately, the infantry was out of the helicopters, running to their assigned positions around the house. Ten seconds after landing, all three helicopters took off in unison, heading south again. In the lead helicopter, Tom was climbing through 100 feet and had crossed a date palm grove when he saw two trails of intense light come streaking up from the ground.

In the left seat, Terry saw a bright green trail of fire racing toward him from below. He instinctively raised his feet off the floor and screamed, "RPG!" just before it exploded against his chin bubble. A ball of flame flashed from under his feet and up through the left side of the cockpit, singeing his eyebrows. Tom flinched as the second RPG blew up in the tail pylon and disabled the tail rotor. Erupting in flames, the Black Hawk spun out of control. Tom yelled, "Shit!" as he stomped on the left pedal, unsuccessfully trying to regain control. It had no effect, so he lowered the collective to slow the spin. The helicopter fell from the sky, landing hard. It bounced and rolled onto its left side in an irrigation canal in a foot of muddy, stagnant water. One of the engines was still screaming loudly at 100%, and the air smelled like hot hydraulic fluid.

Inside the Black Hawk, all four crewmen were injured but alive. Both pilots were sitting on armored crash-worthy seats that could sustain a 16g crash. Upon impacting the ground, the seats stroked down even with the floor of the cockpit on shock absorbers. Tom hung dazed from his seat with his head and arms dangling down loosely over Terry's unconscious body. Unfortunately, the crew chief and the gunner didn't have crash-worthy seats, and both had severe back injuries. Bergman's left leg had been severed above the knee by the blast where the armored seat pan ended. His right leg was broken, and his foot was trapped under the right rudder pedal. Tom reached back behind his head for the engine power control levers and fuel system selectors. He pulled them back to the off position.

One squad of infantry secured the farmhouse and killed the HVT during a short gun battle after he decided he didn't want to be captured. Another squad on the perimeter saw the explosions and crash and ran to the helicopter. They jumped into the canal and pulled Tom and the two crewmen up and out of the wreck. Then they went back for Bergman. Three soldiers climbed on top of the Hawk's right side to retrieve Bergman. The extra weight caused the mud under the Black Hawk to give way, and it rolled another foot onto its left side. Bergman's head slipped into the shallow muddy water, and he drown before the soldiers could free him.

***

The dream returned less and less over the years but still reemerged on occasion. Usually, when something bad was about to happen.

"Tom, wake up. I think the ship has stopped," Gwenn said with concern as she sat up next to him in bed. He continued to snore. She shook him awake and repeated herself, "Tom, wake up. The ship has stopped."

He rubbed his face and tried to reassure her, "I'm sure it's nothing. If there was a problem, they'd announce it over the intercom. Let's go back to sleep." He rolled over and pulled her to him, wrapping her in his arms. Minutes later, a bright light flooded the room through the sliding glass door leading to their balcony. That got their undivided attention. They rolled out of bed and went to the sliding glass door. They looked out to find a USCG Cutter stopped next to their cruise ship about 200 feet away. They watched as an efficient Coast Guard crew winched a small orange and black rigid hulled inflatable boat (RHIB) down into the water, and it headed toward their ship until it disappeared from their view.

"They're probably evacuating someone with a medical emergency, maybe a stroke or heart attack," Tom guessed as he shuffled back to bed. It took a lot to excite him because he had seen a lot. After college, he served as a helicopter aviator in the Marine Corps for eight years. He returned home to the St. Louis suburbs and became a police officer. Nine years later, the World Trade Center was attacked on 9/11, resulting in the deaths of nearly 3,000 and injuries of 6,000 others. Like thousands of Americans, Tom volunteered to come to the defense of the Republic. He thought it was his duty, and he wanted his children to understand that freedom came with a price. He joined the Missouri Army National Guard and deployed to Iraq as a Black Hawk helicopter pilot. After returning home, he traded his police career for that of an aeronautical intelligence officer with the National Geospatial-Intelligence Agency.

"I hope it's not too serious," Gwenn replied as she headed for the bathroom.

Tom watched her walk away. She was over 50 now and still maintained the figure she had 25 years ago. She was still the beautiful Southern belle he had met and fallen in love with during flight school in Pensacola. He closed his eyes and was dozing off when he heard three rapid knocks on the door. He yanked the covers back as he muttered curses under his breath. Before he could roll out of bed, the banging started again. He yelled, "I'm coming, damn it!" He shuffled to the door in his gray St. Louis Cardinals T-shirt and blue gym shorts. He looked through the peephole and saw one of the cruise ship's officers with two Coasties standing behind him.

Gwenn asked, "What is it?" as she padded across the room and threw on her robe.

"I don't know." Tom flipped on the lights and opened the door.

Before he could speak, Gopher said, "I'm sorry for the trouble, Mr. Adams, but these men are here on official business."

"What is it?" Tom said, looking past him at the Coast Guard officer.

"Sir, I'm Lieutenant Commander Finch. Can I come in and talk to you? What I have to say is classified," he replied in a dead serious tone.

Tom opened the door and stepped aside to allow Finch to pass and then closed it.

"I'm Aaron Finch." He held out his hand.

Tom shook it. "Tom Adams, and this is my wife, Gwenn."

She nodded at him sternly while she sat on the edge of the bed with her arms folded and legs crossed.

"I'm sorry for the intrusion, but I have orders for both of you." He reached into the olive drab messenger bag hanging from his shoulder. He handed them both sealed manila envelopes. Red SECRET cover sheets were stapled to the front of both envelopes.

Now Tom was getting concerned. He tore open the envelope and read the orders. He sat down next to Gwenn. "This says I'm being recalled to active duty by the Army for OPERATION BEAR TRAP and I'm to report to Commander Waddle aboard the Cutter Alex Haley."

Gwenn nodded her head. "Mine says the Director of the National Geospatial-Intelligence Agency has canceled my leave and assigned me TDY to the Haley for BEAR TRAP."

Tom rubbed his face and looked up at Finch. "So, what's BEAR TRAP?"

"I'm sorry, sir, but I guess I don't have a need to know because I haven't been read in."

"And what if we say we're not going?" Tom pushed back.

"I have orders to take you both into custody."

Tom laughed. "Bullshit. Whose orders?"

Finch smiled back. "The President's."

CHAPTER 20

Alice was a beautiful twenty-five-year-old woman with brilliant blue eyes and wavy red hair that fell below her shoulders. She was half Amazon warrior, half Viking princess. Tonight, she was wearing a form-fitting green sleeveless dress that ended above her knees with matching four-inch heels.

She was already 6'1", and with the hair and heels, she was pushing 6'6". She didn't get to wear heels very often because when she did, she towered over most guys and their egos couldn't handle it, but that wasn't the case tonight. For the last six months, she had been going hot and heavy with a lawyer named Hunk—er, Hank. He was dark-haired, physically fit, and eight years older than Alice. He was also 6'6", so her height didn't bother him at all.

Alice had been looking forward to spending some alone time with him for weeks. His law firm placed a high demand on his time. Even when he was off, he would receive messages, emails, and phone calls. So far, the cruise had been a lot of fun. Tonight, they were in the ballroom on the dance floor. They had been dancing off and on for over three hours. The music in the ballroom stopped abruptly.

"Ms. Alice York and Mr. Steve Rogers, please report to the bridge," the voice on the ship's intercom said.

She looked at Hank, worried. "I hope everything is OK at home. I better go see what they want."

Hank shook his head. "Let's go."

They asked a member of the crew for help, and he led them to the bridge. Lieutenant Commander Finch was standing with another man who had a pissed-off look on his face.

The man was reading a piece of paper. "Look, Commander, I'm not in the Army anymore. I'm here with my fiancée. I can't just leave her here for the rest of the cruise without me."

"Captain, I'm just a messenger, but these orders are the real deal. You have to report," Finch replied. He turned to Alice and Hank. "Are you Senior Airman Alice York?"

She nodded. "Well, I was, but I got out of the Air Force over a year ago."

"This is Captain Steve Rogers, and I'm Lieutenant Commander Aaron Finch. I have orders for you." He handed them to her.

She shook her head. "This isn't right. Like I said, I've been out of the Air Force for over a year." She looked to Hank for help, and he took her orders and read them.

"I'm Ms. York's attorney. She's not going anywhere with you. Alice, we have waited a long time for this vacation. You can't go with him!" Hank exclaimed.

Finch addressed Alice directly, "Airman York, I have orders to take you into custody if you refuse to comply with your orders. Will you comply?"

Alice looked at Hank. "I'm sorry, Hank, but I have to go."

"I said you can't go! If you leave, we're done! Do you hear me?" Hank yelled at the top of his voice, causing everyone on the bridge to turn and stare.

"I'm sorry, Hank, but I have no choice."

Hank stormed off like a spoiled brat and yelled over his shoulder, "Fuck it! It's over!"

"I'm sorry, Airman, but you and the Captain need to come with me. Captain, you have five minutes to talk to your fiancée. Airman, you have five minutes to change into something more practical for the ride over to the ship. Your new C.O. can explain further when we get aboard the Haley," Finch replied.

CHAPTER 21

0930Z (0430HR EST)
6721 PINE CREEK COURT, MCLEAN, VIRGINIA

Despite the frigid February weather, a crowd of about fifty people from the neighborhood crawled out of bed and gathered outside the yellow "Police Line Do Not Cross" tape that had been strung up around 6721 Pine Creek Court to see what was going on. Now every light in the house was on, including the front porch, driveway, and the backyard. The backup units had arrived within two minutes of the call with their lights on and sirens blaring. The paramedics' ambulance arrived two minutes later also with lights and siren.

Next, the Fairfax County Police Air Unit's Bell 429 helicopter, callsign Fairfax One, arrived overhead, hovered at 300 feet, and lit up the area with its night sun spotlight. Then a steady stream of unmarked police cars began arriving, and men and women in civilian clothes flashed their badges to the police officer manning the tape. He wrote their names down on the crime scene attendance log and raised the tape. They stepped under it and headed for the house. Outside the house, a line of four uniformed officers walked across the property with their flashlights pointed at the ground searching for evidence.

Inside the house, the paramedics realized immediately that the suspects were not only dead but had been dead for quite a while. The blood on the floor was almost dry. They started asking questions that Sergeant Venable couldn't answer, so he called Special Agent Jerry Jerome. Agent Jerome called the Director of the FBI, and the Director called Chief Jon Bucher of the Fairfax County Fire and Rescue Department. Chief Bucher called his paramedics and solved the problem.

The paramedics declared the two dead men dead, packed up, and left. Next, the police dispatcher called the Medical Examiner's Office, and an investigator and two bag men were dispatched to the scene to pick up the bodies for autopsy. This time the Director of the FBI had already contacted the M.E. to pave the way.

One of Joe Venable's buddies, a plain-clothed special operations squad sergeant named Art Bailey from a neighboring district, came by to check out the scene because, well, because he could. Art strolled through the front door like he owned the place. He was a dark-haired fireplug of a man with no neck. He was wearing an unbuttoned bright yellow Hawaiian shirt covered with hula girls over a red hooded Redskins pullover sweatshirt. He refused to wear anything with the team's new logo on it. The house was full of detectives and uniformed cops that were milling around with not enough to do. As Art walked through the crowded home, the police officers parted like the Red Sea before Moses. Art Bailey was kind of a big deal in the department. Even the officers who didn't know him knew of him. He was a bit of a legend. He walked past all of the cops and straight over to Joe.

Art shook Joe's hand. "How are you and your boys doing, Joe?" He gawked at the bodies handcuffed on the floor.

"We're good, Art. Thanks for asking."

Art stepped over, bent down, and shined his flashlight on the bodies. Each body was full of bullet holes. Art was what most other cops would consider a grizzled veteran, but even he wondered if the number of shots was excessive for two cops. Personally, he didn't care.

He looked at Caleb and Danny. "Anybody worth shooting is worth shooting at least seven or eight times. I can't blame you for that." No cop wanted to get shot because he stopped shooting some shitbird scumbag too soon. Art stood up straight, removed his burgundy and gold Redskins stocking cap, and scratched his head. The cap looked rather comical with its golden yarn pom-pom attached to its crown.

He nodded to Caleb and Danny and said with a smile, "Well, if you can't dazzle them with brilliance, riddle them with bullets." Art turned to Joe. "You're a cool customer. When you called in the shooting, you sounded like Chuck Yeager test flying the X-1."

Joe smiled. "Well, this ain't my first rodeo." In twenty-three years on the department, Joe had shot and killed one suspect and wounded another two in three separate shootouts. He had also been shot and stabbed during his career.

Art knew about all of the incidents. He had been involved with one of the shootings.

He smiled back, leaned into Joe, and said quietly, "When the dust settles, come by the house and tell me what really happened." Art slapped Joe on the shoulder and walked out of the house.

***

Down the block at the end of Poole Lane, an FBI surveillance specialist named Garrett Sanders sat in the rear of a blacked-out gray Toyota Sienna minivan. He was one of a team of surveillance specialists who had been dispatched to the scene to help identify any other Russian agents who might come to the scene. He had cameras set up in the back of the van to take video and photographs of all the vehicles and pedestrians that entered and exited the area.

The surveillance specialists weren't special agents. They were unarmed civilian employees of the FBI. They carried gold badges similar to the agents', but they were not armed and were not sworn law enforcement officers, so they didn't have arrest powers. They worked in small teams and conducted physical and technical surveillance on some of the most dangerous criminals, terrorists, and spies in the world.

Their jobs were every bit as dangerous as the agents, but the FBI refused to arm them, simply because the agents didn't want anyone but agents to be armed. The agents would feel less special if the surveillance specialists had guns too. They would never be armed until one of them was killed in the line of duty. Then, of course, the White House and Congress would ask the FBI director why people with such dangerous jobs were unarmed, and then there would be a mad rush within the Bureau to get them all trained and armed ASAP.

Garrett Sanders ran every license plate to see who the vehicles belonged to. Any vehicles that weren't from Poole Lane or Pine Creek Court were flagged and their owners' records checked for anything unusual. Two others from the surveillance team were watching a suspicious car parked in Kirby Park that was probably left there by the two dead Russians. It was a black 2019 Chevrolet Impala from Maryland. A call to the registered owner determined he left it in long-term parking at Washington Dulles International Airport yesterday before he flew to Dallas for business.

***

Jocelyn and Jerry were sitting comfortably across the street from Karpinsky's house on Poole Lane in the home of Supervisory DEA Special Agent Delbert Meyers. After being called by his boss and advised who was parked in his driveway, Delbert climbed out of bed and invited them in for coffee and sandwiches. The three of them sat in his darkened living room watching the show through his massive picture window. News vans from the local Fox and ABC News affiliates pulled up and raised their antennas to prepare to broadcast. Their reporters quickly moved from person to person in the crowd trying to gather information worthy of reporting.

Eventually, Lieutenant Foster from the Fairfax County Police Public Affairs Office walked out of the house. Even though it was in the wee hours of the morning, his police uniform and personal appearance were impeccable. He stepped under the yellow police tape and gave a statement to the reporters. Foster identified himself and said, "I will make a brief announcement about what occurred here this morning. I will not be answering any questions until possibly late this afternoon when the autopsies and prelimi-nary investigation are completed.

"This morning at approximately 3:22 A.M., officers from the Fairfax County Police Department responded to a burglary in progress at 6721 Pine Creek Court. A neighbor reported the homeowner was out of town on vacation and saw someone inside the darkened residence shining a flashlight in the rooms. Our offi-cers responded and confronted two armed suspects in the kitchen. They identified themselves as police officers and ordered the suspects to drop their weapons. The suspects reached for weapons to engage our officers, and the officers fired at the suspects.

"The suspects were declared dead at the scene by paramedics of the Fairfax County Fire and Rescue Department. The medical examiner is en route at this time to take possession of the bodies. The suspects remain unidentified at this time. The identities of our officers will not be released at this time pending further investiga-tion. More information may be released as it becomes available. That's all I have at this time, thank you."

The reporters shouted questions at Foster as he turned, stepped under the police tape, and walked back to the house. Both Fox and ABC broadcast his statement live.

Delbert and his guests watched the Fox report on the TV hanging over his fireplace.

Jerry put his coffee cup down on a saucer on the coffee table. "That should buy us a few more hours. Del, this sandwich is incredible. Would you, please, write down what's in it before we leave?"

Del was a bit of a foodie and said, "Sure, no problem." He left the room to find some paper.

"I don't know how you can eat after what happened earlier," Jocelyn said.

"Firefights always make me hungry. Food tastes better, music sounds better, women smell better, and sex feels better. Everything is just a lot better because you're still alive," Jerry replied.

Minutes later, Jerry and Jocelyn watched as the news trucks drove off and the crowd faded away. Once the coast was clear, they thanked Delbert one more time for his help before they exited his front door and walked to their car. Jerry folded the sandwich recipe and stuck it in his jacket pocket. He climbed behind the wheel, but before he could start the car, his phone rang. Jerry looked at the caller ID, answered the phone, and put it on speaker.

"Hello, this is Jerome."

"Hey, Jerry, this is Garrett."

"Hi, Garrett, we're on speaker with Agent Gillis."

Garrett said, "Hey, Jocelyn. We got a hit on a plate the automated license plate reader picked up on a 2021 black Lincoln Navigator that followed the Fox news truck to the scene. It's a Virginia plate, Adam Boy Tom One One Three Eight. It came back to an address in Annandale. The registered owner's name is Scott Wilkes. He has a Virginia driver's license and a Social Security number, but no other history that we can find so far. No credit reports, no tax returns, and no social media. We captured his cell phone when he drove past the van. We tried to dump his phone, but it must be new because it had no data to take. We're tracking him through his phone right now. He isn't heading back to the address on his DL. He's weaving around all over DC. I can't tell if he's running an SDR or he's lost." Garrett was using a cell phone site simulator to track Wilkes's phone. SDR meant surveillance detection route. They knew if he was a trained Russian operative, it would be likely that he would execute an SDR before meeting with anyone or going home.

The FBI started tracking mobile phones over twenty years earlier when it discovered a new way to spy on the mob. The Mafia dons feared their private clubs were bugged, so they conducted their business as they drove around town in their Caddies. The FBI obtained warrants to listen in through the Cadillacs' OnStar systems and, as a result, locked up a lot of mobsters before they caught on.

"Did you guys get video of him at the scene?" Jocelyn asked.

"Yeah, Angela and Benny got video of the entire crowd. The video of him matches his DL photo. So far, he hasn't made any calls on his cell phone," Garrett replied.

"Have you checked with CIT for facial recognition?" Jocelyn asked.

"Yeah, they're running him, but so far, they haven't found a match except for the DL photo. We do know if he's Russian, he didn't enter the country legally because his photo isn't on file with ICE," Garrett replied. ICE was Immigration and Customs Enforcement.

Jocelyn said, "So, we have a guy who doesn't exist except for a driver's license and SSN. That's strike one. He randomly showed up at Karpinsky's house in McLean around 5:00 A.M., which is nowhere near Annandale, for no legitimate reason. That's strike two. And now, he's driving around aimlessly before the crack of dawn on a Saturday morning instead of sleeping like normal people. That's strike three. And he has a brand-new phone that's never been used. Can you say burner phone? That's strike four."

Jerry smiled. "There is no strike four."

Jocelyn cut her eyes at him. "Whatever, out number four, then."

Jerry smiled. "You only get three outs."

Jocelyn rolled her eyes. "Whatever. We need to stay on this guy until he leads us to his boss. Garrett, tell us which way he's going, and we'll head in that direction."

CHAPTER 22

0958Z (0058HR AKST)
COAST GUARD CUTTER ALEX HALEY,
20 MILES SOUTH OF HOMER

The young Coast Guard coxswain expertly maneuvered the RHIB up to the side of the Haley and held it there while his passengers climbed the ladder to the cutter one at a time. The captain stood at the top of the ladder.

"Welcome aboard, Mrs. Adams," Commander Waddle said as he helped her climb aboard his cutter.

Waddle looked down to the boat when he heard Tom ask, "Permission to come aboard, sir?"

Waddle smiled. "Permission granted, sir."

Tom lumbered up the ladder on to the deck.

"Sir, I'm Commander Dan Waddle, captain of the Haley," he said as he shook hands with Tom and then Gwenn. "Please, follow me inside, and we'll get you up to speed." He opened the hatch.

A moment later, they stepped into the wardroom. They were greeted by another smiling face, a fit-looking man wearing the Army's OCP combat uniform with blue eyes and gray hair. Tom noticed there was no name or insignia on his uniform. He reminded Tom of Race Bannon from the old Johnny Quest cartoon. He held out his hand to Tom, and Tom shook it.

Next, he held it out for Gwenn. "Thank you both for coming. I'm sorry it was necessary to interrupt your vacation."

"It wasn't just a vacation—it's our thirty-second wedding anniversary, and this wasn't a normal cruise! It's a winter cruise! Cruise lines don't normally cruise Alaska in the winter! This is the first time in...well, I don't know how long! A really long time!" Gwenn snapped, making it clear she wasn't happy. She didn't say so, but they had always put off vacations like the cruise throughout the years because they had raised four kids who always needed money for things like braces, dance lessons, college, and, oh yeah, food and clothes.

Mister Gray Hair lowered his hand and dropped his head, indicating he was properly chastised. "I really am sorry, but we need your help. Please, have a seat and I'll brief you."

Tom and Gwenn sat down next to each other at the table.

Smith continued, "The young ladies sitting across from you are Lieutenant Junior Grade Sarah Tuttle and Petty Officer Second Class Cindy McLemore. They are the intelligence cell for the Haley." Tuttle and McLemore nodded at Tom and Gwenn. Smith continued, "My name is Jon Smith, and I'm a CIA officer, but I've been recalled to the Navy for this mission. This wardroom has been designated a temporary SCIF for our use." The SCIF was a sensitive compartmented information facility where classified information could be stored and discussed.

Smith pointed a remote at a large flat-screen TV attached to the wall at the end of the table and turned it on. The screen filled with the image of a pallid old man wearing glasses. He had a high forehead with a gray beard and hair.

Smith said, "As the Berlin Wall came down, this man, a forty-year-old KGB colonel named Oleg Karpinsky, walked into our embassy in Stockholm and defected. Besides giving us the identities of several deep-cover Soviet spies operating in the U.S., he was a treasure trove of information on the Soviet Union's efforts in remote viewing. Have you ever heard of it?"

Tom nodded. "Yeah, I read a book a long time ago written by Chief Warrant Officer Joe McMoneagle from Project Stargate, and we watched a documentary about it on TV a few years ago."

Smith said, "Well, Karpinsky has been helping us with our Technical Remote Viewing program ever since he defected. In 1998, he became an American citizen. When he leaves the DC metro area, he travels with a three-man security detail of deputy U.S. Marshals. For the last five years, he's spent a month in Alaska every winter in a rental cabin at Eek Lake south of Bethel. This year, he moved his vacation up about a month for some reason.

"Anyway, about eight hours ago, NSA intercepted communications from Moscow to one of their special mission submarines, the BS-64 Podmoskovye, that referenced Oleg Karpinsky. The Podmoskovye was being tracked by one of our deep-water sound surveillance system sensors. Right after receiving the Karpinsky message, the Podmoskovye changed course and headed straight for the Yukon-Kuskokwim River Delta in Alaska.

"It's the consensus of the intelligence community that the Russians are going to try to snatch him while he's at the cabin. As I said, he's being protected by three deputy U.S. Marshals, but it's unlikely they'll prevail against Russian Spetsnaz troops. The Marshals Service tried to contact them on their sat phone, but it's out of service. Hopefully, they just forgot to keep it charged."

"OK, hold on a minute," Tom interrupted. "First, Jon Smith's not your name, is it?"

Jon smiled. "No, it's not."

"What did you do in the Navy?"

"I was a lieutenant commander in Naval Special Warfare, and now I've been recalled just like you."

"So, you're a SEAL. What do you need from us? Do you need Gwenn to analyze imagery for you?" Tom turned to his wife.

"Yes, we need her help, but we need you too."

"I'm not an imagery analyst. I supervise a team of aeronautical analysts. I don't know anything about analyzing imagery."

"Tom, we need you to fly that Jayhawk on the fantail and take a team out to recover Karpinsky and the marshals."

Tom laughed. "That's crazy! I don't know how to fly that thing! Besides, the Coast Guard pilots that landed it out there wouldn't let me near it!"

"The guys that flew it out here are both unconscious. They flew me out here earlier tonight and almost put us in the water. The copilot was unconscious when we landed, and right after the pilot got us on the deck, he threw up and passed out. Their crew chief thinks they have food poisoning. The corpsman said they can't fly for at least three days. Look, I read your file, Tom. You flew CH-53 Sea Stallions in the Corps, and you flew over a thousand combat hours in Black Hawks when you were in Iraq with the Guard and a lot of those hours were on NVGs. You still fly Hueys for fun."

Tom replied, "I haven't flown a Hawk in over 10 years, and those were 'A' models with steam gauges. That Jayhawk has a glass cockpit. I don't even know how to start the damn thing," Tom said, shaking his head. "I'm fifty-five years old and thirty pounds overweight. Alaska is full of Army, Air Force, and Coast Guard helicopter pilots. All of them are a better choice than me."

"Tom, I get it, but they're not here. You are. Have you been tracking the weather? We're in a weird weather situation. It's kind of like a giant sucker hole between here and Bethel. Everywhere else is socked in at least until tomorrow. I was on vacation too. I was in Homer at a very nice lodge when the Coast Guard flew in to get me. I got here about an hour and a half ago. We can't get any other assets to Eek Lake in time, and we haven't located the Russian sub, so we really aren't sure how long we have, but we do know the Russians have a big head start."

Commander Waddle interrupted, "Excuse me, but you have an incoming video conference call to take," as he pointed to the large HDTV at the front of the room.

They swiveled in their chairs and were greeted with the smiling face of the President of the United States. Gwenn's mouth dropped open, and Jon, Tom, and the Coasties instinctively sprang to attention.

The President motioned for them to sit. "At ease, at ease. Please, everyone, sit down. I know this is a shock, and you don't have much time to prepare, so I'll be quick. Colonel Adams, I want you to know we wouldn't be putting you on the spot like this if there was another option, but for the next seven or eight hours or so, you're the only option. I had the Pentagon and NSA looking for military helicopter pilots near Homer, and you are the only one close enough.

"I know it's been quite a while since you've flown a combat mission, but the Russians have invaded our country. It doesn't matter if it's a small number of special operators or that it's in a remote part of Alaska. We can't tolerate foreign soldiers operating on our sovereign soil and assaulting or killing American citizens. If you can't stop them, our next option is a cruise missile strike on their sub, assuming we find it on the surface inside our waters. That will cause a huge international commotion and a possible environmental disaster.

"General McKinley assured me you will have no problem flying this mission. He's your biggest fan. We've assembled a big-league team to ensure your success—big-league. Jon will fill you in on the details. The cavalry is ready and standing by at airfields all around you, and they'll launch as soon as possible, Tom, but until then, you'll have to hold the line. Thank you all for your help, and God bless you. It's good to see you again, Gwenn."

Everyone in the room turned to look at Gwenn. She sat there and smiled back at them. She didn't say anything because they didn't have a need to know. They looked back to the TV, but the screen was blank.

Tom looked down, shaking his head and muttering under his breath, "Fuck me." Tom said to Gwenn, "Remind me to punch Whitey in the face next time I see him." Whitey was General Bryan McKinley's callsign in the Flying Tigers. He was so pale he got sunburned by just standing next to a picture of the sun. He was a couple of shades shy of translucent.

Tom turned back to Jon. "I can't believe we're getting sucked into this goat rope. This ad hoc, come-as-you-are shit is going to get good people killed. They trained for months before Operation Eagle Claw, and that ended in disaster. Those guys were the best special operators we had."

Eagle Claw was the secret rescue mission flown deep into Iran to free the fifty-two American hostages being held illegally after the U.S. Embassy was seized on November 4, 1979. The mission failed miserably at the Desert One refueling site when a massive air-taxiing Navy RH-53D helicopter being flown by Marine aviators collided with an Air Force EC-130E. The EC-130E was equipped with internal fuel bladders and was parked on the ground when the air-taxiing RH-53D struck it while repositioning during the refueling operations. The crash resulted in a huge fiery explosion, eight dead soldiers and Marines, and four severely injured. The mission's colossal failure resulted in national humiliation around the world.

"I'd rather explain myself at a court martial than fly into the ocean and kill the team because I'm not proficient. I don't even have a current military flight physical."

Jon replied, "The FAA says you have a Class II medical certificate on file, and the Commandant of the Marine Corps said you can fly this mission single pilot with no problems. He said you trained him to be an aircraft commander when you were flying CH-53s. He also said this isn't your first special mission. He mentioned a time you flew a wave-hopping NVG mission across Manila Bay to the U.S. Embassy during the coup in 1989."

Gwenn shot a look of surprise at Tom. He had never told her about it. She wondered how many other crazy missions he had been involved in throughout the years that she didn't know about. She knew about the time in Iraq when the lead Black Hawk in his formation was shot down during a complex RPG ambush east of Taji, and he and his crew rescued the wounded crew before the anti-coalition forces could reach them. That incident had made the news and been written about in books. One of the soldiers they rescued was later elected to the United States Senate out of Illinois.

And, of course, she remembered when Tom's helicopter was shot down and his friend, Terry Bergman, was killed.

Tom countered, "That was thirty years ago when I was at the top of my game."

Smith took on the role of big brother to the older man. He placed his hand on Tom's shoulder. "Tom, here are the cold, hard facts. For the next day or so on this mission, you are a lieutenant colonel and I am a lieutenant commander. We took oaths when we accepted our commissions, and they don't expire. So, grab a flight suit from the table over there and suit up. When you're ready, I'll bring in the rest of the team, and we can get to know each other and brief them for the mission."

Tom resigned himself to the situation and walked over to the short stack to find a 48 Regular flight suit. Tuttle and McLemore left the room to check on something so Tom started changing clothes. "Did you notice the President got my rank wrong? I was a major, not a colonel."

"You better check your orders again," Jon replied as he typed something into his Toughbook laptop.

Tom zipped up the flight suit and stepped into a new pair of black leather insulated Belleville boots. He grabbed his envelope and thumbed through the papers until he came to the last page. It was an order promoting him to lieutenant colonel signed by the Commander in Chief. Tom accepted his fate. "Alright, look, I'm just a helicopter pilot, and it's been over thirty years since I was trained in infantry tactics, so I will defer to your judgment for all the ground decisions. Bring them in and let's get started. You can do the talking." Tom sat down at the head of the table next to Jon and tied his boot laces.

Commander Waddle opened the hatch and called to his XO to bring the team in. Three enlisted Coast Guard aircrewmen in green flight suits came through the hatch followed by six men and one woman wearing the same OCP woodland green and brown camo that Smith wore.

Smith stood at the front of the room and addressed the group, "Everyone, please, take a seat so we can get started." After they were all seated, he continued, "OK, I'm Lieutenant Commander Jon Smith, United States Navy." Smith gestured to Tom. "Our commander for this mission is Lieutenant Colonel Tom Adams, United States Army Reserve. The briefing you are about to receive is classified TS/SCI. You don't have TS/SCI clearances, so you all need to sign these nondisclosure forms before you can be briefed."

Corporal Davis raised his hand. "Excuse me, sir, but what is TS/SCI?"

"It means Top Secret/Special Compartmented Information. It's one of the highest classifications possible. Mostly, it means this is a big fucking deal, pardon my French." Smith handed a stack of the forms to the first man seated at the table to his left, Chief Petty Officer Ortega, and he passed them along to the others. After the forms were signed and collected, Smith began the briefing. "Please, hold your questions to the end of the brief. As I said, I am Lieutenant Commander Smith and sitting next to me is our commanding officer for this mission, Lieutenant Colonel Adams." Smith motioned with his hand toward Adams.

Adams nodded but remained silent.

Smith spun to look at the large wall monitor. "Back when the Berlin Wall came down in 1989, a KGB colonel named Oleg Karpinsky walked into our embassy in Stockholm and defected to the United States. He has been under our protection ever since."

Karpinsky's Virginia driver's license photo was displayed on the large wall monitor.

Davis raised his hand again. "Excuse me, sir, but isn't Karpinsky a Polish name? How did he end up in the KGB?"

Smith had told everyone to hold their questions to the end of the brief, but he decided to answer him anyway. "Karpinsky's father was a Polish communist and linguist who was fluent in seven languages, including Russian, English, French, and German. He was a true believer in the communist cause, so he immigrated to the Soviet Union in 1935, became a citizen, and joined the KGB. His son Oleg followed in his footsteps and joined the KGB.

"The son, Oleg, was involved in the Russian version of our Stargate Project. He led a team of Russian soldiers and researchers that spied on us and our allies by using a technique called remote viewing. Basically, the spy would sit in a room in Russia and be given a sealed envelope with the name of a target inside it. It could be a person, place, or thing. Without opening the envelope and looking at the name of the target, he would use the techniques he had been taught to travel to the target in his mind and gather all the information possible and then write up a detailed report on the target, including sketches, if possible."

His audience looked around the table skeptically at each other. Eric and Mike tried to make each other laugh by whispering the "Do do, do do," theme from the old Twilight Zone TV show.

Smith nodded. "I know this sounds like science fiction, but people in our government who are a lot smarter than us take him very seriously. After his defection, he came to work for our government. Officially, our Stargate Project was shut down in the mid-90s, but he continues to do research for us. Currently he's on vacation at a cabin at Eek Lake here in Alaska with his three-man protection detail of deputy U.S. Marshals. NSA intercepted a message from Moscow to the special mission submarine, BS-64 Podmoskovye, that mentioned Oleg Karpinsky by name. We don't know if they want him back because he's a traitor or if they fear he has gathered new information they don't want him to divulge. We believe they intend to either kill him or snatch him.

"We've assembled this team to go out to Eek Lake and retrieve him and his protection detail before the Russians arrive. If they already have him, we are going to take him back. Right now, the weather is clear between here and Eek Lake, but most of the rest of the state is experiencing either freezing rain or heavy snow. Due to the unusual weather situation in Alaska, we are unable to bring in any other assets. We plan to launch in approximately two hours, and if all goes well, we will be back to the ship in seven hours and you can all go back to your lives."

The woman in OCP raised her hand and interrupted, "Excuse me, sir, my name is Alice York, and I'm not in the military anymore. I got out over a year ago. This is all very fascinating, but I shouldn't be here."

Jon picked up his clipboard and went to the page with her information. "Alice, you and two of your cohorts have not completed your eight-year initial service obligation, so legally you are still in the Individual Ready Reserve and subject to recall. If you look at the signature on your orders, you will see that the President has recalled you. Your file indicates you're a very talented Air Force Security Forces sniper. We may need your skills when we get out there. All of you were or still are highly trained and capable soldiers.

"How about we all take turns introducing ourselves and briefing our experience and qualifications. I'll start. As I said, my name is Jon Smith, and I work for one of our country's intel agencies. I was recalled from retirement for this mission. I was a SEAL, and my last assignment was with JSOC. Colonel Adams also works for an intel agency and was an aviator in the Marine Corps and Army Guard before his retirement. He was also recalled to active duty. Chief, why don't you go next?"

The man stood up. "I'm Chief Petty Officer Ernesto Ortega. I've been in the Coast Guard for twelve years, and I'm a crew chief on the Jayhawk."

Ortega was from Houston, Texas. He was a good student in high school and played baseball and wrestled. He came from a working-class family where college wasn't considered a necessity. He didn't have money for college, so he decided to join the military. While he was in his senior year of high school, he went to talk to all the military recruiters. He was drawn to the Coast Guard because he was more interested in saving lives than taking them. Plus, he had an Uncle Hector who had been in the Coast Guard, and he gave him the real story of life in the Coast Guard.

Hector told him the Coast Guard bases were usually in good locations. Obviously, most were on the coast, but some were in the Great Lakes and along major rivers like the Mississippi. Hector recommended he get a flying position; otherwise, he might get stuck on a cutter for months at a time. If he was assigned to a fixed-wing aircraft like the C-130 Hercules, he wouldn't have to live on the ships.

Ultimately, Ortega decided to be a helicopter mechanic and crew chief on the Jayhawk. He never regretted his decision. So far, he had been stationed in Miami, Hawaii, and now Alaska. He hoped to become an officer and go to flight school. He had an excellent reputation and been given Taco as a callsign. He told people Taco was short for "Take Charge, Ortega." When he sat down, the man next to him stood up.

"I'm Petty Officer First Class Ed Hicks. I've been in the Coast Guard for eight years, and I'm a Jayhawk crew chief."

Hicks's full name was Eugene David Hicks, so since his initials were E.D., everyone called him Ed. He was a Navy brat. He and his family had followed his father around the world. The old man had been in airfield operations and rose to master chief petty officer. They had lived on NAS Sigonella on the island of Sicily in Italy, NAS Rota in Spain, NAF Atsugi in Japan, NAS Key West in Florida, NAS Oceana in Virginia, NAS Corpus Christi in Texas, and NAS North Island in California.

He grew up around military planes and helicopters and their crews. It was just understood that he would go into the military. His journey continued. After joining the Coast Guard, he had been stationed at Coast Guard Air Stations in Traverse City in Michigan, Clearwater in Florida, and now Kodiak in Alaska. He married another Navy brat right out of high school before he joined the Coast Guard. She followed him into the service. Now, they had two little girls.

The introductions continued with Savage. All he said was, "Petty Officer First Class Chris Savage, rescue swimmer for ten years."

What he didn't say was he started out in the Marine Corps as a mechanic and crew chief on UH-1Y Venom helicopters. He deployed from Camp Pendleton, California, to Afghanistan with the Gunfighters of HMLA-369 and earned his Combat Aircrew Wings. He won his wings as a door gunner, and he was proficient in his duties. He racked up a huge body count of dead Taliban, Al

Qaeda, and Quds Force members of the Islamic Revolutionary Guard Corps.

When he came back to the States, he decided he was tired of killing and wanted to try something else. So, after four years in the Fleet, he decided to volunteer for the search and rescue unit at Cherry Point and became a rescue swimmer. Chris really enjoyed saving people, so when the Corps discontinued the local search and rescue program, he decided to leave the Corps and enlist in the Coast Guard. He had been assigned to Miami before coming to Kodiak.

Next, one of the green-clad men stood up. "Steve Rogers. I was an Army captain in the Finance Corps. I left after five years, and now I've been recalled."

Smith said, "Captain, your file also says you are an Airborne Ranger."

Rogers replied, "Sir, I went to jump school over the summer while in ROTC, and I earned my Ranger tab after graduation, but I never served in the Regiment. My year in Afghanistan was as a finance officer." The regiment he referred to was the storied 75th Ranger Regiment. According to real Rangers, the only way you could be a Ranger was to serve in the Regiment. It didn't matter if you were trained to be a Ranger and had earned the tab. If you weren't from the Regiment, you weren't a Ranger.

Smith said, "Don't be so modest, Captain. It says here you were awarded a Silver Star during your tour. The citation says you killed an insurgent saboteur on the flight line at Bagram Air Base with your pistol, then used his AK-47 to kill two of his comrades before stabbing a fourth insurgent with your Kabar."

Rogers's Kabar was his father's, Steven Rogers Sr., USMC Kabar that he had used during the Vietnam War as a Marine infantry captain. His dad had given it to him when he graduated from Ranger School. As was the custom of Marine officers at the time, Senior had his name engraved on the blade in the blood groove when he bought it while attending the Basic School at Quantico. Back then, the thought was that if he left it stuck in an enemy soldier on the battlefield, he might get it back later because it had his name on it.

That night at Bagram, Steven lost the knife in the confusion. The tango he was fighting was able to run off in the darkness and was found dead after the sun came up with the Kabar lodged in his ribs. The Marine aviator who found the dead tango tracked Rogers down and returned the knife to him. The knife had two small notches on top of the blade near the hilt that had been placed there by his father. Steve added one more.

Smith continued, "Those Taliban terrorists were carrying satchel charges. Your actions saved a squadron of AV-8B Harrier jets and untold lives."

All heads turned to look at Rogers with a mix of respect and admiration. They were truly impressed. Strasburg, Pope, and Davis sat a little taller in their seats.

"Welcome aboard, Captain. Who's next?" Jon motioned to the next in line.

"Mike Harmon, I'm a SERT-qualified Alaska State Trooper." SERT stood for Special Emergency Reaction Team. SERT was what Alaska called their SWAT teams. Alaska was a huge state but only had less than a million residents. They had three SERT teams scattered around the state. "Before that, I was a Marine infantry sergeant for six years, and I had three months left on my obligation before tonight."

Mike grew up in a small town of about 1,200 residents called Cohoe along the Kasilof River south of Kenai. He and his mom, dad, and little brother were the only black people in town. Mike was a three-letter athlete in high school and received good grades. His brother, Russell, wasn't near the athlete Mike was, but he excelled in math, computers, and science. His dad, Mike Sr., was from Memphis, Tennessee, and was an airborne infantryman who served for twenty years and retired as a master sergeant. During his last eight years of service, he was a member of the 4th Brigade Combat Team (Airborne), 25th Infantry Division at Fort Richardson next to Anchorage. His mom was also in the Army. She was a medic, the military equivalent of a licensed practical nurse and paramedic. She served on the medevac helicopters.

After she retired, she earned her Bachelor of Science degree in Nursing (BSN), specializing in trauma medicine. His mom and dad liked Alaska and decided to stay. The day after his dad retired, he started training at the Alaska State Trooper Academy in Sitka. Currently, he was a sergeant with the Soldotna Detachment. Senior taught his boys to be strong and self-reliant. He took them into the wilderness around Tustumena Lake to hunt and fish year-round.

After high school, Mike decided to one-up his old man and become a Marine Corps infantryman. His younger brother, Russell, took the easy route and earned an Aerospace Engineering degree with an AFROTC scholarship at the Virginia Military Institute. He was a new captain flying B-2 Spirit stealth bombers at Whiteman AFB in Knob Noster, Missouri.

"Well, oorah and welcome aboard, Sergeant," Jon said as laughter filled the room.

The man next to him stood up. "My name is Eric Fuller. I'm also an Alaska State Trooper, and I've been in the Air Guard for six years. I'm a staff sergeant and pararescueman."

Eric was born and raised in Seward. During World War II, his great grandfather Bertram was a major in the Army's Corps of Engineers. He helped build Fort Raymond to defend the area from the Japanese who had invaded the Aleutian Islands. The area was important due to its access to docks and the Alaska Railroad that transported goods from ships north to Anchorage and the interior of the territory. After the war, Bertram stayed to work as a manager for the Alaska Railroad. Now it was a major hub for commercial fishing, tourism, and the cruise ship industry.

Eric's dad owned a commercial fishing boat, and his mom stayed home to look after their five kids. Eric spent enough time working on the boat with his dad to know he didn't want a life at sea. He grew up hunting and fishing and was completely at home in the bush. He liked the Air Guard and the idea of being a citizen soldier. He was working on his private pilot's license and had pieced together a bachelor's degree. He intended to apply for a helicopter pilot slot with his unit when they held their next selection board. Serving as a PJ was a common path to becoming a pilot in the Air Guard rescue squadrons. Being a full-time trooper and part-time airman was perfect for him. Eric sat down, and the next man wearing the Army's new OCP camouflage stood up.

"I'm Sergeant First Class Jim Strasburg of the Alaska National Guard. I've served 18 years between the Army and the Guard infantry." He came from Windfall, Indiana. Everyone in his family for four generations farmed corn. When his parents were in high school, classes would let out for a week or two in the fall so the students could help their families harvest the corn.

It was a hard life. Jim was there the day Grandpa didn't come in from the field for lunch. Two of his uncles climbed up in the hay loft and saw Grandpa's big green Jon Deere combine sitting idle in the field over a mile away. They couldn't see Grandpa. They jumped in his old Ford F-100 pickup and raced out to check on him. Ten minutes later, they brought Grandpa back in the bed of the truck. He was dead.

The combine had jammed, and he had tried to clear it by himself. He had probably done it fifty times over the years. This time, it grabbed his sleeve and pulled his right hand into the teeth and chewed it off. He bled to death in the field within sight of the house he had lived in his entire life except for the two years of active duty he had served in the Indiana Army National Guard. He was one of the few who volunteered to go to Vietnam for a year. The family mourned him, and the preacher praised him at the service. Within three days, they were all back in the fields.

Strasburg loved the outdoors, but he did not want to be a farmer. Upon graduating from high school, he enlisted in the Army. He asked for infantry and liked it. After jump school, he volunteered for Ranger School and was assigned to the 3rd Battalion of the 75th Ranger Regiment at Fort Benning, Georgia. Ten years later, he accepted a full-time AGR position with the Alaska Army Guard. Over the years, he saw combat in Africa, Iraq, and Afghanistan.

"Sergeant, were you able to bring everything on my list?" Jon asked.

"Yes, sir, and then some," Strasburg said.

"Excellent. We certainly won't be outgunned. Why don't you go next, Staff Sergeant?" Jon asked.

The man stood up. "I'm Staff Sergeant Nate Pope. I have twelve years with the Army and Alaska National Guard Infantry."

Pope was from Detroit, Michigan. His father worked for the Ford Motor Company for thirty-five years. He worked on the assembly line as a member of the United Auto Workers. His mother stayed home and took care of Nate and his brothers and sisters. Nate was an average student in school, not because he wasn't smart, but because he was bored. He excelled at team sports like football and basketball, but unlike many of the young men he played with, he didn't expect to have a career in professional sports.

He grew up in a time when Detroit was in decline. Gangs and drugs were destroying his neighborhood. After high school, he didn't know what to do. He wasn't ready to go to college, and no good jobs were available. Nate wanted to do something exciting to test his abilities. His father had served in the Army during the Carter administration. He experienced sporadic incidents of racism but, on the whole, had a positive opinion of the Army and was proud of his service. When Nate talked to his father about joining the Army, his father told him the good and the bad. He recommended Nate sign up for a technical MOS, or military occupational specialty, that would help him get a good job after he got out, but Nate decided he wanted an adventure, so he went infantry.

"And last, but not least," Jon said.

Davis stood up. "My name is Corporal Allen Davis, and I've been in the Alaska National Guard Infantry for four years."

"Again, thank you all for your service and your brevity. Just so you all know, everyone on this team has had at least one deployment. So, we all have the T-shirt," Smith said. "As you can see, this is a twelve-man mission. We will have two four-man infantry fire teams. Team One, led by me, includes Sergeants Fuller and

Harmon and Airman York. Team Two, led by Captain Rogers, includes Sergeants Strasburg and Pope and Corporal Davis. In addition to a standard combat loadout, everyone will carry a minimum of three days of survival gear and food. Sergeant Strasburg will supervise the pre-mission inspection."

Tom said, "Excuse me, Commander, but I have a few things to say. First, I want you all to know a little about me. I retired as a major from the Army Reserve five years ago. I had a couple of yearlong combat deployments in Iraq flying the UH-60 Black Hawk. Now, as a supervisory intelligence officer at the National Geospatial-Intelligence Agency, my civilian intelligence rank is equivalent to a military lieutenant colonel, so when the President recalled me, I guess he decided to promote me to that level. I fly a Vietnam War–era Huey helicopter once or twice a month with the Army Aviation Flying Museum in St. Louis, but I have never flown a Jayhawk." Looking at Smith, Tom said, "As I understand it, the President put me in charge of this mission, so everyone here is under my command. Is that correct?"

Commander Smith smiled. "Yes, sir."

"And this is a combat mission to rescue American citizens and to locate, close with, and destroy an enemy military force that has invaded sovereign United States soil?" Tom continued.

"Yes, sir," Smith stated again.

"OK, since you are all under my command, I want you to know that I will not force any of you to come with us. I didn't realize some of you had been recalled for this mission like the Commander and me. If you want out, leave the wardroom now so the rest of us can complete the briefing." He made eye contact with each individual. Surprisingly, no one moved. He thought he might lose one or two of the reservists who had been recalled involuntarily. "Since this is a combat mission, I am ordering field promotions for everyone on the mission, except Chief Ortega. Chief, since you will be my copilot, you will be commissioned as an Ensign. Captain Waddle, I don't have an admin shop. Would you please arrange for all the necessary orders to be written up for my signature?" Tom asked.

Captain Waddle stood up from his chair in the back of the room and headed for the door. "It would be a pleasure, Colonel."

"One more thing, Commander Smith. The flight crew will be a third fire team in the event we have to dismount, so I want them outfitted for ground combat like the other two teams."

"Aye, aye, sir." Smith had originally planned to use the helicopter crew as a third fire team anyway before the pilots became a problem.

CHAPTER 23

Two young boatswains' mates were in the passageway outside the makeshift SCIF swabbing the deck. "Swabbing the deck" was Navy speak for mopping the floor. They pissed off their lead petty officer earlier in the day, and now instead of sleeping or enjoying their free time, they were working it off. As they labored, they saw the strangers in camouflage uniforms walk into the wardroom.

"Who do you think those people are?" Seaman Stokes asked his buddy, Seaman Leonard, as he made long strokes across the shiny deck with his mop. The deck was already clean, but they had to swab the deck until they were told it was clean.

Leonard stopped mopping and cupped his hands on top of the mop handle. "I didn't see no names or ranks on their uniforms. They got to be from one of those top-secret special units."

Stokes kept mopping. "They don't look all that special to me."

Leonard shook his head. "That's the point, Stokes, my man. They're not supposed to look like super soldiers."

"What about that tall Amazon chick? I've never seen no women in the Green Berets or SEALs," Stokes pointed out.

Leonard thought for a moment. "Well then, that chick must be a dude." He nodded and went back to swabbing the deck.

Stokes shook his head. "Damn!"

CHAPTER 24

Deputy Marshal Kevin Bass woke up wet and shivering, surrounded by darkness. The Russians had buried him face down under a foot of snow. It tumbled off his back as he struggled up to his hands and knees. He gasped for air. Then his eyes bugged out, and he screamed as a lightning bolt of excruciating pain shot through his shattered face. The scream sounded more like a guttural howl from a desperate animal. He expelled a large glob of partially coagulated blood onto the snow. It appeared black on the white background. He rolled over onto his back and cradled his face in his trembling hands. He held his mangled jaw up against his face with his left hand. He could feel jagged bone protruding from his jaw. He pulled his lucky bandana out of his back pocket with his right hand. He tied it around his head like a sling to hold his jaw in place.

He had carried the desert camouflage bandana every day since it saved his life in Afghanistan. He had worn the bandana as a skullcap under his helmet while on patrol with his platoon in the Delaram District when it was hit above his right ear with a 7.62mm×39mm round fired from an AK-47. The bullet punched right through the Kevlar helmet but did not penetrate the bandana. He had a hell of a headache but suffered no permanent damage. He bragged to his squad mates afterward that the bandana had saved his life.

It was still dark, but he saw the cabin's silhouette on the white background about a hundred feet away. He didn't hear or see anyone, so he figured the trooper must have left with Karpinsky. He knew he would freeze to death if he didn't get back in the cabin. Kevin rolled over to his hands and knees, and his right hand bumped up against something under the snow next to him. He scooped some of the snow out of the way and felt a flannel shirt sleeve. It had to be Ronnie. The body was already beginning to freeze. He decided not to uncover his face. He didn't want to see it. He felt around with his left hand and felt another body that must be Mark's. He wanted to cry for them, but now wasn't the time. He tried to stand, but the blood loss made him so dizzy it was impossible, so instead, he started crawling.

He remembered regaining consciousness a few times after he had been shot. During one of his more lucid moments, he remembered hearing the trooper talk to the other trooper and saying something about cowboys and policemen and combat. Next, he remembered two men dragging him through the snow by his boots. They were complaining about how heavy he was and how hard it was to drag him through the deep snow. One of the men said if he found out who forgot to pack the snowshoes, he would kick his ass. Last, he remembered hearing the trooper talking to the doctor and the doctor saying he needed to talk to Pichugin about a new weapon. Kevin realized Karpinsky had betrayed them. He wanted him and the trooper's team dead.

Kevin had only crawled about 25 feet when he realized he might actually die in the snow. He had the will to survive, but he might not have the blood. Then a wave of relief flooded over him when he remembered the satellite phone. He reached into his jacket pocket for it to call for help. He knew he couldn't talk, but he could still call the emergency number for the watch officer at the Witness Protection Program office. The watch officer would send help if no one responded to his questions. When he pulled the phone out of his jacket pocket, it came out in several pieces. The trooper's bullet had destroyed it.

Relief was instantly replaced by profound disappointment. Help would not come tonight. No one would look for them until they missed their check-in tomorrow. Kevin was overcome with a surge of white-hot anger. He would have to save himself. It would be easier to lie there and let the cold take him, but he didn't do things the easy way. He never had, and he wouldn't start now.

CHAPTER 25

Commander Waddle had ordered the Haley's mess deck opened up for the team so they could have a hot meal before the mission while snow skis were attached to the helicopter's landing gear. Commander Smith told the team to grab some chow and then report to the hangar. The team walked out of the SCIF after the mission briefing and straight to the brightly lit mess deck, which had a heavily lacquered wooden sign hanging from the bulkhead that read, "The Bering Sea Café."

The room had white painted steel walls and was furnished in a spartan institutional fashion. The stainless-steel tables were bolted to the deck and had six gray backed swivel chairs with blue vinyl padded seats permanently attached to them. The tables were covered with blue vinyl tablecloths the same shade of blue as the seats. A flat-screen TV was attached to the far bulkhead playing the Fox News Channel with the sound muted.

The cooks had already prepared scrambled eggs, steak, bacon, sausage, hash browns, biscuits and gravy, fresh fruit, and assorted cereals. The team went through the chow line with their blue plastic trays and then sat down as fire teams, four to a table.

Mike and Eric were sitting across from each other with Alice next to Mike and Jon next to Eric. They didn't have much time, so they were eating as fast as they could before the equipment inspection in the hangar. Mike had already inhaled his steak and eggs when he choked on a mouthful of Frosted Flakes.

He cleared his throat. "Shit, man! I just figured it out!"

Eric stopped eating. "Figured what out?"

Mike looked around to see if anyone at the other tables was listening and answered as he pointed his spoon at Eric. "We're Red Shirts."

"What the fuck are you talking about?"

"We're Red Shirts like in the old Star Trek show. Every time Captain Kirk beamed down to some fucked-up forbidden planet, he would always take a smoking hot yeoman wearing a mini dress and a couple of red-shirted security men with him that you had never seen on the show before. The Red Shirts would always get killed right after they beamed down, and then Kirk would spend the rest of the show saving the hot chick. Commander Smith is Captain Kirk, Alice is the smoking hot yeoman—no offense," Mike said.

"None taken," Alice replied as she ate her eggs.

"And we're the Red Shirts!" Mike, proud of himself, said with a smile.

The others laughed, and then Eric said, "Well, then, no problem. Just refuse to wear the shirt."

They laughed again, and Commander Smith stood up with his tray. "As soon as you're finished eating, head for the hangar."

***

The Army fire team was sitting nearby at another table. Davis was excited. As he stuffed his face with steak and eggs, he said to the others between bites, "This is turning into a great day. I just got promoted way early, and instead of going to drill tomorrow, we're about to launch out of here on a secret mission to rescue a bunch of federal marshals! We may even get to shwack some commies if they have the guts to show up! Man, their chow here is a lot better than ours. I've never seen steak in an Army chow hall."

Strasburg turned his head from Davis to Captain Rogers and changed the subject. "Sir, if you don't mind, would you tell us a little about your military service? Commander Smith said you have a Silver Star. Was that night the extent of your combat experience?"

Captain Rogers cleared his throat. "Well, no. Like I said, I was in the Finance Corps, but when I got to Bagram as a first lieutenant, I made the mistake of wearing my jump wings and Ranger tab on my ACUs, and my colonel detailed me out to convoy duty and base security. I led a lot of convoys and was involved in quite a few firefights. That night the insurgents came through the wire, I was leading the air base's QRF."

QRF stood for quick reaction force. In this case, Rogers's QRF was a forty-man platoon made up of soldiers who had been detailed from their units like Rogers had been. They were REMFs or POGs. REMFs were rear echelon motherfuckers, and POGs were persons other than grunts. They were cooks, mechanics, admin clerks, and supply guys outfitted for combat.

"That's dope, sir," Davis said. "Sergeant Strasburg was with the Ranger Regiment in Africa and made deployments to Iraq and Afghanistan, and Sergeant Pope deployed to Iraq once and Afghanistan twice. We were all in Afghanistan together during our last deployment. Well, it was my first deployment."

Even though Pope had two slices of pizza in the chopper, he was a big man and was still hungry, so he listened and ate while the others talked. Besides, he always got a kick out of Davis when he spun up. Even when they were conducting PT or in the field in miserable conditions, Davis always seemed thrilled to be there. He consistently sought out new challenges and experiences. His enthusiasm was contagious. It didn't matter if he was talking to another corporal or a general. He was polite and respectful but not the slightest bit intimidated. Davis didn't know it, but he impressed the hell out of Strasburg and Pope. He kept them motivated.

Eric and Mike got up from their table to turn in their dirty trays. As they passed the soldiers who were still eating, Mike pointed at Davis and said, "Red Shirt."

Eric laughed and pushed him forward away from the table.

Davis watched them pass. "What do you think of those cops?"

Strasburg said, "I think they're probably fine soldiers. They've both had plenty of experience."

Davis replied, "They're not soldiers. I see a Jarhead and a Flyboy."

Pope interjected, "Don't kid yourself, Allen. They are both highly trained in the art of killing, and Marines like it more than most, especially Marine infantry. And everybody that takes the oath and carries a weapon is a soldier."

Captain Rogers spoke up, "The thing I admire most about the Marine Corps is that they all consider themselves warfighters. It doesn't matter what their MOS is. In Afghanistan, I asked a Marine pilot one time why the Marine Corps puts their pilots through all of the grunt training before they go to flight school. He said they are taught that when they go into combat, they may have to provide the security for their own airfield because the infantry will be busy on the front lines. The aviators will be leading the patrols outside the wire, keeping the enemy away from their aircraft and runways. Even their lawyers go through the same training as the other officers. Plus, they have their own air support. When a Marine grunt calls for air support, he knows the Marine aviator in that Hornet, Harrier, or Cobra went through the same training he did, and he trusts them to drop ordnance danger close. Close air support is their bread and butter."

Strasburg said, "Excuse me, sir, but I want to say something about the Russians we might be facing. I never went head-to-head with Spetsnaz soldiers, but some of the GRU Spetsnaz units were operating with the Iranians in Afghanistan when I was there with the Regiment. We were briefed on their operations and capabilities. They are highly trained and very dangerous. They will quickly adapt to any situation and are totally ruthless. If they are here, they're probably trained to pass as Americans. Don't hesitate if we make contact with them. Shoot first and ask questions later. As far as I'm concerned, this guy, Karpinsky, isn't worth any one of our lives. I don't care how much help he's been to the CIA. We all get to go home after the mission."

Rogers nodded his head in agreement.

***

Gwenn and Tom were sitting alone at a table in the corner. Tom was taking advantage of a good hot meal before flying all night. He liked to eat. Gwenn sat across from him watching him inhale his food as she drank iced tea. It didn't matter how cold it was outside, she would have iced tea.

She leaned in and said quietly, "Promise me you won't let them pressure you into doing something crazy."

Tom replied, "You mean crazier than what I'm already doing?"

She gave him the wife look.

He nodded as he chewed. "I won't."

She eyed him skeptically, "Really? How many other insane secret missions have you been on?"

Tom put his fork down and swallowed his food. He smiled at her. "Well, if they were secret, I can't tell you about them."

She scowled at him. "What about the embassy in the Philippines? That was thirty years ago. Tell me about that one."

Tom looked around. "It wasn't that big a deal. It was during the coup against President Aquino. We were backing her against the rogue generals. One night, we wave-hopped four Shitters across Manila Bay on NVGs to deliver 120 Marines to beef up the Marine

Security Guard detachment at the embassy. The Filipinos never picked us up on radar. We were really proud of that considering how hard it is to hide 53s from radar."

The great size of the CH-53D combined with its massive six-bladed rotor system gave the Shitter a huge radar signature. The only way to hide a 53 was to get behind the terrain or hug the waves. Sometimes they flew so close to the ground or water they would have to climb a little before they turned to make sure their rotor tips didn't hit the surface.

CHAPTER 26

1020Z (0120HR AKST)
FLIGHT DECK OF THE HALEY

The Haley gently rolled port and starboard and dipped fore and aft as it made its way across Cook Inlet at a brisk eighteen knots. Tom Adams was out on the flight deck with Taco conducting a preflight check of the Jayhawk with their flashlights. It was bitterly cold and windy. They were freezing their asses off. Taco was opening up the access panels so Tom could try to gain a little familiarity with this helicopter.

When they got to the tail, Tom looked up at the tail rotor system. "I'll let you climb up there and check the tail rotor. If I fall off, I might break my hip."

Taco smiled, extended the handholds on the tail section, and climbed up to the tail rotor. He checked the tail rotor blades and linkages for damage and then shined his light at the sight glass to make sure there was transmission fluid in the tail rotor gearbox.

Taco climbed down, and they went on to inspect the left side of the helo. After they finished, Taco climbed in the cockpit and sat in the left seat. Tom took the right seat where the aircraft commander normally sits. They closed the doors to get out of the ice-cold wind.

"Taco, I'm going to be leaning really hard on you to pull this off," Tom told the newly commissioned Ensign Ortega as they sat in the cockpit of the Jayhawk. "I was a Black Hawk pilot in the Guard, but I haven't flown one in ten years, and I've never flown a Jayhawk or any other helicopter with a digital glass cockpit. I know I can handle the physical stick and rudder part of flying the mission, but you'll need to guide me through the engine startup procedures and load the codes into the encrypted radios. I don't have time to memorize the buttonology of this glass cockpit. Are you signed off to do engine run-ups?"

"Yes, sir, and I've flown quite a bit from the left seat while the maintenance pilots did their test flights. Just no takeoffs or landings. I can set everything up for you so you can concentrate on flying. I earned my private pilot license for single-engine airplanes a couple of years ago when I was trying to get the Coast Guard to send me to flight school," Taco replied.

"Good. Let's do a couple of dry runs through the checklist before showtime," Tom said.

CHAPTER 27

The team was assembled in the hangar deck. They stood around three large tables that had been pushed together. They were inspecting their gear and arranging it in their combat packs. They were all wearing baggy white camouflage trousers and parkas over their OCP extreme cold-weather gear.

Sergeant Strasburg called out to the team, "Listen up, everybody. Commander Smith and Captain Rogers are the team leaders and will carry the M4 rifle. Sergeant Harmon and I will be grenadiers and carry the M16A2 rifle with a M203A2 grenade launcher attached. Sergeant Pope and Sergeant Fuller will be automatic riflemen and carry the M249 squad automatic weapon, or SAW. Airman York and Corporal Davis will be riflemen and carry the M4 rifle, and Airman York will also carry a M24 sniper rifle. Everyone will carry ten 30-round magazines for their rifles. Everyone except Airman York will carry a 200-round box for the SAWs. We will carry the Sig Sauer M17 pistol with four 15-round magazines. The Coast Guard crewmen will have their Sig Sauer P229R pistols and M4s, and the helicopter has two M240s and a Barrett M82 sniper rifle.

Strasburg continued, "Everyone will wear Interceptor body armor with SAPI plates, the MICH helmet, a Rifleman Radio, the AN/PVS-14 Night Vision Monocular, white extreme cold-weather boots, and a set of snowshoes. This Rifleman Radio is encrypted and certified up to the Secret level. It also contains a GPS receiver. The Jayhawk and higher command will be able to track our movements on the ground.

"A lanyard has been issued to you for your pistol. I strongly encourage you to use it. I once saw a two-star general's pistol skip across the floor of a Black Hawk and out of the open door as we flew across northern Iraq before anyone could grab it. The General didn't like using a lanyard. After that day, he always had his pistol on a lanyard and made us fly with the cabin doors closed no matter how hot it was. Now everybody, put on all your gear except your packs and snowshoes and jump up and down a few times to see if anything falls loose. After that, roll around on the deck a couple of times."

It took a few minutes, but everyone did as instructed.

"OK, everybody, put your snowshoes on and make sure they fit properly," Strasburg said.

Everyone adjusted the snowshoes to fit over their white Mickey Mouse boots and waddled around the hangar to make sure they wouldn't come loose.

Commander Smith came through the forward hatch and walked across the small hangar to Strasburg. He was also wearing white camouflage trousers and a parka over his OCP extreme cold-weather gear.

"How are we looking, First Sergeant?" Smith asked before he handed him a piece of paper.

Strasburg read it and smiled. It was his promotion warrant to first sergeant. "We're about ready, sir."

"Good. Everyone step forward and get your promotion orders." Smith started handing them out.

Eric stepped around Mike and held his hand out to Alice. "Congratulations on your promotion to staff sergeant, Alice."

She smiled, shaking his hand. "Thank you and congratulations to you, Technical Sergeant."

Eric turned to Mike and said with a smile, "Congratulations on your promotion, Shit Stain."

Mike replied, "Same to you, Dickhead."

Allen Davis was grinning ear to ear as he stared at his promotion warrant and said to Strasburg and Pope, "Sergeant Davis. I like the sound of that."

Strasburg smiled. "It looks good on you Allen. Congratulations."

Davis replied, "Thanks, First Sergeant."

Pope smiled and punched Davis on the arm where the stripes would be on his dress blue uniform. "Congratulations, Sergeant Davis."

After finishing their rehearsal in the cockpit, Tom and Taco walked away from the Jayhawk and stepped through the hatch at the rear of the hangar.

Tom saw Jon and asked, "Jon, do you have the promotion orders?"

"Yes, sir. I already gave them to everyone but Ortega," Jon replied.

"Good. Hand it over." Tom came to attention. "Squad, attention to orders. Chief Ortega front and center."

Ortega stepped in front of Adams as ordered.

Adams continued, "Chief, repeat after me. I, state your name, due solemnly swear that I will support and defend the Constitution of the United States against all enemies, foreign and domestic; that I will bear true faith and allegiance to the same; that I take this obligation freely, without any mental reservation or purpose of evasion; and that I will well and faithfully discharge the duties of the office on which I am about to enter. So help me God."

Ortega repeated the oath.

"Congratulation, Ensign Ortega." Tom shook his hand, and everyone applauded.

Ed Hicks immediately stepped forward with a big grin on his face and saluted Ensign Ortega with his right hand and held out his left hand, palm up. Taco returned the salute and then saw Ed's empty left hand.

Taco smiled. "Sorry, Ed, I don't have a silver dollar to give you." It's a long-standing military tradition that a newly commissioned officer gives a silver dollar to the first enlisted soldier who salutes him.

Ed replied, "That's OK, sir. I know you're good for it."

Waddle and Finch stepped forward to shake Taco's hand and pat him on the back.

"Congratulations, Mr. Ortega," Commander Waddle said.

Ortega replied, "Thank you, sir. Do you really think the commission will stick?"

Waddle responded, "I'll admit yours is a rare case, Taco, but this is a very unusual, once-in-a-lifetime mission. Add in that the President is personally involved, I do think it will be permanent."

CHAPTER 28

Five miles into the trip back to the Podmoskovye, the recently repaired snowmobile's engine sputtered several times and then stalled. They all climbed off the snowmobiles, and Eldon pulled the cover up to examine the engine. He shined his flashlight around the engine but couldn't find anything wrong. Darrin consulted his map and determined there was a cabin only a quarter of a mile away. James and Willie unhooked the sleds. Darrin and Eldon climbed aboard their only operating snowmobile and headed for the cabin to see what they could scavenge.

They covered the distance in a couple of minutes. They stopped about 150 feet from the cabin and quietly walked in closer. They didn't use their flashlights. The cabin was dark, and Darrin couldn't see any smoke coming from the chimney with his commercial third-generation NVGs. A small three-walled pole barn was set about fifty feet from the cabin, and it had two snowmobiles and an old Ford pickup truck parked in it. They went into the barn to check out the snowmobiles and look for fuel. They flipped on their red-lensed flashlights. The snowmobiles looked to be in good condition, but they had electric starters and their batteries were missing. Before they could look any further, two spotlights lit them up from the cabin and four green lasers danced across their chests. They dove for cover behind the pickup.

A voice from the cabin yelled, "Who the fuck are you, and what do you think you're doing?"

Darrin yelled back, "I'm State Trooper Darrin Logan! My partner's hurt and his snowmobile ran out of gas! We didn't think anyone was home!"

The angry voice in the cabin yelled, "Bullshit! Troopers come to the door! They don't steal in the dead of night! Get the fuck off my property! If we see you again, we'll kill you!"

Darrin and Eldon got up and ran for it. The occupants of the cabin popped off a few rounds to hasten their departure. They got back to their snowmobile and cleared out as fast as they could. Darrin yelled over his shoulder to Eldon as he drove away, "Everybody in this fucking country has guns!"

Eldon replied, "At least their aim was bad!"

Darrin shook his head. "They had lasers! If they wanted to hit us, we'd be dead!"

They drove back to the others on the trail.

As they arrived, James asked, "Is everything alright? We heard gunshots."

"Yes, we just ran into some more cowboys," Darrin replied.

James turned to Eldon. "You're a lucky man."

Eldon was puzzled. "What do you mean?"

James grabbed Eldon's parka hood and stuck his fingers through two holes. Eldon's eyes went wide with the knowledge he had almost died. Darrin pulled out his map again to find another cabin. Within a minute, he found another likely candidate about a mile further down the trail.

"This time I'll go to the door," he muttered mostly to himself as he folded his map and put it in the inside pocket of his parka. "Come on, Eldon. We'll give it another shot," Darrin said as everyone, but Eldon laughed.

Eldon climbed aboard behind Darrin with a perturbed or, more accurately, pissed-off look on his face. Darrin started the snowmobile and headed back down the trail again.

They arrived at the cabin about five minutes later. Darrin stopped about a hundred feet from the cabin and killed the engine. The cabin's front door was in the center of the thirty-five-foot-wide porch that spanned the front of the cabin. A neatly shoveled six-foot-wide set of stairs five feet high led to the porch. Darrin saw the interior lights were on and smoke billowed from the chimney. He dismounted and walked about fifty feet closer. "Hello in the cabin. I'm State Trooper Darrin Logan. Is anyone home?"

The porch light next to the door came on, and a few seconds later, the door opened. A large man with a tobacco-stained red beard wearing a red flannel shirt, blue overalls, and fuzzy white bunny slippers appeared from behind the door and pointed a long-barreled shotgun at Darrin.

He yelled, "Who the fuck are—" before he dropped the shotgun and toppled back into the cabin.

Darrin heard two shots from behind him and saw the man fall. A woman screamed from inside the cabin. As Darrin rushed the stairs, he saw the woman appear in the doorway and reach for the shotgun. He shot her twice in the chest with his Glock as he bounded up the steps. He stopped at the left side of the doorway and swept the room with his pistol. The man and woman lay in an unnatural pile on the floor inside the door. Both were bleeding heavily but unconscious. Darrin shot them both in the head. He could hear Eldon behind him coming up the steps. Eldon took the right side of the doorway. They entered the cabin and cleared it quickly.

When they finished, Darrin grabbed Eldon by his parka and shook him. "Why did you shoot him? He wasn't a threat!"

Eldon calmly looked him in the eyes. "He pointed the shotgun at you. I thought he was going to shoot."

Darrin let go of Eldon's parka. He wanted to be angry, but even if Eldon had a chip on his shoulder, Darrin knew he had protected his commander like he had been trained to do. He slapped him on the shoulder and nodded his head. "You were right to follow your training. Let's go check the garage."

They stepped over the dead man and his wife and went outside to the detached three-car garage to the right of the cabin.

"Did you notice his bunny slippers?" Darrin asked.

"No, why?" Eldon replied.

"They were homemade, from real rabbits," Darrin said.

Eldon shook his head and pulled open the large overhead garage door. He found the light switch on the wall and flipped it on. Eldon saw a beat-up old red Dodge pickup truck, an even older red Chevy Tahoe, and a shiny new red Polaris Titan snowmobile. He began inspecting the snowmobile while Darrin stood outside in the dark sweeping the area with his NVGs. "Darrin, we're in luck. The snowmobile is new, full of gas, and has the key in it."

"Are there any gas cans in there?" Darrin asked from outside.

"There are two five-gallon cans, but they're both empty, and I don't see anything to siphon gas from the vehicles."

"Slide the cans under the truck and punch a hole in the bottom of the gas tank," Darrin instructed.

Eldon grabbed a hammer and a Phillips-head screwdriver off the cluttered workbench and loosened the gas cap. Then he crawled under the truck. He pounded the screwdriver into the tank then gas started squirting out all over his glove and sleeve. He pulled the screwdriver out of the hole and the gas started running out mostly into the mouth of the first can. A small stream of gas slowly meandered across the concrete floor. Soon the flow from the tank slowed to a dribble and then stopped. "I caught about four gallons of gas, but the tank ran dry. Do you want me to try the Tahoe?"

"No, we've already been here too long. Meet me out on the trail." Darrin walked away to the snowmobile on the trail.

He started his snowmobile and waited for Eldon. A minute later, he saw Eldon drive out of the garage and turn toward him. He started down the trail slow enough for Eldon to catch up, and then he accelerated as much as he could across the uneven winding terrain.

What neither of them saw was the fire Eldon had accidentally started in the garage when he drove the snowmobile over the stream of gas running across the floor. The hot exhaust from the snowmobile had launched a small ember out of the tailpipe that landed in the stream. It ignited instantly, and a small ribbon of flame flew across the floor to where it had puddled next to the exposed wooden frame of the garage. The dry pine wood provided an excellent fuel supply for the fire, and it readily ran up the wall. Before Darrin and Eldon returned to the others, the garage was fully engulfed.

CHAPTER 29

Special Agents Jerome and Gillis traveled back across the Potomac River into the District of Columbia. For almost an hour, they listened to and loosely followed the surveillance team as they expertly coordinated their movements while tailing Wilkes's black Lincoln Navigator. The team of five specialists took turns following the Navigator so Wilkes wouldn't see the same vehicle twice. Their job was made much easier because the sun hadn't come up yet.

Angela came up on the radio and reported the target vehicle had pulled into the drive-thru lane of the McDonald's restaurant at 66 New York Avenue NE. She rolled through behind him in her gray Ford Escape and picked up breakfast for herself and handed the lead off to Benny. She fell in behind the others.

"Why would this guy drive all the way across the district and pass twenty other McDonald's to come to this one?" Jocelyn asked.

Jerry replied, "Because he's making a drop. We need to leave someone there to see who else comes through the drive-thru. Hopefully, he's arranging a meeting. He might even have a go-between working inside."

Jocelyn called Garrett and put him on speaker, "Garrett, this is Jocelyn. We need someone to set up at the McDonald's and see who else goes through the drive thru."

Garrett responded, "OK. Since I'm in the van, I'll peel off Wilkes and watch Mickey D's until I can get another team out here."

CHAPTER 30

Ensign "Taco" Ortega sat in the left seat of the Jayhawk next to his new, albeit temporary, commander, Lieutenant Colonel Adams. Taco had already started the auxiliary power unit, so they could talk on the Jayhawk's intercom system, or ICS.

"OK, comm check. Taco, Ed, and Chris, can you hear me?" Tom asked.

Taco stepped on his ICS foot switch. "Loud and clear."

Ed Hicks was standing in front of the cockpit with his gloved right hand resting on the nose. His clear helmet visor was down, and his NVGs hung around his neck on a sturdy green cord. He was connected to the ICS by a forty-foot extension cord commonly called a long cord. He gave Tom a thumbs-up with his left hand, pressed the push to talk, or PTT, button that was clipped to his survival vest, and said, "Loud and clear."

Chris Savage was checking the improvised mounting of his M240 machine gun in the left window and responded from the cabin, "Loud and clear, sir."

The Jayhawk didn't have a mount for the gun in the left window. Chris and Ed had used a bunch of heavy-duty bungee cords to hold the machine gun in the window and used its sling as an idiot cord to attach it to the inside of the cabin. They didn't want to have to explain losing a machine gun somewhere in the Alaskan wilderness. Also, normally a gun mount would limit the movement of a machine gun and prevent the gunner from accidentally shooting his own rotor blades. The bungee cords would hold the M240 in the window, but the trick was to not get too excited and accidentally shoot yourself down. Chris would have to exercise extreme caution to make sure he didn't put rounds into the Jayhawk's rotor blades, but he wasn't concerned. His experience in the Corps flying combat missions in the Venom had made him an honest-to-God aerial gunfighter.

"Before we go any further with the checklist, I want to discuss a few things. First, our mission callsign tonight is Mustang 6. Based on the joint makeup of our team, I asked for Rainbow 6, but I was told it's been used before. While we are all flying together tonight, you can call me Tom or by my callsign, Chirp."

Taco smiled and keyed his mic, "Do you mean Chirp like a bird chirps?"

Tom replied, "That's right, and don't ask; we don't have time for sea stories right now. Second, anytime any of you think I'm fucking up or putting us in danger, speak up immediately. Don't ask for permission. I've flown more than 250 missions, but it's been a long time, so don't trust me to know and see everything that you do. Any of you can throw the bullshit flag.

"We'll be in weapons hold status until we are feet dry over the coast and I decide to go to weapons tight or weapons free, but if anywhere along the mission we start taking fire, you may return fire to protect us. Keep in mind, though, that if you see tracer rounds coming up but they are nowhere near us, the enemy may not have night vision devices and they might be trying to get us to give away our position by shooting back at them. In that case, use your best judgment.

"We will be flying at 300 feet above ground level tonight using the radar altimeter. Taco, set your radar altimeter bug for 250 feet, and I'll do the same. If I go below 250, alert me, and if I don't respond right away, start raising the collective. Do you have any questions?"

No one did, but the seriousness of what they were about to attempt was apparent to all of them.

"Oh, one more thing. If we go down, we will unass the helo and meet at the twelve o'clock position. That should keep us clear of the guns if we're on fire and the rounds start to cook off. If we are on fire and I don't get out, come save my fat ass. OK, Taco, I'll read the checklist and back you up while you start the engines," Tom said as he switched on the small blue-lensed LED light hanging by 550 paracord around his neck and opened up the checklist on his kneeboard.

Ten minutes later, the start checklist was complete, the automatic flight control system had been checked, and the NVGs had been attached to their helmets and switched on. The cockpit lighting was NVG compatible and had been turned down to the lowest setting possible to help keep the glare off the inside of the cockpit glass.

Tom keyed his ICS. "OK, Ed, bring the team aboard."

Ed responded by clicking his PTT button twice and turned to wave the team aboard. They emerged from the hangar door led by Commander Smith and walked calmly with their heads lowered to the cabin door. Their gear had already been stowed aboard, and they had rehearsed where they were supposed to sit. The cabin was so crowded they didn't have seats to sit on. With all their gear aboard, they had to settle for the floor or on their packs.

Jon was the only member of the ground team with a headset so he could follow the progress of the mission and talk to the crew. He listened intently, but he knew to keep his mouth shut while they were getting ready for takeoff.

Tom called for Ed to verify the aircraft was unchained from the deck and the chocks around the right main mount tire had been removed. Ed pulled the chocks from around the skis and set them inside the cabin door. He gathered up his long cord and climbed aboard.

He made sure the cabin door was latched closed and keyed his ICS. "The chocks and chains are removed, and we're all set in back for takeoff, Chirp."

Jon cocked his head to the left. He wasn't sure he heard that correctly. It sounded like Ed said "Chirp."

***

Tom had prearranged with Commander Waddle to take off EM-CON, which meant emission control or without radio communications. Tom didn't want to tip off the Russians that they were in the air. He didn't know if they were listening, but he didn't want to risk it.

Taco confirmed, "Takeoff checklist completed, Chirp."

"Taco, give them the takeoff signal," Tom said.

Taco waved his blue-lensed flashlight up and down three times. "Clear left, Chirp."

Tom replied, "Roger that. Clear right, coming up and out to the right."

He pulled up on the collective, and as the helo left the deck, he let the nose drift right and the tail left. He had ten feet on the radar altimeter when he cleared the deck. He kept the nose level on artificial horizon as he scanned the instruments, ensuring he maintained a positive rate of climb. Taking off at night from a ship on NVGs was similar to making an instrument takeoff from the ground into clouds. Taco had already entered the GPS coordinates for the cabin into the flight management system. Chirp climbed to 300 feet above the water and took up a westerly heading directly for the cabin at 140 knots indicated airspeed.

"We should arrive at the cabin in a little over two hours, give or take depending on the winds. Taco, give me a fuel check every 30 minutes," Tom said.

Taco stepped on his floor intercom switch with his left boot. "Roger that, Chirp."

***

Jon's curiosity was killing him. He knew aviators loved giving each other stupid nicknames as much as his buddies in the Teams did, except they called them callsigns. Whenever they talked back and forth to each other on the FM radios, they used their personal callsigns instead of the official aircraft callsign. He knew better than to interrupt the crew while they were flying, but he thought he might know someone who had the answer. He pulled out his secure laptop and sent a message to the Haley. He typed, "How did Tom get his callsign?", hit send, and waited.

***

Gwenn was sitting at her workstation in the Haley's temporary SCIF next to the ship's intel officer, Lieutenant Sarah Tuttle. She received the message and immediately smiled. She took a sip of her iced tea and started typing, with Sarah reading everything she typed, "When Tom was a copilot with the Flying Tigers in 1989, they were TDY at NAS Cubi Point in the Philippines for the presidential coup. He came back to the BOQ right after sunrise after being out drinking all night in Olongapo City with his buddies.

"He staggered down the breezeway to his door, and before he could unlock it, a little bird landed behind him on the chest-high decorative concrete wall and started singing. Tom faced the bird. As he swayed back and forth bleary-eyed, he leaned toward the bird and said, 'Chirp, chirp, fuckin bird, come here and I'll eat your ass.' One of his squadron mates walked around the corner just in time to hear Tom threaten the bird. A few months later when Tom was designated an aircraft commander, he was given 'Chirp' as his callsign. He's used it ever since."

***

Jon's face was illuminated by the green light of his laptop's display as he sat in the dimly lit cabin with the rest of team. He read the message and laughed. He laughed so loud everyone could hear him through their earplugs. They turned to look at him. He looked toward the cockpit and laughed some more, then he passed the laptop around. Soon everyone in the cabin was laughing.

***

Earlier when the squad was staging their gear in the helo, Eric and Mike made sure they would be sitting on either side of Alice. About ten minutes into the flight, Mike pulled out his cell phone and started typing messages to Alice. "Hi, Alice. I'm Mike. So, are you from Homer?" He handed her the phone.

"No, I was on a cruise ship near Homer when I was snatched. I live in Denver," she typed then handed it back.

"Well, when we get back tomorrow, I'd love to show you around town until you have to leave. If you like barbecue, there's a great new Mongolian barbecue place in Homer called Khan's Kitchen," Mike typed.

She smiled and typed, "That would be nice. I don't know how long it will take to get a flight back home."

Mike typed, "Well you could stay at my place. I have a 3BR house on 20 acres. It's especially beautiful this time of year. We could go snowmobiling or cross-country skiing."

She took the phone and replied, "That sounds like a lot of fun. Thanks for the offer."

Eric saw the messages going back and forth and put his hand out for the phone. Alice gave it to him.

Eric started typing, "Hey Mike, tell Alice about how cool your and Cathy's wedding is going to be next summer." Eric smiled innocently and handed the phone back to Alice.

She read the message and frowned as she flipped the phone back to Mike. She refused to look at him after that. Mike read the message and looked at Eric. Eric turned away to look out the window at the darkness. Mike could see Eric's shoulders shaking up and down as he laughed. Mike shook his head. His buddy was a cockblocker. There was no wedding next summer. There wasn't even a Cathy. Mike smiled to himself and thought "buddy" really was only half the word, but that's OK because payback's a bitch.

CHAPTER 31

Once again, Garrett Sanders sat in the rear of his blacked-out minivan. The Sienna was equipped with adjustable electric window tint. He had it dialed up to a point where no one could see him. Minivans were the perfect vehicles for surveillance. They screamed "Soccer Mom." Slap a stick-figure family decal on the back window or a "My kid's an honor student" sticker on the bumper, and it became invisible.

This time, he was parked in the lot of the New York Avenue McDonald's. His conventional, night vision, and thermal cameras were aimed to capture photos and video of the people and vehicles that drove through the drive-thru lane. Every face was instantly sent to the FACE Services Unit. FACE was part of the FBI's Criminal Justice Information Services Division and stood for the

Facial Analysis, Comparison, and Evaluation Services Unit. FACE personnel would run the photo through the Next Generation Identification-Interstate Photo System. He also had an automated license plate reader that was instantly running every plate it saw.

Garrett was getting hungry, but he couldn't get out of the van or roll through the drive-thru. Fortunately, he was used to being stuck in the van, so he was prepared. He reached down and flipped the top of his cooler open and grabbed a Coke and his Jimmy John's Gargantuan sandwich.

He was about to take a bite of his sandwich when a dark blue Ford Crown Victoria pulled into the drive-thru lane. The car had normal Virginia license plates, but Garrett recognized it as a police car right away because of its black sidewall tires, blue emergency lights inside the rear window, and the antennas attached to its roof and trunk. The driver was wearing a Redskins knit cap with a big yellow pom-pom attached to the top. Garrett remembered seeing him and the car at Karpinsky's house. He dialed his phone.

Jerry answered his phone and put it on speaker. "Hello."

Garrett said, "Jerry, an unmarked police car that was at Karpinsky's house just pulled into the McDonald's drive-thru. FACE identified the driver as Arthur Bailey. He's a sergeant with the Fairfax County Police Department."

Jerry asked, "Do you know where he lives? Maybe he stopped on the way home from his shift to get something to eat."

Garrett started typing into his mobile data terminal. "Standby." Moments later, he responded, "Bailey lives thirty miles northwest of McLean in Leesburg, Virginia. According to his cell phone data, he hasn't crossed the Potomac into the District in the last three months. There's no history of him ever visiting this McDonald's. The National Name Check Program indicates he changed his name from Artur Baranov to Arthur Bailey after he immigrated from Estonia in 1980 when he was seventeen years old."

Jocelyn said, "My dad would say, in police work, we call that a clue. Garrett, is he still there?"

"No, he got his order and left. The cashier must have slipped him a message with his food, but now that I have his cell phone, I'm tracking him. It looks like he's heading back the way he came toward Virginia. I'm vectoring the other surveillance team in to intercept him."

Jocelyn asked, "What about Wilkes? Is he still moving?"

Garrett replied, "Yes. He's not heading home either. It looks like he's running another SDR."

Jerry said, "What do you want to bet that Bailey's going to run an SDR too, before they meet up?"

Jocelyn said, "No bet. Thanks for the info, Garrett. Good job putting us onto this cop."

***

Art Bailey turned out of the drive-thru onto New York Avenue and pulled the receipt out of the bag as he drove. He saw the cashier had written "Police Meal" in green ink on it. Police meal meant Art got his food free of charge even though Art was way outside his jurisdiction. It was common across the country for fast-food restaurants and pizza places to give police officers free food. The green ink meant Art had to go to the National Law Enforcement Officers Memorial at 450 F Street NW. It was a good place for him to meet his handler early on a Saturday morning.

The memorial was open 24 hours a day, and it wouldn't be odd for a police officer to visit it after his shift, especially since he had known four officers from Fairfax County whose names were on the marble walls.

CHAPTER 32

1130Z (0230HR AKST) LAKE ILIAMNA, ALASKA

Tom was flying straight and level across frozen Lake Iliamna at 300 feet AGL wishing he'd had a full night's sleep before being ordered to do something this stupid when a big, dark blob filled the windshield in front of him.

"Shit!" he yelled as he immediately dumped the collective and pushed the cyclic forward and left as the object crossed from left to right.

Screams came from the cabin as everyone flew off the floor and hit the sound-proofing insulation attached to the ceiling. They didn't have seats, so they weren't belted down. The sudden maneuver scared the shit out of them. They thought they were going to die. Once clear, Tom pulled up and resumed his course, which dropped everyone back to the floor, causing them to scream again.

"What was that?" Tom asked over the ICS.

Ed Hicks responded, "It was a Piper Cub with skis. It probably took off from the lake. It didn't have any lights on."

The Piper Cub pilot was violating FAA regulations by flying at night without his flashing anti-collision and red and green navigation lights on. He either forgot to turn them on or thought no one else would be stupid enough to be up here tonight. Tom realized he was violating the regulations too because the only lights he had on were the infrared slime lights that could only been seen with NVGs.

"Damn it. I hate near misses. Jon, let the rest of the team know what happened," Tom said over the ICS.

Jon responded, "Will do… I think I peed a little."

Tom said, "Back during OIF II, I flew an NVG mission north from Baghdad to Balad Air Base at 300 feet AGL when something big and ominous flew right over the top of us going in the opposite direction. I could feel the turbulence it generated. It momentarily blocked out the stars. Later, I found out it was a Chinook flying south at 400 feet AGL. Since they were a hundred feet higher, they could see our infrared slime lights, but we couldn't see theirs. The Chinook pilots probably thought it was funny to fly that close to us.

"On another mission in broad daylight, I saw my company commander almost get killed while he was taking off from Washington pad in the Green Zone. His Black Hawk had climbed over the twenty-foot-high concrete T-barrier wall surrounding the landing zone when a British Army Lynx helicopter flew by in front of him from left to right at fifty feet. It was probably going 150 knots. I was about sixty feet behind him in my Black Hawk, and I saw him dive under the Lynx and skim the tops of the palm trees with his wheels. He missed the Lynx by about ten feet, and as he climbed out, he transmitted over the FM radio how remarkably clean the underside of the Lynx was. Later, we found out the Lynx pilots had flown up from Basra and had gotten lost. They accidentally flew across the north side of the landing zone instead of the south side like they were supposed to.

"On my first day at flight school in Pensacola, my entire class of over a hundred flight students and I were seated in the auditorium for a welcome aboard briefing from the commanding officer of Training Wing Six, Captain Carlo 'Pokie' Cipparroni. To impress upon us how dangerous our new profession was, he told us to look around the auditorium at our fellow students. He said if we stayed in the service for a twenty-year career, we had a one in four chance of dying in an aviation mishap. He said that was peace-time accidents. It didn't include actual combat deaths."

"Have you had a lot of near misses?" Taco asked.

Tom replied, "When I was in the Corps, I sat down once and wrote down a list of ten times when I almost died in the air over a four-year period. They were all pilot errors—mine and others— not mechanical problems."

"What happened after that?" Taco asked.

"I stopped counting them," Tom answered.

CHAPTER 33

1135Z (0235HR AKST)
TEN MILES FROM THE CABIN

Karpinsky chafed at being dragged along the trail like a sack of potatoes. He wanted to contribute. He tried to use his remote viewing ability to determine whether they had been discovered. He leaned back in the sled with his eyes closed and tried to concentrate on his unknown target as the sled bumped along the trail. Within minutes, he zeroed in on a target.

He wasn't sure if he was in a trance or dreaming, but he saw a stunning young redhead in a green dress standing at the rail of a ship looking out over a still, dark ocean. Her scent aroused him. She was unaware of his presence as he quietly approached her from behind and threw his arms around her. She resisted, but he held on tight. He bit her neck as he fondled her breasts. Then, his left hand gravitated between her legs. She clawed at his hands and screamed.

He opened his eyes, and he was back in the sled bumping down the trail. He grabbed the side of the sled to steady himself, and a jolt of pain shot through his left hand and up his arm. He took his glove off and discovered that his left pinkie finger was dislocated. He took a deep breath and popped it back into position. He scanned the area around the sled but couldn't determine how he had injured his finger. He bent his fingers a few times and licked his lips. He could still taste her salty skin. He smiled and thought he would have to revisit this target.

In the past ten years, he had made similar visits hundreds of times, always to attractive women. He revisited those he especially enjoyed over and over. Some of the women who were devout Catholics feared they were possessed by demons and begged their priests for exorcisms. Others were so deeply abused they sought counseling and psychiatric help that, on occasion, resulted in institutionalization. A few of the most severely violated committed suicide to escape his torment. He had raped and sexually assaulted hundreds of women over the last decade.

Karpinsky was unconcerned with the damage he caused. He didn't fear being caught by the police. Current laws didn't cover his activities anyway. As a scientist, he didn't believe in an afterlife, much less an all-knowing supreme being, so he was confident there would be no repercussions for his actions.

He had made incredible advances in the field of technical remote viewing. He learned to not only observe targets and gather intelligence, but to actually interact with them in a physical manner. Six months earlier, he argued with a sassy young scientist in his CIA lab. He decided to teach the insolent child a lesson and visited her one night using his enhanced remote viewing abilities. He had his way with her, but in her terror, she resisted with all her strength.

She infuriated him, and in his rage, he mentally strangled her to death. He crossed a threshold and inadvertently made a remarkable scientific discovery. He had murdered another human being with his mind from over five miles away.

The Arlington Police Department, the FBI, and the CIA investigated her death but had nothing to connect him or anyone else to her murder. Normally, a killer would have left behind DNA and other physical evidence, but in this case, there was none. The autopsy revealed she had definitely been strangled to death and had suffered tears in her vagina and rectum, but there were no fingerprints, saliva, blood, ejaculate, or latex residue. He had great difficulty hiding his amusement when the director of the CIA asked him to use his abilities to help find the killer.

If he could get back to Mother Russia and teach his methods to the military, his country could resume its rightful position as a world-dominating superpower. He didn't share this physical aspect of his research with any of his colleagues in the CIA. Russia would have a monopoly. It wasn't exactly mind control, but it was incredible that he could influence people's actions with his mind. His ability to cause physical harm to a target through the power of his mind alone was staggering. His discovery would have to remain secret, but he wondered if the ability to kill with his mind would be worthy of a Nobel Prize.

CHAPTER 34

1135Z (0235HR AKST)
JAYHAWK EN ROUTE TO THE CABIN

Alice sat on her pack with her back against the rear bulkhead of the Jayhawk between Mike and Eric. She fretted about what her boyfriend, Hank, was going to do when she got back to Denver. After how he'd acted earlier tonight, she wasn't sure she wanted to see him anymore anyway. She was watching Commander Smith type something into his laptop when someone's warm breath washed over her neck. She flinched as someone bit her neck and then fondled her breasts. Arms squeezed her from behind and she grabbed them. She didn't see any arms, but she could feel them in her hands. One of the invisible hands slid between her legs. She grabbed the hand and pried a finger back until it popped and then the arms were gone. The attack occurred so fast and ended so abruptly, she had a hard time processing what had happened.

She turned to Mike ready to break his nose, but he was playing a game on his phone. Then she turned to Eric and found him sleeping. She had been molested by a ghost, but she didn't believe in ghosts. She did believe in evil men. A more timid woman would have felt violated and helpless.

Instead, Alice was angry and eager to exact vengeance on whomever had accosted her. She suspected it was someone who practiced this remote viewing stuff the team had been briefed on. She would find this asshole and put a bullet in his forehead or, if she was lucky, choke the life out of him.

CHAPTER 35

"Mrs. Adams, the Global Hawk is on station over the cabin. Their callsign is Hawk 33. I'll bring up the feed on the wall monitor," Petty Officer Second Class Cindy McLemore said.

"Thank you, Cindy, and please, call me Gwenn. Let's see what we have," she responded.

Hawk 33 was an RQ-4 Global Hawk remotely piloted aircraft. The Air Force didn't like to call them drones anymore. It was being operated by a mission control element, or MCE, consisting of a remotely piloted aircraft pilot and a sensor operator. They even wore Nomex flight suits in case the MCE trailer caught fire. Tonight, the pilot was Master Sergeant Krista Nichols, and the sensor operator was a technical sergeant named Roy Kraft. They were members of the 12th Reconnaissance Squadron from Beale Air Force Base,

California. Several years earlier, the Air Force started training enlisted airmen to operate the Global Hawks. They received the same training as the officers but not the same pay.

The Global Hawk provided broad-spectrum intelligence, surveillance, and reconnaissance collection capability to support joint combatant forces in worldwide operations. It was capable of persistent near-real-time coverage using imagery intelligence, signals intelligence, and moving target indicator sensors. It could operate as high as 60,000 feet for 34 hours in all-weather conditions while cruising at 310 knots.

Gwenn and Cindy viewed the infrared video of the cabin at Eek Lake. The cabin glowed white hot compared to the frozen landscape around it. Smoke billowed from the chimney, and the snow on the roof around the chimney was melting. She saw three other heat signatures about a hundred feet behind the cabin. They weren't nearly as hot as the chimney but were easily discernible from the frozen surroundings.

Gwenn transmitted to the Global Hawk, "Hawk 33, can you zoom in on the three hot spots behind the cabin?"

The sensor operator, Technical Sergeant Kraft, responded, "Hawk 33, wilco."

Wilco meant, "I understand you and will comply." He zoomed in on the three heat signatures. Gwenn recognized immediately she was looking at two bodies. She wasn't sure about the third hot spot. She could also see snowmobile trails between the cabin and the south side of Eek Lake. She relayed the information to Commander Smith's laptop.

***

Aboard the Jayhawk, Smith keyed his ICS switch. "Chirp, the Haley reports IR video from Hawk 33 indicates two dead bodies behind the cabin and snowmobile trails leading south away from the cabin across Eek Lake."

Chirp replied, "Roger that, Jon. It sounds like the Russians beat us to the cabin. Have both fire teams ready to go when we land."

CHAPTER 36

The sun was just below the horizon, but there was ample light to see without the streetlights. Sergeant Art Bailey stood in front of the memorial's marble wall. The wind was blowing slightly, which made the frigid February air even colder. Art pulled his Redskins knit cap down lower to cover his ears and stuck his bare hands in his sweatshirt's pockets. He looked at the name of his former captain, Cecil Boone, etched on the wall. When Art was a young patrolman, Cecil had been his sergeant. He had taught Art a lot about being a good cop—especially about doing the right thing even when no one was watching.

Captain Boone had been killed during a domestic violence call. He had shown up on the call to back up his officers and to observe how they did their jobs. As with most domestic violence calls, a woman had been smacked around by her intoxicated husband or boyfriend. That night, it was a husband, and when the officers slapped the cuffs on him as he stood in the kitchen, she became irate. She didn't want the police to arrest her breadwinner. She wanted them to perform some sort of social work magic that changed her husband's mental DNA to remove the gene that told him to hit his wife when he was drunk and pissed off.

She pulled a little Cobra .380 ACP pistol from the cookie jar on the counter next to the stove. Cecil stepped in front of her to shield his officers and tried to grab her gun. She shot him once below the sternum before he pulled the gun out of her hand, but once was enough. Being an old-school copper, he didn't wear body armor even though he mandated his officers do so. Art had been one of the pallbearers at his funeral. As with most officers killed in the line of duty, the service was attended by hundreds of police officers from the surrounding departments.

***

Scott Wilkes parked his Lincoln Navigator in the lot a few spaces from Art's Crown Victoria. The lot was otherwise empty. He was tall, of average build, and had short, curly blonde hair. His mouth was too large for his head, and he looked permanently pissed off. He wore a black hooded wool overcoat to protect him from the cold and help shield his face from any surveillance cameras in the area. The coat was unbuttoned to give him quick access to his pistol if necessary. He surveyed the area but didn't see anyone except Art. He walked over to the memorial and stood about ten feet from Art without acknowledging him. He stood there looking at the names.

***

Art didn't look at Wilkes either, but he soon grew tired of waiting and asked, "What do you want?"

Wilkes said, "I need to know what happened to the two men in Oleg Karpinsky's house."

Art replied, "A neighbor saw lights moving around in the house and knew the homeowner was gone on vacation, so he called the police. When our officers confronted the burglars, they went for their guns, and the officers shot and killed them. The men weren't carrying any ID, so they haven't been identified yet, but they probably will be after the autopsy. Why do you care? Did they work for you?"

Wilkes didn't answer the questions but instead asked more of his own, "Was there anything unusual at the scene? Were any federal agents there?"

Art thought for a minute. "They were both shot at least seven or eight times. At first, I thought that might be excessive, but if they didn't go down right away, it would make sense that the officers would keep shooting until they did."

Wilkes asked again, "Were any federal agents there?"

"No, just local cops, the fire department, and the coroner's people."

Having learned what he needed, Wilkes turned to walk away.

Art turned to look at him. "Hey, wait a minute. When are you guys going to leave me alone?"

Wilkes turned back to Art. "Leave you alone? We own you. Ever since we let you come here from Estonia, we've owned you."

Art yelled angrily, "That was almost forty years ago!"

Wilkes laughed. "It doesn't matter if it's a hundred years. We will always own you."

Art had been an American citizen and police officer for over thirty-five years, and he was proud of what he had accomplished with his life. He had earned his citizenship. He had never spied for the Russians, but they had always kept in touch with him over the years to let him know he was still under their thumb and that if they needed him someday, he would have to help them. He had had enough of living under this shadow. Today, he would make his stand. He pulled his Glock model 23 from behind his right hip and ordered Wilkes to put his hands up and get on his knees. He would arrest Wilkes and deliver him to the FBI. Art would come clean to them and whatever happened would happen.

Instead of complying, Wilkes faced Art and screamed at him, "Are you out of your fucking mind? We will destroy you! And then we'll kill your wife and kids!"

Art yelled, "Shut the fuck up and get on the ground! You're under arrest!"

***

Wilkes didn't like the prospect of sitting in solitary confinement next to Robert Hanssen in the ADX Florence supermax prison for years while he waited and hoped Mother Russia would make a deal for his return, so he went for his gun. As he cleared his holster with his 9mm Glock 19, Art shot him twice high in the chest. Wilkes fell backward and instinctively snapped off several rounds before he smacked his head on the concrete walkway and passed out.

***

The first round missed Art completely. Wilkes's next round blew off his own right big toe. The last round struck Art high on his left shoulder after grazing his body armor. As Art fell over backward, he thought, Shit! I stopped shooting too soon.

***

FBI vehicles and agents immediately swarmed in from every direction and surrounded the scene. The Hostage Rescue Team clad in their tactical gear disarmed, handcuffed, and searched Wilkes and Art. After they were secured, the HRT's paramedics began treating their wounds. Both of them were still alive. Jocelyn, Jerry, and their cohorts had heard everything that Wilkes and Art had said.

Jerry and Jocelyn stood over Art as the paramedics worked.

Art was conscious. "Is he still alive? I tried to hit him high so it wouldn't be fatal. I knew you guys would want to talk to him."

Jerry said, "Yeah, he's still breathing. Sergeant Bailey, the ambulances will be here in a minute to take both of you to the hospital. Are you willing to talk to us?"

Art looked up at the agents surrounding him and winced in pain. "Yeah, I'll talk, and if he doesn't, let me know. I've been following him around in my spare time for the last three years since he's been my contact. I can tell you who he meets with, where he meets them, and where he really lives."

Jerry read him his Miranda rights and started asking him questions as two ambulances arrived.

CHAPTER 37

Chirp keyed the ICS. "OK, we're about six minutes out. Pass the word. Taco, go ahead and give me the landing checklist."

"Tail wheel switch locked, parking brake off, crew, passengers, and mission equipment check."

Ed, Chris, and Jon all started signaling six minutes with their hands. The others nodded in acknowledgment and signaled six minutes to each other. They all started squirming in the limited space, trying to get their packs on and their weapons ready.

Chirp keyed his ICS. "Jon, I'm going to set down about 100 meters to the west of the cabin. We will cover you with the door guns. As soon as you're out, I'll take off and orbit to the north."

Jon responded, "Roger that. We'll leave our snowshoes on our packs for now. My team'll go straight for the cabin, Rogers's team'll circle around and come in from the north, behind the cabin."

The minutes ticked off quickly. Tom lowered the collective to the floor as he pulled the cyclic back to his stomach to rapidly decelerate the helicopter. He was making an aggressive deceleration and approach, but not as aggressive as an air assault landing. He didn't want to damage the helo or get stuck. As they descended through ten feet, Ed slid the door open.

Right before the front skis touched the snow, Smith jumped out, took three steps toward the two o'clock position, and dove to the snow with his rifle pointed toward his front. A second later, Mike dove to the snow about four feet to his right, and a second after that, Alice landed about four feet to the right of Mike. The sequence continued for another five seconds until the two teams were fanned out covering the 180° arc between the helo and cabin.

As soon as the eighth man was out, Ed gave the all clear to Tom and he took off, covering everyone in a layer of snow. Once the helo was flying away, Jon got up and began the fire team rushes they would conduct until they got to the cabin. Rogers's team did the same as they circled around the cabin. The rushes consisted of running through the snow for three seconds and then diving to the snow. The idea was that as two men advanced, the other two were prepared to fire to defend them.

It only took a couple of minutes to get to the cabin through the knee-high snow, but by the time Jon and his team stacked outside the cabin door, they were sucking air. Carrying seventy pounds of gear didn't help. They hit the quick releases on their packs and dropped them on the porch next to the stairs.

Jon lowered his NOD, or night observation device. The others did the same. Jon tried the doorknob, but it was locked. He held up his left hand and counted off three seconds before he squared up in front of the door and kicked it in with his right leg. As the door opened, Mike threw in an M84 stun grenade, also called a flashbang. Jon stepped to the left side of the doorway and waited for it to detonate. Two seconds later, after a blinding flash and deafening blast, he rushed in, covering the left side of the room. Mike followed down the right side. Then Alice followed Jon and Eric followed Mike. Mike found a body in front of the fireplace lying on its right side. A roaring fire burned in the fireplace, and the intense heat in the room was stifling.

Mike covered the body with his rifle and reported loudly to the others, "Hey, there's a body in front of the fireplace!"

A few seconds later, after checking the bedrooms, the others called out all clear. Eric raised his NOD, knelt next to the body, and shined his flashlight on it. The head was wrapped in a blood-soaked tan camo bandana. He pulled it back a little and saw the horrible wound.

"He was shot in the face," Eric said.

Then the body moaned.

"Hey, he's alive. Cover him while I pat him down," Eric said.

"I got you," Mike replied as he continued to point his rifle at the man.

Eric found a Glock model 23 in a holster on his right hip and handed it back to Jon.

Next, Eric found a badge and identification. "This is Deputy U.S. Marshal Kevin Bass."

Alice brought Eric his pack, and he started treating Kevin's wounded jaw. Being a pararescue man, he was a highly qualified paramedic.

Jon keyed the mic to his squad radio. "Mustang 6, this is Mustang 16. The cabin is secured. We found Deputy Marshal Bass alive but unconscious. He is severely wounded with a gunshot to his face. Eric is treating him, but he may not make it. It looks like he's lost a lot of blood. There's no sign of the others."

Captain Rogers interrupted, "Break, this is Mustang 26. We found the other two marshals' bodies buried under the snow about 100 feet behind the cabin. There's also a disabled snowmobile back here. It's been shot up pretty good."

Tom weighed his options in the short amount of time available. His orders were to retrieve Karpinsky, but if he didn't get the marshal to a hospital ASAP, he would surely die. The decision wasn't very difficult at all.

"OK, I'll land next to the cabin and send Chris in with the litter," Tom replied.

As a rescue swimmer, Chris Savage was also a highly trained EMT.

"Commander, look at this." Alice shined her weapon light at the wood floor in front of the fireplace. "The marshal wrote out 'OKXX' in his own blood. What does that mean?"

Jon keyed his mic again, "Chirp, the marshal wrote a message on the floor in his blood that says OKXX. Do you think Karpinsky might have double-crossed the marshals?"

Rogers broke in again, "This is 26. One of the marshals was shot in the back of the head at close range."

Tom landed next to the cabin and transmitted, "Alright, from now on, we will consider Karpinsky as hostile until we can prove otherwise. Get the marshal on board, and we'll get him to a hospital. Steve, bring your team back to the cabin." Tom keyed the intercom and asked, "Taco, where is the closest hospital?"

"Bethel has a level four trauma center about forty miles north of here," Taco replied.

He was referring to Yukon-Kuskokwim Delta Regional Hospital. It was one of only fourteen trauma centers in the state. Five minutes later, Chris, Alice, Jon, and Mike carried Kevin out of the cabin on the litter. Eric walked alongside and held a bag of intravenous fluid high in his hand. In addition to starting an IV, he had also put a tube in Kevin's throat to keep his airway open.

Both teams boarded the helicopter, and as soon as the cabin door slid shut, Tom pulled up on the collective. As the tail wheel left the snow, he pushed the cyclic forward to lower the nose and quickly accelerated to 145 knots. Commander Smith got on his secure laptop and sent a message back to the Haley requesting they alert the emergency room at Bethel they would be there in approximately seventeen minutes.

Chris keyed his ICS button. "Chirp, we need to crank up the heat back here to help keep the marshal warm."

Chirp replied, "Roger that. Go ahead, Taco. Send as much heat back there as you can."

Taco dialed up the heat to the MAX setting and closed the vents blowing into the cockpit to divert more heat to the cabin. Eric and Chris were working frantically trying to keep the marshal alive. They had a hard time finding a pulse or reading his blood pressure, but they knew he was alive because he kept breathing. Eric wrote down what he thought Kevin's vital signs were in a little green waterproof notebook and handed it to Commander Smith. He typed the info into his laptop and sent it forward.

Eric had seen an old pair of dog tags hanging around the marshal's neck earlier in the cabin, but he hadn't taken the time to read them. Now he did. They identified Kevin as a Marine, and he told Ed.

Ed said over the ICS, "Chirp, Eric says the marshal is a Marine."

Tom acknowledged him and gave him a message for Kevin. Ed relayed the message to Eric.

Eric leaned over and yelled in Kevin's ear, "Hey, Marine, if you can hear me, squeeze my hand!"

Kevin's eyes remained closed, but Eric could feel him trying to squeeze his hand.

Eric yelled again, "My colonel says semper fi and to hang on! You do not have permission to die today!"

Kevin's eyes popped open, and he blinked rapidly. He focused on Eric's eyes and squeezed his hand twice.

Eric yelled again, "Kevin, is Karpinsky a traitor?" Kevin squeezed again, hard this time, and then his eyes closed and his heart stopped.

CHAPTER 38

Gwenn watched the live feed from the Global Hawk. It had been orbiting at 25,000 feet over the area from the Eek Lake cabin to the Yukon-Kuskokwim Delta where it emptied into the Bering Sea. She could see the Jayhawk racing away from the cabin heading north to the hospital and over a hundred hot targets burning in the wilderness. Most were heat plumes coming from chimneys keeping homes warm. A few others were small and appeared to be campfires, but one jumped out at her.

"Hawk 33, can you zoom in on target #24?" Gwenn transmitted from the Haley to the Global Hawk.

Hawk 33 had been on station for about an hour and a half. Target #24 was about six miles south of Eek Lake and glowed red hot on the screen. Except in this case, the IR image glowed white hot.

Gwenn said to Cindy, "That has to be a structure fire, probably a cabin or pole barn. I've seen a lot of them while working
disaster relief after tornadoes and hurricanes."

She started typing a secure message to Jon. She included an
image of the burning building, its coordinates, the name of the
owner, and the physical address.

CHAPTER 39

1344Z (0444HR AKST)
YUKON-KUSKOKWIM DELTA REGIONAL
HOSPITAL HELO PAD

"Taco, give me the landing checklist again," Tom ordered.

Taco recited the checklist and held his right thumb up. Tom began a gentle deceleration and descent to the hospital's neatly plowed asphalt helicopter pad. The area was well lit, so Tom decided to rotate his NVGs up out of the way and land using the landing light.

Ed Hicks leaned out of the open right door and called out, "Clear right and below."

Chris Savage was leaning out of the left side window and called out, "Clear left and below."

"Roger, coming down," Tom stated what seemed obvious, but his crew coordination training compelled him to say it.

***

Dr. Jethro "Jed" Pullman and his trauma team waited at the edge of the pad. The gunshot victim coming in reminded him of his two tours as a Navy Reserve surgeon in Afghanistan. He had been forward deployed with the Marines both times. He was extremely proud of his service. It was the highlight of his young medical career, and the experience he gained would help him save lives for decades to come.

As soon as the Jayhawk's wheels hit the pad, he and his team ran forward, dragging a gurney with them. Ed hopped out onto the asphalt and waved them to the cabin door. They slid the litter onto the gurney and swiftly began rolling it toward the emergency room. Eric ran behind them into the building. When the gurney stopped, Eric gave the doctor a quick rundown of Kevin's status and explained they had defibrillated him twice in the last ten minutes. He ripped two green waterproof pages out of his notebook, gave them to the doctor, turned, and ran for the door.

Dr. Pullman yelled after him, "Hey, wait a minute, I need to talk to you!" but it was too late.

Pullman knew something weird was happening. He was used to the Coast Guard flying in with injured hunters and campers, but this medic had been wearing the Army's new camouflage uniform, and it was sterilized. Sterilized meant no rank insignia, unit patches, nor name tapes. Nothing that identified him. He figured one of the military's secret special operations teams must have had a training accident. Pullman had also noticed the machine gun hanging out of the side of the Jayhawk. He had never seen a Coast Guard helo with its gun mounted.

Eric sprinted back to the helo and jumped in. Tom lifted off, pivoted the helo around to the right with a maneuver called a peddle turn, and headed for Bethel Airport. When Tom was a new copilot with the Corps flying from ship to ship, he had been taught to never pass up a chance to get food or fuel. An instructor told him the only time you have too much fuel is when you're on fire. He didn't know how long they would be flying, so he decided to top off his tanks. It only took a few minutes to get to the airport. He didn't call the tower because he didn't want the Russians to hear him. He landed at the fixed base operator's, or FBO's, ramp next to a fuel truck containing Jet-A fuel.

Ed Hicks hopped out and chocked the right main mount. "Chirp, I don't see anybody. It looks like the FBO is closed." He had been to the FBO over twenty times in the last couple of years, so he knew his way around the place.

"Take the master key and get the keys to that truck," Tom replied.

Ed reached into the cabin and grabbed a large set of bolt cutters and ran to the FBO building. He smashed the tempered glass door and stepped through the opening. He hustled behind the counter to the key box attached to the wall. It was secured by a padlock. Ed popped the lock off with the bolt cutters and grabbed the fuel truck keys.

Less than a minute had lapsed when he stepped back through the shattered glass door and ran to the fuel truck. He started the truck while Chris attached the grounding wire to the helicopter and then connected the pressure refueling hose. This system allowed the helicopter to be refueled quickly while the engines were running and rotors were turning. A couple of minutes later, Chirp gave them the cut signal and Chris disconnected the hose and cable and dropped them under the truck. He jumped back into the helicopter. Ed shut down the fuel truck and pulled the chocks from the Jayhawk's right main mount tire before he climbed back aboard and closed the door.

"Sir, we better go. I set off the alarm when I broke into the building, and I see flashing lights coming up the access road," Hicks said calmly.

"Roger that, takeoff checks," Tom replied.

Taco stepped on his floor ICS switch twice and gave him a thumbs-up to indicate the checks were complete. They were climbing through 150 feet when they flew over the police car on the access road. The officer in the car never saw them, but from the deafening roar of the engines and rotors, he thought a freight train was about to run over him. They departed to the south back the way they had come.

Tom called out to the crew and Jon on the ICS, "We'll check the trails in the snow back at the cabin heading south across the lake. I think the Russians came in and out the same way. We'll go back there and see where it leads."

Jon leaned back and opened his laptop. The message from Gwenn was waiting for him.

Jon read it and looked at the images. "Chirp, Gwenn sent me a message with images of a fire about six miles south of the cabin. She thinks it's a cabin or maybe a pole barn. I'll pass the coordinates up to Taco."

Jon wrote them down in his little green notebook and passed it to Chris, who passed it to Taco.

216

CHAPTER 40

Darrin was starting to think they might make it back to the sub on time. Both snowmobiles were working, and although the bumpy snow-covered terrain required them to travel slowly, they were making steady progress toward the pickup point. Then Mr. Murphyski made another appearance. Darrin's snowmobile, the one they didn't steal, started running rough, sputtered a few times, and then the engine stalled.

They all dismounted, and Eldon popped the hood open and started shining his flashlight around the engine looking for the problem. He didn't see anything wrong. They had poured the stolen gas into the tank earlier. Now he wondered if the gas might be bad.

"Darrin, I think the gas we scavenged was contaminated. I'll try to drain the line in case there's any water in the tank," Eldon said. He pulled the fuel line loose from the bottom of the tank and let about a cup of fuel dump into the snow. He reconnected the line and tried to start it again. It cranked but refused to run. He tried several more times with the same results.

"Darrin, I'm sorry, but I can't fix it." Eldon stared at Darrin's boots.

Darrin nodded and pulled out his Garmin Rhino GPS receiver and map. He determined they had traveled fifteen miles from the cabin. He oriented his map and looked for cabins nearby that might have another snowmobile they could grab.

Darrin located a couple of possible targets within a mile. "Willie, unhook the sled. Eldon and I will try to find another snowmobile."

Darrin climbed aboard the working Polaris. "Hop on, Eldon." He did so, and Darrin made a 90° right turn and disappeared into the bush.

After watching them ride away, Hojo spoke up from the sled, "Willie, set up security twenty-five meters further down the trail. James, you go twenty-five meters back to the north."

It took over ten minutes to travel the mile to the first cabin. It was surrounded by trees and was a true log cabin. Darrin didn't see a barn or garage for vehicles, and the cabin looked abandoned. No light came from the windows or smoke from the chimney. Darrin announced his presence but received no response. As he opened the unlocked door, his ears were assaulted with angry screams and growls. He shined his light across the room and saw a family of raccoons standing on their hind legs baring their teeth at him. He closed the door.

Darrin said to Eldon, "Come on. Let's go check the other one."

They arrived at the next cabin in five minutes. It was unoccupied and was in worse shape than the first one. Darrin looked up at the stars in frustration and then down at the snow in resignation. He had a painful decision to make. He turned the snowmobile back to the trail and headed for his team. Fifteen minutes later, they were back with the others. Hojo saw them pull up without a replacement for the disabled snowmobile. He understood immediately what that meant. The success of the mission would require a sacrifice.

Before Darrin could speak, Hojo grabbed his AR-15 rifle and pack and threw them out of the sled. Next, he rolled out of the sled into the snow. He crawled to a large pine tree about thirty feet off the trail and leaned back against its trunk. The twins, James and Willie, grabbed Hojo's pack by its shoulder straps and carried it to him. They dropped the pack next to Hojo. They both shook his hand and headed back to the trail without saying a word. They had too much respect for him to display any pity.

Darrin had followed them with Hojo's rifle and sleeping bag. He brushed the snow off the rifle and handed it to Hojo as he came down on one knee.

Darrin leaned in and whispered in Russian in Hojo's ear, "It has been an honor to serve with you, Lieutenant Petrov. You are a true warrior and patriot. Your dedication to this mission and your duty will always be remembered." Then Darrin kissed his forehead. He stood and walked away. After a few steps, he stopped and turned around. "Hey, Hojo, can I have your DVD collection?"

Everyone laughed. Hojo smiled and gave him the finger.

Darrin rejoined the team. "Transfer the packs to the sled with the Colonel. James, take the point. Willie, take up the rear."

They started slogging down the trail through the two-feet-deep snow. Without snowshoes, they quickly worked up a sweat. Eldon was lucky enough to get the first shift driving the snowmobile, but he knew he would get his turn soon enough. Darrin rode behind him.

***

Hojo watched them until they were out of sight. He didn't want to die, but he was prepared to if necessary. He opened his sleeping bag, pulled it up over his legs, and zipped it up around his body. If he was going to die, he wanted to die comfortably. He thought of his family back home in Moscow. His father was a mid-level civilian manager in the Ministry of Defense. Before that, he had retired from the Army as a colonel. His mother was a practicing pediatrician. His younger sister was in medical school. She intended to treat children like her mother. They all knew Hojo was an officer in the Army, but when his father pressed him for details, he told him he couldn't say anything more. His father knew what that meant.

Hojo wondered what his family would be told about his death. He figured the Ministry would make up a story about him perishing in some sort of training accident. It would have to be something where his body could not be recovered. Maybe a fiery airplane crash or being lost at sea. His family would mourn his loss. His mother and sister would be devastated. His father would take it hard too but would also be extremely proud even without knowing the details of the mission. He leaned back against the tree so he could watch the trail. If any pursuers came down the trail before he bled out or froze to death, he would stop them.

CHAPTER 41

The ambulances raced past several civilian hospitals with their sirens blaring and emergency lights flashing on their way to Walter Reed. Walter Reed was a military hospital with a level two trauma center. It was also much easier to control what, if any, information would be released to the public. Plus, as soon as he was stable, the President was considering pulling Wilkes out of the hospital and sending his ass directly to Gitmo. Gitmo was the Guantanamo Bay Naval Base located on the southeastern coast of the Communist island paradise of Cuba. The FBI was reasonably certain that Wilkes was not a U.S. citizen. The jury was still out on Art Bailey. He was a naturalized citizen, but if he took the oath while he was a Russian agent, then he perpetrated a fraud. Bailey could wind up in a cell next to Wilkes.

Two hours after arriving at the hospital, Art Bailey was resting in reasonable comfort in the ICU. The bullet that wounded him had first hit his bullet-resistant vest at an upward angle and gouged a furrow in the Kevlar about five inches long before it broke his left clavicle. He had a healthy dose of Oxycodone and a high pain threshold, but mostly he felt better because he had finally stood up for himself with the Russians.

Special Agents Gillis and Jerome entered his room and stepped up to the side of his bed.

Jocelyn said, "Sergeant Bailey, do you remember my partner and me?"

Art nodded. "Yeah, you're the FBI. Look, I'm ready to talk to you, but I want to make a deal. I never spied for the Russians or anyone else. I didn't have some secret deal with the Russians in order to be permitted to immigrate to America. They never contacted me until after I had gotten my citizenship and became a cop. After I finished my police field training, a guy approached me. He knew my whole life's story from when I grew up in Estonia. He told me that he might need a favor someday, and if I didn't cooperate when the time came, my parents and brothers back in Estonia would be snatched and carted off to Siberia."

Art thought for a minute. "Over all these years, I've had eight different people, some guys and some women, introduce themselves and let me know they hadn't forgotten about me. Wilkes approached me almost three years ago. This morning was the first time I had talked to him since then. Last night I went to Karpinsky's house because Sergeant Venable was involved in the shooting, and he's a friend of mine. When I walked back to my car, there was a matchbook stuck in the door handle. That was Wilkes's signal to me to go to the McDonald's and pick up a message indicating where to meet him. When we met at the memorial, he asked me about the dead men and if there were any feds involved, but I guess you heard all that."

Jerry said, "You said you wanted a deal, but it sounds like you just gave it all up."

Art shook his head. "Here's my deal. I want immunity from prosecution because I didn't do anything illegal, and I want to keep my citizenship and my job as a cop. I've been a good cop and a model citizen all these years. I've been following Wilkes off and on ever since he approached me. I know that where he parks his Lincoln isn't where he really lives. I can give you his real address where he sleeps and the other name he uses with his wife and kids. I can give you the names and addresses of the fifteen other people he handles. Get my FOP lawyer in here with a signed immunity agreement from the attorney general, and I'll give all of them to you, including his boss."

The FOP was the Fraternal Order of Police. Art was a proud member of the Fairfax County FOP Lodge #77. Every lodge kept a lawyer on retainer to represent their members with legal problems. Usually, it was to protect police officers from their own police departments.

CHAPTER 42

1410Z (0510HR AKST)
FIFTEEN MILES FROM THE FIRE

As the Jayhawk raced south toward the fire, Tom Adams wiggled his helmet back and forth a few times on his head. He was wearing Houdini's helmet, and it had been custom-fitted with padding for Houdini's head. Tom was feeling several hot spots on his head—painful areas caused by pressure points along his skull from the padding. The helmet felt alright when they took off, but now it felt like someone was pressing his knuckles into his skull. Tom had also tried on Lizard's helmet before they launched on the mission, but he had a tiny oblong pinhead, and Tom couldn't get the helmet passed his ears.

Tom pressed his ICS switch. "Taco, I've got some hot spots under my helmet. Take the controls for a minute."

Taco grabbed the cyclic and collective and rested his boots against the antitorque pedals. He wiggled the stick slightly. "I have the controls."

Chirp took his hands and boots off the controls. "You have the controls," he said as he held his hands out in front of the center of the instrument panel.

Taco replied, "Roger, I have the controls." This was called a three-way transfer of controls and left no doubt who was flying the helicopter.

Tom took off his helmet and gray skullcap and rubbed his head vigorously. He shined his small blue LED light into the helmet to see what was irritating him so much. One at a time, he pulled the pads loose from the Velcro inside the helmet and repositioned them. He tried the helmet on to see if it had helped. He repeated the process a couple more times. Finally, he set it up as well as it would get and put the helmet back on. Taco was maintaining airspeed, course, and altitude so Tom let him continue to fly. He slid his seat back and tried to stretch his arms and legs a little to loosen up his stiff body. Tom reached into the lower left leg pocket of his flight suit and retrieved the bag of M&Ms he had removed from one of the MREs he had stripped earlier and placed in his pack. For the next few minutes, he ate the M&Ms and watched Taco fly. He was a good stick.

"Chirp, the barn's at eleven o'clock and about two klicks," Taco called out on the ICS.

Tom slid his seat forward into position. "Roger that. I have it in sight. I have the controls."

Taco and Tom performed the three-way positive transfer of controls again. As the helicopter flew abeam the smoldering remains, Tom lowered the collective and pulled back on the cyclic to slow the Jayhawk to sixty knots and banked into a right turn to orbit the sight.

Ed called out, "Chirp, I see a couple of people in front of the cabin waving at us. I think they want us to land."

"Haley, do you see any other heat signatures in the area besides the two people in front of the cabin?" Tom asked Gwenn back aboard the cutter.

"Negative, but I can't tell if anyone is in the cabin."

"OK, Jon, I don't see anywhere to land near the cabin. I'll hover while you send two guys down on the hoist to talk to them," Tom said.

"I'll take Eric with me." Jon stepped over people and equipment to get to the door.

He motioned for Eric to follow him.

"Yeah, I figured you would go. We'll cover you guys as best we can," Tom replied.

***

Ed slid the door open and grabbed the cable hanging from the hoist. He attached it to the big black carabiner, or D ring, on Jon's combat vest. The heavy-duty carabiner was rated for up to 6,000 pounds. Jon tugged on it a couple of times and then stepped out of the helo. Ed quickly lowered him to the ground.

When Jon unhooked the cable, Ed brought it back up for Eric. Eric hooked on, and Ed sent him down. Jon approached the two people cautiously with his rifle at low ready. They didn't look like a threat, but he was ready to act if they made any aggressive moves. As he got close, he could see one was a man and the other was a teenage boy.

"Good morning, sir. Is this your place?" Jon asked the man.

"No, it belonged to my neighbor, Teddy. He's dead up there in the doorway with his wife, Tina. I live about a mile from here with my family. We heard the gunshots and then saw the fire a few minutes later. I'm Leo Fisher, and this is my son, Albert. Are you with the Coast Guard?"

Eric walked up behind Jon as the Jayhawk flew off to orbit the area. Then Eric sidled off to the right to cover Jon.

"No, sir, I'm Commander Jon Smith, U.S. Navy. I'm sorry we weren't here in time to stop this. I shouldn't tell you, but we're looking for a team of Russian soldiers. They killed a couple of deputy United States Marshals a few hours ago at Eek Lake. We're trying to catch them before they get back to their submarine."

"Son of a bitch!" Leo exclaimed. "Two of them came to our cabin and tried to steal one of our snowmobiles. They said they were state troopers. I knew they were full of shit. I should have shot them when I had the chance, but I thought they were thieves, not fucking Russians. I guess they came here looking for another snowmobile. My neighbors are dead because I didn't shoot those assholes."

"This isn't your fault, Leo. We're going to do everything in our power to make them pay for this." Jon placed his hand on Leo's shoulder. "Can you tell me if they were able to get a snowmobile from Teddy?"

Leo nodded his head. "Teddy had a brand-new Polaris that he kept in the pole barn, and I don't see it. Sir, if it'll help, you can take our snowmobiles and go kill those bastards. They're in real good condition and full of gas. Me and Al can walk home from here after we take care of Teddy and Tina."

"Thanks, Leo. That would help a lot."

Leo nodded and said to his son, "Come on, Al." He walked back to the cabin with his arm over his son's shoulder.

Jon transmitted, "Chirp, the man and woman who lived here are both shot dead on the porch. The two men I talked to are their neighbors, Leo and his son Albert. They said the Russians tried to steal a snowmobile from them at their cabin before they came here. The Russians killed the couple and stole a brand-new Polaris snowmobile from the barn. Leo said the Russians are pretending to be state troopers. He also offered us the use of his two snowmobiles if we want to chase them."

"You're damned right we want to chase them. Steve, get your team down there and give pursuit while we fly ahead and try to intercept them," Chirp ordered.

Rogers turned to his team. "Grab your shit and let's go!" He shouldered his pack and scooted across the cabin floor to the door.

In five minutes, Rogers and his soldiers were on the ground, Eric was back aboard the Jayhawk, and Smith was riding the hoist back up to the helicopter. Davis and Strasburg took the lead with Strasburg driving followed by Pope and Rogers with Pope driving. They headed down the trail using their NODs to guide them. They drove with a sense of urgency, but at the same time, they didn't want to rush into an ambush.

CHAPTER 43

Dr. Jed Pullman stood at the nurse's station in the emergency room sipping coffee from a Styrofoam cup as he filled out a short stack of paperwork. He yawned involuntarily and winced as pain traveled from between his shoulder blades to the base of his skull. He rolled his head up and down and back and forth. He had been on duty for almost twenty hours and had not gotten any sleep. Most nights he was able to get three or so hours of sleep in the on-call room. It was a small room with two sets of bunk beds. He was so tired he was afraid if he sat down, he might nod off. He was still wearing his blue scrubs. He had spent almost an hour performing meatball surgery to stabilize Deputy U.S. Marshal Kevin Bass. Meatball surgery was a form of battlefield medicine he learned in the Navy and practiced extensively in Afghanistan.

He saw similar head wounds in Afghanistan while he was forward deployed supporting the Marines, but this time, the left side of the lower mandible was almost completely detached from the victim's head. The mandible was broken in three places, and four teeth were missing. He temporarily screwed the bones back together, reestablished the blood supply, reconnected the muscle, and then stapled the face back together. Fortunately, being buried alive in the snow helped slow Kevin's blood loss and improved his chances of survival. He required four units of blood. Specialists trained in facial reconstruction would take over in a day or two and take him back into surgery.

Pullman's next task was to call the Bethel Police Department and report treating a shooting victim. He leaned over the chest-high nurse's station counter and pulled the telephone toward him by the power cord. He dialed the nonemergency number to Bethel P.D. The phone was answered by an attractive-sounding female recording that assured him his call was very important to the Bethel Police Department and to please wait. Someone would be with him shortly. As he waited, Pullman saw a man wearing a dark gray suit under an insulated green parka walk through the emergency room's automatic doors. He looked about thirty-five years old with dark hair and a dark complexion. He was of average height and weight. He slid the faux fur-lined hood from his head and stomped his feet on the rubber mat to knock loose the snow clinging to his highly polished black leather wing tips. He approached the receptionist behind her counter and removed a small black leather case from his inside breast pocket. He showed her its contents as he leaned forward and spoke softly to her. She nodded and pointed toward the doctor standing at the nurse's station, and then she buzzed him through the security door.

The man approached Pullman and introduced himself as he displayed his badge and identification card. "Dr. Pullman, I'm Special Agent Byron Wallace with the Federal Bureau of Investigation. Can we talk privately in your office?"

Pullman was both surprised and curious. "Ah, sure. Follow me." He hung up the phone and led Wallace into his small office. Pullman sat down behind his desk, and Wallace sat in front of it.

"Excuse me for a minute," Wallace said. He pulled out his cell phone and made a call. When it was answered, he said, "OK, I'm with Dr. Pullman in his office," and then he hung up.

Instantly, the printer next to Pullman came alive and produced a document. Pullman glanced at the printer and then at Wallace and then back to the printer. Pullman retrieved the paper from the tray and read it. It was an order from the Chief of Naval Operations placing him on active duty and assigning him to the USNORTHCOM under General Peter Harden. Before he could ask any questions, the printer spit out another document. Pullman grabbed it and started reading. It was an order from the Commandant of the Marine Corps placing Staff Sergeant Kevin Bass on active duty.

Pullman looked up at Wallace. "What's all this about?"

Wallace said, "Doctor, what I'm about to say is classified Secret. You still have a Secret clearance, so you can only share this information with others who have a Secret or above clearance that have a true need to know. Staff Sergeant Bass is also a Deputy United States Marshal. He was a member of a three-man protection detail guarding a Russian defector in a cabin at Eek Lake. Russian Spetsnaz soldiers assaulted the cabin and killed Bass's partners and shot him in the face. You are now Staff Sergeant Bass's personal physician and will stay with him until you are relieved. The circumstances of his injuries are classified, so you will not report his shooting to the police. Within a day or two, your replacement will arrive. Until then, the President wants you to make certain the staff sergeant gets everything he needs regardless of the cost or difficulty.

"Also, the team that flew him to the hospital is in the field at this moment actively pursuing the Russians. If they incur any casualties, they will come here for treatment. You need to be ready to receive them. In the unlikely event they capture any wounded Russians, you will also treat them."

"What am I supposed to tell the rest of the staff? State law requires us to report when we treat shooting victims. If we are going to receive casualties from combat, we need to bring in more staff, equipment, and supplies," Pullman said.

"Doctor, I understand your predicament, but for now, you can't make any kind of public request for resources. That may change in a few hours. Help is spinning up from the military, and assets will start arriving soon after the weather clears in other parts of the state," Wallace replied.

***

Forty feet from Pullman's office, Deputy Marshal Kevin Bass opened his eyes and scanned the ceiling. At first, he didn't know where he was or how he got there. The head of his hospital bed was elevated about 30°. The lights in his room were dimmed, but there was enough light for him to see his surroundings. He raised his head off his pillow and groaned loudly as the dull pain he was feeling immediately became excruciating. He quickly lowered his head back to the pillow. He brought his hands up to his face and saw an IV tube sticking out of the back of his left hand. As he took several deep breaths to try to ease the pain, he became aware of the tube in his throat. He touched his bandaged face but knew not to disturb anything.

He continued to breathe steadily and deeply. Slowly, the pain subsided, and his head started to clear. He remembered the attack at the cabin and that his friends Mark and Ronnie were dead. He realized he had survived somehow. Somehow someone knew he needed help and came for him. He vaguely remembered someone saying "semper fi" to him and telling him that he didn't have permission to die. He closed his eyes, and despite his best efforts, he cried. He cried because he was alive and Mark and Ronnie were dead. He had failed them.

Then he remembered that rat bastard, Karpinsky. They had been protecting him for years. The old man had told them about how bad life had been under the Communists and how much better it was to be an American. They had shared meals with him and slept under the same roof. They had trusted him. The level of Karpinsky's betrayal was unbearable. Kevin experienced a visceral, primal hatred. The rage built up inside him, but he couldn't act on it.

He had to alert someone that the Russian was a traitor. He didn't see a nurse call button and he couldn't talk, so he grabbed the pole supporting his IV bag and started banging it against the bed rail, almost like a prisoner banging his tin cup on the bars of his cell to get the guard's attention. The activity spiked his blood pressure and heart rate, which in turn set off the alarm on his monitor.

***

Pullman heard frantic knocking on his office door, and he said, "Yes, come in."

The nurse quickly opened the door and stuck her head inside.

She looked at the stranger and then Pullman. "Excuse me, Doctor, but Deputy Bass is awake, and he's freaking out!"

Pullman jumped to his feet in surprise. He didn't expect Bass to come around for at least another day. He hurried from his office, followed on his heels by Agent Wallace. As Pullman entered Bass's ICU room, he could see his patient was very upset. He couldn't talk because he had a tube down his throat, and of course, he had been shot in the face, but he was straining to keep his head up off the pillow and gesturing wildly with his arms. His face was red and sweat beaded on his forehead.

Pullman came to his bedside. "Kevin, try to stay calm. You could open up your wounds if you move around."

Kevin looked at the doctor and held up his flat left palm and pretended to write with his right hand. Pullman grabbed the clipboard hanging from the foot of the bed. He flipped the top form over and handed it and an ink pen to Kevin. He held the clipboard steady for Kevin.

Kevin wrote, "KARPINSKY TRAITOR KILLED RON-NIE" and then underlined it.

Pullman held the clipboard up for Agent Wallace to see it.

Wallace leaned in. "Deputy Marshal Bass, I'm Special Agent Wallace, FBI. Thank you for your help and what you did out there. I'll make sure everyone knows what Karpinsky did. Try to relax. We'll take it from here."

Kevin groaned as his head sunk back into the pillow and he dropped the ink pen on his lap. He nodded slightly and closed his eyes. As Dr. Pullman picked up the clipboard and pen and turned to leave the room, Kevin grabbed his arm and gestured for them again. Kevin scribbled a note and handed it to Pullman.

Agent Wallace asked, "What's it say?"

Pullman replied, "Where's my bandana?"

CHAPTER 44

Special Agents Gillis and Jerome escorted the FOP lawyer, Phillip Moody, past two deputy U.S. Marshals into Art Bailey's ICU room. Four deputies had been assigned to guard Art and Wilkes.

Moody walked up to the bed and shook Art's hand. "How are you feeling, Art?"

Art pointed to the IV bag. "Not too bad, Phil. They're keeping the pain meds flowing. Did you get the agreement signed by the AG?"

Moody pulled a piece of paper from his brown leather satchel. "Yeah, Art. I have it right here. As long as you don't lie to them and continue to cooperate, you're in the clear." Moody handed it to him.

Art read it. "It looks good to me. Have a seat, Phil, while I fill them in. Jocelyn, Jerry, pull up a chair and get ready to record this. The day Wilkes first approached me, I followed him home to his house in Annandale. He was driving a BMW back then. He pulled into the garage next to a green Land Rover, and instead of going into the house, he hopped in the Land Rover and drove off. After he drove around for about an hour, I followed him to another house in Arlington at 1211 North Frederick Street. It's a single-family two-story house with four bedrooms. That's where he actually lives with his wife and three kids. I think they're a real family.

"He and his wife operate a medical billing service from their home, but they don't do enough business to support their lifestyle. The business is a front for their other activities. The name he uses for his business is Scott Saxton. His wife's name is Cindy. I don't think either of them are American citizens. I couldn't find any record of their existence before fifteen years ago. They just appeared one day as a married couple. I followed him around off and on for about six months after that. I searched the house in Annandale back then. It was obvious no one lived there. There was no fresh food in the refrigerator and no clothes or personal stuff in the house. I think they just used it to stash the Lincoln and maybe as a safe house."

Jocelyn asked, "Have you ever seen anyone else there?"

Art answered, "No, I didn't."

Jocelyn asked, "How did you know when he would be coming over to pick up the BMW or Lincoln to go to a meeting?"

"I didn't at first. Then I put a tracker on his car. Whenever he took it out of the garage, I would receive an alert. If I wasn't busy, I would track him down and see who he was meeting with. Then

I would follow them home and find out who they were. I think a lot of them were people like me who immigrated to America and were then pressured by the Russians to assist them. After a few months, he didn't meet with any new people, so I removed the tracker. However, I do think I saw his boss once."

Jerry asked, "Why do you think it was his boss?"

"I could tell right away by Saxton's body language, plus the guy chewed him out over something. I couldn't hear it, but he was clearly rattled by what he was told."

Jocelyn asked, "So, did you follow the boss?"

Art smiled. "Yes, I did. He ran an SDR for over an hour, but eventually he went to a house in Ashton Heights and swapped cars. Then he drove to the Russian Embassy. I have some photos of him on my phone. They might be good enough to run facial recognition." He continued giving Jocelyn and Jerry the names and information on every contact he saw Saxton make.

***

An hour later, Jerry and Jocelyn were standing in an empty hallway outside the ICU.

Jerry spoke softly to Jocelyn, "That guy, Art, is a fucking gold mine. We haven't even talked to Wilkes—or Saxton—yet."

Jocelyn said, "Let's see what he has to say."

They walked through the door into the ICU and then over to Saxton's room. They acknowledged the deputy marshals at the sliding door and then walked into the room.

Jerry started the questioning. "Mr. Wilkes, I'm FBI Special Agent Jerome. This is Special Agent Gillis. You have already been read your Miranda rights. Are you willing to talk to us?"

Saxton tried to play the scared suburban dad. "Yes. I'll tell you anything if it gets me out of here sooner and back to my family."

Jerry asked, "What's your relationship to Sergeant Bailey, and why did you shoot him?"

Saxton exclaimed, "Is he the nut who shot me? I don't know him! I was visiting the memorial when he pulled a gun on me and started threatening to kill me."

Jerry asked, "Why did you have a pistol with you? Don't you know it's illegal in the District?"

Saxton replied, "DC is a dangerous place. I have a constitutional right to be armed. This is still America."

Jocelyn smiled. "Sergeant Bailey told us you're a Russian spy."

"That's crazy. I've never been to Russia. I don't even have a passport."

Jocelyn looked at her partner. "Jerry, let's stop wasting time and skip ahead a little."

She pulled her phone from her coat pocket and began playing a video of the confrontation between Bailey and Saxton. She held it out for him to see the part where he said, "Are you out of your fucking mind? We will destroy you! And then we will kill your wife and kids!" Saxton's demeanor changed instantly. He had been unconscious from the time his head smacked the pavement until he woke up in the hospital. He didn't know he had been under surveillance.

Saxton calmly said, "I would like to speak to my lawyer now."

Jerry chuckled. "Sorry, no lawyer for you, Ivan or Boris or whatever the fuck your name is. You're an illegal enemy combatant.

Thanks to the Patriot Act, you're on the first Air America flight out of the country, where you can be properly debriefed by some very patient, highly trained professionals. By the way, we've already scooped up your family, if they really are your family. We'll know for sure after we check everyone's DNA."

CHAPTER 45

1500Z (0600HR AKST)
15 MILES SOUTH OF EEK LAKE

First Sergeant Strasburg was slowly driving along the winding trail trying to concentrate on what was out there in front of him. He adjusted his posture in an attempt to alleviate the pain radiating from his hips up his spine to his neck. He wondered how the cavalry troopers handled riding horses all day 150 years ago. As he scanned the trail with his NOD, he noticed a dark object in the trail about fifty meters away. He stopped immediately and rolled off the snowmobile into the snow to the left. Davis rolled off behind him. About forty feet behind them, Pope and Rogers did the same.

Strasburg keyed his radio to talk softly to Rogers, "Sir, something is blocking the trail about fifty meters in front of us. I think it's a snowmobile and sled."

Rogers replied, "OK, you and Davis approach from the left side of the trail, and Pope and I will go about fifteen meters into the trees on the right side of the trail and parallel you."

***

Hojo was getting cold in his sleeping bag, and he thought his leg was bleeding again. He didn't bother to check it. He knew his time was almost up, but he refused to feel sorry for himself. He hadn't been conscripted. He volunteered to be right where he was. Actually, he had volunteered five times over to be where he was. Sitting in a cubicle for the next thirty years wasn't for him.

His eyes were getting heavy, and his chin dipped to his chest several times as he fought his body's desire to sleep. He knew if he did, he would never wake up. Then he heard something. He was instantly wide awake, and his heart was pounding. He realized it had to be snowmobiles coming up the trail. He only heard it for a few seconds before the sound vanished. He sat up straight with his back firmly against the tree. His thumb slowly flipped the selector switch on his rifle from SAFE to FIRE. He didn't know who they were, but he couldn't risk letting them pass. They would have to die.

He could see the blurry silhouettes of the broken-down snowmobile and sled in the darkness to his front, but snow-laden tree limbs blocked his view of the trail to his left where he thought the sound had come from. He concentrated on controlling his breathing while he listened and tried to see anything. He peered over his rifle's barrel with both eyes open. He didn't see any movement, but the shape of the black silhouettes changed. Hojo realized someone was standing next to the snowmobile and immediately began firing. The sound was deafening, and the flash from his rifle blinded him, but he kept firing.

***

Strasburg and Davis cautiously maneuvered along the left side of the trail to the sled and snowmobile. Strasburg whispered, "There's blood in the sled. One of them is wounded."

Davis's eyes traveled from the sled to the trail in the snow. Through his NOD, everything had a fuzzy dark green tint to it. It looked like someone crawled or was dragged away from the sled into the bush. The trail ended at the base of a large tree. Davis was shocked to see one of the Commies sitting against the tree pointing a weapon at them.

As the Russian began firing, Davis yelled, "Get down!" and pushed Strasburg to the snow behind the snowmobile and landed next to him.

Strasburg quickly crawled to the front of the snowmobile and fired four three-round bursts and transmitted, "Contact right!"

Then Strasburg loaded an anti-personnel round into his M203 and fired it into the trees. The round flew through the boughs and detonated twenty-five meters behind the target.

***

Pope and Rogers were about twenty meters to the shooter's left when he started firing. They immediately dropped to the snow and returned fire. Rogers emptied his thirty-round magazine and immediately swapped it out for a fresh one. Pope put several two-second bursts from his M249 SAW into the target.

Rogers yelled, "I'm going to throw a grenade into the trees. When I say now, cover me!"

"Roger that!" Pope replied as he aimed his SAW and fired.

Rogers pulled the pin and shouted, "Now!" as he rolled to his left side and lobbed the grenade with his right arm.

Pope continued his bursts into the target area.

***

The grenade plunged through the snow-covered limbs, landing ten feet in front of Hojo. Three seconds later, it exploded. Shrapnel peppered Hojo from the soles of his boots to the top of his head. He screamed as searing pain surged through his body. Now he really was blind and deaf. He tried to change the magazine in his rifle, but his hands wouldn't work.

***

As soon as the grenade exploded, Pope keyed his radio and yelled, "Pope moving!" and jumped to his feet to rush the target.

He burst through the trees and saw the Russian sitting against the tree fumbling with his rifle. Pope gave him an eight-round burst to the chest and then kicked the rifle out of his dead hands.

Instantly, Strasburg and Rogers appeared at Pope's side ready to fire. Realizing the Russian was dead, Rogers went down to one knee, raised his NOD, and shined his blue-lensed flashlight on the body.

Rogers said, "This guy is wearing an Alaska State Trooper parka."

Strasburg turned to tell Pope and Davis to bring up the snowmobiles and realized Davis was missing. "Where's Allen? Allen, where are you? Allen!" Strasburg ran back to the snowmobile and froze in his tracks as he looked down and saw Allen lying face down in the snow with a dark circle of blood-soaked snow surrounding his head. Strasburg dropped to his knees and rolled him over. Allen had been shot in the throat, and the round hit his spine as it exited. He died instantly. Over his shoulder, Strasburg heard Pope and Rogers run up.

Upon seeing Allen's motionless face and the snow saturated in his blood, Pope shook his head and exclaimed, "Goddamn it! I'm going to kill every one of these motherfuckers!"

Strasburg stared at Allen's dead eyes and sobbed, "He died saving my life. He pushed me out of the way." His thoughts immediately went back to when he had first met Allen. He was a sixteen-year-old kid from the Athabascan Tribe in his junior year at Kenai Central High School. Strasburg was a National Guard recruiter. He was perfect for recruiting duty. He was a better-looking version of a young Mel Gibson who had recently been promoted to sergeant first class. He sported a chest full of ribbons below Air Assault wings, Master Jump wings, and the coveted Combat Infantry Badge from his tours as an Airborne Ranger in Iraq, Afghanistan, and Somalia.

Once a month, Strasburg would come to the school and set up a table in the back of the cafeteria to talk to the seniors during their lunch period, and every time, Allen would bring his lunch over and pepper him with questions about his time in the Army and traveling around the world. Strasburg always answered his questions and couldn't help being flattered by the kid's attention, but he encouraged Allen to finish high school and then decide whether to join the Guard.

Allen had never met his father. His mom was an emergency room nurse and had seen more than her fair share of people who had been maimed or worse. She wasn't thrilled with the idea of her only child joining the Army, but by the time of Allen's seventeenth birthday, he had convinced her to give her permission for him to enlist. When they went to talk to Strasburg at his office in the armory, he told her she should make Allen wait until he graduated before letting him join up. That surprised her. In the end, she decided to let Allen enlist, but before she signed the papers, she made Strasburg promise to look after her boy. Now Strasburg had failed, and assuming he got back home, he didn't know if he could bear to face her.

***

Rogers went down on one knee and put his hand on Strasburg's shoulder. "I'm really sorry this happened, Jim, and I promise you, we'll get these bastards, but we don't have time to mourn right now. We have to get back on the trail."

Strasburg nodded his head and wiped his eyes with the back of his faux fur-backed arctic mitten. "Roger that, sir. Come on, Nate, let's get the snowmobiles." He got to his feet and began walking back down the trail.

Rogers changed frequencies on his radio and transmitted, "Mustang 6, this is 26."

"Go ahead, Steve. What do you have?"

"Sir, we engaged a wounded straggler the Russians left behind on the trail. He was dressed as a state trooper. It looks like one of their snowmobiles broke down, so they had to leave him behind. He is KIA."

"Roger that, well done."

Rogers swallowed hard. "Sir, Mustang 29 is also KIA."

***

Adams looked out the right window into the darkness and yelled, "Fuck!" as loud as he could as he punched the metal framework around his greenhouse window.

Taco snapped his head around to the right as he heard Chirp yell over the roar of the helicopter.

Tom took a couple of deep breaths to compose himself. He keyed his mic and calmly said, "Understood, Steve. Are you mission capable? I don't want you to leave Davis behind."

"Yes, sir. We're ready to fight. The Russians left behind a sled with their snowmobile. We'll use it to bring Davis with us."

"Good. Steve, I know I don't have to say this, but don't take any chances with these assholes. We would like to get Karpinsky back alive, if possible, but if there is any doubt about your safety, kill 'em all."

"Wilco," was Rogers's only response.

Everyone in the Jayhawk except Mike, Eric, and Alice was connected to the intercom system and heard Rogers report the firefight and Allen's death. Smith typed Rogers's report into his laptop and showed it to his team. All three of them had seen friends lost in combat, and they quickly compartmentalized it.

They would mourn for the young soldier after the mission. For now, they would Charlie Mike.

***

Mike thought, Shit, maybe we really are red shirts.

CHAPTER 46

Beams of light pierced the darkness as three snowmobiles raced along the bumpy tree-lined trail. They drove as fast as they could go without throwing their riders. Sixteen-year-old Dave Shepard was driving the lead snowmobile with his girlfriend, Kara King, holding on to him for dear life. She alternated between screaming and laughing. Dave's best friend, Jeff Schmidt, was behind him, running a close second. Jeff's girlfriend, Wendy Jacobs, was riding with him. She was yelling in his ear to speed up and pass Dave. Duncan Williams was bringing up the rear in a distant, conservative third place. His girl friend—not girlfriend—Amanda Haney, was riding with him.

They were in their junior year and had endured an excruciatingly long week of classes and homework. The weather had been miserable most of the week, and it was finally clearing up. Now it was Saturday morning, and they wanted to have fun.

Kara and Wendy had stayed overnight at Amanda's house. Dave and his buddies got permission from their parents to leave their houses early before the sun came up to go rabbit hunting with their .22s. Amanda's father was traveling for work, so he wasn't home. Her mom was a heavy sleeper and tended to sleep late, so the girls had no trouble sneaking out to meet the boys. They planned to be back home long before she woke up.

Dave was the leader of this pack. They had chased each other back and forth across the forest for over half an hour when Dave slowed to a crawl and then turned off the trail. He drove about fifty feet into a small clearing. The boys circled a pile of wood Dave had staged earlier and covered with a blue plastic tarp several times to tamp down the snow. They shut down their vehicles and dismounted.

Dave handed Kara a flashlight. "Here, point this at the tarp."

Dave pulled the tarp off the wood pile and grabbed the plastic bottle of charcoal lighter fluid he had left there previously.

Kara clapped her gloved hands. "Oh, thank you, Dave. My feet are freezing."

He doused the wood with the fluid and then pulled off his heavy mittens. He reached into his front chest pocket to retrieve a small box of wooden matches. He struck a match and dropped it into the pile. The wood burst into flames, and the fire illuminated their little party.

Dave said, "We'll all be plenty warm in a minute."

Next, he unstrapped his backpack from the back of his snowmobile. He unzipped the top and pulled out two large thermos bottles, six red plastic cups, and a box of chocolate-covered mini donuts. The others sat sideways on their snowmobiles facing the roaring fire as Dave served them hot cocoa and donuts. After everyone was taken care of, he sat down next to Kara and poured himself a drink. Kara's eyes had followed him around the circle, and she continued to stare at him as he sipped his steaming cocoa. She was totally smitten with him and had been for two years. He turned to look at her and saw she was smiling at him. When he smiled back, she leaned over and kissed him on the cheek. His cold face brightened even redder, and he leaned forward to poke the fire with a stick.

"Thank you for going to all this trouble, Dave. Everything is wonderful," Wendy said.

The others readily voiced their agreement.

"You're all quite welcome. So, who's going to the game to-night?" Dave asked.

He was really asking Wendy and Amanda. The boys played for their high school's hockey team. Dave was a center and the team captain. He led the team in scoring. He had a good shot at a hockey scholarship, but he was leaning toward going to one of the nation's service academies if he could get an appointment. Jeff played right wing on Dave's line and was second in points on the team. Duncan was the team's starting goalie. Kara had worked hard and made the cheerleading squad this year, so that left Wendy and Amanda.

"It depends on whether or not my mom will need me to babysit my brother," Wendy replied.

Amanda turned to Duncan. "Can I ride with you?"

Duncan smiled. "Of course, you can."

Kara changed the subject. "On the way back, I think the ladies should drive."

Wendy and Amanda both agreed. The boys smiled, giving each other knowing looks.

Dave said, "Sure, why not."

The boys were already looking forward to riding behind the girls and wrapping their arms around them even though they were all clothed in heavy sweaters and parkas. After they finished their picnic, Dave gathered up the trash and thermoses and stuffed them back in his pack. He sat down next to Kara again. He looked deeply into her eyes. He leaned in to kiss her. She closed her eyes and readied her lips to meet his. Just as their cold noses touched, shots rang out in the distance. Everyone turned north, trying to see into the darkness. Gunshots in the Alaska wilderness were not uncommon, even at night, but then they heard an explosion.

Kara was concerned. "What's going on, Dave?"

Then they heard more rifle shots and bursts from a machine gun and another explosion.

Dave told Duncan and Jeff, "Break out your rifles."

Dave reached into his pack and pulled out his stainless-steel Ruger 10/22 takedown rifle. It was designed to come apart in the middle so it could fit in a backpack. He had a couple of ten-round magazines and two twenty-five-round magazines. He quickly twisted the rifle together, loaded it with one of the twenty-five-round magazines, and chambered a round. He made sure the safety was on and slung it across his chest. The boys hastily tossed snow on the fire to extinguish it.

Dave straddled his snowmobile and said calmly to the boys, "Come on. Let's take the girls home."

CHAPTER 47

Gwenn heard the radio traffic reporting the firefight and Allen's death. She struggled to remember which one of the young faces she had seen a few hours earlier was his. She again thought of her husband. He shouldn't be out there. He had served his time in combat; he was retired. She took some solace from the fact that he always came back. He had been in harm's way during many deployments around the world, but he always came home. She would do everything she could to help him today. Gwenn had a reputation in her division at NGA for seeing things in imagery that others didn't think to look for. She looked at the world as a whole differently than others. They even coined a term for it: Gwenntelligence, or Gwenntel for short.

She turned back to her computer screens and redoubled her efforts to find the submarine. The Global Hawk had been orbiting the area from Eek Lake to the coast since it arrived on station. At this point, she had too much information to analyze, so she went back to the cabin where it all started. She followed the Russians' cold trail from the cabin to the barn fire and then to the scene of the ambush, but after that, she lost their trail.

The tree-covered landscape was too thick. Also, people lived in cabins scattered across the landscape, and their snowmobile tracks ran across the ground and frozen lakes like giant spider webs, many of them headed north and south. There were just too many trails, and the canopy was too thick. She could track Rogers's team as they followed the Russians along the trail because of their radios, but she couldn't see what Rogers saw from the ground.

CHAPTER 48

Petty Officer McLemore was monitoring the infrared video feed from Hawk 33 when she observed three snowmobiles. "Gwenn, the feed from Hawk 33 has three snowmobiles heading southwest about three miles south of the ambush site."

Gwenn slid her chair over to see McLemore's computer screen.

Gwenn watched the video for a few seconds. "Cindy, put the feed up on the wall monitor."

McLemore did as instructed, and Gwenn turned to look at the improved high-definition video. She clearly saw three snowmobiles and six riders running along a trail as they alternately appeared and disappeared beneath the snow-laden trees.

Gwenn smiled. "Good work, Cindy. I better call the team."

"Mustang 6, this is the Haley," Gwenn transmitted.

"Go ahead, Haley, this is Mustang 6," Tom replied.

"We have IR video from Hawk 33 showing three snowmobiles with six riders heading southwest away from the vicinity of the ambush site. Their current location is 60°10'43" North 162°01'07" West," Gwenn said.

"Roger that, Haley. We're en route," Tom replied as he turned to a heading of 245°. "Taco, enter the coordinates and give me a more accurate heading." Tom keyed his FM radio. "Mustang 26, this is 6."

"Go for 26," Rogers responded immediately.

"Steve, keep heading south on the trail. We'll investigate the snowmobile sighting and advise further," Tom reported.

"Roger that, sir," Rogers replied.

Gwenn decided to shift her focus to the submarine. She used a classified change detection program called I-Ball to find differences between imagery taken as far back as twenty-four hours ago up to the most recent pass. She compared images of the coast.

CHAPTER 49

Mustang 6 made a beeline for the most recent location of the snowmobiles. The Haley continued to observe the snowmobiles' path along the trail between the trees and guided the Jayhawk to them.

Taco saw them first. "Contact eleven o'clock and a thousand meters."

Tom lowered the collective and pulled back and left on the cyclic to slow down and turn toward the snowmobiles.

"Coming left. Taco, light them up with the IR spotlight," Tom directed.

The IR spotlight switch was on the collective and was controlled by the pilot's left thumb. Taco flipped the switch on and directed the beam with the conical thumb switch. In Tom's day, it was called the Coolie Hat, but the term was no longer considered appropriate. The IR spotlight would help them see the snow-mobiles but would be invisible to the riders if they didn't have night vision devices. Taco guided the beam to the snowmobiles.

Tom keyed his ICS. "I'm going to slow down and orbit them. If they point a weapon at us, light them up."

Chris and Ed replied, "Roger that."

The snowmobiles emerged from the trees and onto a large frozen lake. Tom slowed the Jayhawk down to fifty knots and flew an orbit around the snowmobiles. The snowmobiles were so loud, none of the riders appeared to hear the helicopter. Tom dipped down to 200 feet to give Taco and Chris Savage a better look at the riders and then climbed back to 300 and widened his orbit.

Savage called out on the ICS, "Chirp, the drivers have long guns slung across their chests. The other three riders look like women, and they appear unarmed."

Chirp turned back to the right to reverse the orbit so he could get a look at them.

Chirp repeated the low orbit, this time to the right. "Ed, be ready to shoot if necessary."

As they flew by, Ed reported, "Sir, they look like civilians to me."

"OK, we'll block their path and stop them before they finish crossing the lake. Be ready to shoot from the right side. Taco, switch me up on the loudspeaker. When I start talking, flip on the spotlight," Chirp instructed. He called for the landing checklist and brought the Jayhawk into a fifty-foot hover with the right side of the helicopter facing the snowmobiles. The rotor wash created a mini snowstorm over the lake. When the snowmobiles were within about 500 feet, Chirp called out in his most authoritative voice, "This is the United States Coast Guard; stop your snowmobiles and shut down your engines!"

***

Dave Shepard was feeling much better. They had put over seven miles between themselves and the picnic site. They would have the girls back to Amanda's house in another thirty minutes. The surface on the frozen lake was smooth, and the girls were able to release their death grips on the boys. Suddenly, a voice thundered from the ether, and an intense light in the sky to their front blinded them and lit up the lake. The voice ordered them to stop, and since Dave couldn't see anything anyway, he complied immediately.

The voice spoke again, "Dismount, lay down your weapons, and put your hands up."

Kara screamed in terror.

"Kara, it's alright. They're the Coast Guard," Dave said has he climbed off the snowmobile and laid his rifle down on the snow. He hugged Kara to reassure her then called out to Jeff and Duncan, "Do as they say! Drop your guns!"

***

In the Jayhawk, Ed Hicks manned his M240 mounted to the doorframe and trained it on the snowmobilers, ready to fire. Ed observed them climb off their snowmobiles, put their weapons on the snow, and put their hands up. Chirp started sliding the Jayhawk to the right and landed about 100 feet from the snowmobiles. The rotor wash sent another blanket of snow to cover the snowmobilers.

Fire Team One leapt from the open door into the snow. As soon as they were clear of the rotor arc, Chirp took off and orbited the area at 300 feet AGL. Commander Smith rotated his NOD up away from his left eye and turned on the flashlight attached to the accessory rail of his rifle. The rest of the team did the same. Team One was wearing their snowshoes and traveled easily across the short distance to the snowmobiles. Dave stepped forward and stood in front of the others.

Commander Smith walked up to Dave with his rifle at the low ready position and spoke as his team covered him, "I'm Commander Smith, United States Navy. Who are you, and what are you doing out here this morning?"

Dave's mouth was full of cotton. He swallowed hard and introduced himself and the others, "Sir, I'm Dave Shepard and this is my girlfriend, Kara King." Dave pointed to the others and said, "This is Jeff Schmidt, Wendy Jacobs, Amanda Haney, and Duncan Williams. We were out riding the trails and had a little picnic. We made a campfire and were having a snack when we heard a lot of shooting and some explosions. We decided to take the girls home after that."

Smith nodded. "What are the guns for?"

Dave replied, "After we take the girls home, we were planning to go rabbit hunting." Then Dave shrugged. "Besides, this is Alaska."

Eric nodded.

Mike said, "Fucking A."

Smith gave Mike a shut-the-fuck-up look and then turned back to the teenagers. "I can't go into the details, but there are Russian soldiers in the area pretending to be American, and they have killed several people tonight."

Smith bent over and picked up Dave's rifle. He brushed the snow off, handed it back to him. "Take the girls home ASAP and stay clear of the area." Smith keyed his radio and called Chirp, "Mustang 6, this is 16. The riders are teenaged boys and girls who live in the area. They were close enough to hear the shooting from the ambush. I told them to clear the area and go home. We're ready for pickup."

Smith led his team back to the original landing spot. They all took a knee facing away from each other in an arc to form a small perimeter. Within a minute, the Jayhawk landed next to them and kicked up another snowstorm. Fire Team One clambered aboard, and the helo disappeared into the night.

Dave yelled to the others, "That was fucking awesome!" The others couldn't see the huge grin on his face. Commander Smith was the coolest man he had ever met, and the helicopter was incredible. Now more than ever, he wanted to be an officer in the military. "Come on, let's get out of here," Dave said as he mounted his snowmobile.

Kara climbed on behind him and wrapped her arms tightly around his waist. She pressed the side of her face to his shoulder. She was still scared but was impressed by how Dave had dealt with the officer and how the officer gave Dave back his rifle.

CHAPTER 50

1530Z (0630HR AKST)
18 MILES SOUTH OF EEK LAKE

Darrin and his men had traveled only three miles in an hour and a half. After the first hour, Darrin and Eldon dismounted so James and Willie could ride for a while. Eldon took point, and Darrin followed behind. As Darrin struggled through the knee-deep snow, he wondered if the attack on Karpinsky's cabin had been discovered yet. The doctor had assured him earlier that the marshals weren't scheduled to check in with their watch officer until 11:00 A.M. Darrin had planned on being back aboard the sub well before then.

***

As Darrin slogged down the trail, old man Karpinsky traveled in relative comfort in the sled. It was a bouncy ride, but he didn't complain. He reclined facing to the rear and was actually warm inside his sleeping bag. He was both excited and tired. He was worn out because he was an old man, and he hadn't had much sleep before he was retrieved from the cabin. He was excited because he was back in the game. He was also pleased with himself. He had fooled the Americans for over 25 years, and now he had information for Mother Russia that was vital to her status in the world and possibly her continued existence.

He had used his remote viewing ability to contact President Pichugin telepathically. Not only contact him, but send him enough detailed information that Pichugin was able to send a team to the cabin to retrieve him. It had taken over twenty attempts over a span of two months, but in the end, it had worked. He was fatigued by the events of the night and his repeated attempts to use his telepathic ability to glean intel about any possible pursuers. He was usually most successful when he sat in a quiet room. Unfortunately, he wasn't in a quiet room.

Karpinsky decided he might be more successful if he tried to visit the redhead again. He laid his head back against his pack and closed his eyes. Within minutes, his thoughts drifted to the image of the beautiful young woman. She was standing at the rail of a ship surrounded by darkness. She was wearing an ornate ankle-length purple velvet dress. She was scanning the dark waters in front of her searching for something or someone.

He approached from behind her like he had the first time. As he was about to grab her, he heard a commotion behind him. He turned and saw an angry mob of women coming toward him from the aft end of the ship. There must have been over a hundred. He couldn't see their faces, but they seemed to know him. He turned to run away, but the redhead was there to confront him. He could see recognition in her eyes. Before he could react, she punched him square in the face.

He snapped out of the trance and saw he was back in the sled bumping down the trail. His eyes were watering uncontrollably, and pain radiated outward from his bloody, broken nose. He was frightened, not by his injured nose, but by the realization there was another person out there with psychokinetic abilities that rivaled his own, and now, she was hunting him. He wouldn't have believed it was possible if he hadn't done it himself many times. Until now, he thought his telekinesis discoveries were his alone. Now, he suspected the American military must have an active program separate from the one he had been running for the CIA.

CHAPTER 51

Alice leaned back against the rear bulkhead of the Jayhawk with her eyes closed. She was physically tired and angry but also mentally focused. Back when she was a sniper in Afghanistan, she had a knack for locating her targets no matter how well concealed they were. If she started getting frustrated, she would close her eyes behind her scope and let her intuition go to work. The muzzle of her rifle would float back and forth until she felt it was time to open her eyes. When she did, she was usually on a target. The other Air Force Security Forces airmen knew she had mad skills as a sniper, but they had no idea she had a special ability they all lacked. Of course, there was no way she was going to tell them about her secret. At best, they would think she was crazy. At worst, she would wind up locked in a laboratory being studied like a rat.

She began searching for her attacker. After a few minutes, she felt his presence and understood that he was also looking for her. Before he could get to Alice, he was discovered by an angry mob. Over a hundred bruised and battered women pursued him between the trees and through the snow. They screamed and howled at him. He frantically struggled across the snow-covered landscape running between the brush and trees trying to escape them. Alice stepped from behind a tree and into his path. This time, she had a surprise for him.

When she opened her eyes, she was back in the Jayhawk. She looked down at her gloved right hand. She removed her glove and massaged her sore, swollen knuckles. She had seen him this time and recognized him. Her attacker was Karpinsky, and this time she had made a personal connection with him. She looked at Commander Smith and motioned for him to hand her his laptop. He did, and she began typing. After a minute, she handed it back to him. He read the short note and peered at her. She nodded her head.

Smith keyed his mic. "Chirp, Alice thinks we should set up an ambush at 59°54'11" North 162°03'14" West."

Chirp and Taco exchanged confused looks, and Chirp said, "Why there?"

"She says she gets these feelings sometimes, but they're almost always right. She says if you need convincing to tell you that your wife was born in Andalusia, Alabama, but grew up in Pensacola, and you played baseball for Art's Boys Club in St. Louis when you were a kid," Smith replied.

Chirp keyed his mic. "That's good enough for me."

"Maybe she found the information on your Facebook pages," Taco said.

"We work for an intel agency. We don't have Facebook pages or any other social media. Foreign intel services mine those sites for information on us and our families and friends. Enter the coordinates. Jon, when we get there, we'll drop off your team. Be careful down there. We don't want any blue-on-blue action." Next, Chirp called Major Rogers, "Mustang 26, this is Chirp."

"Go ahead, sir," Rogers replied.

"We're going to drop off Team One about 20 miles down the trail from you. We'll try to pincer the Russians between your teams. After we drop them, I'll send you the coordinates," Chirp said.

Rogers clicked his radio twice in acknowledgment.

CHAPTER 52

1535Z (0635HR AKST)
BS-64 PODMOSKOVYE

The officer of the deck called out to his commanding officer, "Captain, we received an urgent message from the president for your eyes only."

The captain was immediately apprehensive but tried to play it cool.

He replied, "Very well. I'll take it in my quarters. XO, you have the Conn."

"Aye, sir, XO has the Conn."

Captain First Rank Vanya Vyacheslav walked out of the control room and entered his small, but luxurious by submarine standards, quarters. He logged in to his computer and selected the secure message waiting for him. He clicked play on the video. The president of the Russian Federation, Vladimir Pichugin, was sitting at his desk in his office looking directly at the camera. Since he was viewing a recording, Vyacheslav knew the president couldn't see or hear him, but he still felt uncomfortable. He didn't agree with Pichugin's politics. He kept his opinions to himself, but he thought Pichugin was a criminal and a thug.

Pichugin started talking, "Captain Vyacheslav, I have new orders for you and your crew. Under normal circumstances, your training would dictate that you put the safety of your crew and submarine above all else. I am ordering you to disregard your training. Colonel Karpinsky has information vital to the continued survival of the Russian Federation. It is imperative that you retrieve him and return him to Moscow as soon as possible. His safety is paramount. Your submarine and crew are expendable. Do not leave Alaska without him. Failure to follow my orders will result in the most severe consequences imaginable. I look forward to meeting with you and Colonel Karpinsky upon your return home. I will have your family here with me in Moscow as my guests. I am certain they will be eager to see you. You are to remain under EMCON until you are back within Russian territorial waters."

CHAPTER 53

The area Alice designated was a tree-covered hillock overlooking another frozen lake about a mile from the coast. Chirp brought the Jayhawk in low right above the treetops and landed on the edge of the lake. Fire Team One leapt from the helo as soon as it landed and fanned out prone in the snow just as they had done back at the cabin. Their rifles covered the area to the north where they believed the Russians might approach. The helo took off as soon as the team was clear, blanketing them with a layer of snow. The team remained motionless, watching and listening for any hint of the enemy.

After a minute, Smith spoke softly over his shoulder, "Mike and I will advance into the trees at the edge of the lake. After we get in position to cover you, follow us."

All three acknowledged him.

"OK, Mike, let's go." Smith got up and slogged through the knee-high snow.

Mike struggled to keep up. He was younger and probably stronger, but his legs were shorter. As soon as they reached the trees, they dropped to the snow and covered Eric and Alice's rush to the trees. Now that they were under cover, they took turns putting on their snowshoes while the others kept a lookout.

"Alice, where do you want to set up your hide?" Smith asked.

She pointed to the top of the hillock. "Up there, I should be able to cover almost all of the lake."

"OK. Mike and I will cover your movement from here. After you and Eric are in position, we'll move about fifty meters north to cover the trail leading onto the lake."

With their snowshoes on, Alice and Eric made much better time climbing the hill through the deep snow and thick brush. When they got to the top, they saw a rickety wooden shed made of plywood. Eric checked the shed to make sure it was empty. Alice ignored it and went about preparing her hide. She already knew the shed was empty. She and Eric rolled out their gray foam sleeping pads to keep from lying directly on the snowy ground.

Her sniper hide was under a giant pine tree heavy with snow and elevated about fifty feet above the lake, which gave her a kill zone with a 200° field of view that reached out for 1,000 meters. The lake was surrounded by snow-covered trees. She was lying prone behind her rifle scope with Eric lying off to her left looking through his spotter's scope.

Alice whispered to Eric, "Pull our ponchos out of the packs and lay them over us."

"What for? Are you cold?" he asked as he grabbed his pack.

"No, but if we have to shoot, the snow on the limbs above us is going to bury us."

***

Smith and Mike were below them about seventy-five meters to their front. They were watching the closest trail that passed from north to south across the lake. They were well camouflaged, and Alice couldn't see them, but that was OK. She knew where they were anyway.

Eric broke the silence to make a confession, "Back in the chopper, when I told you to ask Mike about his wedding, I was just jerking him around. He's my best friend, so it's easy to mess with him. He's not engaged. He doesn't even have a steady girlfriend."

Alice's head turned from the scope to look in his direction. "You're such a dick. You blue falconed your best friend." She lightly kicked him in the thigh.

Eric smiled. "I was just trying to save both of you from a huge disappointment. His dick is the size of a cocktail wienie."

She giggled again. "Terrible. You guys are worse than my brothers."

"Seriously, he's a great guy. He'll mope around all butt-hurt for weeks if you leave before letting him know that you don't think he's a jerk."

***

Mike pivoted his head to look up the hill. "I wonder what they're doing up there."

Smith whispered, "Shut your hole and Oscar Mike." Oscar Mike meant to stay on mission.

Mike returned his gaze to the Commander. "Aye, aye, sir."

Then, without turning toward Mike, Smith said quietly, "If I was up there, I'd be in my bag with Alice so we could keep each other warm."

Mike snapped his head around to look back up the hill. He developed a mental picture of Eric and Alice naked, making out in the sleeping bag. Smith continued scanning the area with a devilish grin on his face.

CHAPTER 54

1545Z (0645HR AKST) HILLOCK

Alice was doing her thing, letting her scope sweep back and forth over the kill zone, when she stopped, pointing at an area to her extreme left. The area was densely tree-covered at the south end of the lake about 800 meters away. She saw a light green man-sized blob slowly move into position behind a downed tree and lie down. His white camouflage looked green through her scope. "Eric, I see someone dressed in white behind a tree on the edge of the lake about 800 meters out."

Eric noticed where her rifle was pointing and slowly redirected his spotter's scope that way. After about five minutes, he whispered, "I saw something move, but I can't tell what it is."

"It's a man. There's another one about fifty meters to his left crawling on all fours toward a tree stump. He's dragging a pack and a weapon case behind him on a strap. He's a sniper."

"I'll call the Commander," Eric said softly. "Mustang 16, this is 17."

"Go for 16," Smith responded.

"Mustang 19 has spotted two men dressed in white on the south edge of the lake about 800 meters from our location. They are trying to conceal their locations. She believes they are enemy combatants," Eric reported.

"Well done. Keep looking; there are probably four or five more. I'll alert Mustang 6."

***

"Sir, why do you think there are four or five more?" Mike asked.

"Because if I were them, I would have a seven-man boat crew waiting to provide support and lead me back to the sub," Smith explained. "Mustang 6, this is 16."

"Go ahead, Jon," Chirp responded.

"It looks like we're in the right place. Mustang 19 spotted two possible hostiles concealed on the south side of the lake. I suspect there will be four or five more hidden behind them in the trees. The sub is probably close by," Smith reported.

"Roger that; break. Mustang 26, this is 6; do you copy?" Chirp asked Rogers.

"Go for 26," Rogers replied.

"Steve, be careful as you approach Fire Team One's position. We don't want any blue on blue. Fire Team One is set up on the north side of the lake. Mustang 19 spotted two possible enemy combatants on the south end of the lake. There may be more Russians behind them in the trees."

CHAPTER 55

1545Z (0645HR AKST) ONE-HALF MILE FROM THE UNNAMED FROZEN LAKE

Darrin was sweating profusely. Wading through the knee-high snow was kicking his ass. He had unzipped his parka and removed his hat, but it wasn't enough to cool him off. I'd give my left nut for a pair of snowshoes, he thought. He checked his Garmin Rhino GPS. He and his team were about a half mile from the lake when he froze on the trail. He jerked his head skyward. He thought he heard something over the sound of the snowmobile slowly following behind him. He threw his arm up over his shoulder and gave the halt signal. He gazed up through the trees. "Eldon, did you hear that?"

"No, I didn't." Eldon also looked up.

Darrin gave the cut signal to Willie, and he killed the engine on the snowmobile. They all remained motionless, straining to hear. Then they all turned their heads to the east as they heard the sound.

Alarmed, Darrin said, "That's a Black Hawk! Our mission has been discovered! They're looking for us! We have to hurry to the lake! If we can get there, we can make it out!"

CHAPTER 56

"All stations, this is Mustang 16. Heads up. I hear a snowmobile heading toward our location," Smith transmitted. "OK, Mike, this is what we're going to do. When they come out of the trees, as soon as I confirm they're hostile, I'll initiate the ambush. I'll engage the front of their column, and you engage the rear. Our fires will meet in the middle. Try not to hit Karpinsky, but if he picks up a weapon, drop him."

"Sir, let me go out there to the edge of the trees and confront whoever is coming. We need to be dead certain who they are before we start shooting," Mike replied.

Smith thought Mike's cop was showing as he considered the recommendation. He was thinking more like a cop than a Marine. The memory of Clint's head exploding in front of him flashed through his mind. He wanted to say no, but he knew Mike was right. "Alright, Mike, but stay behind cover. Do not—I repeat, do not—expose yourself. Understood? And stay within sight of me at all times."

"Oorah, sir!" Mike jumped to his feet. He shuffled forward about twenty-five meters on his snowshoes and dropped his pack. He proned out behind a large tree stump. Five minutes later, he saw a figure cautiously emerge from the trees. He let him come closer. Next, another man appeared about five meters behind the first, and then a snowmobile towing a sled appeared about five meters behind him. The lead man was about twenty meters away when Mike shouted, "Halt, who goes there?"

The Russians froze in their tracks. They didn't know if there was one guy out there or a hundred.

The second man on the trail called out, "I'm Alaska State Trooper Darrin Logan."

Mike laughed. "Wow, Darrin, you look great! When I last saw you instructing at the Academy, you were twenty years older and fifty pounds heavier."

Immediately, the lead man, Eldon, brought his rifle up to engage Mike, but Smith put three rounds in his torso. Eldon sent his own three-round burst into the night sky as he fell backward into the snow. By the time Eldon went down, the rest of the Russians had hit the deck and were scrambling for cover in the trees. Mike didn't have a target, so he launched a grenade into the snowmobile. It exploded into flames.

***

Up on the Hillock, Alice and Eric could see muzzle flashes coming from across the lake from the two men she had previously spotted. They were firing at Mike. She immediately squeezed off a round from her M24 sniper rifle that struck the Russian sniper hiding next to the stump above his right eye, taking off the back of his head. As she predicted, the snow on the limbs above them blanketed her and Eric. Alice chambered another round and adjusted her aim fifty meters to the left. She saw the Russian under the downed tree begin quickly low-crawling away from the lake toward the trees from which he came. She took a breath, exhaled slowly, stopped, and squeezed the trigger again. Her round struck the Russian in the lower left back and exited below his right collarbone. Then, all four members of Fire Team One heard an ominous "whump, whump" sound coming from the trees on the far side of the lake.

***

Smith hit the deck and transmitted immediately, "Incoming!" two seconds before two 82mm mortar rounds exploded fifty meters short of his position. Next, he transmitted, "Team One, move to RP One!" RP stood for rally point and was a prearranged location for the team to reorganize and, more importantly, get them away from the exploding mortar rounds. They all threw on their packs and hustled through the forest to a point in the trees along the eastern edge of the lake about 100 meters closer to the Russian support team on the far side of the lake. As they hightailed it, they heard two more mortars explode behind them close to their old positions.

CHAPTER 57

1600Z (0700HR AKST)
AMANDA'S HOUSE

Dave and his merry band arrived safely at Amanda's house. They stopped in the trees about 150 feet from the house. They dismounted and walked to the attached garage. They gathered in the vacant half of the oversized three-car garage.

Amanda crept inside the house to see if her mom had discovered their absence. Her mom was still sleeping soundly in her bedroom. She checked on her little brother, Andy. He was sleeping in his bedroom in his homemade tepee. She came back out into the garage with a smile on her face. "We're good! Mom and Andy are asleep! If she caught us, I'd be grounded for a month!"

Jeff said, "I wonder what's going on? If we were under attack, we would be getting alerts on our cell phones. Whatever is happening must be a secret."

Duncan added, "The voice from the helicopter said they were the Coast Guard, but the Commander said he was in the Navy. Why is the Navy flying around in Coast Guard choppers?"

Wendy asked, "Did you notice one of them was a woman? She was tall and redheaded like a Viking."

Dave nodded. "Yeah, I did. She was carrying an M4 rifle in her hands, but she had an M24 sniper rifle with a long-range night vision scope slung across her back. I didn't know we had female snipers." He was thoroughly impressed.

Kara asked, "Amanda, can you turn on the TV and see what's on the news?"

Amanda's dad devoted one bay of the garage to his workshop and had a fifty-five-inch flat-screen TV mounted on the wall. Amanda walked over to the workbench and picked up the remote. She turned on the TV and tuned in to the Newsmax Channel. The weekend talking heads were discussing a threat by the Speaker of the House to impeach the President—again. She flipped through Fox, CNN, and the big three networks. No one was talking about Alaska. "Whatever is happening, no one has reported it yet."

"Well, I guess we better leave before your mom wakes up," Dave said to Amanda. He stepped over to Kara and they hugged goodbye. Jeff and Wendy did the same. Duncan turned to say goodbye to his friend Amanda, but she leaned in and hugged him cheek to cheek. As they separated, he smiled and squeezed her hand. He had been hoping for a closer relationship, but up until now, Amanda had kept her distance, literally and physically.

The boys trudged away from the garage and headed for their snowmobiles. Dave sat down sideways on his snowmobile's seat and said to his best friends in the world, "What do you guys want to do? We could go back to my house and play Call of Duty or hunt for rabbits like we had planned." Muffled rapid fire shots went off in the distance. They turned their heads and scanned the darkness, hoping to see something. They heard a far-off thump, thump sound and were rewarded with two flashes of light that illuminated the tree-lined horizon. Seconds later, they heard two explosions. "Or we could go see what's going on," Dave offered.

Duncan replied, "Why don't we go to the fort?" The fort was on a small piece of high ground about a mile from the coast. It wasn't very tall, but it was the highest point in the area and made an excellent observation point. Two years ago, they had built a hunting blind out of discarded plywood and two-by-fours on top of the hill and furnished it with white plastic lawn chairs. They camouflaged it with green and brown spray paint. It was about eight by twelve feet and had seats for four people.

Jeff said, "I'll go if you guys do."

Dave smiled. "Sweet!" He threw his leg over the seat and started his machine.

CHAPTER 58

Fire Team One arrived at RP One sucking air. It was only 100 meters, but between the heavy packs, snowshoes, and adrenaline, it felt more like a mile.

Smith took a deep breath and said softly, "Report!"

Alice said, "I engaged two on the far side of the lake, both KIA."

Mike reported, "I disabled their snowmobile. You dropped one. The other four Russians retreated west into the trees."

Smith transmitted, "Chirp, this is Mustang 16. We've engaged the Russians. Three KIA. Two from the support team and one from the first group with Karpinsky. They retreated west into the woods on foot. We received mortar fire from the south side of the lake and repositioned to RP One."

"Roger that. We saw the fight. We're looking for the mortar team; break. Mustang 26, this is 6," Chirp transmitted.

"This is 26; go ahead, sir," Rogers replied.

"Join up with Fire Team One at RP One," Chirp ordered.

"Wilco, we'll be at RP One in two mikes."

CHAPTER 59

1610Z (0710HR AKST)
NORTH SIDE OF THE LAKE

Darrin and his team slogged west into the trees as fast as they could. He didn't know for sure if Eldon was dead, but he couldn't go back to check. They heard the mortar rounds impacting behind them and recognized the sounds immediately. They were Russian rounds. Darrin stopped his team after they had gone about 100 meters into the trees and set up a hasty ambush in case they were followed, but no one came. He hoped the mortars found their targets.

Darrin pulled out his satellite phone and made a quick call. "Hi, Dad. I'm on my way home, but I'll have to take the long way. Please ask Mom to have breakfast ready for four." Darrin put the phone in his jacket pocket and announced to his team, "We can't go across the lake as we had planned. That helicopter probably has a FLIR camera. We'll have to go around the western edge of the lake and stay under the trees."

CHAPTER 60

Smith heard Fire Team Two approaching his position on their snowmobiles and called Rogers, "Mustang 26, this is 16. You are about 100 meters from our position. I'll have 18 come out and lead you to us."

Mike went forward out on the trail and flashed the infrared light attached to his rifle at the snow covered ground to alert Team Two to his position. They dismounted and put on their snowshoes before slogging through the snow and heavy brush. They all took a knee around Smith.

"Here's the plan," Smith said to both teams as he began drawing in the snow with his finger like they were a touch football team. "Major, take your team due south and find the highest spot you can within about 200 meters of the beach to set up an ambush. My team will follow the Russians around the western side of the lake and try to push them toward you. I don't think they have snowshoes, so they'll have a hard time going around the lake and walking to their pickup point. Karpinsky is old and out of shape. We should be able to catch up to them.

We really don't know how many Russians are out there between us and the coast, so be careful. OK, let's go."

Pope turned to Rogers and Strasburg and said with deadly calm, "Come on. Let's go kill these motherfuckers."

CHAPTER 61

Dave carefully led his crew down the trail on their snowmobiles. Their headlights lit up the trail for a couple of hundred feet.

He stopped abruptly in the trail, and Jeff yelled, "What's up?"

Dave pointed about seventy-five feet ahead of them. "There's a sled and snowmobile in front of us. You guys cover me, and I'll check it out."

Jeff and Duncan came forward and readied their rifles. They laid down in the snow behind Dave's snowmobile. Dave unslung his Ruger and slowly walked forward on the left side of the trail, careful to stay out of the beam from his snowmobile's headlights. As he got to the sled, he could see it was empty except for an open sleeping bag and four backpacks. He took a few steps further down the trail and saw the still-smoldering hulk of the red snowmobile. Sixty or so feet up the trail, Dave saw something dark blocking the trail. He brought his rifle up, ready to shoot as he slowly advanced. He pulled his flashlight from his parka's pocket and shined it on the motionless form. It was a man lying on his back with three bloody bullet holes in his chest. His dead eyes were open to the dark sky.

Dave yelled back to the others, "There's a dead guy over here!"

Jeff and Duncan joined Dave. They all shined their flashlights on the body. It was still warm, and its chest was soaked with blood, but its eyes were beginning to cloud over. They had all been to funerals and seen dead bodies, but they had never seen anyone who had been shot to death.

Jeff asked, "Do you think we should take a picture to document what happened to this guy? We don't know for sure if he's a good guy or a Russian."

Dave said, "Yeah, you're probably right."

They all pulled out their cell phones and snapped several photos. Dave bent over and retrieved the man's AR-15. It was a Smith & Wesson M&P 15 rifle. He removed the magazine and pulled the charging handle back to see if there was a round in the chamber. There was, and about twenty rounds remained in the Magpul magazine. He flipped the safety switch to SAFE with his right thumb and reseated the magazine. Dave's dad owned several AR-15s and had taught Dave how to operate them several years before. He slung his Ruger over his back and hung the AR-15 across his chest. The three amigos walked back to their snowmobiles and slowly drove past the ambush site. They drove off the trail to the base of the hill and shut off their engines.

While Dave and Jeff put their packs on, Duncan stood still and listened. He said, "Hey, guys, listen for a minute."

The other two stopped and listened.

Duncan said, "I hear the helicopter. Do you? I think it's over there to the south." He scanned the dark sky but couldn't see it. Dave and Jeff didn't hear it. All three of them put LED headlamps on their heads over their wool ski masks and turned them on. Duncan grabbed his pack, and they trudged up the hill to the fort. About twenty feet to the right of the shed, they could see the area where Alice and Eric had set up their hide under the tree.

Dave pointed and said, "Look at that tree. All of the snow is missing from the bottom branches."

They walked over to the fort and saw snowshoe prints in the snow in front of the door. Jeff opened the door, peaked in quickly, and then jumped back. No one was inside. Dave and Duncan laughed nervously and then went inside. Dave opened the two large plywood flaps in the front of the shed that served as shutters and locked them open. Next, they dropped their packs in front of the plastic chairs and sat down in relative comfort. They turned off their headlamps and waited for their eyes to adjust to the darkness. In less than an hour, the sky to the east, which was to their left, would begin to lighten.

Duncan asked, "Dave, do you have any more donuts?"

CHAPTER 62

Fire Team Two made good time on their snowmobiles. They found a spot to set up the ambush on a tree-covered rise about thirty feet above the surrounding terrain. There were no tall trees between them and the frozen shoreline 200 meters to their south, so they had an unobstructed view of the ice field that continued as far as they could see through their NODs. They left their snowmobiles and Davis's body below them, hidden in the dense brush on the east side of the rise. They grabbed their packs and equipment and lugged it all up to their position. It took a couple of trips, and they opened their parkas to keep from overheating. Being the oldest and smallest of the three, the physical labor was hardest on First Sergeant Strasburg, but he was glad he had packed the extra weapon that wasn't on Commander Smith's list.

Strasburg intended to get some payback for Allen at his first opportunity. There would be no invitations for the Russians to surrender. He was going to kill and continue killing until they were all dead or he went Winchester—meaning out of ammo. They unfolded their entrenching tools and started to improve their position by shoveling snow up in front of them to form a packed snow wall about two feet high. The wall provided concealment but no real cover. They left firing ports in the wall about six feet apart for their weapons that allowed them to cover a 90° arc from the west to the south. Next, they unrolled their gray foam sleeping pads behind the firing ports.

Major Rogers lay down in the center position and scanned the frozen coast with his M151 spotting scope. He checked his watch. Morning twilight would begin in about an hour. The sky behind them would slowly turn pink, and the sun would come up about an hour and forty minutes later. Behind him, Strasburg and Pope unpacked and got everything ready.

Strasburg asked Pope, "Nate, have you ever fired one of these things in combat?"

Strasburg could see Pope's green toothy smile through his NOD as Pope nodded. "Yeah, I got pretty good with it in Afghanistan."

They lay down behind their weapons on either side of Rogers.

The major spoke softly to his men, "I know you're probably not hungry, but we should eat something while it's still dark. Once it gets light, we might not be able to eat for quite a while. Pope, you go first and then the first sergeant."

"Roger that, sir." Pope reached back next to his thigh and opened an outside pocket on his pack to retrieve an MRE entrée.

It was frozen solid, so he opened an MRE heater and placed the entrée, shredded beef in barbecue sauce, inside the bag. Next, he pulled a thermos from his pack and poured warm water into the bag up to the line. It began to steam and sizzle. It might not make the food hot in this bitterly cold weather, but at least it wouldn't be frozen. He figured he'd let it go until it stopped heating before he would try to eat it. "Jim, catch!" Pope tossed the thermos to him.

"First Sergeant, how long have you known Sergeant Davis?" Rogers asked as he continued to scan the area through his scope.

"I met him when he was in high school. I recruited him into the Guard. He was a fine young man, and he worked hard to be an outstanding soldier. That's what he wanted most in life. He joined when he turned seventeen and convinced his mom to sign for him. She made me promise to look out for him." He paused for a moment and turned away to wipe his eyes. "I don't know if I can face her."

Rogers said to Strasburg, "Jim, I want to go with you when you talk to her."

Strasburg shook his head and wiped his eyes again. After giving Pope a five-minute head start, Strasburg began heating his entrée, Mexican-style chicken stew. Rogers, being a good young officer, would go last. His meal of choice was beef stew.

CHAPTER 63

Chief Petty Officer Hicks was manning the M240 machine gun sticking out of the open cabin door on the right side of the Jayhawk as it cruised over the trees next to the lake 300 feet above the ground at sixty knots. He had been on hundreds of rescues with the Coast Guard, but he had never been in combat or fired a shot in anger. This morning, he was freezing despite his cold-weather gear. His mouth was dry and his palms were sweating inside his gloves as he tried to squeeze the black off the dual plastic grips on his weapon. He was nervous and wanted to take a leak more than anything in the world. He scanned the trees below the helicopter through his NVGs. Before they launched from the Haley, he and his buddy, Chris Savage, had wagered a hundred bucks on which one of them would engage the enemy first. As he scanned the trees on the right side of the helicopter, he saw a bright green plume erupt from the surface.

He screamed into the ICS, "SAM! SAM! Three o'clock low!" and fired his M240 at the missile as it came up toward the helo.

SAM meant a shoulder-launched surface-to-air missile. He didn't realize it, but the weapon was actually an unguided RPG, or rocket-propelled grenade, but it was just as deadly. Many helicopters had been shot down by RPGs while flying low and slow, especially when landing or taking off. Time slowed down for Ed. The missile looked huge, and he thought they had fired it at him personally. That pissed him off.

***

After Chirp heard Hicks's warning over the ICS, he dropped the collective to put the helicopter into a dive toward the ground and banked sharply to the right toward the grenade. The grenade flew over the rotors and detonated harmlessly beyond the helo. Hicks had missed the grenade but immediately adjusted his aim on the opening in the trees where the RPG had been launched from. He sprayed two Russian soldiers standing next to a mortar tube with a long string of 7.62mm NATO rounds. One of the soldiers held an RPG launcher, and the other held an RPG round he was loading into the launcher. One of Ed's bullets struck the exposed tip of the RPG. The resulting explosion caused a fireball that temporarily shut down Hicks's NVGs. When they came back on seconds later,

Hicks only saw two bodies. If anyone else had been there, they must have scattered into the trees.

"Outstanding, Ed! Good shooting!" Chirp called out on the ICS. "I saw a mortar tube down there with the bodies."

Ed realized he didn't have to pee anymore.

Chirp transmitted, "Mustang 6 to all stations, the mortar crew engaged us with an RPG. We destroyed the mortar and killed two Russian soldiers."

CHAPTER 64

1625Z (0725HR AKST)
THE FORT

The three amigos were kicking back in their chairs munching on chocolate-covered donuts when the Coast Guard helicopter flew over them low and slow heading south. It sounded like a freight train, and the little wood shack shook as if a tornado was passing through. Snow from the trees was dumped on the roof and area surrounding the shack. As the snow cleared, they saw a red streak shoot up from the ground about a half mile south of the fort and explode high in the night sky. The sky lit up briefly, similar to a bolt of lightning, and they could see the top of the white-and-orange Coast Guard helicopter as it fell toward the ground with one of its machine guns firing red tracers. In less than three seconds, another explosion on the ground lit up the underside of the helicopter as it turned away and flew into the darkness.

Jeff exclaimed, "Holy shit! Did you see that?!"

Dave replied, "That was fucking awesome!"

Duncan choked on his donut.

CHAPTER 65

1625Z (0725HR AKST)
USCG CUTTER ALEX HALEY

Gwenn gasped and covered her mouth as she saw the RPG fly toward her husband's helicopter on the Global Hawk's video feed. The RPG attack on the Jayhawk terrified and angered her. When she heard Hicks call out, "SAM! SAM!" she stopped breathing. She imagined Tom dying right in front of her. The Russians were trying to kill her husband, and she would make them pay. She had been looking at imagery taken over the last twenty-four hours of the coast south of the Kuskokwim River Delta for hours hoping to find the Podmoskovye. She was frustrated by her lack of success. Instead of relying on I-Ball, she decided to go back to old-school methods.

Many years ago, before she met and married Tom, she had been a police officer and crime scene investigator in Pensacola. When she was searching a scene for evidence, she would try to reenact the crime in her head. This helped her figure out where to look rather than fingerprinting and photographing everything. Back then, she had pulled a suspect's fingerprints off the skin of a murder victim and recovered a suspect's DNA in a discarded Styrofoam cup. She was the queen of attention to detail. Tonight, time was running out. The sky would start to lighten at 8:15 A.M., and the sun would be up at 9:54 A.M. There was no way the Russians would leave the submarine exposed on the surface after the sun was up.

She pulled up NGA maritime safety of navigation data and determined locations along the coast where the depth would allow the Podmoskovye to come in under the ice and surface close to the shore. She analyzed imagery of the area taken on a pass ten hours earlier and found a breach about 200 feet by 50 feet where the ice had been broken apart.

She transmitted to her husband, "Mustang 6, this is Haley. I found a breach in the ice due south of where you engaged the mortar crew at 59°50'38" North and 162°06'06" West. That's where the submarine dropped off the Spetsnaz team. I'll have imagery from the most recent pass in a few minutes. If the submarine is in the area, I should be able to find it."

"Thanks for the Gwenntel. Great work!" Chirp responded.

CHAPTER 66

1625Z (0725HR AKST)
NORTHWEST SIDE OF THE LAKE

George Schoonover was sleeping soundly in his tent when he heard the familiar sound of automatic weapons fire and an explosion. His eyes sprang open in the dark, and he was instantly alert. He sat up in his sleeping bag. At first, he thought he might have been having a nightmare, but he didn't remember a dream, just the sounds. He shook his wife. "Anne, wake up! We have to get out of here!"

"What? What's wrong?" She flipped on the battery-powered lantern.

"We have to go! We're under attack!" He was near panic.

"What are you talking about? Did you have another bad dream?"

Then they both heard two loud explosions.

"Oh my God! What was that?"

"Mortars! Get dressed! We gotta go!" He had slept in his clothes and was already putting on his boots. He threw on his parka and hat. He turned on his headlamp and ran out of the tent. "Hurry up!" Anne dressed quickly and began helping him tear down their camp. The machine guns and mortar explosions were very familiar to George. He had been a medic in the Army for six years and deployed to Iraq for a year during OIF II. After his Army enlistment was up, he used the Post-9/11 GI Bill to go to college. Now he had a successful dentistry practice in Bethel.

George didn't know what was going on, but he had to get his wife away from the area. They had spent the day driving around on the frozen lake and through the brush in their new Sherp amphibious ATV. The vehicle was a little over eleven feet long, eight feet wide, eight feet high, and had four five-foot-tall ultra-low-pressure tires. The tires had ridges like paddles that enabled the Sherp to run across water, mud, snow, sand, or dirt. It could run on three or even two tires, and it could carry 2,200 pounds while traveling at 25 MPH on ground or 4 MPH on the water.

The night got quiet again and George calmed down some, but not enough to stay there. He wouldn't feel safe until he got back to their home in Bethel.

***

Darrin's team had trekked across the north side of the lake, and Karpinsky was running out of steam. The three soldiers were walking single file in front of the old man to blaze a trail through the snow to make it easier on him. Pretty soon they would have to carry him. He couldn't be left behind. He was the mission. Darrin stopped and held up the hold sign. About fifty meters to his front, he could see lights and hear a diesel engine running. He and his team formed up on line and approached carefully. They saw a man and woman scrambling back and forth loading gear into the back of a Sherp. Darrin smiled because the Sherp was a Russian vehicle, and he and his men had used them before. The man in the camp had a shotgun slung across his back. Darrin signaled to the twins, James and Willie, and the three of them stepped in unison to assault the camp.

George saw the men coming out of the brush and tried to bring his shotgun into action, but James shot him twice in the chest and then again in the face as he lay helpless in the snow. James rolled the body over to free the shotgun. It was a 12-gauge Mossberg 590. He slung it over his shoulder. Willie hurried past James and shot the woman in the back as she ran for the trees. After she fell, he walked over to her and shot her in the back of the head. Darrin headed to the back of the Sherp and swept the interior with his rifle to make sure no one was inside. He grabbed the large red nylon tent bag by the straps, pulled it out, and dropped it on the snow. James took the driver's seat, and the other three climbed aboard through the rear hatch. James performed a zero-degree turn and accelerated out onto the frozen lake headed south at 20 MPH.

Darrin pulled out his sat phone and called Dad again. "Good news, we caught a ride. We'll be home in about five minutes."

***

On board the Podmoskovye, Captain Vyacheslav reluctantly gave the order to surface and told his first officer to alert the landing party to be ready to disembark immediately on his order. Thirty sailors from his crew had been outfitted for ground combat. They wore white camouflage over their cold-weather gear and were armed with every rifle available from the boat's armory. The sailors didn't have enough white camouflage smocks and trousers for everyone, so they had made their own out of bedsheets. Using his sailors as provisional infantry was highly irregular, even for the crew of a special operations sub. They were supposed to deliver the special operators, not be the special operators.

He had delivered two Spetsnaz teams almost twelve hours ago: one for the recovery of Karpinsky and one to provide support. Now both teams had been shot to hell, and he doubted any of them would make it back. This mission had suddenly turned into what the Americans call a Goat Fuck. He was responsible for his boat and crew, and under normal circumstances, he wouldn't risk them for two Spetsnaz teams. These super soldiers could melt into the American populace and make their way home on their own within a week or two. They were trained for that possibility. He would've already set course for home if it had been up to him, but President Pichugin had contacted him personally and ordered him not to leave without Colonel Karpinsky. If the mission failed, he wasn't worried about being court-martialed; he was worried about being planted in an unmarked grave in the Khimki Forest outside of Moscow. Right now, he felt safer in Alaska than back home.

CHAPTER 67

Even humping their packs, Smith and his team were making good time with their snowshoes. They had passed the dead Russian and disabled snowmobile ten minutes ago. Smith didn't know the three young sightseers were sitting above them in their plywood fort. Likewise, Dave and his crew didn't see or hear Smith's team when they passed below in pursuit of the Russians. Now, Fire Team One was having no trouble following the trail Darrin and his group left in the knee-deep snow. Smith's team was spread out along the trail with about five meters between each of them. Mike was on point, followed by Smith, and then York. Eric brought up the rear.

Smith transmitted so Eric and Alice could also hear him, "Mike, we're getting close to them. Be careful. They may have left behind another straggler."

Mike replied, "Roger that. Hey, I think I hear engine noise." He ran forward as best as he could in his snowshoes along the trail. In fifty meters, the brush and trees opened up to a clearing as he emerged on the west side of the frozen lake. He saw large tire tracks in the snow leading across the western edge of the lake. Then he glimpsed a dark truck or ATV with giant tires disappear into the trees on the other side of the lake about 300 meters away before he could get a shot. Commander Smith appeared at his side with his weapon up, ready to shoot.

Mike said to Smith, "It looks like they caught a ride. They have some kind of all-terrain vehicle big enough for six to eight people."

Alice called out, "Hey, there's a body over here," as she turned to her left and pointed her weapon light at the body lying face down in the snow.

Smith yelled out, "Don't touch it! It might be booby-trapped. Back away and let me check it out. Get behind a tree or something just in case."

Smith dropped his pack and took off his snowshoes. He got down on all fours and approached the body slowly as he probed the snow in front of him with his gloved hand. He didn't find anything. Next, he lay down next to the body and reached over and grabbed its far shoulder and pulled it over toward him to expose anything underneath. It was an old combat trick to put a grenade or mine under a body to try to kill or maim your enemies, but this time, there were no tricks. The body had been shot twice in the chest and once in the head. It was still warm.

Smith found the victim's wallet in his back pocket and pulled out his driver's license. "His name is George Schoonover, and his address is in Bethel. Those assholes must have carjacked him."

Eric said, "There's a dead woman over there at the edge of the clearing. She didn't have any ID. I wonder what they were doing out here?"

Mike replied, "By the looks of the ground, they were camping out."

Smith keyed his radio, "Chirp, this is 16."

"Go ahead, Jon," Tom replied.

"We are on the northwest side of the lake. We found two bodies in the snow, a man and a woman; both were killed minutes ago. It looks like the Russians stole a large ATV from them. It was big enough to carry all of them. Mike saw it disappear on the far side of the lake headed for the beach," Smith said.

Tom responded, "Roger that. We'll come pick you up; break. Six to 26, do you copy?"

"Go for 26," Rogers replied.

"Steve, they killed two more civilians and stole a large ATV from them. They should be heading in your direction. You have a green light on the ATV," Tom advised.

***

Rogers replied, "Yes, sir, green light." Rogers spoke softly to his men, "Get ready. They could pop out of the trees any second."

Strasburg loaded an M433 HEDP round into his M203A2. The M433 was a 40x46mm high-explosive dual-purpose round suitable for use against personnel and vehicles. It was capable of penetrating 50mm or two inches of steel armor with an effective range of 350 meters. Strasburg could load and fire seven a minute. Pope had already loaded his M249 SAW with a fresh 200-round box.

Pope held his right fist up over Rogers's back and said to Strasburg, "Let's get some."

Strasburg brought his left arm up, gave Pope a fist bump, and said flatly, "Kill 'em all." He was somber but also grimly determined. He wouldn't be satisfied until he killed a lot of Russians.

Rogers jumped up to his knees. "Shit, where are my earplugs?" as he started checking his pockets. He found them, hastily stuffed them in his ears, and lay back down. He would suffer some serious hearing damage without them after the shooting started. His ears were still ringing from the first firefight.

CHAPTER 68

1640Z (0740HR AKST)
NORTHWEST EDGE OF THE LAKE

Chirp called for the landing checklist.

Taco had the checklist open in his left hand, but he responded from memory, "Tail wheel switch locked, parking brake off, crew, passengers, and mission equipment check," and held his right hand up in front of the center of the instrument panel to give Chirp a thumbs-up.

Chirp executed a no-hover landing to the edge of the snow-covered frozen lake. Hicks swept the area with his door gun to cover Fire Team One as they approached the helo. They hustled out of the brush and clambered aboard with their snowshoes still on. Chirp called for the takeoff checklist.

Taco responded from memory again, "Engine power control levers to fly, systems check, avionics set, crew, passengers, and mission equipment check."

Hicks confirmed they were set in back.

Chirp pressed the ICS switch at the top of the cyclic with his right index finger. "Coming up and left," he informed the crew as he smoothly raised the collective.

Taco turned his head to the left and gave Chirp another thumbs-up as he heard Savage call out, "Clear left," from the port gunner's window.

CHAPTER 69

Fire Team Two was scanning the massive ice field to their front and the tree line to their right. They expected the ATV to come out of the trees any time. Seconds later, a thunderous cracking sound coming from far out in the frozen delta startled them. Pope jerked his head to the left. "What the fuck was that?" About 1,500 meters from the beach, the BS-64 Podmoskovye's conning tower broke through the thick ice field and slowly emerged above the surface followed by the sail and top ten feet of the 547-foot-long hull. It sat broadside to their view. They were momentarily stunned by its incredible size.

Major Rogers quickly recovered from his stupor and transmitted, "All stations, this is Mustang 26. The Russian submarine just surfaced about a klick and a half south of my position!"

Seconds later, Rogers and his team heard a diesel engine accelerating, and he saw a bright green glow shining through the edge of the trees in his scope about 200 meters away to his right. The Sherp with its headlights on burst out of the trees like an NFL fullback hitting a seam in the line of scrimmage and accelerated to its top speed of 25 MPH. It continued due south across the beach, onto the frozen Kuskokwim Delta, and headed straight for the sub.

Pope reacted first. He swung his SAW to the right and squeezed the trigger. Every fifth round he fired was a red tracer, and with the bipod extended, he was able to swiftly adjust his aim to put rounds on target. He fired rapid bursts into the left side of the Sherp, flattening its left-side tires. The Sherp abruptly lurched to a stop.

***

Inside the Sherp, the window next to James erupted from the impact of a string of bullets. He was killed instantly. Darrin and Willie jumped to their feet in the cramped cabin and tried frantically to pull James out of the driver's seat.

***

Strasburg sat up on his knees and fired three grenades from his M203 within fourteen seconds. He didn't bother aiming with the sights. With the target this close, he just eyeballed it. In training, he had put grenades through a passenger car window at 200 meters. The first round landed about ten feet long, which sprayed the right side of the ATV with shrapnel and flattened the right-side tires.

***

Willie screamed out in pain as searing hot metal shards came through the thin sheet metal wall and entered the right side of his body from his shoulder down to his knee. Darrin quickly decided to abandon James's body. He kicked the rear hatch open and yelled to Karpinsky to get out as he pushed him through the hatch onto the snow. A second grenade landed short and was ineffective. Darrin pulled Willie to the hatch, rolled him out, and then jumped after him. A third grenade round landed in front of the Sherp, blowing out the windshield and further damaging James's corpse.

Darrin thrust Willie's rifle at him and yelled, "Take your rifle! I can't carry you! I have to get the old man to the sub! You must stay here and cover us!"

Willie grimaced in pain and yelled back, "I understand! Get him out of here! Make this fiasco count for something!"

Darrin grabbed Karpinsky's arm and started pulling him toward the sub. Willie crawled behind the right rear tire and began returning fire on the line of tracer rounds. The machine gunner on the hill immediately adjusted his fire, and Willie watched in horror as the red hose of death zeroed in on him at the rear of the Sherp.

***

Standing at the bottom of the ladder inside the Podmoskovye waiting for the order to disembark, Lieutenant Yaroslav Saveli said to his friend, Lieutenant Maks Yakov, "So, I guess we're really doing this?"

Maks smiled. "Think about what a great story this will be when you tell it to your grandchildren."

Captain Vyacheslav had ordered them to lead the landing party of provisional infantry. It was an easy decision for the captain. The two young lieutenants weren't members of his crew or trained submariners, so they were expendable.

The order to disembark came, and Maks yelled to the sailors lined up behind him, "Follow me!" as he scrambled up the ladder to the hatch. Russian sailors wearing baggy white camouflage armed with rifles began pouring from hatches on the hull of the sub fore and aft of the sail like angry ants from a kicked-over anthill. They lowered flexible metal ladders down the side of the hull and began descending onto the ice. Four sailors quickly began setting up a mortar tube about fifty meters from the hull, and four others started setting up a Dushka heavy machine gun about thirty meters to the left of the mortar. The remaining twenty-two sailors, armed with rifles and led by the two young lieutenants, ran forward through the snow to assist Darrin and Karpinsky, who were still over a kilometer away.

***

Rogers keyed his radio. "Mustang 6, this is 26. A platoon-sized element has emerged from the sub. They are setting up a mortar and heavy machine gun about fifty meters from the sub. Request immediate air support."

Chirp acknowledged, "Roger that, Steve; we're inbound."

***

Chirp turned toward the sub from two miles to the west. He set his rad alt bug to fifty feet above the ice, dropped dangerously low to that altitude, and accelerated to 150 knots.

Chirp called out to the crew on the ICS, "Taco, we're going in low on the attack, so watch my altitude! Don't let me get below fifty feet! If I do, start pulling up on the collective! Ed and Chris, be ready to fire! You are weapons free!"

Taco, Ed, and Chris responded one after another.

Chirp told them, "I'll flank the sub while its crew's focuses on Team Two." Next, he advised Commander Smith to have his team prepared to dismount. "After our gun run, I'll set down next to the ATV. Check to see if Karpinsky is inside."

Smith acknowledged him and yelled to his team to get ready.

***

Up on the hill, Pope stood up and left his SAW on the snow. He grabbed the Javelin anti-tank system that he and Strasburg had worked so hard to drag up the hill. The FGM-148 Javelin was loaded with a fire-and-forget missile. The system weighed just under fifty pounds, was about four feet long, and consisted of a launcher, a detachable command launch unit (CLU), and a missile. The missile was about five inches in diameter, forty-three inches long, and weighed about 18.5 pounds. Its tandem-shaped, charge high-explosive anti-tank, or HEAT, warhead could penetrate over twenty-four inches of rolled homogeneous armor.

They had carried two extra missiles along for it. Strasburg would have brought more, but three was all he had in the armory. He came from the school of it's better to have it and not need it than to need it and not have it. The Javelin could be fired in curveball or fastball mode. Curveball mode was for top attacks on light tank armor or bunkers. The missile would climb up to 500 feet before diving on the top of the target. Fastball mode was for direct attacks, and this was what Pope would use. He dropped to one knee, hefted the Javelin onto his shoulder, and looked through the thermal sight. He made a conscious decision to aim for the sub and not the mortar and machine gun crews. They were small and easy to miss. He aimed at the base of the sail below the dive plane and launched the missile. It climbed about forty feet and then flew straight and true. It exploded on the sail a couple of feet above the intersection with the hull.

***

In the control room of the Podmoskovye, Captain Vyacheslav was watching the thermal image of the battlefield provided by the periscope extended above the sail. When he saw the initial plume of the Javelin missile being kicked out of the launch tube, at first he thought it was a mortar round exploding on the hill, but then the missile's motor fired and it accelerated right for him. It got bigger and bigger. He was overwhelmed initially but recovered in time to grab the intercom handset and alert his crew, "Brace for impact!" a second before the shock wave from the explosion overhead knocked him off his feet. He heard screams coming from above through the open hatch. A sailor fell through the opening and landed on the deck next to him. He was sickened by the sailor's smoldering black and red condition. He didn't recognize him. His right leg was missing. "Get this man to sick bay!"

***

Back on the hill, Rogers yelled out, "Great shot, Sergeant! The missile exploded near the bottom of the sail. Put the next one into the conning tower where the observers are posted!"

Pope and Strasburg were loading the second missile in the launcher when they heard a far-off whump sound followed by a screeching whistle that got louder and louder. It sounded like the air was being ripped apart. Seconds later, a mortar round exploded thirty feet in front of them. Pope yelled out in pain as he was knocked off his feet by the shrapnel that peppered his left arm and shoulder. His massive frame had shielded Strasburg. Rogers was still safely on the ground with his spotting scope, so he remained uninjured.

Fortunately for Team Two, the first mortar round launched by the Russians had driven the mortar's baseplate down through the unevenly packed snow, and now it sat tilted down to the left, which in turn had aimed the tube way off to the left of their intended target. The Russians couldn't fire a follow-up shot. They had to disassemble the heavy mortar and move it to another relatively level spot on the snow-covered ice.

Strasburg yelled to Pope, "Nate, stay down and man the SAW. I'll handle the Javelin."

Strasburg selected the curveball mode, aimed the Javelin, and prepared to fire their second missile.

Rogers yelled, "Hold your fire! Mustang 6 is approaching from the west!"

Five seconds later, the Jayhawk flew down the starboard side of the sub about ten feet above the top of the conning tower at ninety knots. Tom's instincts were to fly as fast as he could at around 150 knots, but he knew the slower he flew, the more likely his gunners were to hit their targets. Hicks hosed down the Russians manning the tower from his starboard door with his belt-fed M240 machine gun as Savage concentrated his fire from the port side at the Russians manning the mortar and heavy machine gun.

As the Jayhawk flew past the tower, Hicks was within seventy-five feet of his targets. The Russians ducked for cover immediately, but Hicks's rounds ricocheted around the inside of the tower until they hit something soft. Abeam the fantail, Chirp wrapped the Jayhawk into a tight-level decelerating right 180° turn and flew back to the northwest so Hicks could continue his attack on the conning tower. After passing the tower, Chirp banked hard right again to turn north and headed for the rear of the dismounted infantry on the ice. Hicks and Savage targeted individual sailors as they flew over heading for the beach.

"Chirp, we just took some AK hits in the bottom of the helo!" Chris reported.

Taco checked the gauges. "Indications are all normal."

Chirp was way too close to the ice to look inside and check the instruments for himself. The Jayhawk was equipped with self-sealing fuel tanks behind the passenger cabin, so hopefully any rounds that hit the tanks wouldn't cause a fire or catastrophic leak.

***

On the ice, Darrin could see the stream of red tracers raining down from the Jayhawk as it turned north and headed straight for him and the old man. He yelled to Karpinsky, "Lie down and play dead!" Darrin did like the old man and proned out in the snow in an unnatural position. Seconds later, the Jayhawk flew directly over them barely fifty feet from the snow. He knew better than to try to shoot it down. He was happy to let it fly by. Once they were clear,

Darrin got up and helped Karpinsky to his feet. They trudged on toward the submarine.

***

Chirp landed fifty feet north of the Sherp. Fire Team One dismounted and ran forward to use it for cover. Alice left her M24 rifle in the helo and opted for the Barrett M82 due to its extended range and heavier .50 cal BMG round. The Russian Spetsnaz sergeant, Willie, was lying dead facedown next to the right rear tire. He had been riddled with rounds from Pope's SAW.

Mike checked the interior of the Sherp and called out to the team, "The driver's dead. No sign of Karpinsky."

Smith reported to Chirp that Karpinsky was not in the Sherp. York dropped her pack and M4 in the snow. Swiftly, she hefted the massive Barrett M82 rifle up over the side and onto the roof of the Sherp. She scaled the side of the vehicle and proned out on the eight-foot-wide hardtop. She lowered the bipod legs to give the Barrett more stability and pushed it out in front of her. She surveyed the scene with the rifle's night vision scope. She was looking for Karpinsky but would settle for any Russian. She observed a Russian sailor over 600 meters out get up and make a run for the sub. She squeezed the trigger, and green blood and tissue erupted from the sailor's torso. He staggered forward a couple of steps before he realized he was dead and collapsed in the snow. The blast from the muzzle was momentarily deafening, and the shock wave swept over Alice's face. She employed the Barrett in Afghanistan but never got used to the massive force it generated.

Eric followed Alice up to the roof. He proned out to her left with his M249 SAW and M151 sniper spotting scope. He was about to rotate his NOD up out of the way to use the spotting scope when he saw movement on the snow to his ten o'clock position about twenty feet from the Sherp. Two ambitious Russians armed with rifles were scanning for targets as they silently crept forward. They didn't have night vision devices and were relying on ambient light. They were temporarily blinded by the muzzle flash from Alice's Barrett shot. Eric swung his left hand back to his holster and drew his Sig Sauer M17. He shot each sailor once in the chest and followed up with six more. He stopped firing when Mike rushed forward firing his own rapid rifle bursts into the now motionless invaders.

Both sailors were wearing white balaclavas, and one was lying face up. He had been shot in the face several times. His mask was soaked in blood that appeared dark green through their NODs.

As Mike stood over them making sure they were dead, Eric yelled down from the roof, "Hey Mike, take his mask off!"

Mike yelled back, "Fuck you! I know what it looks like!"

***

Darrin had a death grip on the faltering Karpinsky's jacket and was pulling him forward through the snow when they linked up with the Russian ad hoc naval infantry about a kilometer from the sub.

Darrin saw them through his commercial NVGs. He could see they were in disarray from the helicopter attack and the missile that was fired over their heads into the sub. He yelled out to them and identified himself in Russian. He told them to hold their fire and that he had Colonel Karpinsky with him.

Darrin called out, "Who is in charge here?"

A young sailor lying in the snow at his feet said anxiously, "Sir, the lieutenant is dead! No one is in charge!"

Darrin surveyed the scene as green and red tracer rounds zipped back and forth over his head. He could see the able-bodied sailors hiding in the snow among the dead. He realized these sailors were not accustomed to ground combat. They were superbly trained to accomplish their assigned duties aboard the nuclear-powered submarine, but now they were totally unprepared and ill-equipped for this mission. Darrin grabbed two of the terrified sailors by their white smocks and pulled them to their feet and said, "This man is Colonel Karpinsky. Guard him with your lives and escort him back to the sub."

They were eager to comply—anything to get off this killing field.

Darrin yelled out to the remaining ten able-bodied sailors, "I am in command. Get on your feet." He grabbed each sailor individually by the parka and guided them to their new fighting positions. He had the cold, frightened men prone out in a line about three meters from each other facing north toward the Americans. Darrin didn't tell them, but he intended to sacrifice them and himself to give Karpinsky and the sub time to escape. He walked back and forth in front of his men and instructed them, "Conserve your ammunition and fire well-aimed shots as targets expose themselves."

His calm professional demeanor helped stiffen their resolve. He turned around, unzipped his fly, and, facing the Americans, began to urinate in a line parallel to his new defensive position. He confidently bellowed, "The Americans will not cross this line!" The sailors who could see him laughed nervously. They weren't sure if he was the bravest man in the world or just fucking nuts. Mixed in with the erratic heavy-metal cacophony swirling around him, Darrin heard a muffled thump in the distance. As he continued to empty his bladder, he looked up to the dark, starlit sky through the green tubes of his NVGs. At the last moment of its flight, he saw a 40mm grenade come arcing down from the darkness like a small spiraling can of corn heading right at him.

He muttered, "Well, shit," in English right before he exploded.

The two sailors closest to Darrin were splattered with his warm goo. They both screamed hysterically, jumped to their feet, and emptied their magazines into the darkness as they turned and ran back toward the sub. The others followed immediately.

***

Three hundred meters north, as Mike saw the green explosion through his NOD, he yelled out, "Guess who, motherfucker!" He was about to turn and brag to Eric about his excellent grenade shot when one of the Russians' rounds grazed his right calf, and he screamed out in pain, "Fuck, I'm hit!" as he fell to the snow.

Eric, in fear for his friend, immediately jumped off the left side of the Sherp; he and Smith dragged Mike to cover behind it.

Eric looked him over but didn't see any wounds. He yelled, "Where are you hit?"

Mike pointed. "My right leg!"

Eric pulled his EMT shears from his trauma kit and began cutting through Mike's Gortex extreme cold-weather trouser leg, OCP uniform trouser leg, and thermal underwear to inspect the wound. The bullet had plowed a clean furrow about half an inch wide and two inches long across the outside of Mike's right calf. Eric was relieved. The wound was superficial, but to Mike, it burned like hell, and he writhed in pain.

Eric said curtly, "Lie still, pussy! You're a fucking Marine! Besides, girls like scars. They think they're sexy."

Mike stopped wriggling around and propped himself up on his elbows. He looked up to the top of the Sherp. "Really? All girls?"

Alice stuck her head over the side of the roof and said with a smile, "Yeah, all of us."

Eric said, "I think I have a Hello Kitty Band-Aid in my kit somewhere," partly to tease Mike, but mostly to reassure him that his wound wasn't serious. Eric opened a package of QuikClot Combat Gauze to stop the bleeding. He bandaged the wound and then stuck the Hello Kitty Band-Aid on top of the bandage. Then he used 100-MPH tape to close up Mike's trouser leg. It was super strong military OD green duct tape. It was used for many purposes, including to prepare sling loads under helicopters.

Next, he gave Mike an injection of ketamine. "OK, Devil Dog, stop malingering and get back in the fight." The ketamine allowed Mike to regain his focus. The wound still hurt, but the horse tranquilizer helped him not give a shit that it hurt.

***

Up on the hillock, Strasburg viewed the thermal image of the submarine's smoldering sail through the CLU and launched the second missile in curveball mode. It climbed to 500 feet and flew fast and true. It dove on top of the conning tower where the remaining Russian officers were trying to direct the actions of their sailors and exploded. The executive officer's burning carcass cartwheeled out and away from the tower, landing in the snow.

That's for, Allen! You bastards, Strasburg thought.

***

Inside the sub, damage control teams were assessing the damage from the first missile when the second missile exploded and killed several of them. Captain Vyacheslav was still in the control room trying to maintain his composure and determine if he could submerge the boat with the damage from the first missile when the second missile hit. He turned to look at the thermal image from outside, but the signal was gone. The periscope had been damaged by the explosion.

***

Karpinsky was gasping for air and nearing collapse when he and his escort reached the sub. As he struggled to climb the flexible metal ladder attached to the hull, the Javelin exploded above him. He flinched and looked up in time to see the XO's flaming husk fall to the snow on his right. Two junior officers crouching at the top of the ladder quickly grabbed him by the arms and began leading him hunched over to the aft hatch. Inexplicably, Karpinsky pulled away from them and stood erect. He had an overpowering urge to turn around and look back north into the darkness. As he did, he saw a small flash of light in the distance and received Alice's telepathic Fuck you! message.

He shouted, "Bitch!" in Russian right before the massive .50 cal BMG round hit him below his nose. The top of his head disintegrated. His limp body collapsed to the slick deck, slid down the side of the hull, and disappeared into a gap between the hull and the ice.

***

Eric said, "Good shot, Alice."

"That was odd," Alice said dryly.

"What was odd?"

"Well, he was supposed to be psychic, right? You'd think he'd have seen that coming."

Eric let out a short laugh and yelled down to Commander Smith, "Sir, Alice just shwacked Karpinsky right before he could climb down in the sub!"

Smith yelled back, "Are you sure it was Karpinsky?"

Alice said emphatically, "Affirmative!"

Smith transmitted, "Chirp, this is Mustang 16."

Chirp replied, "Go ahead, Jon."

Smith continued, "Sir, Alice confirms she engaged Karpinsky as he was boarding the submarine. He's dead."

Chirp replied, "Understood, Jon. I'm going to attempt to contact the sub's captain. Well done, Alice."

***

One of the Russian lieutenants who had been helping Karpinsky on the deck dropped through the hatch and rushed into the control room.

He yelled, "Captain! Colonel Karpinsky and the first officer are dead! The damage is extensive! There are two holes in the sail! We can't close the hatches! We can't submerge!"

***

Chirp asked Taco to switch to the International Maritime Distress Channel 16, 156.8-megahertz (MHz) on the very-high frequency (VHF) radio. Channel 16 was reserved for emergencies. It was not encrypted, so the Russians would be able to hear him, but so would anyone else who happened to be listening.

Chirp transmitted, "BS-64 Podmoskovye captain, this is the American military forces commander on Channel 16. Respond immediately or your vessel will be destroyed."

"This is Captain Vyacheslav of the Podmoskovye. Go ahead, Commander," he replied instantly.

"Captain, surrender your boat immediately, and you and your men will be treated humanely. If you do not, we will consider you war criminals and send you to the bottom. The next salvo of missiles will come to your bridge," Chirp advised. This was a huge exaggeration considering he only had one Javelin left.

***

Vyacheslav looked around the smoke-filled control room at his men. They met his gaze with a mixture of fear and frustration: fear for what the future might bring and frustration for being put in an impossible position by an arrogant ass of a politician back home. They were bright young men, the best Russia had to offer. He refused to allow their lives to be squandered by an idiot 7,000 kilometers away in Moscow. He had already lost over thirty of his men on this fool's errand. He refused to lose any more, and he also needed to buy more time.

Vyacheslav transmitted, "Commander, if I have your word my men will not be mistreated, I surrender my ship and crew to you."

Chirp replied, "Captain, you have my word. You have five minutes to muster your crew on the deck aft of the sail and prepare to be processed as prisoners. Any tricks will be dealt with severely." Chirp said to Taco, "Switch back to FM."

Taco switched the radios and gave Chirp a thumbs-up.

Chirp transmitted, "All stations, the Podmoskovye has surrendered. Mustang 26, ask First Sergeant Strasburg to give Commander Smith a ride to the sub to accept the surrender from the captain. Everyone else, maintain your positions and be prepared to resume the attack on my command."

Strasburg jumped to his feet and threw on his pack. He stepped into his snowshoes and hustled down the backside of the hill to the snowmobiles. He passed the first snowmobile but stopped for a moment next to Allen's body in the sled.

He took a knee, placed his gloved hand on the poncho covering him, and spoke softly, "We got them, Allen. We fucked them up real good." He started the other snowmobile, raced around the hill, and headed straight for the Sherp. In two minutes, he pulled up next to Team One.

Smith climbed aboard behind him, tapped him on the shoulder, and yelled, "Let's go before they change their minds!"

Strasburg nodded and opened up the throttle. Smith grabbed him to keep from falling off as they sped away toward the sub. It took three minutes to get to the sub. Strasburg had to keep slowing down to weave between the dead sailors scattered across the ice. When they arrived at the bottom of the aft ladder, Captain Vyacheslav had his crew standing in formation aft of the sail as ordered. Strasburg covered Smith as he scaled the ladder, and then Smith did the same for Strasburg. Captain Vyacheslav saluted as Smith approached.

Smith returned the salute. "I am Commander Smith, United States Navy. My commander, Colonel Adams, sends his compliments and thanks you for agreeing to cease any further hostilities."

"I am Captain Vyacheslav. As ordered, my crew is ready for processing, but I must report, my second officer is unaccounted for."

Smith's demeanor changed immediately, and he keyed his radio. "All stations, the captain of the Podmoskovye is reporting one officer unaccounted for. He could be below deck attempting to scuttle the boat. We need to get more people out here to guard the crew while we search the sub."

***

The second officer heard everything that was being said. He was above them, proned out on the rear of the observation deck armed with a rifle. He aimed his rifle over the rounded edge of the steel hull as best he could to get a shot at the Americans.

***

Everyone on the sub, except the second officer, flinched as they heard a supersonic smack overhead and then a gunshot from over 1,300 meters away. A rifle fell to the deck at Smith's feet.

Smith heard Alice transmit, "Now he's accounted for. All clear."

***

As Eric lay next to her looking through his scope, he said, "How in the hell did you hit him? I couldn't even see him."

CHAPTER 70

1710Z (0810HR AKST)
THE FORT

Dave and his crew had a front-row seat to the most incredible fireworks show they had ever seen during their short lives. Red American tracers had flown south and west in front of them, while green Russian tracers had flown north and east. Then a missile had been launched from a small rise to their south toward the ocean and detonated. In the flash of the explosion, they saw the massive submarine. It must have been an enemy sub. Next, the Jayhawk helicopter flew in and attacked the submarine. The boys couldn't see the sub, but they saw the rounds bouncing off the hull. A couple of minutes later, another missile was launched, but this one climbed high in the sky before dropping on top of the submarine. Again, the explosion exposed the submarine, and the three amigos could see it for a couple of seconds before it disappeared back into the darkness.

CHAPTER 71

The sky would begin to lighten in five minutes, but the sun wouldn't actually be up for another hour and forty-four minutes. This was the period when the sun was still below the horizon but was beginning to bounce light off the atmosphere onto the ground. Aviators called it pinky time. Soon it would be too bright to wear the NVGs. Chirp had set up an irregular orbit at 300 feet AGL about 1,500 meters north of the sub just in case Smith and Strasburg needed help.

Taco keyed his ICS with his foot switch. "Chirp, a flight of four A-10s from Eielson AFB is two mikes inbound from the east, callsign Hawg 44."

"Sweet. Dial them up," Chirp replied.

Taco's right hand drifted to the center console between their seats, switched radios, and gave Chirp a thumbs-up.

Chirp transmitted, "Hawg 44, this is Mustang 6, do you copy?"

A seductive reply came back immediately, "Yes, sir. Go for Hawg 44."

Chirp transmitted, "44, I have accepted the Russian submarine commander's surrender, and two of my people are on the sub guarding the crew. Would you please conduct a low flyby to reinforce my team and encourage the Russians' continued cooperation?"

***

The young female USAF captain, Alexis Acevedo, callsign Ace, responded, "Yes, sir! With pleasure!"

Ace switched to her FM radio and transmitted to her flight, "Gumby and Blinky, stay up here and cover us. Booger and I will make a low pass." She was referring to her wingman, Captain Martin Bolger, callsign Booger. "Booger, follow me!" she called as she rolled inverted to dive from 5,000 feet AGL down to 100 feet AGL. Her section of two Warthogs flew over the Podmoskovye about thirty feet above the conning tower at 350 knots and then banked left to orbit south of the sub. The flyby had the desired effect. It startled and intimidated Vyacheslav's crew, but they were disciplined and remained in formation on the deck.

***

Taco keyed his ICS foot switch again. "Chirp, a flight of three C-17s, callsign Husky 12, is inbound in five mikes with 300 Rangers. They're going to drop them on the ice between the beach and the sub. I told them the show's over, but they are going to jump anyway."

Chirp replied, "That works for me. As soon as they're on the deck and ready, we'll hand this fucking mess off to them and they can babysit the prisoners until somebody decides what to do with them. Besides, we need to fly our causalities back to the hospital in Bethel while we still have enough fuel."

CHAPTER 72

Husky 12 flew over the ice flow from east to west at 1,250 feet AGL and 120 knots followed in trail by his two wingmen. Inside the cargo area of Husky 12, two Air Force loadmasters wearing gray flight helmets and parachutes were preparing for airborne operations. They slid the jump doors up out of the way, locked them in place, and leaned out of the doorways to make sure it was safe for the soldiers to jump. Once satisfied, they stepped back out of the way.

The Ranger Jumpmasters had their Rangers on their feet and lined up ready to file out the doors on either side of the plane. As they stood in line, each jumper checked the parachute of the jumper in front of him and patted him on the shoulder to let him know he was good to go. The jumpmasters anxiously waited for the disembarkation lights to turn green. Finally, it happened, and the jumpmasters yelled, "Go!"

Lieutenant Colonel Dragon stepped out into the cold, pre-dawn sky followed by his men. Their parachutes were attached to the aircraft by static lines, and they opened immediately after the jumpers exited the aircraft. Dragon hit the snow-covered ice forty-five seconds after jumping. Within three minutes, 300 Rangers were on the ice looking for someone to kill. Dragon and his battalion staff landed right in the middle of the cluster of dead Russian sailors where Darrin had made his last stand. Dragon sat down on his pack and strapped on his snowshoes.

He yelled to his executive officer, Major Henry Henderson, over the roar of the C-17s flying overhead, "Sasquatch, let's stage our packs right here. I'm going to take Sergeant Mendoza and Corporal Franks to the sub with me. Stay here and organize the companies. Oh, and make sure all these assholes are really dead. I don't want any of our boys getting shot in the back by a dead Russian."

"Yes, sir, will do!" Henderson yelled back.

***

About three hundred meters to the north, Alice, Mike, and Eric were sitting on the roof of the Sherp with their feet dangling in front of the blown-out windshield. The dead Russian driver sat motionless below them. Eric had taken pity on Mike and let him sit in the middle next to Alice. It was the least he could do after screwing him over earlier in the chopper. They were enjoying the air show being put on by the Warthogs and the Rangers through their NODs.

Eric exclaimed, "Those lucky bastards!" as he watched Rangers float down from the sky and land all around them.

Alice asked, "What do you mean?"

Eric explained, "Every one of these Doggies is going to get a set of combat jump wings for jumping into combat on U.S. soil. I don't even know if any of the soldiers who fought the Japs in the Aleutian Islands during World War II got combat jump wings. These guys might be the first, and they didn't even fire a shot."

Two Rangers approached the trio with their rifles at the ready and challenged them, "Identify yourselves!"

Mike responded, "Fuck you, Dogface! The Marine Corps already owns this beach! Get back in your plane and go home."

Eric interrupted, "Actually fellas, we do need your help. Can you call Triple-A for us? We need someone to fix our flat tires."

Alice and Mike busted out laughing. Tires wouldn't help this Sherp. It was shot to shit. The two young Rangers didn't have a witty reply, so they faded away into the darkness headed south. A couple minutes later, an officious young butter bar approached them. He identified himself as Second Lieutenant Poindexter. The trio stifled their laughter, and Eric and Mike started a new routine. They flashed their badges and identified themselves as Alaska State Troopers. Mike advised the lieutenant that his soldiers were contaminating an active crime scene and ordered him to evacuate the area immediately. Poindexter ran off looking for his captain. He didn't want to get arrested during his first combat operation.

CHAPTER 73

Dragon stood at the bottom of the sub's ladder sweating like a pig. He had opened his parka and removed his helmet and balaclava about halfway into the 1,000-meter hump through the knee-deep snow, but despite his snowshoes, he still overheated. This shit wasn't as easy as it was twenty-five years ago when he was a twenty-year-old private first class, or PFC. He had risen through the ranks to staff sergeant and, after eight years, accepted an officer's commission. He had served twenty of his twenty-five years in Ranger assignments. Mendoza and Franks stood in front of him looking like they had just woke up from a nap. They weren't even breathing hard. They looked at Dragon with big grins on their faces.

He said, "Fuck both of ya. You'll get old someday." Dragon kicked off his snowshoes and climbed the ladder. He met Commander Smith aft of the sail about halfway to the Russian formation. Steam was rising off Dragon's bald head as he called out, "Permission to come aboard, sir."

Smith smiled. "Permission granted, sir."

They exchanged introductions and handshakes.

Dragon glimpsed beyond Smith's shoulder to the Russian formation. "We're here to save you, but it looks like we're too late."

Smith grinned. "Better late than never. Besides, we're a little understaffed. Do you mind sending your men aft to give First Sergeant Strasburg a hand guarding the Russians? He lost a soldier tonight, and he's still pretty hot. We shouldn't leave him alone with them."

"Sergeant Mendoza, Corporal Franks, go give the first sergeant a hand," Dragon called out over his shoulder.

Both Rangers responded with a loud, "Hooah!" and quickly passed them.

***

Mendoza walked up to Strasburg and introduced himself and Franks. "We're sorry to hear about your soldier, First Sergeant," Mendoza said soberly.

"Thanks. Sergeant Davis was a fine young man and soldier," Strasburg replied without looking away from the sailors. He studied the Russian formation. He had been awake over 27 hours, and he was bone tired. He was trying to fight it, but his anger and hatred were slowly melting away. Earlier he had wanted to kill everyone on this boat, but now he saw a lot of cold, scared young men. He wondered how many of these sailors grew up on farms like he had and joined the Navy to escape. They had been doing their jobs, just like he and Davis had been doing theirs. He realized the people to blame were actually back in Moscow in their nice warm homes and offices.

***

Smith led Dragon toward the Russian formation and called Captain Vyacheslav forward to them. Smith said, "Captain Vyacheslav, this is Colonel Dragon. His men will be searching your boat. Are you certain none of your men are hiding below waiting to ambush them? No more second officers? If there are, you will be held responsible."

Vyacheslav shook his head. "None of my men are below, but please, instruct your men not to touch any of the controls. This boat has two nuclear reactors. They could accidentally cause a horrible catastrophe."

Smith responded, "Actually, aren't there three nuclear reactors down below?"

Vyacheslav looked surprised. "I don't understand."

Smith stepped forward, invading the captain's personal space, and tried again, "Sure you do, Captain. There are three reactors below because there are two submarines. The A-12 Losharik, also known as Project 210, is attached to the bottom of the Podmoskovye. Isn't that correct? Before you answer, you should know that we have two fast-attack subs waiting for the Losharik. If it tries to escape, it will be destroyed. I believe it's crewed by twenty-five officers, right? Do you want to add them to the dead sailors lying out there on the ice?"

Vyacheslav was trying to think of a way to help the Losharik get away, but he was out of ideas, so he remained silent.

Dragon felt like a kid who had missed the first week of summer school and piped up, "What the fuck is the Losharik?"

Smith replied to Dragon while looking directly at Vyacheslav, "It's a 200-foot-long nuclear submarine that's capable of descending to about 20,000 feet. It can conduct peaceful scientific deep ocean research, deep water rescue of personnel in disabled subs, cut internet lines, or wiretap our most classified undersea communications. The undersea cables used to be out of reach, but now subs like the Losharik can tap them or cut them. But most importantly, the Losharik can deliver a smaller short-range variant of the nuclear-powered Kanyon torpedo that carries a 100-megaton warhead. When detonated under 3,000 feet of water, it would generate a tsunami that could inundate several hundred miles of our coastline and kill millions of people. The land would be contaminated for over 100 years. Isn't that right, Captain?"

Again, Vyacheslav remained silent.

Major Henderson appeared behind them and announced, "Colonel, I have Alpha Company standing by at the bottom of the ladder and Charlie Company deployed about 100 meters away to provide support."

Dragon replied, "Major, send a squad aft to help guard the Russians. Send the rest of Alpha below to search the sub and then post a Ranger at every hatch. Tell them not to touch any switches or controls."

Smith interjected, "I'm going with them, and when I find the hatch leading to the Losharik, I'm going to drop a couple of thermite grenades through it."

Smith started walking toward the hatch.

Vyacheslav yelled, "Stop! Alright, Commander, let me go to the control room so I can call the Losharik. I will order the crew to surrender."

***

Ten minutes later, twenty-five Russian Navy officers from the Losharik joined the Russian formation on the deck, and Commander Smith accepted the surrender of another Russian sub. He thought, That must be some kind of record. It sucked that he wouldn't be able to tell anyone.

Smith turned to Dragon. "OK, Ike, this kabuki dick dance is all yours. You can babysit these guys until somebody decides what to do with them. Chirp is going to fly our team back to Bethel to get our wounded treated at the hospital. Then, we'll head for home."

"Who's Chirp?" Dragon asked.

"It's Colonel Adam's old callsign from his Marine Corps days." Smith told Dragon the whole story about how he earned it.

Dragon laughed and shook Smith's hand. "You guys did a hell of a job last night. I don't think anyone could ask for better. It was quite a coup to kill a traitor and capture two subs. I guess it was a good thing you were able to get those fast-attack subs into position to keep the Losharik from slipping away."

With a cocky grin, Smith replied, "Well, actually, that was bullshit. I don't think the subs are here yet. I told Vyacheslav that to help convince him to give them up. I guess after seeing 25% of his crew get wiped out and two massive holes put in his boat, he figured we were serious. Shit! I almost forgot!" He turned and disappeared through a hatch in the sail and reappeared seconds later at the top, standing in the conning tower's observation deck. It was already occupied by two young Rangers. They were looking at the ass end of the second officer's dead body.

Smith said, "Excuse me, gentlemen," as he stepped between them. Blood and tissue were scattered everywhere, and Smith was trying to be careful to not get any of it on his white smock. He glanced up at the assortment of antennas and masts overhead. The Russian naval ensign was fluttering in the breeze about ten feet overhead. It was a white flag with two light blue diagonal stripes known as the St. Andrew's cross. It showed some damage from multiple bullet strikes and the Javelin explosion, but it was still in one piece. He drew his bayonet from its scabbard and cut the halyard loose. He pulled down the flag, folded it several times, and stuffed it inside his parka.

"Do either of you have an American flag on you?" Smith asked.

One of the young PFCs responded, "Yes sir, I have one in my cargo pocket."

"Good. Hoist Old Glory over this tub. You'll never get another chance for as long as you live." Smith disappeared back down through the hatch. He popped out on the deck next to Dragon and called Chirp, "Mustang 6, this is 16."

"Go ahead, Jon."

"Colonel Dragon and his Rangers have assumed control of the Russians. Strasburg and I are ready for pickup."

"Roger that. We'll be there in two mikes; break. Mustang 26, meet us on the ice at the ATV. Then we'll fly our wounded to Bethel."

Rogers replied, "Wilco, sir. We'll be there ASAP."

Smith looked up and saw the Stars and Stripes being raised over the sub. He said to Dragon, "Ike, check it out. Our flag flying over a Russian sub. I bet we'll never see that again." Smith changed the subject, "We have two snowmobiles that we'll be leaving with you. They belong to Leo Fisher. He lives a few miles north of here. He offered them to us last night after he found his neighbors dead on their front porch. Please, make sure he gets them back."

Dragon wrote the name down in his notebook before sticking it back in his pocket. "Will do, Jon."

CHAPTER 74

Rogers and Pope packed up the Javelin launcher and remaining missile. They put on their snowshoes and donned their packs and weapons. Then they dragged the Javelin's case down the hill. They stopped next to the sled, and Pope paused to look down at the poncho covering Davis's body.

Rogers stepped up next to him. "I'm sorry this happened, Nate. I don't know what I could have done differently."

Pope shook his head. "It wasn't your fault, sir. I just feel sorry for Allen. All he ever wanted was to be a soldier. He would've been a thirty-year man. He loved every bit of it. The only reason he joined the Guard instead of the Regular Army was because he wanted to stay in Alaska. I just wish he had had more time."

They loaded the Javelin and their packs into the sled next to the body and headed out to meet up with Team One at the shot-up ATV. Two minutes later, they came to a stop behind the Sherp. Pope observed the bullet- and shrapnel-ridden Sherp and smiled with pride at the destruction. Then he saw the dead Russian behind the right rear tire. The damage to the body was so extensive that he had to look away.

Rogers noticed Mike's blood-soaked trouser leg. "How's your leg, Staff Sergeant?"

"Fine, sir. It just grazed me. You should see the other guy. He's scattered all over the ice out there," Mike said, gesturing over his shoulder.

Rogers keyed his radio to transmit, "Chirp, the rest of Teams One and Two are assembled at the ATV ready for pickup."

"Roger that, Steve, we're inbound." Tom turned to Taco and keyed his ICS, "OK, Taco, take us back to the sub. When we get close, I'll take over for the landing."

Taco clicked his ICS switch twice to acknowledge him. Minutes later, the Jayhawk landed on the ice next to the submarine and whipped up a snowstorm that covered the Rangers and Russians in a fresh layer of snow. Smith and Strasburg trudged over to the helo and clambered into the cabin. The Jayhawk lifted off again, dusting the Rangers and Russians. Chirp pedal-turned to the right and flew north directly toward the Sherp at 50 feet AGL. He landed next to it. Steve, Nate, Alice, Eric, and Mike carried Allen's poncho-covered body to the helo.

As the Rangers in the area saw what was happening, they came to attention and presented arms. Strasburg, Smith, Savage, and Hicks received the body and gently placed it inside the cabin. The rest of the team boarded the helo. Second Lieutenant

Poindexter appeared at the open cabin door, pulled an American flag from his trousers' cargo pocket, and handed it to Commander Smith. Poindexter saluted and then hustled back away from the rotor arc. Hicks slid the door closed as Smith and Strasburg spread the flag out and placed it over Davis.

Chirp had watched what was happening over his shoulder, and when the young Ranger handed Smith a flag for Davis's body, he lost it. He turned to the right toward his window and cried. Taco observed him but didn't interrupt. After a minute or so, Chirp slowly regained his composure and wiped his eyes. Chirp called for the takeoff checklist. Taco read it off and gave him a thumbs-up.

Hicks called out, "Clear right."

Savage followed, "Clear left."

Chirp responded, "Coming up," as he raised the collective and pushed the cyclic forward slightly to lower the nose and accelerate across the ice.

He headed north directly for the hospital in Bethel.

Five minutes later, Smith keyed his ICS switch. "Chirp, Nate and Mike are requesting we disregard going to the hospital. They say their wounds are not serious, and they would rather return to the Haley with the rest of the team. Eric and Chris looked them over and believe it is safe for them to come back with us."

Chirp asked, "What about Davis?"

"The team and I believe Davis should come back to the ship with us. Strasburg said he was sure Davis would have wanted it that way."

Chirp glanced down to check how much fuel he had remaining.

He thought about it for a minute. "He's probably right. OK, let's go home. Coming right." Chirp turned the helo to the east and headed back to the Haley. After a few minutes, Chirp keyed his ICS, "Taco, how are you feeling? Do you want to take over for a while?"

Taco replied, "Yes, sir, I'm good. I have the controls."

Chirp thought, Oh, to be young.

They went through the three-way change of controls, and Chirp showed Taco his hands. He slid his seat back away from the controls and stretched his arms and legs as well as he could in the small cockpit. He was so tired he was afraid he might nod off, and if he did, he didn't want to while he was at the controls.

The lack of sleep and stress of the mission had worn him out, but the death of Sergeant Davis was devastating. He had never lost a soldier under his command. He had been present when soldiers died, but he wasn't in charge of those operations. This time as the commander, he was responsible. He didn't know much about the young soldier but judging by how his death affected Strasburg and Pope, he assumed Davis had been special. Tom wished he'd had the opportunity to know him. He yawned deeply as he stared out his door's window. His head bobbed a few times, and he leaned his head back so his helmet would lay against the headrest. He really wished he could get up and move around a little to get his blood flowing.

His mind started to drift. He remembered the old days when he was in the Marines flying Shitters. The CH-53s were so big he could unstrap from his seat and walk back to the cargo area to stretch his legs whenever he needed to. It was so big; you could drive a Jeep and its trailer up inside it. They used to call it the Sikorsky Hilton because it was big enough for the crew to sleep in when it broke down in the field. Chirp closed his eyes for a minute.

Taco tapped Tom's left shoulder. "Chirp, it's time to take over. We're here."

He opened his eyes, blinking back sleep. Taco had flown them back across Alaska and navigated them to Cook Inlet to rendezvous with the Haley. Tom felt like he had barely closed his eyes, but he had actually been sleeping for two hours. He didn't remember dreaming about anything, but more importantly, he didn't dream about the shootdown outside of Baqubah. Maybe today would be a good day.

Taco said, "Chirp, we're about ten miles from the Haley. Are you ready to take over?"

Tom slid his seat forward, rubbed his face, and took the controls back. "OK, Taco, call the Haley for permission to land and give me the landing checklist."

Taco did as requested, and minutes later, Chirp made an uneventful landing aboard the Haley like he had hundreds of times before in the Corps. Chirp held the controls as Taco went through the shutdown checklist. As the rotors came to a stop, Boatswain's Mates Leonard and Stokes came out of the hangar with a stretcher for Davis's body. When they got to the helicopter, Rogers accepted it from them and both fire teams gently lifted Davis's body onto the stretcher and carefully carried it into the hangar, making sure the flag covered him. Commander Waddle called all his crew present to attention, and they saluted as the body was carried past them. Gwenn stood at the edge of the large hangar door waiting for Tom. She watched the team carry Davis's body inside and noticed the respect Waddle and his men paid to it and the team. She dabbed tears away from her eyes as she thought of how his death would affect his parents.

Taco and Chirp were left alone in the helicopter. Chirp said, "Taco, you did an outstanding job last night. I couldn't have flown this helicopter without you. Are you still interested in going to flight school?"

"Yes, sir, I'd love to, but I've already been turned down once and I'm getting close to the age limit."

"Look, I learned a long time ago that when the military tells you no, it really means not right now. The first time I tried to get into Marine Officer Candidate School with a flight contract, they politely told me to go pound sand, so I went next door to the Navy, and they said they'd take me but I would have to wait six months. About three months later, I got tired of waiting and called the Marines again. This time, they scooped me up right away. They put me under contract immediately so the Navy couldn't have me.

"When 9/11 happened, I joined the Missouri National Guard to fly Black Hawks, but the National Guard Bureau in Washington kept rejecting my application for designation as an Army Aviator. It turned out there was a crusty old warrant officer there that had a hard-on for Marines. It took me a year and a half and three attempts before my Army flight orders were approved. Six months later, I was in Iraq flying combat missions every day.

"What I'm trying to say is, if you want it, you should keep trying until it happens, and if you do hit the age limit, request a waiver. The military has waivers for everything. I heard about a kid one time that got a waiver to join the Army with one eye. I know of a Force Recon sergeant who stayed on active duty after losing a leg below the knee in a HALO accident. He retired as a sergeant major. So, never give up. Plus, after they read my after-action report, they're going to be begging you to go to flight school. You're a Coast Guard officer with combat flight time who captured two Russian subs. They'll want to keep you in the Coast Guard. Come on, let's get inside and warm up."

They climbed out of the cockpit and headed for the hangar. As soon as Tom stepped through the door, Gwenn threw her arms around him and kissed him long and hard. She hugged him tightly and whispered in his ear, "Never do that again."

He whispered back, "Sounds good to me."

CHAPTER 75

Pichugin's face was red with rage. Watching Fox News Channel, he could see his submarine surfaced on the ice behind a row of American Chinook helicopters. The Podmoskovye had an American flag flying over it. When he was last briefed a few hours earlier, the extraction mission was underway and there were no reported problems. Now the operation had gone to shit, and no one could tell him why the captain of the Podmoskovye had allowed his submarine and crew to be captured. Why would he risk his boat and crew for Karpinsky and a handful of Spetsnaz operators? It didn't make sense. Was the captain a defector? Pichugin stood up and furiously pounded his fists on the top of his desk.

Spittle flew from his mouth and landed on the desk as he yelled at the Russian Federation's minister of defense, General of the Army Sergei Gennady, "How could you allow this to happen?

Your incompetence has cost us two submarines and 150 men! You should do the honorable thing! You are not fit to serve!"

Pichugin wasn't talking about resignation. He wanted Gennady to drive out to his dacha in the country and eat his gun. That way, Pichugin could blame the entire fiasco on the senile old general. Gennady had been a soldier for forty-five years and was willing to take a bullet for Mother Russia. In fact, he had on three separate occasions, still carrying shrapnel in his thigh from Afghanistan, but Gennady wouldn't let this sorry little excuse for a bureaucrat push him around. Pichugin was a petty criminal. His corruption was well known. Gennady's staff referred to him as President Pikachu.

General Gennady replied, "Excuse me, Mr. President, but you must recall that I advised against this operation in the strongest possible terms. I explained to you the risks far outweighed the possible benefits of retrieving Colonel Karpinsky. If it was really vital that we bring Karpinsky out, we could have smuggled him out from his home in Virginia. There was no need to risk the Podmoskovye."

Pichugin couldn't tell the general that he had been receiving information from Karpinsky in his dreams for the last several months. Karpinsky was haunting him. He couldn't sleep. He couldn't eat. He had to follow Karpinsky's instructions or he would go mad.

General Gennady continued, "Mr. President, I suggest you call the American president and tell him that this was a rogue operation conducted without your knowledge. Tell him we will conduct a full investigation and punish those responsible. Negotiate the return of our people and submarines. Perhaps offer to stop interfering with the American elections."

Pichugin retorted, "The Americans have been interfering in our elections for decades! They tried to have me thrown out of office! They secretly spent millions of dollars trying to defeat me."

Gennady replied, "Then, perhaps offer to pull our support from President Assad in his civil war." Bashar al-Assad was the president for life, or dictator, of Syria. Russia had been propping up the Assad family for almost fifty years in exchange for permission to operate a naval base at Tartus on the Mediterranean coast for its Black Sea Fleet. It was Russia's only overseas military base.

CHAPTER 76

Connie Huff and her team were standing around the table in their conference room on the third floor of Operations Building 2B at Fort Meade. Like Pichugin, they were watching Fox News when the reports from Alaska came on. When they saw the BS-64 Podmoskovye surfaced on the ice behind the Chinooks, they cheered loudly and started congratulating each other. Huff was a branch chief supervising a group of computer experts that had been tasked with creating a Deep Fake video of Vladimir Pichugin.

Unknown to the Russians, an attractive CIA asset had engaged a married Russian Navy officer assigned to their embassy in Vienna in an extramarital affair. The officer's wife happened to be the daughter of a high-ranking admiral in the Kremlin. The officer was very amenable to finding a way to keep the affair secret.

He agreed to provide the asset with access to the Russian Navy's submarine communications network. Within hours of gaining access to their encrypted communications, the U.S. had learned of the Russians' interest in Karpinsky. The access would only be available for a few hours.

Huff's team exploited the gap in the Russian Navy's cyber-security defenses. Her experts used a video of Pichugin recorded from his office earlier in the day to create a fake video of Pichugin ordering the captain of the Podmoskovye to not leave Alaska without Karpinsky. The video was inserted into the Russian Navy's communications system. It was also designed to delete any trace of its existence two hours after it was viewed.

CHAPTER 77

The Coast Guard Jayhawk flew across the bay 500 feet above the waves. As it approached the beach, the pilot lowered the collective and pulled the cyclic back to decelerate and assume a landing profile. He came to a ten-foot hover over the beach, kicked the tail around to the right 90°, and landed. The crew chief slid the cabin door back, jumped out, and put the chocks around the right main mount tire.

Jon Smith, now back in his civilian clothes, hopped out after him and followed him to the edge of the rotor arc. The crew chief saluted, and Jon returned it despite being out of uniform, then they shook hands. The crew chief wheeled around, gathered his long cord like a cowboy's lasso, and hustled back to the Jayhawk. Jon stood there and watched as the crew chief pulled the chocks, climbed aboard, and closed the door. He looked to the pilot and saw him give Jon a thumbs-up. Jon nodded and waved as the helicopter sprang from the ground. He squinted and turned away as the sand and pebbles reached his face. The Jayhawk turned left as it headed back out over the water. It still amazed him how well those guys handled their helos.

Jon walked across the narrow beach and up the steps onto the deck. He grabbed his empty beer bottle off the deck rail and slid the glass door open. He walked across the kitchen and put the bottle on the counter next to the cap. He grabbed another Blue Moon from the icebox and walked over to the sofa. He removed his parka, pulled his holster off his hip, and set it down on the coffee table. He sat down on the sofa and kicked off his Merrill's. He picked up the TV remote off the coffee table and switched it on. He put his feet up on the table and took a long draw from the bottle. He hoped he could get a few hours of sleep before Aunt Faye called again. He decided to turn off his phone just in case, but then remembered that it wouldn't matter anyway. He went to his contacts and scrolled down to Sarah Tuttle's information. He was already looking forward to their first date next week after the Haley returned to port. He put down his phone and picked up the remote. He scanned the available channels and settled on Fox News.

The talking heads were announcing a Fox News Alert. They were running a shaky cell phone video provided by a young man in Alaska. Jon smiled as he recognized Dave Shepard and his two amigos. The video bounced around as Dave talked about what they had seen. Dave was standing with a small crowd of people who lived in the area of the Yukon-Kuskokwim River Delta. Most of them were armed with hunting rifles and shotguns, but Dave had an AR-15 slung across his chest. Jon smiled as he realized where Dave must have gotten it.

Before the sun came up, the local residents had heard machine gun fire and explosions and a helicopter buzzing around the area. After sunrise, they got on their snowmobiles and came out to see what was happening. In the video, they were being held back by a line of U.S. Army Rangers wearing white camouflage.

Behind the Rangers in the distance was the silhouette of a huge black submarine. Five massive dark green Army CH-47F Chinook helicopters were sitting on the snow in front of the submarine with their rotor blades turning. Well over a hundred men were lined up behind the first four helicopters. They weren't dressed like the Rangers. Their coats and uniforms looked black. They were being guarded by the white-clad Rangers. In unison, they began trudging through the deep snow toward the rear ramps of the Chinooks. Their arms appeared to be held behind their backs. Several fell face-first into the snow and didn't break their falls with their arms. They were helped to their feet by the Rangers and continued shuffling to the Chinooks with their faces and the front of their coats caked white with snow. Another group of Rangers appeared to be carrying body bags into the fifth Chinook. There were a lot of bags. The video went back to the submarine and focused on the two holes in the sail.

Jon could see the Stars and Stripes flying proudly over the Russian sub. That made him smile. He glanced over at his parka laying across the chair next to the sofa. Part of the Russian Navy flag was sticking out of the large inside breast pocket. He decided he would hang it on the wall above the TV. When his buddies arrived, they would see the battle-scarred flag and assume he had been involved in capturing the Podmoskovye. They would ask him a ton of questions, but he would let them wonder. He examined his hand and realized the tremors had been gone since he left the lodge for the mission.

The talking heads on Fox began speculating about what they were viewing. Their military expert was a retired Air Force major general. He was a former commander in the Air Mobility Command. He was an expert on aerial refueling and the logistics of moving cargo by air, but he didn't know shit about submarines or Alaska. He was making his best guess—no, make that a wild-ass guess—about what they were seeing. Was this a no-notice joint military exercise or a submarine accident, or could it actually be a real military operation? Jon was tired and getting more bored by the second. By the time he had downed half of his beer, his head slid back against the cushion, and he was asleep.

CHAPTER 78

2400Z (1500HR AKST)
YUKON-KUSKOKWIM DELTA, ALASKA

Well into the afternoon, Dave Shepard was still standing out on the ice with his buddies watching all the action. U.S. military helicopters of all sizes were coming and going. Two giant U.S. Navy air-cushioned landing crafts came hovering across the ice from the south at high speed and stopped about a hundred yards east of the submarine. Dave and his friends couldn't see the ship they came from. Their ramps dropped, and two Marine light armored vehicles drove off each ramp.

When Dave's cell phone rang, he answered it, "Hello."

His mother asked, "David, are you alright? We just saw you and the boys on the news. What's going on out there?"

Dave replied, "We're fine, Mom. We saw our military capture a Russian submarine and kill a bunch of enemy sailors."

His mom replied, "Well, that's nice, but it's time to come home. We have to leave for your hockey game in a couple of hours."

~The End~

Thank you for reading BEAR TRAP. I sincerely hope you enjoyed it. Please, do me a huge favor and leave a review on Amazon. Indie authors, like me, struggle to get reviews for our books. I've read typically only one of 200 readers leaves a review. Reviews on Amazon help move my book up in the rankings and give me a more competitive chance as I compete with more well-established authors.

Also, please join my Newsletter using the link below for updates on future Jon Smith novels and short stories and I will give you a FREE copy of my Jon Smith Short Story, SMOKE SIGNALS. I promise I won't sell or share your email address with others. Bob Asher Books Newsletter - https://bookhip.com/HXFQKLV

GLOSSARY

- **ACP** – Automatic Colt Pistol

- **ADX** – Administrative Maximum Facility, Federal Prison

- **AGL** – Above Ground Level

- **AGR** – Active Guard and Reserve

- **AKST** – Alaska Standard Time

- **AST** – Arabia Standard Time

- **BOQ** – Bachelor Officer Quarters

- **CIT** – Cyber-Intelligence Team

- **EMCON** – Emission Control

- **FACE** – Facial Analysis, Comparison, and Evaluation Services Unit

- **FGM-148** – Javelin Anti-Tank Missile System

- **FLIR** – Forward Looking Infrared

- **FOV** – Field of View

- **GRU** – Main Intelligence Directorate. Military Intelligence for the Russian Federation

- **HMH** – Heavy Marine Helicopter Squadron

- **HMLA** – Light Attack Marine Helicopter Squadron

- **IC** – Intelligence Community

- **IED** – Improvised Explosive Device

- **IMSI** – International Mobile Subscriber Identity - Catcher

- **JCS** – Joint Chiefs of Staff

- **JSOC** – Joint Special Operations Command

- **MOS** – Military Occupational Specialty

- **MRE** – Meal Read to Eat

- **MSK** – Moscow Time

- **NOD** – Night Observation Device

- **NORTHCOM** – US Northern Command

- **NSA** – National Security Agency

- **NVGs** – Night Vision Goggles

- **OCP** – Operational Camouflage Pattern

- **PETT** - Kamchatka Time Zone

- **PJ** – Pararescueman

- **PST** – Pacific Standard Time

- **RHIB** – Rigid-hulled Inflatable Boat

- **RP** – Rendezvous Point

- **RPG** – Rocket Propelled Grenade

- **SAM** – Surface to Air Missile

- **S&W** – Smith and Wesson

- **SCIF** – Sensitive Compartmented Information Facility

- **SEAL** – Sea, Air, and Land Team

- **SF** – Short Frame, Some Glock pistols offer a short frame model

- **SMU** – Special Mission Unit

- **SVR RF** – Foreign Intelligence Service of the Russian Federation

- **TDY** – Temporary Duty

- **X-1** – Experimental rocket powered aircraft (Bell Model 44)

- **Z** – Zulu time. Also, UTC (Universal) time or GMT (Greenwich Mean Time)

NGA QCC

Why is this statement here and what does it mean? It's here because I had to present my novel to the federal government for prepublication review before I could publish it. And why did I have to do that? Because I am an Intelligence officer employed by the National Geospatial-Intelligence Agency (NGA) and I signed a nondisclosure agreement as a condition of my employment swearing to keep classified information secret under threat of imprisonment.

So, after an exhaustive one year and four-month review conducted by NGA, NSA, FBI, CIA, NRO, and the Office of the Secretary of Defense (OSD), which required numerous changes and redactions, my book has been approved for public release. And, no, I'm not bitter. Rest assured, they made me redact some pretty cool stuff. None of it was classified, in my opinion, but they definitely didn't want it appearing in print written by a US intelligence officer. Some of the material they objected to frustrated me to no end because other thriller novel writers like Brad Thor and Mark Greaney refer to that same material frequently in their novels. For example, here are a couple of the minor issues. You know that Army Special Operations outfit books and movies are written about, the tier one group that Rangers and Green Beret compete to join, the one that comes after Charlie Force and before

Echo Force? Yeah, that one. I can't mention it in my book. If it does exist, it isn't even called by that name anymore.

I can write about SEAL Team Five or SEAL Team Seven, but not the one between them. I can write Green Beret, JSOC, and special mission unit (SMU). Here's another, remember that terrorist detention center operated on Naval Station Guantanamo Bay, the one that 60 Minutes did an extensive story on? It was called Camp something or other. Well, I can't write that in my book either, but I can refer to the camp as Gitmo. The FBI really didn't like me writing about cell site simulators, also known as IMSI catchers. Which I thought was odd because they are commercially available. City and state police agencies around the country use them every day. The funny thing is they let me write about the black bag jobs, the FACES Services Unit, the Next Generation Identification-Interstate Photo System, and the automated license plate readers. Even funnier, the CIA asked me if Operation Bear Trap was based on a real operation. I wanted to respond, "Yeah, don't you remember that time we killed a bunch of Russian Spetsnaz operators and sailors up in Alaska and captured two of their special mission submarines. It was on CNN and Fox News," but I thought if I did, they might hold my book back for another year.

SNEAK PEEK OF THE NEXT

JON SMITH NOVEL

ESCAPE FROM DONETSK

CHAPTER 1

Jon was the fourth man in a tight stack of six standing along the back wall of a secluded stone and brick farmhouse on the outskirts of Dnipro, Ukraine. It was a little after 0100hr local time and even though it was a pleasant 70°F this July morning, he was sweating under his helmet and plate carrier. The team and he were wearing Ukrainian Army uniforms tonight and carrying suppressed HK416 carbines with IR lasers. The rest of their gear was also obviously of American origin but since the United States and most of NATO were sending weapons and equipment to help the war effort it didn't matter as long as the administration could say no American combat soldiers were operating in Ukraine. That was technically true. Jon's team was not from the US military, although most were retired from American military special mission units. They fell under the often-used euphemism OGA or other government agencies.

He tried to focus on the op but couldn't help flashing back to two years earlier when he had been in a similar stack in Mosul, Iraq when he saw an explosively formed penetrator explode through a cinder block wall, vaporizing, his best friend, Clint's head as he stood just a foot in front of him. Even now, he could smell the burnt flesh and taste the brain matter that he almost swallowed. Jon tried to shake off the memory. *Get your head out of your ass and focus,* he thought. He had experienced bouts of PTSD ever since, though he refused to acknowledge his diagnosis from his personal civilian doctor, whom he paid in cash. His doctor had transitioned into calling it PTS to hopefully alleviate any stigma attached to the word disorder. There was no way in Hell he would use his military retiree Tricare health insurance to pay for the counseling. He didn't want it popping up in his medical records so to be sure, he used another alias. *Fuck you, PTSD. You can't stop me. I'll operate until I die.* On occasion, he had numbness and tingling in his hands and an annoying twitch in the corner of his right eyelid but only when he was safely in the rear, never while he was on an operation.

Through his Ground Panoramic Night Vision Goggles or GPNVGs, he could see the stack and his team leader, Charlie One, although the team just called him Boss. The four-tubed goggles aka four bangers were a giant leap forward from the dual-tubed goggles he had used in Iraq. Boss was standing at the front of the line facing his team as he began counting down from five with his gloved fingers. When Boss signaled three, Charlie Six cut the electricity to the house. On two the breacher let go of his carbine to let it hang from its sling as he reached back, bringing the duckbilled Mossberg 590A1 shotgun into action. He pressed the end of the barrel against the door between the doorjamb and the deadbolt, before squeezing the trigger. The wood exploded, leaving a four-inch hole. Boss kicked the door open, tossed an M84 stun grenade into the kitchen, and stepped back. After the grenade exploded, he rushed into the darkened room followed by the stack. Instantly, six IR lasers were darting across the room hunting for targets.

They were looking for a Russian SVR officer named Fyodor Nikolaev who had expressed his desire to defect to a CIA case officer. He was sharing this safe house with three other SVR officers who without prior notice or legal process evicted the Ukrainian owners at gunpoint. Jon thought they were no better than the mercenary Hessian troops the Redcoats employed during the American Revolution. The Hessians were infamous for their brutal treatment of the colonists. No one was safe from their outright thievery and physical brutality. The defector was to be identified by his red tracksuit top and excessively submissive posture on the floor with his empty hands on his head. The plan hit a momentary snag when the team encountered four men staggering around the first floor in varying stages of undress, none wearing the required red tracksuit top and all holding handguns. A man wearing a white wife beater and boxers ran into the darkened kitchen. He was looking down while trying to load a magazine into his pistol. Boss shot him with three rounds to his chest from his suppressed carbine.

"Drop your weapons! You are under arrest!" Charlie Five yelled in Russian as loud as he could amongst the chaos, hoping the Russians would stop resisting and make themselves easier targets. Only one Russian was going to leave this house alive. Charlie Two engaged an SVR officer in the family room as he dove behind the overstuffed couch in front of the fireplace. Charlie Two saw half of a bare foot sticking out from the end of the couch. He blew the toes off and was rewarded with a loud yelp, encouraging him to empty half a mag into the couch, instantly killing the man. Charlie Three shot the third SVR officer in the back as he ran for the front door. Jon and Charlie Five saw a man's naked legs disappear up the stairs to the second floor. Charlie Five was Jon's friend Angus "Angie" Hawkins recently retired from the Australian Special Air Service Regiment or SASR. He had been hired as a contractor for this mission thanks to Jon's recommendation and his fluency in Russian and Ukrainian. They followed the naked legs cautiously upstairs, no reason to rush to your *death. Slow is smooth, smooth is fast, Jon thought.*

"Surrender and you will not be harmed!" Angie yelled in Russian.

From the far bedroom, a voice replied in thickly Russian-accented English, "Do not shoot! I surrender, I am Fyodor Nikolaev."

Jon took a quick peek into the room with his NVGs, then carefully entered ready to fire followed immediately by Angie. They saw the man sans trousers face down on the rug, his hands on his head, and his legs bent upward at the knees and crossed at the ankles. His tracksuit top had been hastily draped across his back like Superman's cape. Jon yelled out, "We have the package! Don't move motherfucker." He covered the man while Angie searched him.

"You idiot! Why didn't you have the red tracksuit jacket on as agreed? We almost killed you!" Angie scolded him in perfect Russian.

"It was hot up here in bed and you weren't supposed to be here for another hour. I thought I had plenty of time to get ready," SVR Officer Nikolaev slurred his words. Too much vodka.

Arriving early was a smart way to reduce the team's ambush risk. Jon grabbed Nikolaev's trousers off the chair next to the bed, checked the pockets, and tossed them to him. "Put your pants on," he said.

Boss entered the room as Nikolaev rolled back and forth on the floor trying to get his skinny jeans over his hips. "Damn, he looks like Gru from that movie, Despicable Me," Boss said after laughing. "Fyodor, what are you doing? We told you what to do when we got here."

"The others wanted to drink vodka, so I had to drink with them. It would have been odd for me not to drink. They all know how much I love vodka," Nikolaev replied in slurred English.

"You don't seem very upset over us killing your friends," Boss said.

"They are not my friends. I never worked with them before we came here for the war. We would have all been dead within a few weeks anyway. Our operational security is shit. We are dying every day. Take me to America. I will tell you everything I know," Nikolaev replied.

"Why didn't you just resign and go back to Russia?" Boss asked.

"I am SVR. Is like Bratva. My country is run by criminals now. The only way you leave SVR is to die," Nikolaev explained. The Bratva was the Russian version of the American Mafia, except much more brutal and effective.

Three transmitted over the team radio, "Boss, Six and I went to get the vehicles, but the Russians are already there. They're setting up an ambush for us. We're coming back to the house now."

"Negative, Three, disregard coming back to the house. We're moving to the secondary exfil site. Go ahead of us, and secure the

LZ," Boss transmitted back. He switched radios and transmitted, "Ghost 21, Charlie 1."

"Go for Ghost 21," the agency pilot and air mission commander of the MH-60 Direct-Action Penetrator or DAP Blackhawk responded as he and his wingman, Ghost 22, randomly orbited about five minutes to the northwest. Ghost 21 was a retired Army CW5 who had served over twenty years in the 160th Special Operations Aviation Regiment known as the Night Stalkers.

"Ghost 21, our ground exfil has been compromised. We are moving to the secondary exfil site," Boss replied.

"Roger that, Ghost 21 five mikes out. Advise when the LZ is secure," the pilot replied.

Boss turned to Angie and said, "Five, zip him up and we'll head out," and then yelled downstairs, "We're coming down."

Angie zip-tied Nikolaev's hands behind his back and led him out of the room to the stairs. He said in Russian, "Be careful. We don't want you breaking your neck on the stairs after we went to all this trouble coming for you."

"Do not worry about me. I have been drinking vodka since I am nine," Nikolaev replied as he effortlessly sauntered down the stairs. He was happy to be leaving the war behind him.

They followed Boss down the stairs and stepped over the bodies as they made their way through the kitchen to the back door. Boss cracked the door open and listened for a few seconds.

Two transmitted from the far side of the backyard, "It's all quiet, you're clear."

Boss checked for himself. "Let's go," he said quietly before he led Jon, Nikolaev, and Angie quickly across the yard where they disappeared into the trees and thick brush.

Two took point and signaled for the group to follow in single-file formation. They fell in behind him at five-meter intervals except for Angie who kept one hand on the Russian. A hundred yards into their trek something growled nearby. Two threw up his left fist to signal the group to freeze. He listened for a few seconds. The group heard something large hurrying away through the brush. Two gave the dog signal with his hand and then motioned for them to follow him. They carefully but swiftly made their way through the woods for about another half mile to the secondary exfil site, a small elementary school playground, where they linked up with Three and Six. The others spread out and covered Angie as he pulled a harness out of his three-day pack.

"Raise your left leg," Angie whispered to Nikolaev.

Nikolaev was confused but complied. "What are you doing? Why do I need a climbing harness? We are flying out in a helicopter, yes?" he asked.

"Sort of, yeah. Right leg," Angie replied as he tugged at his right leg.

Nikolaev raised his leg, but he still didn't understand. He asked, "What? What is sort of?" as the whine of turbine engines grew to an ear-splitting volume just before a large black mass blocked out the stars to hover above him at treetop level. The rotor downwash enveloped them in an invisible cyclone of dirt and debris. Anything not anchored to the ground was flying. The team ran to the center of the playground and grabbed the thick rope that dangled from the bottom of the helicopter. Individually they attached the large D-rings on their harnesses to the rope. Angie finished tightening Nikolaev's harness, and he and Jon pulled the confused Nikolaev along with them. Angie connected Nikolaev's primary D-ring and secondary safety D-ring to the rope before attaching his own.

"Wait, this no good. What is this? Why am I, wait!" Nikolaev shouted as Boss signaled the Blackhawk's crew chief that they were ready. The helicopter leaped toward the stars yanking the team along beneath it. Nikolaev screamed in terror, the sound lost in the roar of the helicopter. The climb was so severe he thought his shoes would come off. He watched wide-eyed as the trees and buildings fell away from him as he rose to sixty meters above the ground before quickly accelerating away in an unknown direction. This high-risk extraction technique was called the Special Patrol Insertion/Extraction or SPIE system. It was not for those with a fear of heights.

"I, I think I will be sick," Nikolaev shouted.

Jon reached above his head and slapped Nikolaev's shoe. "Like fuck, you are! If you puke on me, I'm gonna climb up there and cut you loose! If you throw up, do it inside your shirt!" Jon yelled.

Angie was hanging above Nikolaev laughing. "Relax mate! A little vodka and half-digested Borsch won't hurt you!" Angie shouted to Jon between laughs. A string of green tracers interrupted his laugh and tightened his sphincter as they zipped across the sky toward the helicopter from a road intersection about 500 meters to the east. The helicopter was briefly silhouetted against the lights in the distance.

The crew chief on the right side returned fire with devastating effect from his window-mounted M134 minigun, silencing the machine gun. The M134 was a six-barreled 7.62mm Gatling gun capable of firing up to an incredible 6,000 rounds per minute or

100 rounds per second. The well-disciplined Night Stalker pilot continued on course without any abrupt evasive maneuvers.

"Charlie 1 are you boys still in one piece down there?" the pilot of Ghost 21 calmly transmitted.

"Roger that, looks like we're all here and no one's leaking. I hope that shithead didn't nick our rope," Boss replied.

"Well, if he did you won't have to worry about it very long," Ghost 21 said.

"Three, two, one," Three transmitted on the team radio before he and Six pressed send on their MK152 - remote radio detonators. Almost three miles away, the tree line erupted in spectacular orange and red flashes as the team's SUVs exploded, taking a platoon of Russian Airborne Infantry off the board, and sending large chunks of steel skyward. The SUVs carried an abundance of exotic weapons and ammo. Three and Six shared satisfied smiles and an exploding fist bump. The crew chief sitting behind the right minigun nodded his approval.

CHAPTER 2

Sister Joan was so pissed off she wanted to punch someone in the throat just as her father had taught her when she was thirteen years old. She stood in the kitchen pantry looking at empty shelves that, hours earlier, had been overloaded with food. Only a small fraction remained. She locked the door and hurried away to find the father. She stormed into the large classroom in the basement of the church. It had been hastily converted into a nursery and playroom. Rows of old army cots filled the room. In the two weeks she had been at the church Father Del Toro, and she had taken in almost a hundred children ranging from newborn infants to young teenagers. Some were displaced kids whose parents were fighting the Russians, but most were orphaned by the war.

Father Del Toro, the Spanish priest, was sitting on a tiny red chair between their cots, entertaining them with a spirited reading of a story from a book of Ukrainian folktales. They laughed at the story and his difficulty reading Ukrainian. Sister Joan waved from across the room to get his attention.

"Oh, yes, sister," he said quietly as he waved back. "Excuse me, boys and girls, Sister Joan needs my help," Father Del Toro said as he stood. He handed the book to an older girl. "Katya, please, finish the story for the children." The children moaned their disappointment. "Oh, please, don't upset Katya. She is much better at reading Ukrainian than I am." She sat down and delivered a spirited reading of the fairytale. As he crossed the room, he could see the concern on Sister Joan's face. He placed his hand on her shoulder and whispered in English, "Don't be cross sister. I know it is late but one of the children woke up crying from a nightmare which caused several others to wake up."

Sister Joan shook her head and led him out of the room so the children couldn't hear her.

"What is wrong, sister?" the father asked.

"Food is missing from the pantry, a lot of food. We have maybe a day's worth left," she said quietly as she struggled to control herself.

Father Del Toro was shocked. "How is this possible? We keep the pantry door locked. We should have food for five days," he said.

She rolled her eyes. "Please, Father, you know who took it, it's obvious. There's only you, me, and Yurochka here," she replied. "He stole it while we were busy with the kids." Yurochka Yecoshenko was the church gardener and handyman. He lived in a small cottage behind the church next to the barn and cemetery. He had become more and more unreliable as the days passed under Russian occupation. They walked through the kitchen at the other end of the large basement. The pantry was in the rear of the kitchen. Sister Joan unlocked the pantry door, and they walked inside.

Father Del Toro slowly surveyed the empty shelves, his anger quickly surpassing Sister Joan's. It had been very difficult to keep the pantry stocked as every day more and more hungry children were placed in his care. On his last foraging trip, he had to trade everything of value the church possessed. "He must have worked for hours moving the food out of here. If only he worked this hard at his daily duties, the church would be pristine. I will speak to him to give him a chance to explain his actions and then we will bring the food back to the pantry," Father Del Toro said. He wasn't afraid of confronting the thuggish, Yurochka. Father Del Toro had earned his green beret in the Unidad de Operaciones Especiales or Spanish Army Special Forces before entering the priesthood.

"Father we should change the padlock. Only the two of us should have keys," Sister Joan said.

"I am sorry to say you are right. I have another lock in my desk. Come with me, we'll get it now," Father Del Toro replied, "While I'm there I will try to call the bishop and ask him to evacuate the children again."

"It's late. He's probably sleeping," Sister Joan warned.

"My children are awake and soon they may be hungry. He can be awake too," Father Del Toro said. He wasn't afraid of bishops either. The father kept an Armor of God challenge coin in his pocket to remind him of what was important. He knew who he answered to.

They walked up the stairs and as they passed the church's front doors, they heard the rumble of trucks coming up the long gravel driveway. They shared concerned looks and Father Del Toro cracked the door open to peek into the darkness. The streetlights at the entrance to the church property had stopped working weeks before. He saw a convoy of headlights coming toward the church. "They must be military trucks, Russian or Chechen, I'm not sure. Stay in here and I will go out to talk to them," he said. He walked outside, closing the massive wooden doors behind him. He stood on the edge of the driveway as three large green military cargo trucks came to a stop. Twenty Chechen soldiers climbed out of the trucks and stood in a semicircle around the priest. Their commander stepped forward. He was a tall, overweight man with a long graying beard.

He smiled and said in English, "Father, I am Colonel Marvan Sultanovich of the Chechen Special Forces." He offered his hand to the Father.

Father Del Toro smiled back politely, shook his hand, and said in English, "It is good to meet you, Colonel. I am Father Domingo Del Toro. How may I help you tonight?" as he scanned the soldiers arrayed in front of him.

"Father, I have received reports that many children are being housed in your church. This is a war zone, and they are not safe here. I am concerned for their well-being. I am responsible for all civilians living in my sector. I am here to evacuate them to a safe area where they can be properly protected," Sultanovich replied.

"Thank you for your concern but there is no need for worry, Colonel. This is God's house," Father Del Toro said as he motioned to the sturdy brick and stone church behind him, "The children will always be safe here under God's protection."

Sultanovich nodded and said, "I have also been told you are running out of food to feed them. There are no stores left in this sector for you to get more food. It will be much better for the children if they come with me." His men stepped toward the doors and the priest stepped in front of them.

Now the father smelled a rat. How could the Colonel know the food was gone unless he was working with Yurochka? "Colonel, I assure you we have plenty of food for the children," Father Del Toro said as he backed up to the doors and grasped the handles behind his back to keep them closed. He knew what the Chechen had planned for his children, and he would not permit it. There were numerous reports of Ukrainian children being rounded up by the Russians and Chechens only to be taken out of the country never to be seen again.

The Colonel took a deep breath and expelled it quickly in exasperation. "Very well, I grow tired of this charade, teach the priest a lesson in exchange for his insolence," Colonel Sultanovich said with a smile. The soldiers moved forward sensing fresh meat. Father Del Toro dropped the first man with a swift kick to his groin and the second with a left jab that destroyed his nose. The soldiers swarmed Father Del Toro, two grabbing his arms. Father Del Toro headbutted the one on the left and drove his right heel into the other's knee. He was rewarded with a satisfying crack as it bent unnaturally sideways, and the soldier fell to the ground. More arms grabbed him, and he was able to elbow a soldier in the temple causing him to collapse unconscious. The rest of the swarm enveloped the father, taking him to the ground. They pummeled the priest with their fists and kicked him back onto the driveway.

They took turns stomping and kicking the poor priest in the head and torso like a bunch of drunken soccer hooligans. He was hopelessly outmatched against so many men. *I must stay alive for the children*, he thought. He cried out, "Por favor, no se detenga más no más!" in his native tongue. His eyes were swelling shut and he couldn't breathe through his broken nose. A gash on the back of his head where his skull was cracked covered his neck with blood and spinal fluid. *Father, forgive them for what they do,* was his last thought before he died.

Sister Joan cried helplessly as she watched the beating from the window. Tears ran across her hands as she covered her mouth, hoping they wouldn't hear her. She was frozen in terror. She prayed for a miracle to save the good father, but none came. In her young life, she had never witnessed anything so callous and brutal, totally devoid of humanity. It was akin to a pride of lions eating a baby impala while it was still alive. The soldiers were laughing, except for the five that required medical attention. Then she thought of the children, she didn't worry about herself. How could she save the children? She prayed again, then looked around for something she could use as a weapon.

"Bring out the children!" Sultanovich bellowed to his men as he rubbed his hands together while stepping over the dead priest's body. He was already imagining the huge stacks of euros he would be depositing in his Zurich safety deposit box.

Sister Joan stood just inside the doors with a sturdy five-foot-long oak coat rack held above her head. She would make the fat colonel pay for his sins.

But before he could step inside the threshold a young baby-faced captain yelled to the colonel from the cab of the second truck, "Colonel, the Ukrainians have mounted a counterattack on the airport. The base is in danger of being overrun."

Sultanovich stopped three feet short of having his skull caved in, turned to look at the captain for a moment, and then back to the church lobby. He weighed his options and finally turned toward his truck and said, "Very well, our retirement plan will have to wait. Mount up. We will come back for them later." The trucks roared to life and the lead truck made a hard left turn, plowing deep furrows in the manicured lawn with its massive offroad tires quickly followed by the others. He would never know the Ukrainian Army saved his life.

Sister Joan remained frozen with the coat rack above her head. She was stunned by what had just happened. She had been given the reprieve she asked for. Why would the Lord save her but not his faithful servant, Father Del Toro? There was so much she didn't understand. She needed help, so she would call the one person in the world who had always fixed her problems. She ran to the church's office and sat down behind the father's desk. She looked at the phone and made another silent prayer. Telephone service had been intermittent for weeks. She picked up the receiver and got a dial tone. She called her mom in Norfolk, Virginia.

"Please, answer! Please, answer! Please, answer!" she begged.

"Hello," her mom said.

Sister Joan was so excited she tried to say everything all at once. She sounded like a scared thirteen-year-old girl, "Momma, it's Kimmie! I need help! Chechen soldiers came to the church and killed Father Del Toro! They beat him to death, Mom. We're trapped behind the Russian lines!" And then the phone went dead again. "No! No! No! Please, Lord, help me!" Sister Joan cried as she prayed aloud with her head bowed, "Oh Jesus, our beloved Lord and Savior, please, help me protect these innocent children. I ask this through Christ, our Lord, Amen." She tried the phone again but there was no dial tone. She tapped the plunger several times, but the line was dead. At least her mom had heard her. She knew Kimmie needed help. Now she thought of her immediate problem. She had to bury Father Del Toro.

CHAPTER 3

The two passengers observed the scene below through their NVGs as their Mi-2 transport helicopter flew low and slow over the smoldering remains of the two Agency Chevy Suburbans. The SUVs' white-hot metal framework glowed bright green in their goggles. A platoon of soldiers moved about in the darkness retrieving the bodies and body parts of their comrades to stuff into rubberized bags. The Mi-2, NATO codename – Hoplite, landed a kilometer down the gravel road near the farmhouse where Jon's team had collected their defector only an hour and a half before. The two men jumped from the Hoplite and hunched over as they hurried out from under the rotor arc. They walked with purpose as they passed the soldiers forming a loose perimeter around the house. No one dared confront them. They raised their NVGs out of the way as they entered the brightly lit interior of the farmhouse through the front door. Three body bags were lined up on the floor. A lieutenant colonel, the battalion commander, was standing beyond the bodies near the kitchen with his back to the men as he gave orders to his officers. The older, taller man bent over and unzipped the first bag to see the occupant's face. He quickly zipped it up and moved to the second bag. He zipped that bag up and moved to the final bag. He unzipped the third bag and froze for a moment. He dropped to one knee and took his glove off to touch his younger brother's bloody face. His partner knelt next to him and put his arm around his shoulder. Tears fell from the older man's face as he closed his brother's dead eyes. He wiped his tears away, approached the colonel, and asked, "Colonel, where is the fourth SVR officer, Fyodor Nikolaev?"

The colonel looked over his shoulder and said, "I will talk to you in a moment. I'm issuing orders to my officers," before turning back to his men.

The man grabbed the colonel by his arm and spun him around, "You will talk to me now, Colonel. Where is SVR Officer Nikolaev? We need to determine if he has been abducted or is a traitor."

"Get your hands off of me! Who do you think you are? This is my AOR. What is your authority here?" the battalion commander demanded to know as he looked down on the man.

The man looked up at the colonel and punched him in the face with his right fist sending him to the floor. The colonel's officers moved to defend him. The man's partner raised his rifle and shouted, "Stop or you will join these men in the bags!"

"Who are you? What is your rank?" the colonel asked loudly as he held his bloody nose between his fingers.

The man straddled the colonel's waist and bent over. He pointed to the embroidered patch stuck to the side of his MICH helmet that read M22. "I am SVR Zaslon Officer M22." He pointed to his partner behind him and said, "He is Zaslon Officer M29. We have been ordered here to track down a hostage or a traitor. I can kill you if it is my wish without any concern. I can remove any trace that your wife and children ever existed. That is my authority. Now, where is SVR Officer Nikolaev?" Zaslon was Russia's most secretive special-purpose or Spetsnaz unit within the Russian external security service, Sluzhba Vneshney Razvedki or SVR.

"He was taken by a team of American Spetsnaz. They flew away in a Blackhawk helicopter," the colonel replied.

"We need transportation. Where is your car?" M22 asked.

"Fuck you! You can't have my car!" the colonel yelled. He had stolen the Ultimate Black Metallic Land Rover Defender 110 fair and square from a Ukrainian bank president.

M22 shot him in the face with his rifle. The colonel's young officers recoiled in horror, frozen by the violence. "Who is the executive officer?" M22 asked the men. The two lieutenants pointed to the man standing between them. "Come with us, Major, and bring his key fob."

Minutes later, M22 drove past the soldiers manning the perimeter around the burned-out Suburbans. M29 sat next to him, and the major sat in the backseat. M22 left the headlights off and relied on his NVGs to navigate along the road. He slowed to 40 KPH and said, "Thank you for the escort, Major. You may go now."

"What? The car is still moving!" the major complained.

"You are the mighty Airborne Infantry. Jump," M22 said.

M29 turned in his seat, displayed his pistol over the seatback, and said, "It will only get faster from here," before he motioned with his pistol for the major to jump. The major reluctantly opened his door and launched himself out of the vehicle. He tried to protect his head as he hit the gravel.

M29 watched him roll to a stop and stagger to his feet through the back window before he turned back around to speak to M22, "I don't mind throwing an occasional major out of a moving vehicle, but you must stop executing battalion commanders. Eventually, someone will complain."

CHAPTER 4

After an uncomfortable fifteen minutes of being dragged along behind Ghost 21, it finally landed in a clearing long enough for everyone to climb inside. Jon was sitting in the right rear seat. Nikolaev sat next to him in the middle seat with sound-suppressing headphones over his ears under a black hood. Nikolaev spread his legs wide and complained loudly, "My balls are on fire! I think the harness strangled them! I have been castrated! Tell the medic to check my testicles!"

Jon pulled the sound-suppressing cup about three inches from Nikolaev's ear and yelled, "Shut the fuck up or I'll cut'em off for real!" Jon let go, allowing the cup to slam into his head. The startled defector shut up immediately.

Angie sat on the other side of Nikolaev. He was chugging some local imitation of Red Bull that Jon knew from personal experience tasted like artificially sweetened tiger piss. He choked on his drink as he laughed after hearing Jon's threat. Boss and the rest of the team were sipping coffee provided by the aircrew. Jon was looking out of his window trying not to fall asleep when his satellite phone vibrated. He had turned it back on after getting inside the helicopter. He disconnected the comm cord from his team radio and plugged it into the sat phone. He answered, "Hello."

"Jon, it's Carol! I need your help! Kimmie called me about an hour and a half ago. She's in danger! You have to help her! Please, Jon!" she cried out.

Jon sat up straight in his seat. "Whoa! Slow down, Carol, take a breath! What's wrong?" Jon asked. He was wide awake now.

She took several deep breaths and said slowly, "Don't tell me to calm down. Kimmie needs help. You know she's a nun now, right? She's called Sister Joan. She volunteered to leave her church in Austria two weeks ago to help with the humanitarian relief efforts in Ukraine. They sent her to St. Michael's Church in Donetsk. It's behind the Russian lines now. She said the Chechens came to the church and murdered her priest. They beat him to death, Jon. She is scared to death. She needs help getting out. Jon, please, help her."

"Jesus Christ, Carol! Why did you let her go to Ukraine? It's a damned war zone! Are you fucking stupid?" Jon yelled into the phone. Angie and Boss heard him over the roar of the helicopter and turned to look. Even Nikolaev moved his head around under the hood like Stevie Wonder searching for the origin of the phantom sound. Angie and Boss had never seen Jon that pissed off, even in combat.

"Don't yell at me, dammit! She's an adult! I didn't let her do anything! She gets to decide what she does now! She was in Donetsk before she even told me! Now, stop yelling and help me! You're the only person I know that can get her out of there!" She started crying again.

Jon was on the verge of hyperventilating. He followed his own advice and took several long deep breaths to calm himself.

"Jon? Hello? Are you still there?" she asked between sobs. She sounded weak and small now. Like her only hope of saving her daughter had faded away.

"Yeah, I'm here, Carol. I'm sorry I blew up at you. I know this isn't your fault. I happen to be less than a day away from Donetsk. I'll get her out," he replied.

Relief rushed over her. She could breathe again. Carol worked to regain her composure. "She was terrified, Jon. She said she needed help. She didn't actually say she wanted out. What if she won't leave?" Carol asked.

Jon looked at the phone like it must be malfunctioning. "Carol, are you serious? When I find her, she's coming out! There's no question about that!" Jon replied, "Give me the number to the church. I'll try to call her." She read off the number and Jon wrote it on his left forearm, before programming it into his sat phone. "Try not to worry. I'll get her. Hey, why did you wait to call me?"

"I couldn't find the number for your damn sat phone. I've been turning the house upside down," she replied.

"I left it on the front of the fridge, remember?" Jon said.

"Yes, that's where I found it," she replied.

"Okay, I better go," Jon said.

"Thank you, Jon, and Jon, be careful," she said like she was going to cry again.

BOB ASHER

"I will. No worries," he replied.

"I love you, Jon," she said quietly.

"I love you too. Talk to you soon. Say hi to the kids," he disconnected the call and wiped his eyes. He started shaking his head and cursing out loud to himself.

Boss leaned over and touched Jon's knee to get his attention. He tapped his ear signaling Jon he wanted to talk. He waited until Jon reconnected his radio. "What the fuck was that?" Boss asked Jon over the team radio.

Now everyone on the team would hear about Jon's private business but he really didn't care. They were all good people. After training together for four months and then operating together for six more they had become like brothers. "That was my old swim buddy Clint's widow. She said my goddaughter, Kimmie, who now happens to be a Catholic nun named Sister Joan called her and said she's trapped behind enemy lines at her church in Donetsk. The Chechens came to the church tonight. She saw them beat her priest to death," Jon explained.

Boss shook his head and said, "Those shitheads are savages. I've seen them skin people alive."

"Boss, I'm sorry about this, but I have to go after her," Jon said as a matter of fact. He wasn't asking for permission.

Boss nodded. "No shit. Of course, you do. You do anything for family. I'd drop this SVR asshole off at the Polish border and go with you, but I know the Agency would have a shitfit. They'll say some bullshit about the Russians already threatening to go nuclear if there is any American intervention in Ukraine and forbid me from helping you. But as I remember, you have a bunch of use or lose leave on the books. So, if you want to go on vacation for a couple of weeks, I'll approve it," Boss replied.

"Thanks, Boss," Jon said.

Boss waved his hand in the air to signal no thanks was warranted. He wrote down an address in his notebook and ripped the page out. He handed it over to Jon. "This is the address to our cache house in Lviv. We'll drop you off nearby. You'll find a black Chevy Suburban there and all the weapons and equipment you'll need."

"Boss, if it's all the same to you, I'd like to go with Jon," Angie said.

Boss turned to Angie and said, "Well Hawkins, you did a fine job with us on your first contract. I hope we'll be able to work together again." He held out his hand and they shook. "I think we'll be able to manage the rest of the way to Poland without you guys," Boss replied.

Jon reconnected his sat phone to his headset and called the church's number. *Come on, Kimmie, answer the phone,* he thought. He tried several times, but the call never went through. *Lord, please, let her be safe until I can get her out of there,* he prayed silently.

CHAPTER 5

Sister Joan quietly walked between the cots until she got to the girl she was looking for. "Katya, wake up." The girl looked up at the sister. "Please, wake up the six oldest children. Tell them to get dressed and meet us outside the nursery," Sister Joan whispered. Katya spoke English and was able to translate for the sister. Five minutes later she led the group upstairs. "Katya, please tell everyone to sit in the last pew," Sister Joan said. Katya translated the message into Ukrainian for her.

"I'm sorry but I have terrible news. Chechen soldiers came to the church tonight. They intended to take all of you away to Chechnya where your families would never see you again. Father Del Toro fought them for us and hurt many of them before they killed him," Sister Joan said. Katya translated as she cried. She was quickly joined by the others. Sister Joan gave them time to compose themselves.

"When will they come back? We should run away before they come back," a frightened boy said.

"Calm down. We must be strong for the little ones. I will ask Sister Joan," Katya said in Ukrainian before switching to English for the sister. "He is scared. He wants to run before they come back to get us."

"Tell him not to worry. Father Del Toro told the bishop to send people to evacuate us and I called home to get help. Have faith. Help will come for us," Sister Joan said in her most confident voice. Katya relayed the message.

"Now, we have to bury the father before the children wake up. They can't be allowed to see his body," she said. She handed out the shovels she retrieved from the barn and said, "Follow me."

CHAPTER 6

05002 (0100HR LOCAL)
OFFICE OF THE WHITE HOUSE
CHIEF OF STAFF

A portly, balding man hurried down the empty hall as fast as his short legs could carry him toward the White House Chief of Staff's office. Flop sweat flowed from every pore. His damp bowtie was about to strangle him. He pounded rapidly on the office door and then entered before receiving a response. He flipped on the light switch. "Harold, we have a problem!" he said near panic while trying to catch his breath. Harold was Harold Lamb, White House Chief of Staff, the President's right-hand man.

"Of course, we do, Pres, it's," he squinted in the bright light as he looked at his watch, "another early Tuesday morning in the White House," Lamb replied unimpressed from underneath his Harvard University fleece blanket. He sat up on his couch and rubbed his eyes. "Well?" he asked.

Pres took his glasses off and cleaned them with his handkerchief. "A CIA paramilitary officer, with the cover name, Jon Smith, is on an unsanctioned mission in Ukraine to rescue his goddaughter. She's a Catholic nun at St. Michael's Church in Donetsk," said the National Security Advisor, Preston Alexander.

"So what? Who gives a fuck? Wait! That's under Russian control, right?" Lamb asked.

"Yes, and if we don't get him out of there, he could ruin Wynken's trip to Belarus," Alexander replied. Wynken was Secretary of State Anton Wynken. His trip to Belarus was scheduled to occur in two days. He would meet with the Russians to discuss a peaceful resolution to the illegal invasion of Ukraine. Oddly, the Ukrainians weren't invited to the peace talks that could very well determine their nation's future.

"Wait a minute. Let's think this through. He's just one guy. How much damage can he do?" Lamb asked, "He'll probably get killed before he can cause any problems."

"Actually, there are two of them. His teammate, a contractor from Australia named Angus Hawkins went with him," Alexander said.

"Okay, two guys. Big fucking deal. I'm tired of everybody acting like these special operations guys are supermen. They're a bunch of knuckle-dragging gun monkeys. They're expendable like toilet paper or MREs. There's always another dumbass farm boy dying to take their place.

"Make sure the DNI and DOD are told not to help them under any circumstance. If they go to Donetsk, they're fucked. They'll never get out alive." Lamb scratched his scruffy gray beard. "Track their progress and report back if they stir up any shit that might cause a problem. I have to be up at 5:30. Turn out the lights and close the door," Lamb said as he lay down and curled up under his blanket.

"Shouldn't we tell the President?" Alexander asked.

"What's the point? He won't remember it in the morning anyway," Lamb replied.

Alexander stood there like they had unfinished business. "Go away, Pres!" *Fucking academics,* Lamb thought. He changed gears and thought, *I should call Suliman. He might be able to use this information.*

CHAPTER 7

0500Z (0800HR LOCAL)
DONETSK AIRPORT FOB

The fat Chechen colonel was sitting at his private table in the dining facility about to bite into his hot breakfast when his nephew, the captain, appeared in front of him to report. The colonel returned his utensils to the table. "What is it, Captain?" he asked.

"Colonel, the fighting has ended. The Ukrainian attack has been repulsed. We killed fifteen and recovered ten of the wounded they left on the battlefield. The prisoners are being interrogated as we speak. We incurred twenty-five dead and 42 wounded," he replied.

"Yes, yes, very well. What about the broker? Any news from him?" Sultanovich asked.

"Yes, sir. The broker wants every child we can obtain, and he promises the auction results will be better than the last. He also said he will pay a premium for the Catholic nun if she is delivered undamaged," he replied.

"How much more?" Sultanovich asked.

"Twice the usual amount for a female of her age," the captain replied.

"Excellent! Pass the word to the men. If any of them damage the nun, I will cut off one of their hands for stealing from me," the colonel said.

CHAPTER 8

Boss and his team had been sitting in the relative comfort of the Blackhawk's nylon seats for hours except for a twenty-minute period when they set up a security perimeter while the helicopter refueled in a temporary FARP on a bomb-damaged general aviation airport. Now they were rapidly approaching Lviv. Jon was asleep in the back row with his helmeted head resting in the corner between the aft bulkhead and the right-side crew door when Boss tapped his knee and transmitted over the team radio, "I called the brass back home and informed them of your situation. They took it all the way up to the DDO. He was sympathetic but refused to provide any support. He specifically forbade me from helping you, so sorry, but I can't help," he said.

Jon didn't bother moving his head but replied, "I understand, Boss. Thanks for the cache house. That will help a lot."

Boss shook his head at Jon and gave him the cut signal before he transmitted, "What was that? I think you broke up for a second."

"Oh, okay. Thanks anyway," Jon replied.

"Also, I just received intel that an air attack is imminent on Lviv. Heavy bombers and cruise missiles are inbound so don't be surprised if we drop you off in the middle of a maelstrom."

"A what?" Jon asked.

"An enormous clusterfuck," Boss clarified.

"Roger that, Boss, easy day. Are you hearing this, Angie? It's not too late to change your mind," Jon said.

"Fuck it, mate! Let's get this party started!" Angie feigned excitement.

***

Boss's intel was good. Twenty minutes later as the Blackhawk approached the outskirts of Lviv from the south everyone sitting on the right side of the helicopter could see a steady stream of cruise missiles coming toward the city low and fast from the east followed at high altitude by the bombers and their escorts. "Damn! It looks like the old black and white newsreel films of London being attacked by the German V2 rockets," Boss said. They were transfixed by the scene they were witnessing and by the knowledge the seemingly peaceful landscape they were approaching would soon be engulfed in flames and destruction. Innocent people were going to die, and they were helpless to prevent it.

Ukrainian air defense missiles, launched from sites ringing the city, raced toward the Russian missiles and bombers. Many of them were intercepted, their fiery debris tumbling from the sky well short of their intended targets, but many more were not. The Russian missiles slammed indiscriminately into civilian apartment buildings seemingly at random throughout the city. None could be even remotely considered valid military targets. The explosions caused massive fires and burning debris flew in all directions causing further death and destruction. Steel beams and concrete rubble rained down into the streets crushing vehicles and people.

Boss snapped out of his stupor. "Hey, that's a Patriot missile!" he transmitted on the team radio as he pointed out the window. The anti-aircraft missile was launched from the city's eastern edge and was flying directly toward a TU-95 Bear bomber at Mach 4.1. The missile exploded on the Bear's left wing causing it to roll upside down before spiraling toward the ground. The bomber didn't have an ejection system for the aircrew. Boss watched as the six-man crew began bailing out of the disintegrating bomber before it impacted the ground causing an even greater explosion. "There's one, two, three. I see three good chutes," Boss transmitted.

"Those boys are in for a rough day. The first rule of bomber flying is to not bailout over the target you just attacked," the Ghost 21 pilot said over the team radio frequency.

"Actually, I don't think they had time to release their load," the copilot replied.

"I don't think the kind people of Lviv will make that distinction," the pilot said.

Next time stay in Russia, Jon thought as he grew angrier by the second watching the ongoing destruction spread. He also didn't relish the idea of being dropped right in the middle of it.

"Okay, Jon, we're going to drop you off about three miles from your target, so we don't draw any unnecessary attention to the house. The area is built up so we're going to land on the flat roof of an abandoned building. Your target will be due north. Get ready, we'll be there in about three minutes," the pilot transmitted.

"Roger that, we'll be ready," Jon replied. He looked over at Angie and received a thumbs up.

"Landing checklist," the pilot called out on the ICS.

"Tail wheel switch locked. Parking brake on. Crew, passengers, and mission equipment check," the copilot replied as he held his thumb up in front of the instrument console where the pilot could see it.

"We'll see you guys when we get back," Jon transmitted to the team. The other guys responded with fist bumps and handed over their extra rifle magazines to make sure Jon and Angie had a full combat load when they hit the ground.

"If you get down there and you are absolutely out of options call me. I don't know what I'll be able to do but call me anyway. Otherwise, you boys be careful," Boss said.

The sun had been up for two hours when the Blackhawk came into a hover next to the flat roof of an old bombed-out two-story warehouse in a secluded wooded area on the outskirts of Lviv. The pilot slid his helicopter to the right and placed his right main mount tire on the corner of the roof as he maintained a steady hover. All the while, the Russian air attack continued around them. Jon's teammate, Charlie Three, slid the right door open and Jon and Angie, carrying their rifles and packs, stepped out of the helicopter onto the roof. They hunched over under the spinning rotor blades and hurried away to the stairs leading off the roof.

Ghost 21 climbed away as Charlie Three closed the door. The crew chief waved goodbye from behind his minigun.

Jon and Angie shouldered their heavy packs before running down the stairs to the ground floor of the gutted building. All that remained of the original structure was part of the roof and the brick walls. Everything else had been scavenged long before the most recent Russian aggression. They headed north right away without looking at their GPS receivers. For now, they just wanted to create some distance between themselves and the drop-off point. The roads were empty in the immediate area. All of the sane people in town were taking cover below ground. They took turns bounding forward. One would run forward for three to five seconds while the other covered him. They continued the process for about ten minutes. Every step brought them closer to the chaos and destruction caused by the air attack. Cruise missiles continued to explode in front of them.

"I hope we don't get killed before we even start heading to Donetsk," Angie said as he ran by Jon.

ACKNOWLEDGEMENTS

To Gwenn, Bevy, Hillary, Bill, Jeff, Wilson, and Ernie.

Thank you to my beta readers, proofreaders, and armchair editors who volunteered their time to find and help me fix the mountain of errors I missed the first six or seven times I read it. Also, many thanks to Karen at Comma Queen Editing, who came in after all of us and still found copious mistakes.

ABOUT THE AUTHOR

Bob is a retired supervisory intelligence officer. He grew up in and around St. Louis, Missouri. By the time he was in high school he knew he wanted to do two things with his life; he wanted to fly in the military and he wanted to work in law enforcement. After graduating from Parks College of St. Louis University with a degree in Aeronautics he earned a commission in the USMC and became a Naval Aviator flying the CH-53D Sea Stallion helicopter. He returned to the St. Louis area after his active duty and worked as a police officer. When the Twin Towers were attacked, he joined the Missouri Army National Guard and flew Black Hawk helicopters in Iraq during Operation Iraqi Freedom II. While in Iraq he applied for and accepted a position with NGA. Now he and his wife live a quiet life in the country surrounded by trees.

www.ingramcontent.com/pod-product-compliance
Lightning Source LLC
Chambersburg PA
CBHW060218030726
47499CB00004B/1100